Blessings from Acorn Hill

Tales from Grace Chapel Inn

Blessings from Acorn Hill

JUDY BAER

Guideposts
New York, New York

Blessings from Acorn Hill

ISBN-10: 0-8249-4907-2
ISBN-13: 978-0-8249-4907-5

Published by Guideposts
16 East 34th Street
New York, New York 10016
www.guideposts.org

Distributed by Ideals Publications, a Guideposts company
2630 Elm Hill Pike, Suite 100
Nashville, TN 37214

Library of Congress Cataloging-in-Publication Data for *Slices of Life* and
The Way We Were on file.

Cover by Deborah Chabrian
Interior design by Marisa Jackson
Typeset by Aptara

Printed and bound in the United States of America
10 9 8 7 6 5 4 3 2 1

Slices of Life

For Jennifer and Jay Abrahamson—I love you guys!

Chapter One

$\mathcal{H}$i, Clarissa. What do you have for me today?"

The screen door banged shut behind Jane Howard as she entered the Good Apple Bakery. Clarissa Cottrell's best marketing tool was to open her bakery door wide and allow the delicious aromas to escape through the screen door into the street. Her customers, led by their noses, could rarely resist stopping in for muffins, cookies or doughnuts.

Jane paused in front of the display case and felt her mouth water.

"How many guests do you have up there at Grace Chapel Inn?" Clarissa asked. "My yeast doughnuts are mighty good today, but there are only five left."

"I never worry about the number of guests, you know that. Everything I buy here gets eaten by someone." Jane patted her flat belly. "Usually me."

"Wouldn't know it to look at you."

Neither, Jane thought, would anyone think that Clarissa ever tasted her own wares. She was tall and very thin. She worked off any of her products that she might have had time to eat.

"Seems to me you need some fattening up. How about a chocolate éclair with lots of filling and a nice big glass of milk?" Clarissa offered.

Jane remembered her sister Louise's stories about Clarissa's parents, from whom she had inherited the bakery. They had done the same thing for Louise when she was a child. The Cottrells knew that once someone got even a bite of their baked goods, she would be back for more.

Jane chuckled to herself. So many people wanted to fatten her up since she had moved back to Acorn Hill. If she let them, the friendly people of Acorn Hill, Pennsylvania, would have her weighing three hundred pounds.

"I'll take the biscotti, some of each kind, lemon, chocolate…"

"I'll give you all I've got then. That makes a dozen." Clarissa grabbed a sheet of thin white paper from the box on the counter and started filling a white paper bag printed with the bakery's slogan: "If You Love It, We Baked It at the Good Apple." Clarissa counted out loud to fourteen.

"That's more than a baker's dozen," Jane reminded her. "You're giving away your product. Is that good for business?"

"You come back, don't you?"

"All the time."

"There you go, then." Clarissa handed Jane the bag and winked. "I'll put it on your tab. I expect Louise to be in any day to pay your bill."

"You're a lifesaver, Clarissa." Jane sat down on one of the spindly wrought iron chairs by a matching table. Clarissa always said that she didn't want people to get too comfortable and linger too long at the bakery; the Coffee Shop was for that kind of business. Her policy paid off when the Coffee Shop became her very best customer. The shop made its own pies, but every slice of bread, muffin, cookie and doughnut served there was baked at the Good Apple. Symbiosis was how much of Acorn Hill worked and thrived.

"You've made my work at the inn so much easier." Jane bit into the éclair that Clarissa insisted she have and delighted in its vanilla flavor. "Since your breads, sweet rolls and scones are without equal, I can concentrate on making the specialties I use for our teas and for the guests' breakfasts."

"And to tinker with those candies of yours," Clarissa added. "How is Madeleine and Daughters faring these days?" Madeleine and Daughters was Jane's brainchild, a small candy company that used only Jane's recipes and those of her mother.

"Quite well, thank you. I've been able to sell some recently. It's been a nice boost to our income, which, as you can imagine, we always welcome."

"Like pouring money down the drain," Clarissa said obliquely, referring to Jane's rambling Victorian home. "Too bad the upkeep on these big old houses is so expensive, but I'm grateful you and your sisters decided to convert your family home into an inn. It's a landmark here in Acorn Hill." Then Clarissa chuckled. "Doesn't hurt my pocketbook either."

The wrinkles that marked Clarissa's features as she laughed were a shock to Jane, who rarely paid attention to age. *Had Clarissa always had those?*

Before Jane had time to consider the question, the screen door burst open and two people hurried into the room. They were Jane's Aunt Ethel and Ethel's friend Lloyd Tynan. Lloyd's trademark bow tie was askew, and his thinning hair looked almost messy. These were true signs of agitation, for the mayor of Acorn Hill was never unpolished or undignified.

Ethel was trembling from head to toe. In her maroon polyester pantsuit and dyed-red hair, she reminded Jane of a quivering bowl of plum jelly.

"Now, Honey Bunch," Lloyd clucked, "don't believe everything you hear. There's lots of gossip going around about the big reunion, and we don't know that any of it is true."

Honey Bunch? Jane almost laughed but caught herself in time. Lloyd must really be in a pickle with Ethel to call her "Honey Bunch."

Jane's aunt lived in the small carriage house next to Grace Chapel Inn. She had been there since her husband Bob Buckley had passed away some years before. Always a bit of a busybody, Ethel often meddled in the affairs of the inn—if she was not riled up about something else going on in Acorn Hill, that is.

Lloyd, the mayor and Ethel's "beau," was nearly as excitable as Ethel was, and the two of them in concert were like rubbing matchsticks together. It was inevitable that some sparks would fly.

Ever since Daniel Howard, Ethel's brother and pastor of Grace Chapel, had invited her to live next door, Ethel had "adopted" the Howard girls as her maternal project. It was no wonder, Jane thought sometimes, that the three Buckley cousins always thanked them for "taking over Mom." Being mothered by Ethel must have been a full-time job for her children. Neither Jane nor her sisters really minded Ethel's involvement in their affairs. After all, she was a loving aunt, and her late husband, a man of great faith, had been very close to their parents. Until she and Lloyd became friends, Ethel must have been terribly lonely. She did, of course, have a good friend in Clara Horn, but since adopting a potbellied pig, Clara had been involved in her own form of nurturing and motherhood.

Today's uproar was, apparently, about the upcoming all-school reunion scheduled to take place in less than two weeks. Several small towns, including Acorn Hill, had agreed to join with Potterston in a countywide gathering that was, according to the excited residents, "the best thing that's happened since Ben Franklin flew that kite."

"What's the matter?" Jane asked. "You two don't look very happy."

"We were just over in Potterston to pick up the reunion book that was printed for the Acorn Hill graduates and heard in the café that..." Ethel jumped, a reaction to Lloyd's gently poking her with his elbow. He made a policy to be loyal to Acorn Hill businesses and never liked to be caught being unfaithful—even by drinking a cup of coffee on what Lloyd considered foreign territory.

"We just stopped for a cup of coffee, no food or anything, if you don't count that piece of pie we shared," he explained.

"And my, oh my, what inferior pie they have over there," Ethel commented. "Why, between the Coffee Shop and the Good Apple and, of course, you, Jane, our people can out-bake their people any day."

"With one hand tied behind our backs," Jane said, winking at Clarissa. Then she directed her aunt back on course. "And?"

"It seems that Orlando's Restaurant in Potterston has the sole contract to serve food for the reunion. They presented a bid to the planners without being asked, and everyone assumed that no one else would *consider* trying to take on a big job like that, so they gave it to them. Why this wasn't common knowledge until now is beyond me."

In other words, Ethel felt left out of the loop. She had determined long ago that it was necessary for her to know everything that happened in Acorn Hill *as* it happened.

"And I hear the owner isn't even from Pennsylvania but somewhere in the Southwest. Disgraceful." She turned to Jane. "Can't you *do* something?"

"Me?" Even Jane, who was familiar with Ethel's convoluted thinking, was surprised.

"You're Sylvia Songer's closest friend, and she's on the reunion committee. Why can't you do the catering?"

"For one thing, I haven't been asked. For another, I don't have a staff or the kind of kitchen it would require. And finally, Orlando's will do a fine job. It's too late anyway. There simply aren't that many days until the reunion begins."

"Where's your civic pride, Jane? Acorn Hill needs to put its best foot forward, and you are definitely one of those feet." Ethel grabbed Lloyd and managed to turn him toward the door. "We need to talk to Sylvia about this. Come, Lloyd, don't dally."

Jane and Clarissa stared at each other for a long moment before bursting into simultaneous laughter.

"Hoo, hoo, hoo," Clarissa chortled. "One of Acorn Hill's best feet."

"I've been called a lot of things," Jane said, wiping her eyes, "but that was the zaniest yet."

"That Ethel is on a real mission this time." Clarissa had known Ethel for years, and even she had been taken aback. "I had no idea she felt so strongly about our part in the reunion. I suppose Lloyd has been fanning the flames of civic pride."

"Well, forewarned is forearmed," Jane said philosophically. "Now this 'best foot' must go home and get some work done." She picked up the bag of biscotti.

Clarissa wiped her hands on her apron. "See you tomorrow?"

"Of course. I glanced at the reservation book before I left, and we have two new guests coming in."

"You're one of the reasons I keep on with this bakery, you know." Clarissa's face wrinkled once again as she smiled, her eyes bright. "I'd miss all the wonderful people who pass through these doors, and you most of all."

Jane walked around the counter and gave Clarissa a hug. "And I'd miss you, but I'm counting on your being here for a long time. You're an institution in this town. Don't you forget it."

As Jane went out the door, Clarissa shook her head sadly as she thought that even institutions have to close someday.

Jane's walk back to the inn was interrupted by a steady stream of Acorn Hill neighbors. She met José Morales on the corner across from Fred's Hardware. Joe, as he preferred to be called, was pushing a wheelbarrow full of yard tools, clippers, hand trowels, a hand rake and an assortment of products for fighting weeds, bugs and crabgrass.

"Off to work, I see."

Joe beamed at her. "Sì. I'm going to work in Ms. Reed's yard. Mr. Humbert is letting me take all these things from the hardware store, and I will pay him back when I earn the money from my yard jobs," Joe explained. Sunlight glinted off his black hair, and his teeth flashed white in his nut-brown face.

Joe had built up Fred Humbert's rental service for the mowers and snow blowers by offering his own services to run them. Fred now had a waiting list for rentals of his machines.

"How is the decorating progressing in your apartment?" Jane asked.

Joe lived in a tiny apartment that Fred had prepared for him above the hardware store and had gone to Jane the week before to ask for help in making it seem homier.

"I've painted," he said proudly. "I like the colors you suggested. I like the red best." A perplexed expression flitted across his features. "But I don't know what to do next."

"I'll tell you what, Joe, I'll paint a picture for your wall. We'll find a few baskets and some dried flowers and a new bedspread and you'll have the coziest place in town."

"I'll pay you. ..."

"It's my gift, Joe." Then she saw the consternation on his face. Joe was proud, and tried to have obligations to no one. "Well, if you must pay me, then just come over and help me out at the inn some time."

"I could do that." Joe's head nodded in agreement. "Are you having any more teas?"

Since Jane had opened the inn for occasional afternoon teas, she called upon the town gardener to be a waiter sometimes. He had been working on his English while Jane brushed up on her Spanish, and they made an effective team when there were a dozen ladies waiting to be served in the parlor.

"Stop over and we'll look at the schedule." Two figures appeared out of the door of the pharmacy across the street from them. "I'm sure I've got work for you and Justine and Josie as well."

"Jane!" Josie cried, jumping up and down and waving both arms. "It's me!"

As if the adorable little girl could be missed. She was a common sight around town, and Jane had grown close to her recently.

Mother and daughter walked across the street hand-in-hand. Josie danced on tiptoe like the eight-year-old ballerina that she was. Both mother and daughter had masses of blond curls and eyes blue as cornflowers. "I got a candy bar. See?" She held it up. "Mr. Ned gave it to me."

"*Tsk, tsk,*" Jane said in mock concern. "He's going to run Chuck Parker's store out of business if he keeps giving away the merchandise."

Ned Arnold was the fill-in pharmacist who spent a good part of every month running the store so that the Parkers, who were reaching their retirement years, could travel. A handsome fellow with prematurely gray hair, Ned stayed at the inn when he was in town and had practically become a part of the family. Often, he took his meals in the kitchen with Jane, Louise and Alice when no other guests were booked. They had even quit counting him when they referred to the number of guests they had.

"He put money in the till," Josie informed her. "He treated me."

"That was very nice." Jane knelt down and gave Josie a hug. They had become friends months before when Jane noticed Josie, in old skimpy clothes, riding a rickety bicycle in the Grace Chapel parking lot. Since then, Jane had often provided extra work opportunities at the inn for Josie's mother, a struggling single mom. Justine had proved to be a capable waitress for the inn's teas.

Jane's next encounter was with Viola Reed. Around sixty and heavy-set, Viola always made a fashion statement with her penchant for bright colors and dramatic scarves. Today she wore a vivid blue tunic and a scarf of red, yellow and green wrapped around her neck. Viola was among Louise's best friends. They shared a passionate love of books and learning. As the owner of the Nine Lives Bookstore, Viola took it as a personal affront if someone did not like to read.

"Your aunt's book on lowering cholesterol came in," Viola said. She peered into Jane's eyes. "Do you think it's for her? She hasn't mentioned having high cholesterol to me. I do know a few things about the subject, since it runs in my family. Or could it be for Lloyd. They've both put on a few pounds since you opened the inn. . . ."

"Aunt Ethel and Lloyd are in town somewhere. I saw them not long ago in the bakery. They were in a dither about the reunion."

"Well, the bakery is certainly the wrong place for someone with high cholesterol." Viola suddenly looked fierce. "This whole reunion thing is getting completely out of hand. I don't see why we couldn't have handled our reunion by ourselves. I just got a call from a bookstore in Potterston. They want to set up a booth and display popular books from the forties, fifties, sixties and so on. They have the idea that everyone will want to reminisce. They think that if we offer a selection of the most popular books of each decade, we could sell quite a few."

Jane thought it sounded like a great idea, but was wise enough not to say it out loud. She already knew what had set Viola on her high horse, the single word *popular*. It was Viola's theory—and she therefore felt it should be shared by everyone else in Acorn Hill—that good literature and popular literature were not necessarily the same. Good literature could be redeeming, yes. Educational, enlightening and edifying, certainly. Uplifting and informative, of course. But *popular?* Did that not imply frivolity? For Viola, popular fiction was defined as facile, inane, simplistic prose meant purely to entertain. Viola thought people entertained themselves much too much as it was. To rectify the situation, she had been giving readings at her store of the writings of authors on her approved list—most of them long dead.

"It would be a wonderful way to let others know about your shop," Jane pointed out. "Great advertising."

"It would be sinking rather low, don't you think?"

"Not everyone views the written word the same way, Viola. Look at Hope."

Viola snorted. Her eye twitched a little with the tic that always seemed to appear at the mention of Hope Collins' name. Hope, an avid reader, had said that she would buy all her books on-line if Viola didn't bring in new releases and best sellers. She had even threatened to have June Carter, the owner, sell books at the Coffee Shop. Jane figured that Hope had doubled Viola's business, even if Viola insisted on displaying those "simplistic" books on all the lower shelves in the store.

"Think of it as a service to the people of our communities," Jane suggested, knowing Viola's soft spot. "I know how much you care about our community."

"When you put it that way . . ." Viola gave a gusty sigh and started off again, frowning. It was always perplexing to her when someone made a good argument for having an opinion opposed to her own.

Jane took the mail from the box at the end of the driveway and sauntered toward the nineteenth-century

Victorian home that was now called Grace Chapel Inn. After the death of their father, the three sisters reunited and started the small bed-and-breakfast. Though she had viewed its exterior countless times since its renovation, she never failed to be pleased by its appearance. The cocoa-colored exterior, highlighted with eggplant, green and creamy white, was striking. The house restoration had turned out better than she had imagined, and the place truly spoke "welcome" to its guests.

Wendell, the inn's house cat now that his former owner, Rev. Daniel Howard, had passed on, sat sphinxlike on the top step. A gray tabby with coal-black stripes, white paws and a black-tipped tail, Wendell still assumed that the house was his property and that he was allowing these interlopers to stay only because they had been feeding him rather well. Sometimes Jane had the uncomfortable feeling that the cat was right.

It had not been easy making the transition from the Blue Fish Grille in San Francisco to her childhood home and to living with her two older, still occasionally bossy, sisters. Alice, a nurse at the Potterston hospital, was kind and caring. Louise, a widow, was also good-hearted but her staid demeanor often made her seem aloof. A pianist, Louise was always in demand to teach students and to play for events. But they all loved running the inn together.

Jane sat on the top step and scratched Wendell's head until he rumbled an appreciative purr. "Hey, big guy, what's going on inside? Have our guests left yet?"

He yawned and plopped onto his side for a belly rub.

The screen door opened and Ted and Millie Larken stepped onto the porch. They were carrying suitcases, and Millie had a sun hat anchored on her graying hair. Jane jumped to her feet. "Leaving already? You don't have to check out until noon, you know."

"I'm afraid we have to go, though both of us wish we could stay right here for another week. This is the sweetest, most relaxing place we've ever visited." Millie put down her luggage to adjust her hat.

"I'll agree with my wife," Ted, a retired executive from a large Philadelphia bank, added. "We've already made reservations for another visit next summer."

"Good. Then we don't have to say good-bye," Jane said with a smile. "Just see you later."

"What's this about a big reunion that's about to happen? I suppose Grace Chapel Inn will be busy then."

"It's the first time anyone has ever tried this sort of thing. There are a number of small towns like Acorn Hill in the county. This will enable all of us to share the same celebration. There will be class reunions, music, meals and entertainment."

"What a charming idea. In fact, everything about this place is charming." Then Millie frowned. "Except for that crabby man in the room next to ours."

"Mr. Enrich is certainly interesting," Jane said.

Jane had quickly discovered that people who passed through their doors were all fascinating in their own ways. Sometimes it took a little longer to dig through the outer shell of a person to find the kernel of good inside, but it was always worth it. Some had, of course, considerably harder shells than others.

"Before we leave, I've been meaning to tell you how attractive your clothes are." Millie eyed Jane's hand-painted, oversized T-shirt and leggings.

"Thanks. I decided to doctor up these things to make them a little more interesting." She turned her ankle so Millie could see the little cat whose tail roped around the bottom of one leg. "It's fun."

"It's talent," Millie corrected. "You should be selling things in boutiques. Have you considered it?"

Jane had, but hadn't found the time to pursue it. Being chef at the inn was a full-time job, and her painting and jewelry design were on hold until after the reunion.

"I took a few of your cards," Millie continued. "I plan to tell my friends about this perfect town."

Acorn Hill was a perfect small town in many ways, with its quaint shops, picturesque churches and friendly people. Lloyd, and therefore Ethel, wanted to keep it just that way. His campaign slogan and the motto by which Lloyd performed his duty as mayor was: "Acorn Hill has a life of its own away from the outside world, and that's the way we like it."

At first, Lloyd had worried that the inn might bring too much change to Acorn Hill but had come to realize that it brought even more charm to the town. It was just fine with Lloyd that the inn existed—he had eaten enough meals there with Ethel to pack on fifteen extra pounds—but he still didn't want an influx of visitors ruining the ambiance of the town.

Jane reminded herself to order more business cards and brochures before the reunion.

Both Louise and Alice had gone off somewhere and the house was quiet. Over the year, her sisters had also become her good friends. Jane couldn't imagine not having them to consult, chat and laugh with every day. Still, Jane relished going into the library, sitting there alone among her father's books and feeling his spirit. She and her father had always shared a love of the Psalms, and it was in the library where they had had their theological discussions.

There was no time for reminiscences today, Jane reminded herself. She had dinner to fix for herself and her sisters. She slipped into an ankle-length apron she had sewn and wrapped it around her waist. Regular aprons were little protection from flour dust and splattering stains. She thought of her creation as a raincoat that protected her from food showers. After putting a pot of potatoes on to boil and starting a pan of eggs in cold water so that they wouldn't crack, she took a knife from the cupboard and marched down the back steps and into the garden with her eye on the huge-leafed rhubarb with its succulent red stalks growing there.

Rhubarb always reminded Jane of her mother Madeleine, whose recipe book was full of rhubarb recipes. It was through the personality-packed annotated pages of the recipe book that Jane had come to know her mother better.

Jane was dicing rhubarb, cooling the potatoes and preparing to shell boiled eggs when Sylvia Songer rapped on the back door and walked in.

"If I cooked as much as you do, I'd weigh a ton," Sylvia said. She went to the cupboard for two glasses, took them to the table and then removed the peach iced tea from the refrigerator. Sylvia was the owner of Sylvia's Buttons, a fabric store in town, and was gifted with a needle.

"It's a good thing you're the seamstress and I'm the cook, then." Jane scraped the red crescents from the cutting board

to a bowl and began rapping boiled eggs on the side of the sink
to crack and peel them. She always worked on at least two
projects at a time. "My pleasure comes from making food, not
eating it. Speaking of food, how's the reunion progressing?"

Sylvia groaned, leaned forward and buried her face in
her hands so that all Jane could see was the top of her head
with its soft red hair. "Tell me again why I'm on this
committee."

"You were trapped into it, if I remember, because of
your creativity and organizational abilities. Serves you right
for being so unerringly capable." Jane rinsed the eggs, put
them in another bowl and joined Sylvia at the table.
"What's up now?"

"Something I thought we had under control until Ethel
and Lloyd paid me a visit today. They believe that we
shouldn't have accepted the first proposal we got for catering. Lloyd and Ethel think it was unfair not to give everyone
an opportunity to bid."

"Pay no attention. With the reunion so near, there's
nothing you can do about it now. Besides, they're so thrilled
with the entire event that they'll be on to something else by
tomorrow."

"The trouble is, I think they're right."

Jane's eyebrows raised practically into her hairline. "No
kidding?"

"Orlando's is making noises about the job being too large for the amount of money they bid, which is, of course, their own doing. I think they've realized that with the influx of people for the reunion, they're going to be swamped at the restaurant itself and are trying to squirm out of some responsibility."

"They should've thought of that a little earlier." Jane had done plenty of catering and knew the enormous amount of work it could involve. "But they can't squirm far in only a few days."

"I'm blaming the inexperience of the new manager," Sylvia murmured. "Otherwise I'd feel like strangling him." She looked up hopefully. "Do you have any ideas?"

"Sylvia, there's no time left."

"Just pretend there is time, Jane," Sylvia pleaded.

"How much money do you have to work with if you relieve Orlando's from some of the responsibility? That usually tells the tale."

"If I find out, will you brainstorm with me?"

"With what little brain I have left."

Chapter Two

I'll need vitamins if I'm going to be in charge of a car wash!" Alice said as she entered the kitchen. Obviously agitated, she stopped short when she saw that they had a visitor. "Oh, hello, Sylvia."

"Hello, yourself."

Alice dropped into the chair. "I should have my head examined—and offer Pastor Kenneth the same service. What made us think the reunion would be a good time for the ANGELs to earn money for their charity projects and the youth group's mission trip?"

"Because it's the perfect opportunity," Jane said. "There'll be more people in Acorn Hill during the reunion than there will be for the rest of the year. *That's* why you thought this would be a good time to have a fundraiser."

"Having a fundraiser is fine, but we should never have let the *kids* pick the event. At least we should've told them to choose something tidy. All that water is going to make a mess."

"I have to admit that the committee was surprised at the choice," Sylvia said, adding with a smile, "but we decided that it would be *clean* fun."

Alice moaned at the joke. "There's only one redeeming thing about this car wash," she said, her voice muffled as she held her head in her hands. "The younger kids love the idea of it, and they enjoy working with the high-schoolers. They'll do anything to make it happen."

"Everything will work out beautifully," Sylvia said. "The kids are also planning to sell caramel apples and lemonade, and they're bound to have a big success."

"Call me vain," Alice said, "but I'd hoped that when I saw my old friends and classmates, I'd be doing something a little more laudable than wearing a rain slicker and running a car wash."

"I think you look very fetching in your slicker," said Jane.

"Thank you. I feel *so* much better," said Alice with a rare touch of sarcasm in her voice.

Sylvia studied Jane across the table. "And how do you feel about the reunion, now that it's practically here?"

Jane and Alice exchanged a telling glance. "Mostly I'm excited," Jane said.

"Just 'mostly'?"

"Jane had an unpleasant experience in high school with one of her classmates." Alice said. She paused and the others remained silent. "You know that our mother died when Jane was born."

Sylvia nodded.

"Regrettably, our father decided not to tell Jane all the circumstances of her birth when she was growing up. Our mother had complications during childbirth and didn't live long after. He felt that there was no need to connect sadness with the joy we felt at having a new baby in the family. Mother would have wanted it that way—or, at least, that's what he thought."

Jane took up the story. "I never asked too many questions about that time and never connected Mother's death with my own birth."

Sylvia waited.

Finally, Alice spoke again. "Shirley Taylor was always an odd girl. More than once, one of Jane's friends commented on how jealous she was of Jane. We all chalked it up to immaturity."

"Then Shirley took it upon herself to tell me the circumstances of my birth and my mother's death. I suppose she'd heard it from her own parents."

Sylvia leaned forward. "How nasty!"

Jane looked down at her hands. "I could barely fathom it—if I hadn't been born, my mother might have still been alive. I was devastated."

"We had no idea how hurt Jane would be. Father later grieved over his choice not to tell her, but it was how he'd decided to handle it and he couldn't go back." Alice murmured.

"It would have been easier if I'd known from the time I was a child," Jane admitted. "Hearing the story that way for the first time was heartbreaking. It wasn't until I came back to Acorn Hill and helped my sisters open the inn that I was really able to put it in perspective." She smiled faintly.

"It was the cookbook," Alice said. Her eyes glowed. "The one with the truffle recipes in it."

"It was so full of Mother's handwritten thoughts, comments and ideas, that it was as if she came to life right before my eyes."

"And she gave you a gift, didn't she, Jane? Madeleine and Daughters, I mean," Sylvia said.

"So, so many gifts."

"And Shirley Taylor?" Sylvia asked. "Whatever happened to her?"

"I have no idea. I haven't thought of her in years."

"Of whom?" Louise asked as she entered the kitchen, a stack of sheet music under one arm. She took the fourth chair and sighed with relief. "I thought I would never get done choosing music today. Pastor Kenneth wants everything to be especially familiar and welcoming with all the visitors we will be having." She poured herself a glass of tea and took a sip.

"Who were you talking about when I came in?"

"Shirley Taylor."

Louise looked as if the name rang no bell with her and then recognition began to show on her face. "Oh, you've been looking at the reservation book. We have a Shirley Taylor staying here during the reunion. The name sounded so familiar, but I couldn't place it."

The room grew so silent that they could hear Wendell snoring on the windowsill.

"There are a dozen or more Taylor families in this county. . . ." Louise paused and looked at Alice, then at Jane. "*That* Shirley Taylor? But why would she make reservations here, of all places?" Louise appeared stricken. "I am so sorry. I would never have taken her reservation if I had known who she was."

"It may not be the same person," Jane said soothingly. "And if it is, then it's time to clear the air and settle what's hung between us all these years. We were just kids—young, thoughtless kids."

God has a way of working things out, Jane knew. She did not really want to see her again, but if *the* Shirley Taylor was coming to stay at the inn, then Jane had no doubt that He had had a hand in the reservation.

Late the next morning, Alice came up behind Jane and put her arm around her sister's shoulders. "What are you so busy with today?"

Jane leaned back in the chair and pushed a box of stationery aside to make room for Alice as she sat down. "Catching up on some letter writing. A friend from San Francisco has written to me twice. I thought it was time to respond."

Alice peered at the quotation Jane had scrawled on the bottom of the page.

> "Hide not your talents. They for use were made.
> What's a sundial in the shade?"
>
> —Ben Franklin

"Ben Franklin?" Alice asked, raising an eyebrow.

Jane nodded. "Did you know that his autobiography is considered by some to be the first really great work of American literature?"

"No."

"Or that as a teenager he was a troublemaker who thought he was ten times smarter than his parents?"

"No."

"And he *was*! It was true. Think of trying to raise a child like that."

"I had enough trouble raising you, and you aren't more than four or fives times smarter than I am."

"Very funny, Alice." Jane grinned at her sister.

Alice smiled and stood. "I'd better go upstairs and write a few things down myself. I'm so afraid I'll forget to do something over the busy weekend." She peered out the window. "Besides, I think you have company coming up the walk."

"Can Jane come out and play?" A childish voice piped the question to Louise, who was sweeping the porch.

Jane peeked out the window to see Louise stop sweeping and rest her arm on top of the broom. As usual, Louise was dressed in what her sisters called her "uniform," another variation on her trademark skirt and sweater combination. Her signature lace handkerchief peeked out of one pocket. Louise, who loved discipline and order, never made the radical clothing statements that Jane enjoyed. Today Josie made a smile tweak the corners of her lips.

"Jane? Well, I don't know. She might not have all her chores done yet."

Josie's small shoulders drooped. "Oh." Then she perked up again. "I got my chores done really fast today. Maybe I could help her."

"What a generous offer," Louise said, smiling. They had all grown to love Josie, who, after meeting Jane, had promptly adopted all the sisters as her surrogate family.

Jane often took Josie with her when she escaped to Fairy Pond to sketch. With Sylvia's help, she was also teaching Josie to sew buttons back onto her own clothes and had promised that someday they would work together on a quilt for Josie's doll. Alice had once taken Josie to an ANGELs meeting, and she had been adopted promptly as the group's mascot. Josie, with her tangle of blonde curls and cornflower eyes, was easy to love.

Jane came to the door. "Did I hear an offer of help out here?"

"Me! Me!" Josie danced on her toes.

"Okay, but it's something very difficult."

"I don't care. I'm big."

"You'll have to help me finish my grocery list and help me shop."

"That's not hard." Josie opened the screen door. "That's fun."

"I'm glad somebody thinks so," Jane murmured to Louise.

"You just have to do it too often," Louise commented. "Maybe one day you can train Josie to do it for you."

"Not a bad thought," Jane said. "Not bad at all."

Later Josie and Jane strolled the aisles of the General Store looking for the items on Jane's list. Rustic as it was, the store provided Jane with most of what she needed. She especially liked their produce from local farms.

Josie pushed her own miniature cart, which the store provided to entertain shoppers' children, while Jane filled her big one.

"Bananas. And apples and oranges, I think."

"Bread?" Josie stopped in front of the case. "And cookies?"

"We'll get that at Clarissa's. Why don't you find me some dishwasher soap?"

As Josie scampered off, Vera Humbert turned her cart down the aisle toward Jane. "You have a helper today, I see."

"If she were a little bigger, she'd be my right-hand girl," Jane said with a laugh. "Now she can't reach groceries on the top shelves." She eyed Vera's cart, which was piled high with everything from lasagna noodles and butter to cereal boxes and frozen vegetables. "Looks like you have plenty of cooking to do."

"I never realized we had so many relatives—especially who graduated from high school somewhere in this county. They're all coming back for a visit and expect to stay—and eat—at our house. I'm trying to get food prepared and in the freezer so I can have a break too. Fred is already threatening to put cots in the attic and basement for the overflow. You don't have any more space at the inn, do you?"

"Not unless Alice, Louise and I sleep in the same bed, which might stretch the sisterhood thing too far."

Vera laughed and nodded. "The reunion will be fun, though, won't it?" She turned so that Jane could see her sideways. "Do I look thin to you?"

"You've definitely lost a few pounds."

"Good." Vera's eyes twinkled. "Fred's old girlfriend is coming to the reunion, and I don't want him to think that he picked the wrong woman."

"No danger of that."

"I dug out a miniskirt for me and a polyester leisure suit for him. I thought we could dress up for our class social. Fortunately Fred said that he wouldn't wear the suit, so I didn't have to admit that my mini would only fit around one of my thighs." Vera shook her head. "I'd forgotten what a little thing I was." Vera was all wound up in the reunion mode. "Do you remember Bill Paige and Betty Loomis? They got married right out of high school. You know the ones—Acorn Hill's only flower children. They're coming back and I'm dying to see them now. Do you think they still have ponytails or do you think they've turned into corporate CEOs?"

"We'll know soon."

"If only poor Sylvia and Joseph Holzmann get the food problem straightened out." Vera clucked like a mother hen.

"'Food problem?'"

"Didn't you hear? Just this morning Orlando's Restaurant in Potterston asked that the committee find some other place to cater the class breakfasts and afternoon teas in Acorn Hill. They decided they'd taken on too much." Vera sighed. "We just aren't accustomed to the kind of crowds that this event promises." She looked sideways at Jane. "But you are."

Jane held up a hand. "I'm hoping no one remembers that. It would be nice to go to something and be on the eating end once in a while." No wonder Sylvia had been asking her for ideas. She must have suspected that this would happen.

"I'm sure, but people know what a treasure you are. It's likely that your name will come up."

Vera was one of Jane's best customers at the inn; her teachers' group held teas there regularly. Jane had also begun to create new pieces of jewelry with them in mind because they loved her bright, eccentric pins and bracelets. The last time they had come, Jane had painted and framed some miniatures, mostly of local birds and wildlife. Every one of them had sold. It felt good to Jane to be selling her art again—and having time to pursue it.

Vera eyed her cart and sighed. "I suppose I'd better get a move on. I still have to red-up the house today." "Red-up" was Vera's way of saying ready up the house for company.

Jane and Josie drove home with the groceries and put them away. Then Jane held out her hand to Josie. "Want to come to the Good Apple with me now? It's a nice day for a walk."

Josie's eyes glowed. "Yes. It smells really good in there."

When they arrived, Clarissa was sitting on a stool behind the counter. She had a cup of coffee and a cookie in front of her. Wearing a flowered house dress, white socks and nurse's shoes, with her hair tied back from her face and hidden under a hairnet, Clarissa did not seem the least bit surprised to see Jane and Josie. They were often a pair on the streets of Acorn Hill.

Jane went around to the back of the counter and helped herself to a cup of coffee as she often did when Clarissa was rolling cookie dough or frosting a cake and didn't want to stop.

"Have a peanut butter cookie too." Clarissa waved in the direction of the display case. "I outdid myself this time, if I do say so myself." Then she looked at Josie, who was eyeing the brownies in the display case. "And I suppose you'd like one of those."

Josie's eyes were round as saucers when Clarissa put two fat brownies in a bag and handed them to her. "Why don't you take one of those home to your mother and eat the other yourself?"

They both laughed as Josie threw her arms around Clarissa and then around Jane, babbling thanks, before she darted out the door toward home.

Then Jane dropped into the seat across from her old friend. "Taking a break, I see."

"It's that lull between my morning shoppers and three o'clock when everyone begins to realize they're out of bread or buns or need a dessert for dinner."

"And then you'll go home, fall into bed exhausted, get up at three tomorrow morning and start all over again," Jane added.

"Pretty much." Clarissa took a sip of her coffee. "I appreciate talking to you, Jane. At least you understand how hard it is to be in the food business."

Clarissa put her cup down and absentmindedly rubbed her hip, something Jane had never noticed her doing before.

"Is it getting harder to stand on your feet?" Jane inquired gently, remembering all the thick-soled shoes and rubber mats she had used during her own years in the restaurant kitchen.

Her thin face looking drawn, Clarissa smiled ruefully. "You caught me. My bones are creakier by the day, and I'm not sleeping as well as I used to, but you know me, I love this place. The Good Apple is all I've ever known. My parents had it before me. My husband and I raised our family while working at the bakery. My children played in the big yard out back where we kept a swing set and a sand box. What would I do without it?"

"The Good Apple isn't going anywhere, and you've told me yourself that business is the best it's ever been."

Clarissa's expression flickered with unexpected sadness and a hint of confusion.

"True, my dear, but though I hate to admit it, *I'm* the one who's not quite what she used to be. But if I weren't baking for the Good Apple, what would I do? I don't even have a hobby other than baking."

"Oh, Clarissa, I know it's hard to believe, but you're so much more than just the bakery. Though the business has been a part of you for what seems like forever, it's not your identity."

Clarissa considered that for a moment before asking with amusement, "Then who am I?"

"Mother of three. A much loved grandmother—I've seen photos of those children hanging onto your hands like they never wanted to let go. Churchwoman. Community supporter. Pillar of the community." Jane stretched her hand across the table and put it over Clarissa's. "Friend."

Then Jane's voice softened. "I'm saying things to you that at one time I didn't believe about myself. There was a time when I forgot I was anything more than chief cook and bottle-washer. I know how it is to totally identify with work. I put so much of myself into mine that it became 'me.'"

A grin spread across Jane's face as she continued. "For a moment there, I was giving you the lecture that I always hated to hear from everyone who thought I was too focused and working too hard. But I have found there's much more to life than my work." She rolled her eyes. "God had to drag me all the way back to Acorn Hill to discover that." She waggled a finger at Clarissa. "Who knows what wonderful thing He has in store for you?"

"Thanks for understanding," Clarissa said softly. "My family thinks I'm being a silly old woman about it. I'm glad someone knows what I mean."

On the way back to the inn, Jane noticed their guest, Mr. Enrich, leaving the Nine Lives Bookstore. The man had a way of looking unapproachable and gloomy no matter what he was doing. When he walked, he hovered near the buildings, as if trying to make himself unnoticeable.

Instead of turning north on Chapel Road, Jane impulsively crossed the street and walked toward Nine Lives herself. The store always reminded her of an old English shop with its large baskets of flowers and swinging sign. She had often wondered why Viola had not named the shop something Dickensian in honor of one of her favorite authors, but clearly Viola had preferred to dedicate it to her feline friends.

Viola Reed was behind the counter talking on the telephone. She waved a welcome but was obviously engrossed in placing an order. Jane found Rev. Kenneth Thompson crouched on the floor in the back corner of the store where Viola kept her popular fiction and best sellers. Engaged in a losing battle with the readers of Acorn Hill to get them to "enlighten" their minds with "fine" literature, her desperate tactic of hiding "modern" books in the back corner had only made that the most popular part of the store.

"What are you doing back here?" Jane said, hunkering down beside the pastor. "Don't you know this is as close as Viola gets to having to an X-rated section in her store?"

"Just think, if Viola *wanted* people to buy these books, she'd only sell a few. By boosting the curiosity factor, she's got them flying off the shelves." He gestured toward the shelves. "People want to read for themselves what's so scandalous."

They looked at Viola's "shocking" titles, which included everything from *New York Times* best sellers and a coffee-table book of contemporary artists to a dictionary of slang.

The pastor stood with a groan. "There's going to come a day, however, when I'll scrunch down there to read the titles and won't be able to stand up again." He looked at Jane and smiled. They had become good friends since he arrived in Acorn Hill shortly after Jane's return home and he took over the pulpit that Jane's father had once filled.

"By the way, I'm glad you came in," he added. "I wanted to give you a 'heads up' about the reunion."

"I'm not really involved," Jane said. "That's Sylvia's department. I'm just the innkeeper."

"You did hear that Orlando's in Potterston thinks it—pardon the restaurant pun—bit off a little more than it can chew?"

"Yes …," Jane said cautiously.

"And that your aunt and the mayor have offered to solve the problem by involving you?"

"Oh no, they won't," Jane said firmly, recalling her promise to help Sylvia brainstorm. Thinking and cooking were two entirely different activities, and those lovable but irritating busybodies had not even consulted her. "Neither of them has any idea about what they're asking. I don't have a facility big enough to prepare large volumes of food. I have no staff, unless you count Alice and Louise, who are busy with the reunion themselves. They'll just have to find another solution to their problem."

"Uh-huh," Rev. Thompson said in doubtful agreement.

When Jane arrived at the inn, all was quiet. She picked up Wendell, who was sleeping in a porch chair, scratched him under the chin, and carried him into the house. The sleepy cat was heavy and relaxed in her arms, and a purr rumbled from deep within his chest. Jane buried her nose in his soft fur and thought she could smell a hint of Alice's perfume there. This was not a neglected animal, Jane thought with a smile as she carried him into the parlor and curled up with him in a big chair. Wendell yawned widely, burrowed into Jane's lap and promptly fell asleep again.

She picked up the Bible from the table next to her chair and began to skim its pages. She almost always settled on the Psalms. Her father had loved poetry and had quoted it occasionally, and often it had been the poetry of the Psalms. She had always treasured the fervor of the Psalms and the honesty of those who had written them. The verses dealt with the depths of despair, the pinnacles of praise. She read in Psalm 150:6,

"Let everything that has breath praise the Lord.
Praise the Lord."

With Wendell heavy against her legs and the parlor warm with sunlight, she began to read out loud from Psalm 111.

"Praise the Lord.
I will extol the Lord with all my heart
in the council of the upright and in the assembly.
Great are the works of the Lord;
they are pondered by all who delight in them.

Glorious and majestic are his deeds,

and his righteousness endures forever.

He has caused his wonders to be remembered;

the Lord is gracious and compassionate.

He provides food for those who fear him. …"

"Then it would be smart for us to be fearful right now," a voice suddenly interrupted her.

Both Jane and Wendell jumped. Neither had heard Sylvia come into the inn or step into the parlor.

"You startled us," Jane protested mildly. Wendell gave Sylvia a slit-eyed glare and went back to sleep.

"Sorry. I knocked and called but you didn't answer. I could hear you talking in here so I knew you were home. I just couldn't get your attention. I see why now."

"Have a seat. Do you want some iced tea or lemonade?"

"Nothing for me." Sylvia sank into a cushiony chair.

"And what did you mean, 'It would be smart for us to be fearful'?"

"So you haven't heard about our catering upset," Sylvia said. "What I worried would happen, has."

"Oh, I get it. 'He provides food …'" Jane laughed.

"Looks like He'll have to. Orlando's certainly won't. They have asked us to find another vendor to serve the breakfasts. It appears they want someone to take over and do everything they don't want to do."

"I've been looking for someone like that myself," Jane said.

"If I live through this reunion, remind me never, ever, to volunteer for anything again. If I do, stop me, and if you can't stop me, have me committed. We'd drop Orlando's completely, but we need them. It's too late to find anyone else now. This reunion is a logistical nightmare."

Sylvia paused and took a breath before asking, "Is there *any* chance that you would consider saving my sanity by taking over the rest of the catering?"

"Sure. Right after I perform my own appendectomy on the kitchen table." Jane snorted at the ridiculousness of the idea. "We are only days from this thing starting, Sylvia. You don't want me. You want a miracle worker."

"You tell me one person who is better suited. You've run huge kitchens."

"Will everyone be happy with cereal and milk for breakfast?"

"Come on, Jane, consider it. We're desperate here."

"No way. Besides, I'm planning to enjoy the reunion myself."

"How can you enjoy it when you know that people are missing meals, that I'm having a nervous breakdown and that the entire committee will be humiliated?" Sylvia pleaded.

"It will be hard, but I'll manage," Jane responded cheerfully. She stood up and put the limp Wendell in her seat. "What I *will* do is make you a nice cup of tea."

"*Ja-a-ane* . . ." Sylvia almost wailed as she followed Jane into the kitchen.

"Look at the size of this room, Sylvia. It's nowhere near big enough to do what needs to be done for the reunion. I can't cook for the masses in here."

"Maybe someone could help you? A group effort?"

"I'm not sure you can find enough crazy people in Acorn Hill to make a group like that. Unless . . ."

Sylvia's head shot up. "Yes?"

"Oh, never mind." Jane gave a dismissive wave of her hand. "Just a silly idea."

"All ideas are welcome, Jane. Even the silly ones." Sylvia gave her a pleading look. "Please?"

"The only way I could see it happening is if I subcontracted the food. The Good Apple is the only place that can bake in that kind of volume, but we could have a buffet breakfast of sweet rolls, muffins, bagels, pecan sticky buns and the like. Fruit bowls, fresh juices and yogurt—things that don't have to be cooked on the spot. We're serving out of tents after all."

Sylvia kept her mouth closed as Jane spun off into the topic she liked best.

"In the afternoon, a pie social would go over well. If June Carter and Hope Collins at the Coffee Shop would agree to make pies and prepare the fruit for breakfast, then Wilhelm Wood from Time for Tea could set up a tea buffet. The General Store could be in charge of ice cream for the à la mode and the town's church ladies could serve coffee and..."

"So you'll organize it then? We'll pay you well. We have more people registered than expected, and we would be generous to anyone who helped us out in our time of need."

"Wait just a..."

"I'll assemble the church ladies myself," Sylvia interrupted. "Pastor Ken can help me. It will be perfect. No one has had more experience serving food than church ladies have. We'll have the tables up and ready, and we'll do anything you ask. Just get us out of this mess."

Jane groaned inwardly, knowing full well what she was getting into. "Oh, all right."

I've lost my mind, Jane thought. *Well, perhaps for the next few days I'm better off without it.*

"Thank you, thank you, thank you!" Sylvia flung her arms around Jane. "Now I can sleep tonight."

"You'll be able to," Jane said, "but I won't."

"You agreed to do *what*?" Louise asked over the dinner table.

"You don't have to say a word," Jane assured her sister with a smile. "Alice has already offered to take me somewhere to have my head examined. It won't be that difficult. I've already spoken to Wilhelm and June. Both are more than willing to pitch in. So is the General Store. The only one I haven't talked to yet is Clarissa. Pastor Ken called about a half hour ago and says the presidents of every church ladies group in town are working to gather helpers. He says it won't be a problem."

"I am amazed," Louise murmured. "Just when people will be so busy with their own families, they are willing to take this on. There are some remarkable people in Acorn Hill, that's all I can say."

"I'm not surprised," Alice said. "I think Acorn Hill was feeling a little overlooked in this entire reunion. You know how upset Lloyd and Ethel were at the thought that some of the catering business wasn't coming our way. Besides, it will be good income for the businesses that take part."

"I suppose, when you put it that way." Louise still didn't look completely convinced. "Jane, you will be awfully busy. You do need to take care of yourself." Louise blushed slightly. "Am I sounding like I'm your mother again?"

Jane reached for another piece of apricot walnut bread. "I know you care, but you don't have to worry. It's what I've done for years, Louise. It might be fun to get right out there and mix with people. I'm actually—and don't you dare tell Sylvia this—rather enjoying the idea." Then she frowned.

"What's wrong?" Alice asked, noticing immediately.

"The only one I'm worried about is Clarissa. We may have to keep the baked goods menu very simple."

"Nonsense," Louise proclaimed. "Clarissa can bake rings around anyone in Potterston."

"True, but she's not as young as she used to be."

"None of us is." Louise eyed Jane. "Except, perhaps, you."

"Is there a problem with Clarissa?" Alice asked.

"She's tired, that's all." Jane could picture Clarissa absently rubbing her hip when they had visited. "I wish she had some help. Bakery hours wear a person out."

"Could she train someone to step in occasionally?" Alice asked. Then she responded to her own question by saying, "But who?"

Chapter Three

*T*he three sisters sat in the library after dinner. Soft lamplight filled the room, and a bowl of potpourri gave off a delicate lavender scent. Louise was working on the intricate piece of needlework that she planned to give to her daughter Cynthia for Christmas. Alice was sorting through a pile of magazines and papers, and Jane was paging through a biography of Benjamin Franklin.

Jane never tired of reading about Franklin. She had already laughed out loud several times at Ben's sage advice. She particularly liked, "If a man empties his purse into his head, no man can take it away from him. An investment in knowledge always pays the best interest."

Wendell, who was curled into a tight ball on a pillow on the floor, opened one eye each time she chuckled, as if to ask what this human was up to now.

Ben Franklin was a model of industriousness, and every time Jane thought about all that he had managed to accomplish in a lifetime, she felt that she should accomplish more in her own. She put down the book. There must be things to do that she had been overlooking. "Alice, are we caught up on everything for the reunion?"

"I doubt it, but I can't think of a thing we've missed. Louise, what do you think?"

Louise pondered the question. "I can't think of anything right now. If we missed something, then we'll deal with it."

Jane glanced at the small clock on the bookshelf. "Our new guests are late checking in."

"Yes, and Mr. Enrich hasn't returned yet. That's odd." Alice's brow furrowed.

"We're not his keepers, Alice," Louise pointed out gently.

"I realize that, but there's something about him...."

"You mean that he's the crabbiest guest we've ever had?" Jane asked. "That a smile or a 'thank you' might kill him?"

"That is not gracious," Louise said.

"Oh, Louie," Jane teased her sister with the nickname only she dared use. "Don't try to kid me. I saw you bite your lip when he told you the bed linens were 'rough.'"

"Well, I do try to keep the Egyptian cotton on the guest beds. We were so busy the night before that I used our ordinary sheets. I never dreamed anyone would notice." Louise was unaccustomed to being criticized.

"He told me he expected telephones and televisions in the rooms, and an Internet hook-up," Alice added. "Didn't he read the brochure I sent him?"

Jane chuckled. "He told me white chocolate and cranberries had no business being in scones. He suggested that if I found a good bagel shop, I could stop trying so hard."

"No!" Alice looked horrified.

"Don't worry about it, Alice, I've got a tough skin where finicky eaters are concerned. I'm good at what I do. If someone complains, I always chalk it up to differing tastes, not a personal affront. Besides, despite all his complaints, he keeps hanging around."

Mr. Enrich had initially planned to stay one night as he traveled through Acorn Hill. Then it became two, then three, and now this was his fourth night at the inn.

"He must not have a fixed schedule," Louise observed. "I thought he would have checked out by now."

"I did tell him that we had an open room until just before the reunion," Alice said. "Ned told me today he'd be going home very soon because the Parkers want him to come back and fill in at the pharmacy during the reunion so they can enjoy the event. The Parkers knew we'd be busy, so Ned will stay with them for those nights."

"Remember what we told ourselves when we were planning our purpose for the inn," Jane said. "We would welcome people with open arms and unconditional love. Just enough Martha and a lot of Mary," she said with a smile, referring to her favorite biblical hostesses.

"Jane's right," Alice concluded. "It's just harder to get your arms around some people than others. I've been compelled to pray for Mr. Enrich ever since he arrived."

"So have I," Louise added.

"Me too."

They all stared at each other, startled.

"Well, this changes everything," Alice said.

"Indeed," Louise intoned.

Jane could not agree more.

"If God has all three of us praying for Mr. Enrich, then he is here for a reason," Louise said. "We must also pray that we are the tools that God needs."

"I think of all the people who passed the poor man who was robbed and lay beaten on the road from Jerusalem to Jericho," Alice said. "The thieves who beat him and left him for dead, the priest and the Levite who moved to the other side of the road. Even the innkeeper only tended him because he was being paid."

"But the Samaritan had the heart and the attitude of Christ, and he cared for him," Jane added.

They were all silent, thinking of the commitment they had made when they had opened the inn, but the quiet was soon shattered by the slam of the screen door, announcing that Mr. Enrich had arrived. The sisters glanced at each other.

"I'll go," Jane offered. "I heard him mention a couple days ago that his favorite pie was apple, so I made one today. We can treat him and have something to welcome our new guests too." Jane's custom of providing late-arriving guests with a hospitable dessert was one of the most appreciated niceties that the inn offered. It was a chance for them to sit down, meet the other guests and relax a bit while one of the sisters—usually Alice—checked them into the inn.

"Mr. Enrich?" Jane came upon the man in the hall and was startled by his appearance. His dark hair was disheveled and he looked haggard and drawn, as if he had aged since morning.

His brown eyes darted toward her, hostility in his expression. "What?"

She felt a stab of fear for him. He seemed desperate. It was as though he were a drowning man and she had the means to rescue him.

"I ... ah ..." She was not even sure that she should continue after seeing that look in his eyes, but she couldn't stop herself. "I baked you an apple pie. Would you like a slice? With vanilla ice cream?"

He paused as he processed her invitation. "You made me a pie?"

"Yes. You said you liked apple best. We have two new guests coming in later, but why don't you join me and my sisters in the kitchen. We could have ours now."

He looked as though the invitation baffled him. Though he took a quick glance up the stairs toward his room, his gaze finally settled on Jane. "That would be . . . nice."

"Good. Do you like it heated? One scoop of ice cream or two?"

They gathered to eat around the big kitchen table. Alice brewed tea while Louise took napkins and cups from the cupboard. Mr. Enrich observed their busyness as though they were aliens.

When he took a taste of the pie, his eyes opened a little wider. "This is good."

"Thanks. I'd hoped it would be," Jane said serenely.

He said very little as they ate, but he didn't have to. Louise regaled them with a story about one of her piano students that day, a young boy who had come with a note he claimed was from his mother, a college professor. Louise took the note from her pocket and passed it around. It read, "Randy couldn't practis this week cause he had the flew."

They all laughed at the work of the professor's "ghost writer."

Then Alice began talking about the book she had begun reading. It was about God's gifts and how much each individual has been given. She turned in her chair. "What do you think your special blessings are, Mr. Enrich?"

He started in his chair. "Me? Uh...maybe you're asking the wrong person. I've never been very religious. God's never done very much for me."

"Really." Jane put her elbows on the table and her palms beneath her chin. "How do you know?"

"Because, well...just look at me."

"You look perfectly fine to us," Louise said.

"Handsome, even," Jane said. Even as she said it she wondered why those particular words had slipped out of her mouth.

"You don't know me," he protested, but he didn't sound angry or put out. "There are lots of things I've wanted, and none of them happened."

Three curious pairs of eyes stared at him, and he felt compelled to continue. "I wanted a wife and a family," he stammered, "but my wife left me and took our son. I rarely see him any more. Now that he's a teenager, he doesn't want to hang around with his dull old dad. I wanted my own business and that went belly-up a year ago. Does any of this sound like God's been working for me?" His laugh was bitter. "I don't think so."

"So God's been ignoring you?" Jane asked.

"Sure seems like it. If He exists at all, that is."

Alice's eyes grew moist. "He exists, all right. We all know Him personally."

His eyes narrowed. "Yeah, right . . . whatever."

"Don't let us make you uncomfortable, Mr. Enrich. It's just that each of us has had the experience of God's generosity." Jane smiled a little. "And He didn't give me what I thought I wanted either."

At his doubtful expression, she continued. "I wanted a marriage that worked, a successful, well-known restaurant, money, a taste of fame . . ." She spread out a hand and gestured to the expanse of the room. "And here I am, in the house I grew up in, in a little town in Pennsylvania that very few people have even heard of—and happier than I've been in years."

"I don't get it."

"Neither did I. I still don't, sometimes. It's amazing how God can turn a life around and make something mundane or unremarkable into a gift."

"Why are you telling me this?" His eyes narrowed and he scowled.

"I have no idea," Jane admitted cheerfully. "My mouth seems to be in gear without my brain tonight. More pie?"

He begged off, but not before thanking her for the dessert. He then excused himself and retreated to his room.

The kitchen was quiet for a long time after he had left.

The doorbell rang just after Louise had threatened to give up on the new guests and go to bed. Jane never minded staying up for late-arriving guests because, years before, she had grown to like the late hours that she had kept at the restaurant. Of course, now no one let her sleep late the next morning. Alice, who was equally accustomed to unpredictable hours as a nurse, was also flexible.

"Just in time," Alice said as Jane jumped up to get the door.

Two faces were peering through the screen door when Jane entered the hall. "Welcome," she said to Nancy and Zack Colwin as she opened the screen door to let them enter.

Jane suspected they were older than they looked. At least, she hoped that was true because the pair looked all of nineteen years old. The woman had thick black hair that fell to midback, a ruddy complexion, rosy cheeks and a big smile that revealed slightly overlapping front teeth. She was robust and altogether pleasant looking.

Her husband was very thin. He wore khakis and a white-and-blue striped shirt. His light brown hair was cut in a boyish style and his smile was even wider than his wife's.

"Sorry we're late," said Nancy. "We took more time than we'd planned looking at restaurants in little towns along the way. We had no idea how many there are out here."

"Looking for something to eat?" Jane inquired, thinking of her pie.

"Not that, although we did have an excellent blue-plate special at a place called Henrietta's Diner somewhere. Do you remember the name of the town, Zack?"

"Not a clue." He looked around the foyer and peered up the stairway to the second floor. "This is a great place."

"Thank you." Jane gestured toward the dining room. "We have pie for a bedtime snack if you wish. You can eat while Alice is checking you in. Or if you aren't hungry ..."

"I'm always hungry," Zack said, enthusiastically rubbing his flat stomach.

"You'd never know it to look at him," Nancy grumbled cheerfully. "The thing I envy most about my husband is his efficient metabolism. He burns off calories sitting still."

Louise, yawning behind her ever-present white hankie, introduced herself before going off to bed. After registering the new pair, Alice settled them at the dining-room table and gave them some tips about the inn and Acorn Hill while Jane dished up pie and ice cream in the kitchen.

"This is the best pie I've ever had," Zack said enthusiastically. He looked up from his plate before taking another bite. "Believe me, that's saying quite a lot."

"Zack's a sweets freak," Nancy explained. "Some people have a sweet tooth. Zack has an entire set of them. It's a good thing he does what he does for a living."

"And what's that?" Alice asked politely.

"He's a cook, baker, chef, whatever. Just an all around 'food guy.'"

"Really?" Jane sat straighter in her chair. "Tell us more."

"Nancy and I have been working for a lunch and supper place that is open from eleven in the morning to eleven at night. It's been good work and good pay, but it was recently sold. The new owners closed the place for two weeks to remodel and gave us vacation time. So Nancy and I have been driving around, looking at scenery and scouting out restaurants."

"Our favorite pastime," Nancy chimed in.

"Some people like movies and popcorn. You just like restaurants," Jane said. "It makes perfect sense to me."

"Someday Zack and I would like to have our own restaurant," Nancy said. She glanced warily at Zack before continuing. "But we have a few details yet to iron out. We can't seem to agree on exactly what we want."

"Not really," Zack corrected his wife. "I think we're sure of the direction we're going."

Nancy stiffened. "Maybe you are sure, Zack, but I'm not."

A slight tension seemed to dance in the air until Zack stood up and said, "We have lots of time to relax and discuss it here, Nancy. Are you ready to go upstairs?"

After she had said good night to the Colwins, Jane loaded their dishes into the dishwasher and set it on delay so that it would start after everyone had fallen asleep. She absently brushed a tiny crumb from the counter and turned out all but a small night-light in the dining room. She always left that on for late-night snackers who sometimes raided the cookie jar.

So, Nancy and Zack wanted to buy a restaurant—if they could settle on a single vision. Jane wished she could help them or give them some direction. Perhaps she could put them in touch with her old boss, Trent Vescio at the Blue Fish Grille. Maybe he could give them some ideas. But this was not California, and it was not easy to make restaurants succeed.

"Morning, Jane," Fred Humbert greeted her as she entered the hardware store. "What's new with you on this fine day?"

"Same old, same old," Jane replied. "I ran into Vera and she told me your daughters are coming home."

"For the school reunion. Just like everyone else who's ever passed through the doors of Acorn Hill's school. Vera is beginning to panic. She doesn't know where'll she put all the company. I told Joe just this morning that if it got much worse, I'd have to rent out his room and let him sleep in the basement." Fred looked up. "Didn't I, Joe?"

"Sí." Joe, his dark eyes sparkling, nodded in agreement. "And we could put a mattress on the floor too. We wouldn't have to charge so much for it."

"You've made him into a regular entrepreneur, Fred," Jane said as Joe grinned and returned to his work, loading bins with various sized nails.

"He's done it himself." Fred's eyes glowed with gratitude. "I don't know how many times I've silently thanked you for introducing me to Joe. I thought I was helping him by giving him a room and a job, but he's given me much more. Business has never been better since he started his lawn and snow removal services out of this place. People are so happy with his work that they come in and walk out with more bags of peat, fertilizer and weed killer than ever before. One day I had two ladies in here arguing over whose house Joe should go to first."

Jane looked at Joe, who had modestly hung his head. "Good for you, Joe."

When he looked up to shake his head, there were tears in his eyes. "Not me. You, Miss Jane, Mr. Humbert—and especially God."

Jane did not have any doubt of that.

"But back to business," Fred said. "What can I get for you?"

"Just one of those special picture hangers for plaster walls."

"I'll get it, Miss Jane." Joe smiled happily, and for some odd reason Mr. Enrich popped into Jane's mind. Why couldn't everyone be happy and smiling like Joe? Mr. Enrich was often as surly and irritable as Joe was sunny.

After making her purchase and saying her good-byes, Jane left the hardware store and headed for the Good Apple, where she found Mayor Tynan and her aunt Ethel seated on iron chairs on either side of a small table. From the powdered sugar on Lloyd's tie, Jane deduced that he had had doughnuts with his coffee. Ethel, who had lately been claiming to be watching her figure, had remnants of a blueberry Danish on her plate. Apparently she was, in fact, only "watching" her figure, not doing anything about it.

"Come sit down," Ethel invited, "and tell us what you've been up to."

Tell us the latest gossip, Jane translated mentally. Out loud, she said, "Thanks, but I just came in to visit with Clarissa. . . ."

"She's out back. Someone came to pick up a huge order of buns and cookies for the Methodists. They must be having something special this evening."

Jane was surprised that her aunt didn't know exactly what was going on, what time it started and who would attend. Were Ethel's information-gathering skills slipping?

"I thought you knew," Lloyd said. "Big meeting with Potterston Methodists tonight. They're kicking off a new fund-raising campaign for missions. I'm going to pledge something myself."

"By the way, Aunt Ethel, are any of my Buckley cousins coming for the reunion?"

Ethel looked crestfallen for a moment but rallied immediately. "No, I'm sad to say. None of them has any vacation time left at work, but they all plan to visit Acorn Hill as soon as their jobs allow." She beamed. "We're thinking about a little family reunion. You girls, of course, will be the first to know. My place is so small that I'm sure that they'll all want to stay with you at the inn."

"Naturally," Jane said, sighing inwardly. *Another party where I'll be in charge of meals.*

"Ethel's not feeling too bad about it though," Lloyd said proudly. "You're taking it rather well, aren't you?"

"I will get to see them," Ethel said logically. "And there will be so much happening now that I'd hate to miss . . . be tied down . . . *er*, not be available to help wherever I'm needed."

The truth had come out. Ethel was relieved that she would not miss a thing at the reunion.

"Any new guests at the inn?" she asked, eyes bright. A good share of Ethel's entertainment was observing the activity at the inn. She was always tuned in to what was happening next door.

"A young couple checked in last night. We didn't visit much, but I'll bet you'll see them around today." Jane was careful not to divulge too much information about her guests lest Ethel take it and run with it—all over town.

"That's it?" Ethel was obviously disappointed.

"Believe it or not," Jane said, amused, "life at the inn isn't a laugh a minute or excitement all the time. I did experiment with a few recipes for tea cookies and made a pie yesterday. Oh, and I spent part of the afternoon sketching at Fairy Pond." The little pond tucked far off Chapel Road into a lush grove of trees was one of Jane's favorite retreats.

"*Harrumph.* I've always thought that was a silly name for a pond," Ethel said. "What were people thinking? That fairies actually lived there?"

"Maybe she's seen one, Ethel. It's a pretty magical place," Lloyd said.

Jane smiled. Fairy Pond had charmed Lloyd too. It was a delightful, serene place, surrounded by a canopy of trees, vines and delicate ferns. Even the deer seemed tamer and the birds less timid around Fairy Pond. There she had done some of her best creative work—sketches and jewelry designs that took on the lacy, delicate feel of the place.

"*Tsk, tsk*," Ethel clucked disapprovingly.

There was nothing of the dreamer in Ethel.

Jane and Lloyd exchanged an amused glance. It was not often that the conservative mayor and the resident artist of Acorn Hill shared the same imaginings.

Ethel dusted a bit of sugar off her blouse and looked at her watch. Jane noticed with some satisfaction that her aunt was giving up on her. Too boring.

Feeling a little sorry for being so dull, Jane offered, "I was in the attic yesterday and found something interesting."

Ethel's upright posture became even more erect. "'Found something'? What did you find?"

"A box of old toys. I haven't had the time to look through them."

"I remember your mother showing me some of her childhood toys. There was a mechanical bank—cast iron as I remember—and some china-headed dolls, tops, things like that." Ethel's expression grew distant. "The toys you found were probably your mother's. Daniel was never given anything 'frivolous' as a child. I fared better because our father had mellowed by the time I came along." Ethel shook her head slowly. "You might think that Daniel would have resented me and the better treatment that I got, but he was such a wonderful brother. So kind." Ethel used her napkin to dab at her eyes, leaving a smudge of powdered sugar on the bridge of her nose.

Jane reached over and gently flicked the sugar away.

Daniel and Ethel were actually half-siblings, but Ethel had always looked up to him and loved him so dearly that rarely did anyone remember that they had had different mothers.

"I'll bet he took good care of you, didn't he, Ethel?" Lloyd asked.

"Oh my, yes." She launched into a long memory of how Daniel would send her little gifts when he was away at college or studying for the ministry. Then she segued into a story about a bag of marbles, a girl with long golden curls, hopscotch and a purloined lunch.

Knowing that this recitation would take some time to wind down, Jane patted her aunt's hand. "I want to hear the story sometime, but I need to talk to Clarissa. Would you excuse me?"

"Run along, dear. We'll come for dinner one night next week, and I'll tell all three of you girls the whole story."

Jane was not sure she had made much of a bargain. Now she would not only have to listen to one of Ethel's rambling stories, but she would also have to cook dinner for Ethel and Lloyd.

"Hello, Jane. I didn't hear you come in," Clarissa said. She looked tired.

"Were you lifting and carrying things you shouldn't have been?"

Clarissa chuckled. "You mean like coarse, heavy buns and cookies hard as rocks? Why, Jane, you know my baking is always light as a feather."

"You should take it easy, that's all."

"Now you sound like my children. They're always saying, 'Take it easy, Mom. Don't work so hard.' *Harrumph*. As if they don't know that my work sent them to college."

"I'm sure they appreciate your work, Clarissa, but maybe they just think you should slow down a little."

Furrows formed across Clarissa's brow. "If I slow down, I may stop. And if I stop, I'm done for."

"Whatever do you mean?"

"Oh, it's Arthur. He's been giving me some trouble lately."

Jane searched her memory banks for someone named Arthur and could not think of anyone in Acorn Hill.

Clarissa laughed at the expression on Jane's face. "You don't know about Arthur? Arthritis. *Arthur-itis*. Get it?"

"You caught me that time," Jane admitted. "That joke is so old that I forgot all about it."

"I'm old, it's old, but you didn't come in to hear my antiquated jokes, now, did you?"

"I actually did have a purpose for stopping by. I wanted to talk business with you."

Clarissa didn't respond, but waved at Lloyd and Ethel, who were making their way to the door. When they had gone, Clarissa looked at the empty display case. "I'll just close up shop first. I'm already eaten out of house and home." As she moved to lock the door and pull down the shade that indicated to the town that she had run out of baked goods for the day, Clarissa spoke over her shoulder to Jane. "I hate to admit it, but I like to close up before the end of the day once in a while. I'm glad when I've misjudged the product I need and run out early on." Then she returned to the counter and filled two cups with the last of the coffee. "Cream or sugar?"

"This is fine."

Clarissa bent under the counter and came up with an old-fashioned cake plate holding two cinnamon scones. She smiled impishly. "And look what I found just for an occasion such as this."

"Who were you saving those for, Clarissa? Surely not me." Still, Jane helped herself to one of the luscious beauties when Clarissa offered it.

"I usually keep something back for myself at the end of the day. I'd be round as a ball if I didn't limit myself to just one sample a day. And I always save two, hoping my last customer will have a few minutes to visit."

"Then I'm very lucky this afternoon," Jane concluded.

"No luckier than me." Clarissa sank into a chair with a sigh. "Ah, that's better."

Jane eyed Clarissa's feet. The woman wore white, lace-up, support shoes, the kind Alice wore for work. Jane could only imagine how many hours a day Clarissa was on her feet. And she could not be younger than seventy-four or -five. No wonder she was tired.

"Maybe this isn't the best time to ask what I've come to ask," Jane ventured. "Why don't I come back tomorrow, when you've rested up?"

"Don't try wiggling out of it," said Clarissa, wagging a finger at Jane. "Now you've tickled my curiosity. What's that inventive mind of yours hatching now?"

Jane's heart sank. Clarissa's eyes were tired behind her smile, she had flour and cocoa powder up and down the front of her apron, and a wisp of gray hair had escaped her hairnet.

Oh well, Jane thought. *Say it anyway.* "You know all the hubbub about the reunion, and how we talked about the catering being too much for a restaurant not set up for events this large?"

Clarissa nodded suspiciously.

"Well, it's come to this. Orlando's has bowed out of catering the breakfasts in Acorn Hill, and the committee has asked me to cater them and the afternoon socials."

"So late in the game? The reunion is practically upon us." Clarissa whistled under her breath. "Better you than me."

"That's the challenge, Clarissa. It won't happen unless it's me *and* you." Jane hurried on before Clarissa could say no. "I don't have the equipment to cater. The only way we can provide for the reunion guests now is if everyone pitches in. The Coffee Shop is willing to make pies, Wilhelm's Time for Tea will be offering afternoon tea, and church ladies from around town will be serving coffee. I can't even name everyone who's volunteered to help out. But the only one who has the skill and capacity to do the baked goods is you."

Clarissa's eyes lit for a brief moment and then faded. "I'd love to, Jane, but the Good Apple will keep me busy enough. I've already started getting orders from townspeople who are having a gaggle of relatives staying with them. There's no way I can do it. I'm only one woman."

"What if you were two or three people?" Jane asked.

Clarissa chuckled. "Then I could do about anything. But I have enough trouble just keeping someone here to help in front while I'm baking. Catering an event the size of this reunion? I don't think so."

Jane's shoulders sank. She knew Clarissa was right. She also knew that she was fresh out of ideas for making it work any other way. Lloyd had suggested they have everything made in Acorn Hill so, as he put it, "we can strut our stuff." Pride, the downfall of nations. Maybe it just was not meant to be. Jane dreaded breaking the news to Lloyd and Ethel.

She put her hand on Clarissa's. "I understand, but if any miracles occur back there in the bakery and somehow you can manage it, let me know."

"I'd love to, Jane, you know that, but it would have to be a miracle."

"Then I guess I'll start praying that the right thing happens—whatever it might be. I can be content with that." Wanting to change the subject, Jane went on, "Is Olivia coming home for the reunion?"

Olivia, usually called Livvy, was Clarissa's oldest daughter, a dark-haired beauty who had recently become the superintendent of a large school in Oregon. She was smart, organized and used to taking the helm. Louise often talked about what a good example Livvy must make for her students. Livvy was a loving but formidable person, much, Jane had heard, like Clarissa's late husband.

"Oh yes, Livvy will be here. So will my sons, Kent and Raymond. They're coming together for a quick trip and will bring their families along later when I'm not so busy. Kent is a youth pastor now, you know. He's married and has two young children. Raymond still runs the automotive garage in South Dakota. It will be good to get my children all together again." Clarissa said the last part so oddly that Jane looked at her questioningly.

"Oh, I love my children with all my heart, it's just that sometimes..."

"Yes? I'm all ears."

"Well, they're the *bossiest* group of human beings on the planet. Each of them calls me up all the time to tell me what to do with my life. Sometimes they turn the tables on me and treat me like a child. 'Mother, do this. Mother, do that. Get a new stove. Save your money. Move to an apartment. Retire.' Mercy, sometimes those children drive me nuts."

"They love you and they think they're helping."

"Well, they aren't. I may be an old gray mare, but I'm not ready for the glue factory yet." She paused to chuckle. "And if they'd heard me say that, they would have told me to 'get with it' and not use those old sayings anymore."

"You're worried that the reunion will be a prime time for them to gang up on you and give you some unhelpful advice."

"That's it in a nutshell. And if they saw me tackling the reunion baking alone, they'd have me committed."

"You know best, Clarissa," Jane said gently. "You're one of the smartest businesswomen I know. But remember, miracles can happen."

"I know. I've seen many in my lifetime, but never in the back end of my bakery."

Laughing, the two parted: Clarissa to go home and soak her feet, and Jane to tell the committee that she was not going to be able to pull the catering together.

Lloyd and Ethel, knowing exactly when the sisters sat down to eat, sometimes managed to arrive for a visit just in time for the evening meal. Jane would put a couple of extra pork chops in the pan or stretch dessert by adding a few candies to the plate and invite them to stay.

Tonight, however, Jane was way ahead of them.

She had been feeling a strange urgency about Mr. Enrich ever since he had checked into the inn. He spent most of his time either in his room or in Daniel Howard's library reading her father's old books on philosophy. For whatever reason, Jane felt compelled to reach out to him in a way she usually didn't for their other guests. The inn's policy was to provide only breakfasts for guests, but sometimes, on certain occasions, the sisters would invite them for a light dinner in order to get to know them better.

That was Jane's intention for the evening. She made a gigantic pot of white chicken chili, crusty baguettes, and a caramel apple cheesecake for dessert. She invited

Mr. Enrich, Ned and the Colwins to join them for dinner. Ned, as Jane thought he would, declined so that he could catch up on paperwork at the pharmacy, but the Colwins agreed eagerly. Mr. Enrich also agreed, but in a somewhat confused manner.

Alice put an extra leaf in the dining room table, and Louise set out red-and-white-checked placemats and napkins while Jane made a centerpiece of fresh fruits and vegetables. The table was festive and welcoming by the time the guests arrived.

Chapter Four

*T*hat was one mighty fine meal," Lloyd said as he pushed away from the table. "Mighty fine indeed." He dusted the crumbs off his vest and sighed contentedly.

"It was delicious, my dear," Ethel agreed, "even if chili is supposed to be red and not white."

"Just great," Nancy Colwin said. "We want your recipe."

"Jane's going to do an entire cookbook," Ethel informed the Colwins proudly. "Then you'll be able to get all of her recipes."

"Terrific. Where do I sign up?" Zack asked.

Jane enjoyed the young couple. They were so enthusiastic and full of energy—as she had been early in her career. Jane was, of course, still enthusiastic and energetic, but her energy would not last forever. Jane thought of Clarissa and how her business had worn her down.

"I hear all three of Clarissa Cottrell's children are coming for the reunion," Ethel announced.

Louise's eyes brightened. "Good. I would love to see Livvy again. She was an excellent pianist, very talented. She played for me one summer when I was here visiting. I do hope she has kept it up."

"Probably," Ethel said. "If she made up her mind to do something, she never gave up. Remember all the trouble she gave her mother over redecorating the Good Apple?"

"Redecorating?" Jane frowned. "The Good Apple hasn't changed much over the years."

"Oh, Clarissa held fast. Said people didn't come in to see psychedelic colors and lava lamps. Fortunately, the older Livvy got, the smarter Clarissa seemed to become too.

"A couple years back," Ethel added, "Clarissa told me Livvy had admitted that she was *glad* Clarissa hadn't changed the store. Too bad she didn't figure that out before she caused her mother all that gray hair."

"Now, with the responsibility of being superintendent of a big school district," Alice said, "she probably needs all that fire and more."

"What became of the boys?" Louise inquired.

Jane noticed that the Colwins and even Mr. Enrich seemed pleased by the homey conversation. She said nothing as Ethel happily repeated to the guests what Clarissa had told Jane earlier.

"Kent is a youth pastor in Oregon," Ethel informed them. "He was so quiet I never thought he'd be able to speak in public, but Clarissa says he's wonderful with children."

"Such a kind young man," Alice recalled. "He was in our church youth group at one time."

"How long have you worked with Grace Chapel's youth?" Nancy inquired.

"For the past twenty-five years." Alice put her hand to her cheek. "My, that certainly dates me."

"And Ray still has a garage in South Dakota," Lloyd added. "Always loved working with his hands. Never had much time for talking, that one."

"He is the one with Clarissa's sense of humor, though," Louise said. "His eyes were always twinkling over something."

"Do you know *everyone* in Acorn Hill?" Nancy asked. Jane could hear wistfulness in her voice.

Ethel stared at her as if she had sprouted a second head. "Of course. Why wouldn't we?"

"Nancy came from a smaller community in Michigan. I lived in a city where we never knew many people outside our immediate friends and family." He turned to his wife. "Maybe you're a little homesick."

"I think it is so...cozy...here," Nancy said. "I love it. I hope you all realize how nice you have it—friends, extended family, community, fellowship."

Zack's head bobbed. "Growing up, I would have given anything for that." A longing expression flitted across his face. "But the city is what I'm accustomed to."

Lloyd emitted a horrified sound. "Terrible! That's no way to grow up."

Jane smiled to herself. Lloyd's ideas about cities were similar to his ideas about freeways and traffic snarls—no place for human beings to be.

Louise cleared her throat. She didn't want her guests to feel insulted. "Well, getting back to Clarissa, she has a talented family, no doubt about that," she concluded.

"But...," Lloyd started.

"But bossy?" Alice put in.

Although Louise tried to look aghast at Alice's and Lloyd's candor, the description was no surprise.

What was a surprise, however, was Mr. Enrich's foray into the discussion. "Sometimes being a smart-aleck catches up with you," he said, looking startled even as he said it.

To make him feel comfortable, Jane said, "I agree. It's not until we figure out that we don't know much of anything and submit to God's wisdom that we get wise."

That brought nods from around the table, and Mr. Enrich retreated into silence.

"Since we're speaking of Clarissa," Jane began, dreading to tell Lloyd and Ethel her news, "I'm sorry to tell you that she's not able to do the baking for me. I'm afraid that means that I won't be able to cater the reunion breakfasts."

"Doesn't she know how important this is?" Lloyd sounded shocked.

"I'm sure she does. She also knows that she's the only one baking. There's no way she can do it alone."

Ethel cleared her throat. "I'm afraid she's right, Lloyd."

The three sisters just about sprained their necks swiveling them to stare at their aunt. Ethel, not agreeing with Lloyd? Would wonders ever cease?

"I've done a fair amount of baking in my day, and that much work would be difficult for anyone—especially one getting on in years."

Lloyd sputtered, "But, but…"

"When's this reunion of yours?" Zack asked.

Jane gave Zack the date.

"That's barely a week away."

"Yes, that's why everyone is in such a tizzy."

Zack sat in thoughtful silence for a moment and then said, "We'll still be on vacation. If you'd like, maybe Nancy and I could help out your friend. It would be okay with you, wouldn't it, honey?"

Nancy looked surprised, but not annoyed. "I suppose so."

"You can't break into your holiday to work for complete strangers," Alice protested. "This is your vacation."

"Why not? It's a worthy cause, right? We can sightsee with Grace Chapel Inn as our home base as well as using any other spot in Pennsylvania," Zack said cheerfully. "If a couple days of help would make it easier, let us know. Besides, it might be fun. Sounds like the reunion parties are going to be an event."

"You aren't serious, are you?" Jane asked.

"Nancy and I will talk it over tonight."

The entire group turned to stare at Nancy.

"Someday I'll grow accustomed to Zack surprising me like this," Nancy said, looking unfazed. "His parents are always volunteering in a soup kitchen or nursing home. Last year when we arrived for Thanksgiving, we found a note on the door saying 'Meet us at the Mission on Fourth Street. You two are serving turkey and dressing.' He comes by it naturally." She appeared resigned, if not delighted.

"We'll let you know for sure in the morning." Zack paused. "But even if we can help, maybe your friend doesn't want to do it at all. You should probably consider other options anyway."

"I'll deal with Clarissa." Lloyd announced this with an authority that everyone knew was all bluster, but the entire table could see how grateful he was for the offer.

"One thing at a time," Jane suggested. "On the off chance you *do* help out, we insist that you and Nancy stay on at the inn. The reunion days will be free of charge, of course."

Louise looked surprised. "But the rooms..."

"Oh, we'll manage just fine," Jane said confidently. "Alice and I have bunked together before. We can always set up a cot in the library for an emergency. Someone might need a place to stay and would be willing to rough it for the weekend."

"Maybe I could stay in the library."

Mr. Enrich had stunned them twice this evening. No one had anticipated his having any input into the conversation, considering how uncommunicative he had been. And after his critical comments about the inn during his first days there, no one had dreamed that he would want to bunk in the inn's library.

"You?" Louise blurted. "Why?"

"What my sister meant," Alice hurried to explain, "was that since you aren't an alumnus..."

"I know I'd planned to leave before your reunion guests start arriving, but it looks like it might be..." his face twisted, as if he had difficulty spitting out the next word, "fun."

Everyone stared at the man. *Mr. Enrich is looking for fun?* Jane thought. *Who would have guessed?*

"If it's a problem..." he added.

"Not a problem at all," Jane said firmly before Louise could speak. "None at all. We'll be delighted to have you. We'll consider you 'family' during the reunion, if you don't mind."

Louise and Alice looked at Jane as if she had lost her wits. This was not how they treated guests, banishing them to sleep in the common rooms of the inn.

Mr. Enrich, however, seemed faintly pleased. "I don't have any other plans. And it's been . . ." he paused to search for something to say, "nice, here. I didn't really expect to be around this long." A strange, pained look crossed his face. "But here I am." Even he looked mystified.

"It's settled then," Jane said. She had no idea what drew her to this odd man or made her feel responsible for him, but she had learned in her life that it was always wisest to follow God's nudging, even when it sent her in a strange direction. Why she thought this was from God, she was not sure, but she also knew that if the reclusive Mr. Enrich expressed any interest whatsoever in what was going on around him, it was worth encouraging.

"If you're willing, I'd appreciate your giving me a hand during the reunion. We'll be very short on help, and it might make the weekend more interesting for you." Where had that come from? Since when did she order her guests to work?

Since just now, she decided, as Mr. Enrich nodded.

God, this is weird, but I believe You're behind it, so take it and run with it and let me know what I'm supposed to do, she prayed silently.

"Well, well, well," Lloyd spluttered, his face red and beaming, "if everything falls into place, this is going to be a dandy reunion."

"Dandy." Jane certainly hoped so.

"You look like the dog ate your socks," Jane commented as she entered Sylvia's Buttons. Sylvia Songer was sitting on a high stool by her cutting counter staring at papers that were spread out across it like leaves after a windstorm.

"If only that were it," Sylvia moaned. She and Jane had become close friends since Jane's return to Acorn Hill, but lately they had not been seeing as much of each other socially as they would like. The all-school reunion was taking every waking moment—and some of Sylvia's sleeping ones too, by the look of it.

She pushed away the piles of papers and supported her head with her hands. "This reunion is never going to work. Never."

"I don't believe that for a moment," Jane said calmly. "I'm going to make tea." She went into the back of the store where she could always find hot water in an insulated carafe and a basket of assorted teas from Tea for Two.

She put two bags of peppermint tea into a small pot, filled it with water and carried it on a tray with two cups to

Sylvia, who was still at the table. Jane poured the tea and set a cup in front of her friend.

Finally Sylvia roused herself. Taking the steaming cup in her hands, she moaned, "The logistics of this are going to kill me. Whatever made me think this would be fun? I'll be a pariah after the debacle I've created."

"What's today's crisis?" Jane asked evenly. Sylvia had been on a roller coaster of emotions for weeks, and her state was getting worse as the reunion date neared.

"Too few booths for vendors, too many people wanting places to stay, too few parade entries, too many complainers and," she eyed Jane glumly, "too few caterers to get the job done."

"Maybe, and maybe not." Jane told her about the Colwins.

"What did Clarissa say?"

"I haven't asked her yet. I'm almost scared to do it."

"Think she'll say no again?"

"Possibly. But she's feeling so tired that I'm almost afraid she'll say yes." Jane tugged on her own hair. "I'm getting the idea that Clarissa's children won't enjoy seeing Clarissa working that hard either."

"Clarissa knows her own mind," Sylvia assured Jane. "Just because she's got gray hair, it doesn't mean her mind is aging too. My mother always said her biggest frustration was that when she got older, people wanted to treat her differently."

Jane nodded in agreement. "I know I feel younger than I am, younger than when I was young, actually. I have a much stronger sense of myself and my relationship with God and others. I finally understand what George Bernard Shaw meant when he said that youth is wasted on the young."

Sylvia nodded, sighed and went back to shuffling her papers.

Clarissa, somewhat to Jane's surprise, was delighted that the Colwins were considering working with her.

"You mean it? You found help for me? Somebody who's actually had experience?"

Jane retold the story of Zack and Nancy's offer. "They haven't said for sure. They were going to talk it over last night, and I left the inn before they came down for breakfast, but I think they'll help. So, what do you think?"

"I think I've been feeling sorry that I couldn't contribute any more to the reunion and was saying 'poor old me' last night." She gave a happy grin. "The only thing worn out about me is my body, Jane. I want to be involved. Maybe this will allow it."

"They're pretty young," Jane warned. "They might think they have better ideas than yours."

"Don't worry about that. Remember, I raised Livvy, the most opinionated young woman in three counties. I can handle them. In fact, after Livvy, the Colwins will be a pleasure."

∽

"Has anyone seen Mr. Enrich lately?" Jane asked as she entered the kitchen and found her sisters poring over the inn's finances, their heads nearly touching as they studied the books in front of them.

"No. Not since breakfast." Alice looked up from the ledger and pushed her hair away from her face.

A few minutes later, Jane ran into Mr. Enrich coming out of the library. He hadn't shaved. A stubbly shadow covered his jaw. Neither had he combed his hair, which stood in dark spiky points on his head. As always, Jane was startled by the haunted look that never seemed to leave his eyes.

"Been reading?" Jane eyed the C. S. Lewis books under his arm. She doubted that some of her father's books had been read since Daniel passed away, so she was glad someone was finally using them.

"You've got quite a library," Mr. Enrich commented.

"My father did. He'd rather buy himself a book than a pair of shoes or trousers." She chuckled. "That may or may not tell you something about the look of his wardrobe."

A stiff smile contorted the corners of Mr. Enrich's lips.

How long has it been, Jane wondered, *since the man's laughed?*

"Mr. Enrich, I've been noticing the titles you've chosen. Most of our guests read the lighter fare. You've even had out a few books my father used when he was in seminary years ago."

"Never read anything like that. Thought I'd try."

Wendell came strolling out of the room yawning and stretching. He was even staggering a little, as if he was having difficulty waking from the deep sleep he had been enjoying. He glided over to Jane and wound himself around her ankles, purring.

"I see you had company for the day," Jane said. "I wondered where he'd gone."

"He kept meowing at the door until I let him in. I hope that was okay."

"Sure. Wendell actually owns the house. We simply live here as his slaves. He was my father's cat and grew accustomed to long days in the study, dozing, while Dad read."

Mr. Enrich looked at her oddly. "I've never been in a place quite like this," he said after a long pause.

"The inn, you mean?"

"Where people are so willing to share what they have with others. Even the cat is sociable. My wife had a cat and it didn't like anyone but her. It never did quit hissing and spitting at me when I came within three feet of it."

His life was none of her affair, Jane reminded herself. None at all. But Mr. Enrich must have felt her curiosity.

"I had a turn of bad luck with business and was spending an inordinate amount of time working. One night I came home late and went to bed. It wasn't until I woke up in the morning that I realized that not only was my wife's side of the bed not slept in, but her clothes, her cat, our son and the living room furniture were gone." He seemed to marvel as he said it. "Can you imagine?"

Then, like a clam snapping shut, Mr. Enrich closed his mouth. It was clear that he regretted his revelations.

Although he had just said more about himself than he had since he first arrived, Jane knew that this information was just the tip of the iceberg.

As Jane slowly maneuvered the staircase carrying a load of freshly washed linens, she heard low, urgent voices coming from the Colwins' room at the top of the stairs.

"If you'd just make up your mind it would be much easier."

"Make up *my* mind? You're the one who's changing her ideas every five minutes."

"That's not fair, Zack. I think the restaurant we work at is just fine. Pretty soon, we'll have saved enough for a down payment on a house and we can start a family..."

"And support it with what?"

"It's you, Zack, who keeps thinking there's something big over the horizon, some pie in the sky, a jackpot. We don't have to have a fancy restaurant right away. Maybe we'll never need one. I'd rather have a little house and a family, remember?"

"Come on, Nancy. Be realistic. Kids cost money. Houses cost money. We've got to get our finances in order before we start any of that."

"But what if there's always something else out there that you want to do first." Her voice had a painful catch in it. "I grew up in a sweet little neighborhood like this one. I want my children to experience the things I had."

"And just who is going to pay for all that? My folks didn't have any money. I know how that feels, and I also know it's something I never want to experience again. First things first."

"That's what I am doing, putting first things first—a baby, a happy life, settling down and not thinking up one fantastical thing after another to pursue. One day you're going to run out of rainbows, Zack."

Jane had just reached the top step when the Colwins' door burst open and Nancy, tears glistening on her cheeks, shot past Jane down the stairs and out the front door. Zack closed the door to their room without looking after his wife.

First Mr. Enrich and now this. What was wrong with her guests? She had never seen such turmoil and distress.

Mr. Enrich wandered into the dining room and was obviously surprised to find a tea party in session. Josie and Jane were having a tête-à-tête over miniature sandwiches and cookies. "Oh, excuse me," he stammered and started backing toward the door.

"Would you like to join us?" Josie asked, sounding forty years old as she said it. She pointed a finger at one of the empty chairs. "Just don't sit on my doll," Josie instructed firmly. "You may have your own chair."

Josie, wearing a pair of Louise's old dress shoes, a shawl Alice had dug out of her closet and a floppy hat of Jane's, presided over the tea party. The chairs around the dining table were filled with teddy bears and ragtag dolls that Josie had dragged from home.

It always delighted Josie when Jane dressed up for these impromptu play dates. So, Jane wore a flowing golden pants and blouse outfit with sandals made of faux-leopard leather. She completed the ensemble with a wide-brimmed, tan felt hat decorated with colorful feathers and a beaded band. She looked as exotic as a day in the Serengeti.

"Tea?" Jane asked primly. Jane loved these play teas she and Josie concocted. Normally they were held in the kitchen, but today they had decided to be special and use the dining room.

"*Puleeeze*, Mr. Enrich," the little girl cajoled as the man shook his head and began backing from the room again. "It would make me *sooo* happy."

He stopped and then walked stiffly toward a chair. The child was impossible to resist.

They ate with their pinkies in the air at Josie's insistence. When Josie decided that her baby doll needed to be changed and trotted off to do some intense mothering, Jane and Mr. Enrich switched from cookies to the plate of Madeleine and Daughters chocolates Jane had set on the table.

"Do you do this a lot?" Mr. Enrich asked.

"Sometimes," Jane said. "It's kind of fun, don't you think?"

"Yeah . . . *er* . . . fun," he muttered as Josie returned.

Moments later, Lloyd, Ethel and Sylvia found them there, looking like escapees from the Mad Hatter's Tea Party, finishing up the tea and the tidbits left on the plates, pinkie fingers all high in the air.

Chapter Five

I'm sure you're a wonderful chef," Alice said to Zack as they visited after breakfast the next morning. Everyone had finished eating, Ned had left for the pharmacy and Nancy had gone upstairs. Mr. Enrich sat unsmiling as usual but hadn't made a move to leave the table.

"Yeah, and I love it. I had a great job as a salad chef and then pastry chef at a well-known restaurant. I saw how a famous restaurant works—from the ground up. Ever since then, I've known I wanted to create my own special signature place." His eyes were shining. "What a great challenge!"

"How fortunate you have such a wonderful vision for your future. I wish I could say the same for some of the young people I've been working with lately. A few of them can't see the future beyond their own noses. They can't imagine how good their lives and relationships could be and how much they have to offer the world."

Mr. Enrich unexpectedly cleared his throat and spoke. "What if they don't have anything to offer and no fulfilling relationships? What if there is no good future for them?"

Alice gave as emphatic a response as Jane had ever heard from her sister. "Of course they have a future."

"How do you know?"

"Because God made them. He knit each one of us in our mother's wombs. He gave us gifts to use and a reason for being. It's up to us to bring out the best of His gifts."

"You say that like you believe it," Mr. Enrich said mildly.

"With all my heart." Alice straightened.

⌒

"What are you two up to?" Louise asked. "What are those bumping and scraping sounds coming from the library?"

"Mr. Enrich and I have been putting up his cot," answered Jane. "We're also going through that carton of toys that I brought down from the attic. I just came in for a drink of water."

When she returned to the library, Mr. Enrich had unwrapped all the toys and was just removing a smaller box from the storage carton. He handed it to Jane.

"*Hmm*," she said as she knelt on the floor and opened it. Whatever it was had been packed with newspaper dated from the nineteen-fifties. She lifted a paper-wrapped object out of the box and peeled away the layers. "Well, look at this."

Mr. Enrich stared curiously.

It was a vase about eight inches tall—flat on one side and curved like a regular vase on the other. The colors, mostly orange and black, covered an embossed surface. When she turned it over, Jane saw a flat picture hook on the back. "Looks like this was meant to hang on the wall. I wonder what they put in it."

"Air ferns," Mr. Enrich said.

"What are those?"

"My grandmother used to have little vases like that all over her house. She'd put in some rootless little ferns that she called air ferns. As a child I thought the ferns must be magical because they never needed water or soil. I never did find out what they actually were—maybe something like dried flowers."

Jane stood up with the odd little container in her hand. "Let's see what Louise knows about this vase."

As they entered the kitchen, Louise announced, "I'm making lunch."

"Great. What are we having?" Jane asked.

Louise paused. "*Er*, what were you planning?"

"I've spoiled you, haven't I?"

"You *have* spoiled us," Louise admitted. "I have begun to assume that when I open the refrigerator door, my meal will be there." Louise pulled at the refrigerator door, and it opened to reveal a plate of ham sandwiches cut in triangles and covered with plastic wrap. There was a bowl of potato salad decorated with parsley and next to it a pitcher of lemonade. "And you never fail us."

She wagged a finger in Jane's grinning face. "You could have told me you had already planned lunch."

"And Louie, you could have thought of cooking something earlier."

"You like to tease," Louise accused her.

"It's good for you," Jane retorted happily.

Shaking her head, Louise set the table with woven straw placemats and yellow napkins. "What have you got there?" she asked, nodding at the box in Jane's hands.

Jane held up the vase.

"My, my. I haven't seen that in years."

"You remember this vase?"

"Why, yes. It hung on the dining room wall for years. I think Uncle Bob bought it on a trip he and Aunt Ethel had taken somewhere. I was visiting Father when Alice took it down and packed it away. Odd little thing, isn't it?"

"You were right, Mr. Enrich," Jane said to the man who had followed her into the kitchen. She looked again at Louise. "He remembers these from his grandmother's house."

Impulsively, Jane held out the little ceramic vase to Mr. Enrich. "Here."

"What am I supposed to do with it?"

"I don't know. Hang it in your room. Take it home with you and put it in your living room. Keep it as a reminder of your grandmother and of the days you spent at Grace Chapel Inn."

"I couldn't do that." He sounded shocked.

"Why not? No one here has a great attachment to it, and you, at least, seem to have fond memories connected with it. We'd like you to have it, wouldn't we, Louise?"

"Certainly. Our walls are full to overflowing as it is."

Jane thrust it toward him.

Mr. Enrich reached out and respectfully took the small decoration. "I loved my grandmother's house," he said, almost in a whisper.

"Good. Enjoy. Think of us when you look at it."

He stared at her so strangely that Jane felt a shiver down her spine, but he took the vase and carried it carefully to his room.

After the lunch dishes had been cleared, Jane began cooking.

"May I come in?" Nancy Colwin stood in the kitchen door and observed Jane. The sleeves of Jane's pale denim shirt were rolled to her elbows. She was browning sausage for the *strata* she was making for the next morning.

"Sure. I'm just putting this together for breakfast tomorrow," Jane responded. A glass baking dish filled with crustless bread sat nearby. Eggs, milk and an assortment of spices were on the counter close to Jane's elbow. "It needs to be in the refrigerator overnight."

"Yum." Nancy pulled a stool nearer the counter and sat down to watch Jane cook.

"These days I have to be on my toes because Mr. Enrich is always so prompt for breakfast," Jane said as she moved the pan of sausage from the burner. "For that matter, so is Ned. He likes to get to the pharmacy early to prepare for the day. But he moved to the Parkers' house this morning to make way for our reunion guests, so I don't have to worry about him right now." She whisked together the milk, eggs and seasonings. "I like this recipe because it's delicious and it's easy. I'll just pop it in the oven in the morning, cut fresh fruit, make coffee and we'll be set."

"You're a wonderful cook," Nancy said.

"That's a real compliment coming from another professional," Jane said. She was happy to see Nancy so cheerful. The Colwins, though obviously in love, certainly had a tendency to bicker and easily take offense at each other's words. Maybe this was part of the reason they were on vacation—to recover from the stresses of their lives that made them so short with each other. Jane silently prayed that they could find common ground on which they could grow together.

One of Jane's own failings was impatience when she was tired or under stress. Fortunately, the pace of Acorn Hill did not tire her much, and the stress of living with her sisters again was practically nonexistent now. In fact, Louise's and Alice's quirks and foibles had become endearing. Ethel was the one who could still most easily upset Jane, but when Ethel was meddling, she was usually trying to do some good or was suffering from boredom or loneliness. The more troublesome she became, the more Jane felt like giving her a hug.

"I ran into Mr. Enrich in the hall," Nancy said idly. "He's not much of a talker, is he?"

"That's an understatement. You're probably lucky if you got him to say 'hello.'"

"Oh, he did that. I even got him to talk about the breakfasts we've had. He says he likes your Belgian waffles best."

"My, my, a regular chatterbox," Jane said with a chuckle. "I'll put Belgian waffles on my menu this week."

"What's his first name?" Nancy wondered. "All I've ever heard anyone call him is 'Mr. Enrich.'"

Jane paused and set down the mixing bowl she was holding. "I have no idea." She wiped her hands on the big colorful apron she wore. "I'm going to get the reservation book and find out."

She returned a moment later, shaking her head. "It's the strangest thing, but we don't know his first name. The reservation, the slip he signed when he checked in, and his signature in the guest book are all just 'Enrich.'"

"Weird," Nancy commented.

It is *weird*, Jane thought. That, she was sure, had never happened before. Alice, who enjoyed taking reservations and checking in visitors, was always very conscientious about getting as many details as she could about their guests. If there was something special a guest liked—a certain soap, flavored coffee, or a late sleep—the three sisters wanted to know so that they could make the guest's stay more enjoyable. For Alice not to get someone's first name was almost beyond belief. Unless, of course, Mr. Enrich did not care to divulge it. He was one of the most reclusive guests that they had ever had. He seldom talked, never used the telephone and rarely went outside the inn. There was so little that they actually knew about him. They had no idea what he did for a living, although Jane and Louise had speculated that he might be a writer since his light seemed to be on all night.

"I'll have to ask Alice," Jane said. "There is a slim chance that she just forgot to write it down."

"Where's Zack?" Jane asked.

Nancy shrugged her shoulders nonchalantly. "I'm not sure."

Jane looked up sharply. "Is something wrong?" she asked, and then added, "Please feel free to tell me if it's none of my affair."

"Zack and I really want our own business sooner or later, but the way we're going, it's going to be later, much later." Nancy's eyes grew teary. "It's the first major issue that Zack and I haven't agreed about, and it's a huge one."

"Tell me more." Jane sealed the baking dish with aluminum foil and slid it into the refrigerator. Then she took out a tea chest filled with gourmet teas from Time for Tea and set it and two cups on the counter.

"We, being chefs and all, both want to have a restaurant, but our visions of what it is that we want are so different that we aren't getting along well."

Jane put a plate of oatmeal raisin cookies and sour cream bars in front of Nancy. Then she pulled up a stool and sat down.

"Zack has an image of himself in a high white hat, concocting new recipes and creating perfectly artistic presentations of food. He wants to open something trendy, the kind of place people go for special occasions, for meeting friends and for out-of-this-world food. Something unique."

"That sounds lovely," Jane said, thinking of the Blue Fish Grille and all that she had left behind when she moved from San Francisco back to Pennsylvania. "And you?"

"Me? I'm a down-home girl. Meat and potatoes, fresh vegetables, fabulous hearty breads and soups—comfort food. Customers like something delicious that they don't have to identify with a foreign-language dictionary. No morels or sushi. I can make cheesy-potato bread that, served with chowder or soup, will make a banquet. Belly-warming stews and, of course, desserts—that's really what I'm about—decadent chocolate cake, homemade ices and ice creams, Frisbee-sized chocolate chip cookies served with a bottomless cup of great coffee."

"I'm getting hungry just thinking about it," Jane acknowledged, "but I also see your problem."

"Zack wants to make a name for himself somewhere. He'd love a place that's a diner's destination. You know, so good that people would be willing to drive from other places just to experience his food. He's already got a name picked out. Zachary's." Nancy said it a little scornfully. "Great name, huh?"

"And what would you name *your* place?"

"I'm not sure . . ." Nancy gestured at herself. "I'm not fancy. I love comfortable clothing and shoes, the natural look. I'd like a place that would be open only during the day." She blushed a little. "I'm ready to start a family. I'm just plain, I guess."

Plain nothing, Jane thought. Nancy had a healthy fresh-scrubbed look that most other women would give their eyeteeth to achieve.

"Maybe I'd name it something like the places in Acorn Hill," Nancy speculated. "'The Coffee Shop.' There's no doubt what they offer there—great breakfasts, good pie and long conversations with friends."

She called that right, Jane thought. One could get a stack of flapjacks, biscuits and gravy, or any number of other things to fuel up on for the day.

"And I love the bakery's name," Nancy continued. "'The Good Apple.' Quaint. Cheerful. Maybe I would name my place 'Nancy's.'" She sighed. "It's no wonder Zack and I haven't been getting along. I'm afraid the situation will turn into one of those if-you-really-loved-me-you'd-do-this-my-way things. Yet if either of us gives in, I know it will be a source of resentment. We've both worked hard learning our craft and making our dreams come true. Neither of us expected that the one standing in the way would be the other, the one we love most."

"You do have a problem," Jane agreed. "Is there a compromise in this somewhere?"

"Not that we've come up with," Nancy said sadly. "I've been praying for a solution, but so far, no answer."

"Don't give up," Jane urged. "If God's got a hand in it, it will turn out right."

Nancy nodded, but by the way her shoulders drooped, it was obvious that giving up was a very real option for her.

Later that day Jane found Zack sitting in a chair on the front porch holding Wendell. Wendell, she had noticed, was very popular with guests who were feeling disheartened or sad. The big cat seemed to know when a person was troubled and would linger on the lap of someone who needed cheering or consoling. Sometimes Jane wondered if the cat had learned the value of a comforting presence from her father.

"Hi." Zack kept scratching Wendell behind his particularly itchy ear.

"Hi, yourself," Jane responded. "Where's Nancy?"

"She went for a walk."

"I see."

"I wish *I* did," Zack said, shaking his head. "She's upset with me, and all I want to do is make the best possible life for us."

"*Hmm.* The best possible life for whom?"

"Us." His voice faltered. "At least *I* think it's the best life for us."

"I see," Jane said again. Zack was doing just fine without her input.

"She doesn't listen to me. I keep telling her that my way is the fastest way to get what we want—a home, children, a successful business."

"And she doesn't listen?"

"No. I kept telling her but..."

"What does she do?"

"She just keeps saying that I'm not paying attention to her feelings, that I'm not hearing her ..." Zack stopped short and considered what he had just said. "Oh."

Jane remained silent.

"Maybe I haven't been listening as well as *I* should, but we're husband and wife. If she really cared about me, she'd try to help me make this happen, don't you think?"

Jane said nothing.

"I do," Zack continued, completely unaware of the one-sidedness of his conversation. "But I don't want to fight with her. I love her. Even when she's driving me crazy, I love her."

He picked up Wendell and put him gently on the porch floor. "Hey, thanks. I appreciate your input. Maybe I'd better find Nancy and see if we can talk."

Jane watched him go down the walk before she picked up Wendell and buried her nose in his fur. "Wendell," she said. "I see now why you're such a good counselor. I'm going to do it your way from now on. You know how to keep your mouth shut and listen."

Chapter Six

*L*ouise came into the kitchen looking distressed. Jane, who had heard her enter the house, had a glass of lemonade ready for her. As Louise sat down, Alice raised one eyebrow as if to say, "Now what?"

"This reunion is going to make everyone in town crazy," Louise announced as she took out her handkerchief and dabbed at her brow dramatically. "Even Pastor Kenneth has been swept up in the nonsense. Alice, do you know that he is letting the ANGELs use the entire church parking lot for their car wash?"

Alice blushed. "I suggested it, Louise. Where else could we put it?"

"What has happened to the citizens of this community? Everyone is sweeping sidewalks, pruning hedges and washing windows as if the president were coming to town."

"Oh, this is much more important than the president," Jane said. "You know people really like an excuse to fuss, and this reunion is as big an occasion for most people in town as a family birthday, a wedding or a graduation."

"This all-school reunion is going to be the death of us yet," Louise predicted. Then a genuinely concerned expression spread over her features. "I am worried about Clarissa Cottrell for one."

Jane straightened. "Is something wrong with Clarissa?"

"Only that she is about to drop in her tracks. I stopped at the Good Apple on the way home and it was full of people, all buzzing about the upcoming festivities. Clarissa was behind the counter doling out baked goods, looking as though she was about to fall over at any minute. She wouldn't admit it to me, but I know she wasn't feeling well. Why she agreed to let the Colwins help her just so that she could take on more work for the reunion is beyond me."

Alice frowned. "Maybe I should go over there and check on her. I've got my blood pressure cuff ...."

"It wouldn't do any good," Louise said. "She won't stop for you. Everyone keeps telling her what a good job she is doing and what a wonderful baker she is, and you know Clarissa. The more they praise her, the harder she tries."

"Well, wouldn't you? Work hard, I mean," Jane said, "if people were praising you all over the place? You love it when people enjoy your playing the piano. Clarissa has her own art form—baking. She bakes and decorates beautiful pastries, and her displays are breathtaking."

"I believe Jane has something there," Alice added. "What people want most is to be useful and to have a purpose. The Good Apple is Clarissa's purpose. Maybe she's afraid that if and when she does give up the bakery, she'll lose her personality with it." Alice grew reflective. "One of the reasons our father was so happy in his later years was that he never stopped being useful. Younger pastors would stop by to visit and go away wiser for the experience. And as he slowed down and wasn't so busy with the church, he had time to sit with friends who were ill or to comfort those who were suffering. In fact, in some ways, I believe his ministry deepened as he grew older."

"You've got to give yourself some credit too, Alice," Jane said softly. "It was because you were here, cooking for Dad, making a home for him and being vigilant about his health, that he was able to continue to thrive and to contribute. Not everyone is so fortunate as to have someone like you in his life."

Alice dismissed the acknowledgment of her dedication with a wave of her hand. "It was my gift too."

"Clarissa should be nearer to her children," Louise concluded. "That's what she needs."

Jane recalled Clarissa's words about her bossy family but didn't speak. No use judging. She would wait and see for herself just what Clarissa considered "bossy."

"You are surprisingly quiet on the subject." Louise said to Jane. Though she didn't say it, her words implied, *for once.*

"I don't blame Clarissa for wanting to stay independent," Jane said. "Her mind is great, sharp as a tack. She'll go absolutely mad if she can't keep active. How can a woman who's run her own business for years suddenly sit down and twiddle her thumbs and be happy?"

"That is what *you* might experience," Louise said, "but is it what Clarissa would feel?"

Jane had a hunch that it was. She and Clarissa both had a bit of the maverick in them. Unlike Clarissa, however, Jane had been born in a time that allowed her a little more freedom.

"I do wish Clarissa could be nearer her children," Alice murmured.

Silently Jane wondered if Clarissa were up to it. Pleasing her family sounded like almost as much work as pleasing her customers.

There was a knock on the door, and then the sisters heard the screen door open and close.

"It's just me." Sylvia appeared in the doorway. Her red hair looked as if it had been hastily brushed and her light, freckled skin was paler than usual.

Before anyone could speak, Sylvia said, "Give me two minutes to catch my breath before asking me anything about the reunion."

"Seems to me you're going to need two months to catch your breath," Jane observed. "You look awful."

"Thanks so much. I'm so glad I came here for support."

"You're welcome." Jane smiled. "How about a little pick-me-up? I made chocolate-chocolate brownies with fudge frosting today."

"Be still my heart." Sylvia looked around the room. "Where are they?"

Once Sylvia was settled with a cup of calming herbal tea and a plate of brownies, the others watched her with amusement as she took a bite, closed her eyes, leaned back in her chair and purred, "*Ahhhh.*"

It took two brownies and a refill of her tea before Sylvia signaled that she was ready to talk.

"You don't know how good it is to have someplace to go where, when I say I don't want to talk about the reunion, they believe me."

"You're safe with us," Alice assured her with a smile. "But …"

"I know, I know, you want to be in the loop too." Sylvia arranged her hair with her fingers only making it worse. With her wild red hair and with brownie crumbs on her lips, she hardly looked like one of the masterminds of this upcoming event, or as Sylvia often referred to it, "the logistical nightmare."

"This reunion is like a snowball rolling down the side of a mountain. It's been picking up size, energy and momentum ever since we got the idea for the celebration, and now it's about to crash down upon our village burying us. And," Sylvia predicted gloomily, "I'll be at the bottom of the pile."

"Going that well, huh?" Jane said. "Welcome to my world. Catering is the same way. It sounds easy enough when you agree to do it. A few canapés here, a dessert buffet there, something with swordfish for the entrée. And the date is months away. There's not another thing on the calendar to prevent you from spending all your time making it perfect."

Louise raised an eyebrow but Jane kept talking.

"Then, just when you think you've got it under control, someone comes along and says all the guests are allergic to swordfish and asks if we can we serve meatballs and mashed potatoes instead. And there are forty or fifty more guests coming than first planned so the event is being moved across town. And they all love Black Forest cake and want to end with a taffy pull or some such craziness."

"A taffy pull is the *only* thing someone hasn't suggested," Sylvia said. "Don't say a word about it or someone will think that's a good idea too. Where was everyone when we were planning this reunion? Thirty people showed up for the meetings. Now we're getting input from three hundred."

"Other than that, how's it going?" Alice said, chuckling.

"I hate to say this, but Lloyd Tynan and your aunt are going to be the death of me, if Viola and Orlando's don't get to me first."

"'Now, Sylvia,'" Sylvia mimicked Lloyd's fussy way of worrying a subject to death. Jane could just imagine him looking both vexed and determined not to be left out of the action. "'You're representing our little town properly, aren't you? There's nothing planned that would make people think badly of us? I heard a rumor that you're considering blowing off those fireworks on the football field. You know how messy fireworks can be. Maybe you could move the fireworks outside the city limits . . . . What? You checked that out and there's not enough parking spaces? And you've already arranged a cleanup crew? Oh my, I hope you didn't make any hasty decisions about that. You can't have just anyone on a cleanup crew, you know. You need someone with some maturity and common sense. Why don't you drop off the list of candidates and I'll tell you who to pick. Then you can call them and give them the word. That's what this committee is for, after all, right?'" Sylvia waved her hand just as Lloyd might and concluded in his tone, "'Don't worry, it's no problem for me. Glad to be of service. This is my reunion city too.'"

Alice and Jane were hooting with laughter at Sylvia's imitation of the mayor. Even Louise, who treasures propriety, was smiling.

"Can you believe it?" Sylvia shook her head. "Everyone is trying to micromanage this event, and they're all getting into the action months too late. My cleanup crews were formed in January, and now we're in the countdown to reunion day. I'm not going to change a thing now, even if Lloyd does think they might be a bit 'immature' or 'flighty.' He nearly had a heart attack when I told him who was in charge of cleanup. What's wrong with Boy Scouts anyway?"

"Lloyd wants you to fire Boy Scouts?" Jane said, still laughing helplessly.

"Oh dear," Louise murmured. "That sounds un-American."

"I wonder if the Brownies are available." Alice hiccupped with mirth. "Maybe he would think that girls are more mature."

"You'd think we needed a medical team to come in and surgically scrub the football field after the fireworks. And you don't know the half of it."

Sylvia pulled out a big calendar with the month of August on it. Across the top of the calendar, she had scrawled "Countdown to Reunion." Then, in red marker, she had crossed out the word *Reunion* and replaced it with the word *Chaos*.

"This whole thing is just bedlam. How will we ever pull it off?"

"You're too close to the action to see how well everything is going," Alice assured her. "How can it not be a success? Most people are having their families and friends come home. There will be food, music, games, even hot-air-balloon rides. There are class dinners, socials and a parade planned. Everyone I've talked to is just happy that you're providing a setting for them to reacquaint themselves with old friends. When you hand out that program of events and locations, the reunion will practically run itself."

Sylvia looked at Jane. "Is that how you see it?"

"It's not quite that simple," Jane said. "I know, having been in on the planning and execution side of things, but Alice has the general idea. If people simply do what they're assigned to do—Boy Scouts clean up, church ladies serve, car washers wash cars—then it will happen."

Sylvia took a deep breath. "The plans look good on paper. We think we've thought of every contingency. I even ordered extra porta-potties and Fred has stocked umbrellas in case it rains...."

"And the marketplace is ready?" Jane referred to the sea of white tents Sylvia had planned as marketing booths for anyone who had something made locally that they wanted to sell.

"Yes. It's full. Every booth is taken. Several people are doing pottery, others are making pins and headbands or dying shirts and kerchiefs emblazoned with the date and logo of the reunion. The committee is selling mugs, posters and T-shirts to pay for our expenses. Several artists, potters and woodworkers have rented tents, and so has a group of ladies who are making personalized reunion sweatshirts and quilts. There's no need for anyone to forget they've been here for a celebration."

"And the parade?" Louise asked. She wasn't sure what a parade had to do with a high-school reunion, but at least it sounded like fun.

"Several registrations have come in just in the past two days. First I worried that we wouldn't have enough entries to make a good parade, and now I'm worrying if we have enough streets for the procession to move on."

"And the food?" Alice asked.

Sylvia turned quickly toward Jane. "Jane is the only one who can pull that off."

Jane made a mental note to stop by the Good Apple again and see for herself how Clarissa was faring.

Just then, Nancy and Zack came into the kitchen laughing hysterically. Jane asked them what had amused them so.

"There was this woman . . ." Zack doubled over and held his midsection.

"And she had a ..." Nancy, so overcome with laughter that she couldn't speak, put her hands on the sides of her head and waggled them.

"And it was dressed in ..." Zack pulled at his T-shirt.

"She was ..." Nancy made a backward and forward motion with her hands.

"It was ... the funniest thing ... we've ever seen."

Jane gestured them into the untaken chairs. "Either the two of you saw an elephant in dress clothes vacuuming, or you ran into Clara Horn pushing her pig Daisy in a baby buggy."

"And Daisy was dressed for the outing," Alice added.

"You *know* about this?" Zack wiped tears from his eyes.

"It's a long story," Alice said calmly. "Just enjoy Clara and the pig and don't ask about the rest. We've all actually become quite fond of little Daisy."

Nancy and Zack broke again into hoots of laughter.

By that time, the noise had roused Mr. Enrich, who had been reading in Daniel's library. When his face with its questioning expression appeared in the kitchen door, *everyone* started laughing.

Although he blushed, Mr. Enrich did not skitter away. Instead, he held his ground while Jane explained to him about Clara Horn and how she enjoyed taking her pig Daisy for walks.

"By the way, we stopped at the Good Apple and introduced ourselves to Clarissa," Zack reported.

"We just loved her," Nancy added. "She will be so easy to work with—and fun too."

"She's got a great kitchen with plenty of room. I'm sure we can handle whatever you want done. We're actually looking forward to it."

Nancy looked at Zack with such intensity that Jane deduced they had been talking about their futures again. She felt a small, uncomfortable flip in her stomach. *Why, she wondered, did so many troubled people and people in transition land on their doorstep?*

Because God wanted it that way, that's why. There was no doubt in Jane's mind that God was using her and her sisters and the inn for some bigger plan. There were times, however, when she wondered what, exactly, it might be. She had a true sense of rightness and belonging here that could not be wrong. She had followed her instincts to create some of her best entrées, her best artwork and her most amazing jewelry. Surely, she could use it here at the inn with the people who passed through.

Looking from Nancy and Zack to Mr. Enrich, Jane had an overwhelming feeling that she needed to follow her instinct with these guests. God had something in mind. She just knew it. What she didn't know was what part she was to play in it.

Chapter Seven

$\mathcal{J}$ ane had taken to stopping daily at the Good Apple to see how Clarissa was faring. Today the bakery was busy when Jane arrived, filled with customers stocking up for the frenetic days ahead. Clarissa, tall and straight as if she were seventeen instead of seventy-plus, was filling orders, chatting with customers and generally running an efficient ship. And, Jane observed, she was beaming.

"...best in town."

"My Becky says she wants these for breakfast every morning."

"And Jim immediately asked if they were from the Good Apple..."

"You're the best, Clarissa. I hope you'll make extras tomorrow because I'll be back for more..."

The praise and pleasure were fast flowing around Acorn Hill's resident baker, and she was soaking it in like a sunbather enjoying the warmth on a summer's day. It took, Jane noticed, at least fifteen years off Clarissa's age to see her so happy. How could Clarissa even consider quitting something she loved so much? Jane knew the answer resided with Clarissa's children. They wanted their mother happy, of course, but by their own definition of happy: safe, secure, no long hours on her feet, near them so they could stop in when they were free. Clarissa's definition of happy, Jane mused, was probably quite different: busy, purposeful, needed, independent.

Clarissa caught Jane's eye and waved her into the back of the bakery. "Help me put out some more buns and dough-nuts, will you? I'm almost out of cookies and rolls and it's barely noon. I'll have to double my batches tomorrow."

With practiced hands, Jane did as she was told. When the crowd had subsided and the stragglers went off lament-ing the empty shelves, Clarissa poured two cups of coffee and invited Jane to sit down with her.

"Feels good to take a load off," Clarissa sighed.

"You're having fun, aren't you?"

Clarissa grinned and her face pleated with happy wrin-kles. "I've loved this my entire life. Sometimes I've worried about making a living in this little town, but this reunion is becoming its own little gold mine. I'm going to have some money to bolster that retirement fund of mine." The grin faded. "Not that I want to use it anytime soon."

"That's just being prudent, not a sign you're going to quit."

The frown cleared. "You're absolutely right, no matter what she says...." Clarissa's words drifted off.

"Who says?"

"Oh, Olivia called last night. She's asked for a couple extra days off from work and will be here tomorrow. 'To help you, Mother,' she said. *Harrumph.* Help me into an early grave, most likely." She put her thumb and index finger to the bridge of her nose and rubbed the soft indentations on either side.

"You're one of the most self-sufficient, independent women I know," Jane reminded her. "Don't let Livvy make decisions for you if you don't agree with them. You're perfectly capable of deciding things for yourself."

Clarissa looked doubtful, as if Livvy were more than a daughter—more a force of nature to be reckoned with, perhaps.

"What *do* you want?" Jane asked.

"What am I going to be when I grow up, you mean?"

"Something like that."

"I feel like a teenager having an identity crisis, Jane," Clarissa admitted. "I know it's happening all because the kids are coming home for the reunion. They haven't been in Acorn Hill together since high school, and I have this bad feeling that they're going to 'gang up' on me."

"For what?"

"Look at me. I'm past 'retirement age.' They all have the idea that they're being 'bad' children if they don't make me stop working. I can handle their phone conversations one at a time, but all three of them here at once ..."

"That has to do with their own guilt. They just want to do the right thing for their mother."

"And the 'right' thing in this case is to leave Mother alone," Clarissa said. "If that was only possible."

Jane could see Clarissa's worry and her frustration, and was glad that she and her sisters had never tried to talk down to their father or assumed that just because he was old he was unable to think for himself.

"What do your kids want you to do, Clarissa? What are your options?"

"The only option is for me to stay in the bakery business until they carry me out like a sack of flour." Clarissa's eyes crinkled and twinkled again. "It's my kids who think there are other options."

"Such as?"

"Assisted living, an apartment near one of them, a 'companion' to help me, maybe a nursing home. Nothing I'm interested in, that's for sure." Clarissa took a sip of her coffee. "I've been considering getting a new car. I've got nearly a hundred thousand miles on my old one. And the kids are trying to talk me out of renewing my license."

"Not very tuned in to you, huh?"

"They only get back here once a year or so. How could they know how I live? When they're here, of course I get exhausted. I'm cooking all their favorite meals, watching the little ones so they can go out, doing laundry, picking up toys…"

"The bakery's a breeze compared to that, right?"

"Piece of cake, if you don't mind my saying so." Clarissa smiled. "I love them all dearly. Ray is most like me but they all resemble their father, bullheaded, opinionated and loyal as the day is long. It's just that their best qualities are sometimes also their worst ones." She wiped a tear from her eye. "I wish he were here. He'd know what to do."

"Perhaps it won't be as bad as you're anticipating. Maybe they only want to have a good time at the reunion."

Clarissa looked at Jane as if she had lost her mind. "Maybe. But don't count on it."

After leaving Clarissa's, Jane ran a few errands and when she returned to the inn she indulged in some work on her jewelry projects. Then she showered, changed and headed over to Sylvia's house for dinner.

"This is great beef stew," Jane said, dabbing her lips with her napkin. "Is there any more in that pot?"

Sylvia nodded and carried the pot over to Jane. "I'm flattered. I'm always a little scared to invite the great chef Jane Howard to dinner for fear my cooking won't stand the test."

"Don't be silly. Sometimes I'm so tired of cooking that I'd give anything for someone to wait on me. This is absolutely perfect, Sylvia. You're a wonderful cook." Jane looked at her friend speculatively. "Did you ever think of settling down with someone special? Or do you like your independence too much?"

"Oh, I thought about it all right. In fact, I assumed that I'd have been married for twenty years by now. Funny how things turn out sometimes." She went to a shelf that held several pictures and chose one in a small silver frame. "And this is who I'd planned to marry."

Jane studied the black and white photo of a military man. He was stern and handsome, staring directly into the camera lens.

"That's James Marcot Wilson," Sylvia said softly. "The love of my life."

Jane held the framed photo gently. "Tell me more."

"Oh, there's not so much to tell. The older I get, the smaller the portion of my life was spent with James. We were college sweethearts." A smile played on Sylvia's soft features. "I was so in love with him that I barely remember a class I took. He wasn't much better but managed to graduate with honors anyway. He became a military pilot. Doesn't he look handsome in that uniform?"

Jane studied the photo again, and then nodded. "What happened?"

"Life intruded on our love story." Sylvia picked up a dishcloth and scrubbed an already clean area on the table. "He decided that the best route for us was for him to stay in the military. I didn't mind. All I could think about was having a military wedding." She smiled ruefully. "I'm a sucker for a man in uniform."

"I didn't know you were married."

"Oh, I wasn't. I only dreamed of it. James spent a lot of his time flying. He loved that more than anything. He talked about his plane with as much affection as he did me."

Sylvia's expression became distant, remembering something long since past. "He promised to take me up in a plane some day."

"And did he?"

"No. There was an accident and James quit flying. A fire broke out in the plane on a routine mission. His crew was badly burned trying to put it out. He was able to land the plane and come out unscathed but for a broken leg, but his navigator didn't make it. He died a month later from the effects of the burns. He was in excruciating pain and James wouldn't leave his side."

"I'm so sorry."

"It was awful," Sylvia said. "I thought James would lose his mind. He felt responsible for what happened."

"And then?"

"And then he changed. He couldn't get over it and he couldn't forgive himself for the accident. James did this." She opened her hands wide and then slowly curled her fingers in upon themselves until she made tight little fists. "He refused to talk to a counselor or anyone who might have helped him. It was as though he wanted, or needed, to do penance for what had gone wrong."

Sylvia recounted her story in even, unemotional tones, but Jane knew that her outside calm was only a cover for the emotions eating away at her. "He changed after that, became distant and absentminded. Sometimes it was as if he didn't even hear me when I spoke."

"But the wedding..."

"We kept putting it off, hoping that he'd be better soon. But he never got better."

Sylvia shifted in her chair. "I never lost hope, even after his first breakdown. I thought that once he was out of the hospital, things would get back to normal, but for James, there was no 'normal' anymore. He was in and out of institutions for six years before I accepted that the man I'd loved didn't even exist anymore. All that was left was a pale shadow that I didn't even recognize. James disappeared in front of my eyes."

"Where is he now?" Jane's heart ached for Sylvia.

"I don't know. As long as his parents were alive, I kept in touch with them. He'd live at home and work for a while at some job or other and then disappear. Eventually he'd come back to try to pull himself together and the cycle would start again. They never gave up hoping something would turn around for him, but they went to their graves waiting."

"So he's just ... gone?"

"His sister writes to me every couple of years to tell me if she's heard from him. The last I heard she didn't know where he was."

"Oh, Sylvia, I'm so sorry."

"I wouldn't have believed it if I hadn't seen it for myself. He could never forgive himself for his friend's death and could never quit reliving it or punishing himself for letting it happen."

"But it wasn't his fault. It was an accident."

"I know that and you know that. Even James knew it on some level, but he just couldn't get beyond it." She looked at Jane sharply. "Things happen to a person that can have a profound and lasting effect. It doesn't always make sense. It may be perfectly clear to everyone else how to deal with whatever it is, but to the one who's hurting..."

Sylvia looked at Jane with a speculative expression of her own in her eyes. "But you know how that is, to have something that happened in your youth affect you for years to come."

"Shirley Taylor, you mean?" Shirley had been on Jane's mind a lot lately. She had been replaying the video of that fateful moment in high school in her mind. She felt a pang of empathy and sadness for James Marcot Wilson. The burden he had carried was far, far worse.

"She probably had no idea how deep the wound went," Sylvia commented. Her eyes were warm and compassionate as she looked at Jane. "Just as none of the rest of us ever really knew what James had felt." Sylvia was steering the conversation away from herself and back to Jane. "What was Shirley like? Otherwise, I mean."

Jane sat back and pondered the question. "Quiet, mostly. She never seemed to hang around with anyone special. She just attached herself to whatever crowd was available. She was like a . . . a chameleon, changing colors to blend in. The only time I ever really saw her animated was when she was around a couple of the guys on the football team."

"Really? I wonder why?"

Jane's expression grew distant. "Jeremy Patterson, my high-school sweetheart, was on the team. Jeremy Patterson. Quarterback, weight lifter, all around cutie. He was so sweet to me—and to everyone."

"How so?" Sylvia tucked her feet beneath her and settled in for a long story.

"He just was. It was his nature to be considerate and thoughtful. He always saw things that no one else seemed to see. He knew when people were hurt, upset or disappointed and he always acknowledged it, even when he couldn't do a thing about it." Jane sighed. "For a time, I really thought I loved Jeremy."

"And?"

"And I suppose I did—not mature love so much as appreciative love. I was so grateful that I was fortunate enough to know a person as kind—and handsome—as he."

"A lovable teddy bear," Sylvia murmured.

"That pretty much sums up Jeremy."

"Where did you meet him?"

"He belonged to our church, Grace Chapel. He was the only boyfriend I ever had that my entire family approved of. Even Father trusted Jeremy." Jane felt sad. "But after the trouble with Shirley, even the thought of Jeremy couldn't keep me in Acorn Hill."

"What if that was her motive? Maybe she loved Jeremy too."

"Of course. Everyone did."

"I mean *loved*. You were in her way. Maybe she thought that if you weren't in the picture, Jeremy would be free to love her."

"No . . . that couldn't be . . . even if . . . he wouldn't have . . ." Jane paused to stare at Sylvia. "You could be right. It wouldn't be surprising if she cared about Jeremy. Every girl did. There's no way she could have known. . . ." Jane's voice trailed off.

"Known what?" Sylvia persisted.

"That she was one of the few people that Jeremy actually didn't like. He was uncomfortable around her."

"No wonder," Sylvia commented. "Good intuition, that Jeremy."

Jane sat back and pondered the discussion. "And I was oblivious to it all."

"That's how it is with the popular kids, Jane. They have no idea how jealous others can be." Sylvia's eyes clouded. "Believe me, I know. I was on the outside."

Jane was overwhelmed with compassion. "Were you hurt a lot?"

"Not so that it broke me. I was lucky. I was always wearing these amazing clothes my mother made for me. I might have been poor, but I was also interesting. It gave me an edge."

"Would you like to see James again?" Jane asked.

"I'm not sure. In some ways, I want to remember him as he was when we met. And in others ..." she sighed.

"Yes?"

"I suppose I never quite got over him. I love who he was, if not what he is now." Her eyes misted. "But I would also be afraid."

Then she seemed to shake off the melancholy that thoughts of James inspired. "One more question," Sylvia said. "Whatever happened to Jeremy Patterson?"

"Is that a dragonfly? Why do they call them dragons? Are they really dragons or is it just because they look like them? What do real dragons look like? Do they breathe fire like they do in storybooks? My mom says ..."

Jane closed her eyes and shut out Josie's endless string of questions. It had seemed like a good idea at the time to invite the little girl to join her at Fairy Pond. The child, after all, had been playing in the inn's driveway, patiently waiting for her mother to get home from work, which was nearly two hours away. Better her here than dodging traffic, right?

"Fern is a funny word, isn't it, Jane? Furrn—like on a kitty, right? Fur-urn. Why are some ferns like lace and others kind of clumpy and not very pretty? Why do they call them all ferns? My mom says that her grandmother always had a fern on a stand in her living room. Fern. Fuuuurrrrrrnnnn. Furn. Furniture. Furnace. Fern…"

Josie, even sitting still, seemed to be in action. Her little bottom bounced on the tree stump that she had claimed as a chair and her curls seemed to be animated by a life of their own. Her mouth never stopped. It was always smiling or asking questions. And given permission, her pert nose would poke into everything and everybody's business.

There was to be no soothing, mind-releasing sketching today, Jane thought. With Josie around, the only thing she could think to draw were whirligigs, Ferris wheels and children doing cartwheels.

Suddenly Josie stopped squirming and turned to Jane. "Is the ree-union going to be fun?"

"I hope so."

"I've never been to one before. Mom says I'm not old enough to have a ree-union. But I'm old enough to go to this one, aren't I?"

"Oh yes. And I think you'll like it. There'll be lots of food, a little carnival, music…"

"And a car wash!" Josie chortled. "Mom says it's *Alice's* car wash. Isn't that funny, Jane? I didn't know Alice liked to wash cars." Josie giggled and kicked her feet.

"Alice's car wash." That, actually, was what it had come to be called, much to Alice's dismay. Every streak and spot left unpolished on those cars would be Alice's responsibility. Poor Alice was having a minor nervous breakdown over the entire affair. She had never washed a car in her life, other than using the automated one at the gas station. As the reunion neared—and it was almost the Day—Alice became more and more edgy.

When Jane had finally gotten Josie to settle down with a pad of sketch paper and a handful of colored pencils, she started drawing the large old stump that had been challenging her on her last few visits. The thing had personality with its gnarled shape and rough bark. It was a very old stump and sometimes Jane tried to imagine what the tree had seen in its lifetime—and what the stump had seen since. Generations of birds, rabbits and deer, squirrels and fox, insects and humans, no doubt. As she tried to imagine the old stump alive and speaking, she could see a crack in the base that could very well be a mouth. And the knothole to the left, an eye, definitely an eye ...

She was so engrossed that it took her some time to realize they were no longer alone at Fairy Pond.

The crash and clatter of footsteps breaking their way through the delicate environment sounded like a harsh intrusion after the whirr of wings and warbles of birds. Even Josie's little voice had seemed at home in this place, but not the loud clomping that was coming their way.

Jane was about to gather Josie close to her when Mr. Enrich broke through the wall of forest and stumbled into the magical land of Fairy Pond.

His clothes were rumpled, as if branches and twigs had been pulling at him, and his hair was decorated with leaves and spiderwebs. He looked utterly out of place in the severe dark clothing he always wore, and it was obvious that the trek through the woods had damaged his shoes.

It was he, not Jane and Josie, who was startled. "You!"

"Hi, Mr. Enrich, how are you today?"

"What are you doing here?" Josie asked.

Jane had thought to ask the same thing but the question sounded much sweeter coming from the child.

"We came to draw pictures and paint," Josie went on without waiting for an answer. "Sometimes Jane brings me here. Do you want to see what I drew?" Josie dived for the picture, which might have been the ferns around the pond—or just about anything else in the woodsy tangle of greenery.

"Very nice," Mr. Enrich stammered, taken aback at finding someone here, in the middle of nowhere.

"Did you come to draw too?" Josie inquired. "Do you want to use some of my paper?"

He looked so out of place and befuddled in his black loafers, dress pants, and dark shirt and tie that Jane had to stifle her laughter. No doubt he had left his suit coat in the car before venturing into the woods.

"No, I, *ah* . . . I just wanted to take a walk."

"And you found us!" Josie concluded delightedly. She turned to Jane. "Isn't it time for lunch yet? Can we share it with Mr. Enrich?"

Jane glanced at her watch. "I think it's exactly time for lunch and I made plenty." She looked at Mr. Enrich. "Will you join us?"

It was Josie who had him trapped. She had already dragged out the picnic basket, found the red-and-white checked flannel-backed plastic tablecloth and was spreading it across the tree stump Jane had been sketching.

Mr. Enrich shot Jane a pleading glance, as if to say, "Help me get out of this," but Jane had no intention of doing anything to help him escape. Instead she pulled a bowl out of the basket. "Three-bean salad with my secret dressing. Ham sandwiches, fruit and Josie's favorite caramel cake for dessert."

"And don't forget these." Josie held up a bag of salt-and-vinegar potato chips and a thermos of lemonade. "And," her voice lowered, "Jane says there's a surprise in the bottom of the basket if we're good."

Jane wasn't sure Mr. Enrich would be tempted to behave by a coloring book and a packet of crayons, but who knew with him anyway?

He sat down on the ground in front of the stump and gave a little groan, like an old man whose joints had frozen. Misery seemed to be his middle name. Of course, Jane reminded herself, they didn't even know his first name yet.

Josie presided over lunch like a queen over her subjects, handing out sandwiches, serving lemonade in plastic cups and generally taking charge.

"Do you want to say grace, Mr. Enrich?" Josie asked. "Jane and I always say grace."

Mr. Enrich's terrified deer-in-the-headlights expression compelled Jane to say, "I'd like to pray today, Josie."

"Oh, okay." The little girl folded her hands and bowed her head. Mr. Enrich, following her lead, mimicked her pose.

"Dear Heavenly Father," Jane began, "thank You for this lovely place You created and the miracle of every tree and bug and flower. Thank You for the food we are about to eat. Without Your gifts, we have nothing and are nothing. And thank You for our little trio of friends today. There are no coincidences, Lord, and for whatever reason we're here together. Help us to make the most of this opportunity to share food, friendship and support. We ask it in His name. Amen."

Josie heartily echoed, "Amen."

Mr. Enrich made a strangled little sound halfway between a sob and a sigh.

Three-bean salad and ham sandwiches seemed to be on Mr. Enrich's list of top ten foods, Jane observed, and she was glad she had, as usual, packed far more than she and Josie could eat. Generally she sent the leftovers home with Josie so her mother wouldn't have to cook dinner that night, but today there wouldn't be a crumb left behind.

After she ate, Josie spread out on a bed of soft grass, her arm beneath her head, and began to grow sleepy. As her eyelids drooped she struggled to keep them open, but eventually she dozed off.

"I suppose I should move along..." Mr. Enrich began.

"Not for me, you don't. Now that Josie's asleep, there's nothing that will keep me from sketching. If you'd like, take a nap yourself."

"It's tempting but..."

"But what? You're on vacation."

For a moment, Mr. Enrich looked startled, as if he had not remembered that was his purpose, but he did lie down on his back and gazed at the canopy of green decorated with bright birds and filtered rays of sunlight. When Jane turned from her sketching to speak to him, he, too, was fast asleep. Resting, some of the worry lines in his face faded, and for the first time Jane realized what it might look like to see Mr. Enrich at peace.

She was packing the last of her equipment when Josie and Mr. Enrich awoke.

"Done already?" Josie asked disappointedly.

"It's been over two hours, sleepyhead."

"Two hours!" Mr. Enrich sat up straight. "I haven't had a two-hour nap in . . . well, I can't remember when."

"Good. It was time then. Come on, Van Gogh, come on Raphael, it's time for me to see what's happening at the inn."

They trudged back to the road and to what Jane called "civilization," though she had always thought Fairy Pond was one of the most civilized places she knew.

Alice met Jane at the door. "Jane, would you do me a favor?"

"Sure. What's up?"

"I have a meeting at the church. Could you go to the Good Apple? I left an order with Clarissa for the meeting's refreshments, and she said she'd have it ready about now."

"Okay, I'll be back in a few minutes. I'll take them to the assembly room for you."

"Thank you, Jane." Alice put her hand to her head. "I've had so much to do...."

Poor Alice, Jane thought as she jogged toward the Good Apple. If her heart were any bigger for the youth of the church, it would burst. It wasn't an easy job keeping up with that kind of youthful energy.

When she got to the Good Apple, the door was already closed and the blinds pulled. Clarissa must have run out of baked goods very early today. Jane walked around to the back of the building and called through the screen door. "Clarissa? It's Jane. Sorry I'm late to pick up Alice's order. I didn't think you'd be closed this early...."

A small gasp escaped Jane's lips. The large wooden kneading table in the center of Clarissa's kitchen was piled high with baked goods—bags of buns and cookies, loaves of bread and two intricately decorated cakes. Clarissa was obviously not out of product.

"Clarissa!" Jane called more loudly. The lights were turned off in the back of the bakery, but she stepped into the dimness anyway.

"Don't trip."

The voice came out of the far corner where Clarissa's tiny office was located. It, too, was dark, but as Jane's eyes adjusted to the dimness, she could see Clarissa inside, sitting in the dark, leaning back in the old office chair she had had since before her husband had died.

"Are you okay?" Jane made her way toward the office. "Why are you sitting here in the dark?"

"I'm hiding, mostly." Clarissa sighed. "You're welcome to hide out with me if you like."

Eyes adjusting, Jane found a second chair and sat down just outside the doorway of the office. "What are we hiding from?"

"Reality."

"Would you like to explain?"

"Olivia arrived this morning."

"How nice."

"Yes." Clarissa sounded as happy about it as she had when the plumbing broke at the bakery a few months back.

"Not so nice, then? Let me try to interpret this," Jane suggested. "Livvy arrived even earlier than expected and caught you working here in the wee hours of the morning. She thought you were working too hard and scolded you about it."

"Close." A chuckle grew out of the dimness. "When I wasn't at the house, Livvy, unable to believe that I still went to work that early, decided I'd had a heart attack or been kidnapped or wandered off in a vacant elderly haze. Without even checking out the bakery, she went to Fred Humbert, because she knew he's always willing to help, woke him out of a sound sleep to come with her to find me." Clarissa shook her head. "That girl has been watching too much television."

"And what did Fred say?"

"Not a thing. He knew Livvy as a little girl and recalled all her theatrics. He just went along with her. Said he'd be happy to go along and 'save your mother's life.' Besides, he stops at the Good Apple for coffee almost every morning before I open the store, so he knew good and well where I was."

"And when she saw you, was your daughter embarrassed over her histrionics?"

"Not in the least. She said it just proved that I worked much too hard and that I needed 'more care' than I was getting."

"'More care?' As in . . ."

"A retirement home, probably, so I can start acting like the grandmother I am."

"I hate to say it, Clarissa, but your daughter is a little deluded about you. . . ."

"Livvy is dead set on 'helping' me quit working."

"Do you want to?"

"Not on your life." Clarissa paused. "It wouldn't hurt to ease up a little, to take a trip once in a while or sleep in until six, but that's as much 'quitting' as I want to do."

"So tell her that."

Clarissa gave Jane a withering look. "Livvy's a woman in search of a cause, Jane. I'm afraid this is her cause at the moment. And things are going to be even worse when her brothers come along."

"Wow." Jane sat back and folded her arms over her chest. "Do any of them know how unempowering that attitude is?"

"Opinionated, like their father," Clarissa said, as if that explained everything. "And I know they love me so much they think they have to 'protect' me. Trouble is, I don't want to be protected. If I can just get through these next days without the people I love most in the world driving me crazy, I'll consider the reunion a success."

She paused. "Oh, by the way. That nice young couple stopped in, the ones who are going to help me during the reunion. I think we'll get along just dandy. Thanks, Jane, for finding them for me."

"For Acorn Hill, more accurately, and especially for Lloyd. He's convinced that an event without your baked goods will fail on that point alone."

They were chuckling when they heard the screen door open and crash shut.

"Mother? Mother? Are you in here? Are you okay?"

An overhead light flicked on, leaving Jane and Clarissa blinking stupidly for a moment until their eyes adjusted.

"What on earth are you doing sitting in the dark...oh, hello. I didn't realize Mother had someone with her."

"Hi, Olivia," Jane greeted her.

Olivia Cottrell was even more beautiful than she had been as a child. She was as slim and tall as Clarissa, but while her mother appeared long and wiry, Livvy looked like a model—willowy and regal. She wore her nearly black hair pulled back into a severe knot that accentuated her already exotically slanted eyes. Clad in pristine white trousers, a lemon-yellow cotton-knit sweater and a navy double-breasted jacket emblazoned with the crest of a well-known designer, she looked as though she had stepped off a page of a slick fashion catalogue. Her lips and her nails were an identical shade of blood red and the gold jewelry at her ears and on her wrists was undoubtedly real. She was a beautiful and intimidating woman.

Jane's heart sank a little. She saw immediately what Louise, Alice and Clarissa had meant. Livvy was obviously accustomed to getting her own way. In fact, the way she carried herself and her air of confidence hinted that anyone would be foolish to disagree with her.

"I'm Jane Howard, Livvy," Jane stood and thrust out her hand. "You probably know my sisters better—Alice and Louise?"

"Reverend Howard's family." Livvy gave Jane a beautiful smile. "As a little girl, I thought your father was the most wonderful man in the world. We'd leave church on Sunday mornings and he'd reach out to shake my hand, just as he did all the adults, and greet me as if my presence had made his day. Such a good, sweet man."

"I fully agree," Jane said, touched. "He had a love for children."

"I know. I think more than anyone, he influenced me to become a teacher and even a school administrator. I never forgot how valued and respected he made me feel, even as a little girl. I hope I'm doing some of that for the children I have in my charge now."

Jane glanced at Clarissa, who was beaming with maternal pride. No wonder Clarissa loved her so—and no wonder she wanted to avoid any sort of confrontation. A woman with such passion and fervor for her beliefs would be hard to convince that any opinion other than her own could be right.

"Now back to my original question: What are you two doing sitting in the dark?"

"Enjoying the calm before the storm," Jane said deftly. "We're gearing up, that's all."

"What do you think of my mother still working like a slave in this bakery?" Livvy asked.

"I think your mother is remarkable. She and the Good Apple are a tradition in this little town. I'm delighted that we're going to have plenty of opportunity to taste the best baked goods in the entire state."

Livvy opened and closed her eyes owlishly. That was not the sentiment she had expected—or wanted—to hear. "But don't you think it's hard on her? Isn't it time for her to relax and enjoy herself?"

"Quit talking about me like I'm not here, child," Clarissa chided.

Livvy rolled her eyes a bit as she turned toward Jane, as if they were discussing an errant child just out of earshot.

"Maybe the bakery *is* a way for her to relax and enjoy herself," Jane suggested. "Granted, it's been hectic lately, but generally it is a wonderful way for her to see all her friends every day when they come to shop."

Clarissa nodded emphatically at that.

"But think of all the *fun* things there are to do. Mom, you could be in a craft club, doing senior water aerobics, going on the senior bus to plays and concerts..."

"Crafts! More stuff to fill my house with? And water aerobics? Livvy, have you ever, in your entire life, seen me enjoy the water?"

"You went fishing with Papa and me once."

"And sat on the shore and waved at you two in the boat."

"And you came to every single play, concert or event any of us kids were in during our school years."

"Got my fill then," Clarissa retorted. "Honey, my fun, my relaxation and my hobby is this business. Don't try to take that away from me."

"I've seen how stiff you are in the morning."

"And coming here limbers me up."

"You were tired when I arrived, I know you were."

"And a cup of coffee with my regular customers wakes me right up and cheers me for the entire day."

"And you're not as young as you used to be."

For that, Clarissa had no answer.

Chapter Eight

$\mathcal{I}$s there something wrong with you?" Louise asked Jane. "You've been moping all morning."

"I'm not moping, really," Jane said, "but I am concerned." She told her sisters about the conversation she had had with Livvy and her mother.

"Frankly, they both have a point," Louise said reasonably. "The Good Apple *is* a lot for Clarissa. She will admit that to anyone but Livvy, because Livvy is set on making her mother take it easy. Clarissa wants to decide for herself what her next step might be."

"Livvy doesn't realize that the most fun her mother ever has is in that bakery," Alice said. "Why, Clarissa told me once that decorating cakes day and night would be her idea of a good time. As long as I've known Clarissa, she's never had another hobby other than her work."

"And, you might have just hit the nail on the head," said Jane. "If she weren't at the bakery, I think Clarissa might just die of boredom."

"Well, she won't be bored this week," Louise said. "Nancy and Zack went to visit with her. They are eager to get started." Louise shook her head. "That's another topic of conversation. I wish those two could agree on what they want to do with their lives."

Clarissa and Livvy. Nancy and Zack. Mr. Enrich. All troubled souls. As Louise poured more coffee for herself and Alice sipped her tea, Jane reached for the small Bible that always lay somewhere in the kitchen and flipped to the thirty-seventh chapter of the Psalms:

"Though he stumble, he will not fall,
for the Lord upholds him with his hand."

Lord, Jane prayed silently, *there are people here who are stumbling. Reach out Your hand to each of them and send them on the right path, the path You want for them. Amen.*

At that moment, Nancy arrived in the kitchen. "Jane, Zack sent me to tell you that you should come and convince Mrs. Cottrell to take a break this afternoon. We can handle the bakery now that we've got our strategy planned for the reunion. He thinks she should rest up. What do you think?"

Poor Clarissa. Everyone was either trying to send her to bed or out to pasture—and they all thought they were being kind doing it.

"She's sturdier than Zack thinks, but it's lovely of him to be so considerate." Jane paused before adding gently, "Next time, you might just ask *Clarissa* what she feels like doing."

Nancy bobbed her head agreeably, as if that were an option that neither of them had considered.

When Nancy left, Louise spoke up. "Why does everyone think age is a disease? Clarissa could teach those youngsters a thing or two."

"Everyone has to reinvent the wheel," Alice said quietly. "I see young people do it every day. It's as if they know a better way than anyone who's gone before them."

"You didn't do that to Father," Louise pointed out. "You always deferred to his wisdom."

"That's because he had so much of it," Alice said. "I still miss the talks we use to have."

"I wish Livvy would listen to her mother. She could learn a lot too."

There was a knock at the door, interrupting their conversation. "Anybody home?"

"Hi, Vera, we're back here," Jane called, recognizing their friend's voice.

Vera came into the kitchen looking frazzled. "Do you have any vacancies for the reunion? A single would do."

"Sorry, Vera. We're full. Did you get an unexpected guest?"

"No. Everybody is expected and everyone is coming."

"Then who's the room for?"

"Me." Vera dropped into a chair and groaned. "I told Fred we might as well install a revolving door on the front of the house. Both girls are here and some of their old classmates have descended already. It's like high school all over again but worse because they have no curfew and I can't say, 'No, you can't do that, not as long as you live under my roof.' And they're the best behaved of our relatives. The rest of them will flock in, leaving Fred and me to cook and clean while they can go out and enjoy the reunion."

"Don't cook or clean," Jane suggested. "There will be plenty of things to eat—especially for breakfast. I've never been known to skimp on portions. And you can clean the house after they leave. That's when it will need it."

"See? That's why I need to run away from home and come to a place where there's some common sense. I can't even think in my own house."

"We are full—top to bottom—or we would help you out. Every nook and cranny is filled, even some that shouldn't be," said Louise.

"What do you mean?"

"Mr. Enrich is staying for the reunion and has agreed to sleep in the library on a cot, of all things," Louise told her. "Jane thinks it's a fine idea but I think it's awful—what kind of innkeeper would do that?"

"The kind that won't kick someone out onto the street because they want to hang around and enjoy the fun," Jane said calmly. "Besides, it makes him happy. I think he's enjoying this."

"How can you tell?" Louise said dryly.

Jane shot her sister a look. "I think I saw him smile yesterday."

"Who made that miracle happen?" Louise asked.

"Josie."

"Oh. That explains it. She can make anyone smile."

Vera glanced at her watch. "If you can't take me in, can you at least promise that if things get too out of hand, I can come and sit in your garden instead of my own?"

"We'll even give you some iced tea—and an aspirin," Jane assured her.

How, Jane wondered, was she supposed to get Clarissa out of the bakery mid-afternoon to take a rest? Zack and Nancy were trying to be considerate of Clarissa, but getting her to leave the bakery was nearly impossible. On impulse, she picked up the bag of sketchbooks and pencils that she and Josie had used the other day as she was walking out the door.

Sylvia waved her down as she was walking toward the Good Apple. She looked surprisingly calm, considering that the countdown clock to the reunion was ticking noisily.

Jane commented to that effect.

"Oh, I've given up," Sylvia said cheerfully. "What happens, happens. We've tried our best. Now all we can do is point people in the right direction, put out fires, and hope and pray for success. It's in the hands of our volunteers now. I'm going to start enjoying things."

At that moment, Wilhelm Wood joined them on the sidewalk. He addressed Jane. "I've got everything settled about the beverages and more than enough helpers. When the time comes, speak up and tell them what you need them to do."

"Then I think we're set." Jane turned to Sylvia. "Everything's covered."

"Music to my ears."

"Not quite everything," Wilhelm interjected. A smile played around his lips.

Sylvia leaned forward. "What do you mean?"

"Obviously Viola hasn't found you yet this morning."

"I've been hiding from her, actually. She's in a twist over the books we've asked her to order. 'Too silly,' according to her."

"Oh, it's more than that now. . ."

Wilhelm's comment was interrupted by a vociferous *"Yoo-hoo! Yoo-hoo!"* from across the street. Viola charged toward them without looking to the right or to the left. Poor Carlene Moss, editor of the *Acorn Nutshell*, had to slam on the brakes of her car as Viola trotted in front of her.

Viola was a palette of color in her teal blue pantsuit and rainbow-colored scarf. Her face was bright pink under her rouged cheeks. "I have something to say."

"Yes?" Sylvia asked tentatively.

"I want to file an official protest with the reunion committee. I have been forced to order boxes and boxes of books, tapes and CDs that will never be purchased. I will have to return them all. That 'good idea' to have a reunion bookstore in the marketplace was misguided. Who will purchase ridiculous tapes of music from the sixties and seventies? What kind of character would want to read a book, *Autobiography of a Flower Child* or *What They Wore in 74* or some such nonsense? Reminiscing is one thing, but ..."

"Actually," Sylvia said, "I'll buy a copy of *What They Wore in 74*. I don't have that one in my collection of books on fashion. Do you have any others like it? I like collecting vintage clothing, the word's gone out about it and I get calls from people searching for certain garments. The seventies are far enough in the past to be collectible. Please put one aside for me. I'd hate to have them sell out without getting one."

The look on Viola's face was worth a thousand words. *No, maybe a million*, Jane thought.

Deflated, Viola walked off, now apparently worrying that she might be in danger of actually selling some books and thereby ruining her reputation for carrying fine literature.

It was not until she disappeared around the corner that the trio erupted in laughter.

"Shame on you, Sylvia," Wilhelm chided. "Being interested in a 'silly' book."

"Hardly silly. I didn't even know it existed until now. I can't wait to see it."

"I'm not sure what Viola fears most, not selling her books or selling them." Jane glanced at her watch. "I should go. I'm a woman on a mission."

When Jane arrived at the bakery, Clarissa was sitting out front having a conversation with Craig Tracy from Wild Things. Nancy was behind the counter pulling empty trays from the displays and replacing them with full ones. Jane could see Zack moving around in back with swift, efficient steps.

"Hi, Craig. Are you ready for the onslaught?"

"As ready as I'll ever be. How about you?"

"If I've learned anything over the years, it's plan well, hire the best and enjoy the ride. The planning is done. We obviously," and Jane tipped her head toward Clarissa and then the Colwins, "have hired the best. Now all that's left is enjoying the ride."

"Well said, Jane." Craig clapped his open palms on his thighs before he stood up. "I'm going to take your advice. I'd better go back to the store and make sure my floral orders are caught up. Cheers, Clarissa."

Clarissa waved.

"Look at you," Jane said to Clarissa after Craig had departed.

"Sitting around like a queen," Clarissa acknowledged with a smile. "I had no idea it could feel so good."

"Just 'sitting around,' you mean?"

"No, sitting in my own business and overseeing a staff as smart and quick as the Colwins. I should have hired help years ago."

"What's stopping you now?" Jane inquired.

Clarissa's eyes twinkled. "At the moment? Livvy is stopping me. She got some of those stubborn genes from me. I want it to be *my* idea, not hers. Livvy understands children and school systems but I think that girl needs to learn a little more about old people. They don't like being bossed about and having decisions made for them any more than young people do. I may be wrinkled but I'm not weird. And I'm younger up here," Clarissa tapped her head with her index finger, "than many people. Probably even Livvy."

"I love it." Jane sat back and grinned. "You teach 'em, Clarissa. But how about an even bigger break from the grind before this reunion gets into full swing and engulfs us all?"

"What do you have in mind?"

"Josie and I were at Fairy Pond yesterday and it was just lovely."

"Fairy Pond. I haven't been there in years. Why, my husband and I used to go out there." Clarissa blushed.

Jane smiled, trying to imagine Clarissa and her husband kissing under the canopy of foliage encompassing Fairy Pond. "Then it's past time that you make a return visit. I've got apples and water in my bag. It's not much, but we can pretend it's lunch."

"I've got tuna fish sandwiches," Clarissa offered. "And all the cookies we can eat."

"Done."

"Done." Clarissa rose to get ready for her first picnic in twenty years.

"It's even more beautiful than I remember." Clarissa sat on the stump Josie had used the day before for a table. "How everything has grown. Some of these trees were just saplings and now they're giants."

"It's one of my favorite places," Jane admitted. "I come here to sketch or design jewelry. There's inspiration here."

"I see that."

"Do you draw, Clarissa?"

"Just my breath, nothing else."

"I can't believe that. Look at all the beautiful cakes you've made over the years."

"That's with a pastry tube and a little butter and sugar, hardly the real thing."

"Don't sell yourself short." Jane reached into her bag and pulled out the sketchbook Josie had used. "Want to try it?"

"Sure. Then you'll see that I'm telling you the truth, and I can shut my eyes and take a nap out here." Clarissa reached for the paper and colored pencils Jane handed her.

They were quiet then, Jane intent on her design for a brooch that reflected the mist of ferns hovering near the lake. Neither spoke for a long time.

Finally, the design satisfactory, Jane looked up. Clarissa was absorbed in sketching, her tongue caught between her teeth and her brow furrowed. Whatever she was drawing, she was working hard at it.

Clarissa raised her head and looked embarrassed. "This is kind of fun."

"I think so. May I see your drawing?"

"It's not much yet, but…" She held up a full-page drawing of Fairy Pond dotted with lily pads. From one of the lily pads, a frog was jumping, his green body stretched its full length and—Jane wasn't quite sure how Clarissa had managed it—an intent, do-or-die sort of expression on his tiny face. His mottled green skin seemed to glisten in sunlight.

"That is absolutely marvelous!" Jane exclaimed. "And you told me you couldn't draw."

"Didn't know I could." Clarissa studied the picture. "Huh. How about that? I started working at the bakery when I was a little girl and just never quit. My parents never thought to encourage me to do anything but the family business. I learned to decorate cakes by watching my parents do them. I never saw either one pick up a pencil to draw." She held it out and squinted at it. "It kind of looks like the pond, doesn't it?"

"Clarissa, it is an amazing likeness. And you've even improved upon the pond. I love that frog."

"His name is Ed."

Jane did a double take. "What?"

"The frog's name is Ed. I drew a few other sketches of him and decided he needed a name." She flipped back the pages to other sketches. Ed poised on the lily pad. Ed diving into the water with only the back half of his body showing. Ed sitting on a tiny stool, and Ed on his back legs peeking through a faint sketch of a window.

Jane laughed out loud. "This is marvelous! How inventive. Clarissa, I've seen children's books illustrated with much less creativity than this."

"Go on. You're just trying to make an old lady feel good about herself."

"Not where art is concerned. This is great. Maybe *I'll* start decorating cakes for practice."

"Don't be silly. This is nothing like what you do."

"No? Probably not. It has the potential to be even better."

Clarissa rolled her eyes at that.

"I wonder how your kids will react when they learn that you can do this."

"It will be a surprise. All they ever saw me do was work— at the bakery, at home, in the garden, at church. Of course, I didn't have much choice once their dad was gone. I had to earn a living and keep them clean and fed." Clarissa's expression saddened. "Sometimes I wonder if Livvy's work habits are my fault. I didn't teach her much about resting."

"And the boys?" Jane sensed this was a direction Clarissa wanted to go.

"They're a little better. I'm thankful that they married wives who made them slow down for the sake of their families." She leaned back and gave a gusty sigh. "I wish I'd thought to bring them out here."

"It's not too late. You have grandchildren, you know."

"They're far away and I'm an old woman now. . . ."

"Now that's the lamest excuse I've heard in a long time."

Clarissa chuckled. "It sounded pretty bad to me too. But until I get Livvy—or the bakery—off my back, I'm not going to have much time for anything else. That girl has practically said that she thinks it's time I consider a nursing home. Well, maybe not that, but somewhere I can have 'meals, a social director and company my own age.'"

Jane wrinkled her nose. "'Company your own age'? What fun is that? Variety is the spice of life."

"Tell that to Livvy."

"Just promise me this. Now that you've started drawing, will you keep it up?" Jane took extra sketchbooks, pencils and a little watercolor kit with brushes from her bag. "I want you to have these."

"I couldn't take those. They must have cost you a fortune."

"I'll trade you then. For one of your pictures."

"You're getting the raw end of that deal," Clarissa said, shaking her head.

"That's for me to decide. Will you take them?"

Clarissa looked longingly at the equipment at her feet. "It was fun to draw that frog...."

"Then do it for Ed."

That settled it. Clarissa gathered the art materials and stuck them in her own bag.

〜

"Jane, someone from your graduating class called to remind you about 'the big party.'" Alice was carrying clean towels through the kitchen toward the upstairs bedrooms.

"'Big party?' Isn't that what this entire reunion is? One big party."

"No, something else. Something formal. She said you should bring a guest."

Jane groaned. "Oh, that's the reception for all the graduates on Friday night. Every school in the county is having one in their hometown. You're going to it, aren't you? After some mingling time, the classes are supposed to congregate. I suppose that's when we get to look one another over and see who's got the most gray hair, jowls, wrinkles and chins."

"Well, it certainly won't be you. Sometimes I think you're even prettier now than you were in high school, so ... what is it the kids say?...so 'together.'"

"That is very sweet of you, Alice, but I can already feel my insecurities flaring. Besides, someone had the brilliant idea that this event should be a formal affair. Can you believe it? What are we supposed to do? Squeeze into our old prom dresses and tuxedoes? Ridiculous."

Louise, who had entered the room mid-speech asked, "Insecurities? You? Jane, whatever do you have to feel insecure about?"

Alice shot her older sister a look.

"Oh, you mean that thing Shirley Taylor said? Don't pay one bit of attention to that. You were both young."

"Of course," Alice said slyly, "you don't want to go to the formal party without an attractive man on your arm—just like in high school."

"I don't need anyone else with me to feel complete." Then her eyes began to sparkle. "I have to admit, though, that it would be fun to bring a handsome man to the festivities just to get people talking. I know the women from my class would find it most interesting." Then she groaned. "Even saying that makes me sound like an adolescent."

"Reunions do that to people. Frankly, I think you should get one. A handsome man, I mean."

Louise and Jane stared at Alice as if the top of her head had come off.

Alice looked girlish as she spoke. "For fun. I know *I'd* like to come to the reunion in a lovely dress with a good-looking man on my arm instead of wearing a rain slicker and working a car wash. At least one of us should go the glamorous route." She looked at Louise. "Unless you want to be the one."

Louise held up a hand. "Don't look at me. I am committed to helping Viola with the bookstore and keeping her sane. I already have my hands full. Besides, at my age, my classmates thought something more sedate might be in order.

"And Pastor Ken and I promised a pizza party with movies to our young people. He is going to hold down the fort until I get there after the reception."

"That doesn't sound like much fun," Jane commented. "Doesn't he want to get out and see the celebration?"

"He says that as a newcomer to Acorn Hill, it's his duty to see that everyone else is free to enjoy the event. He's happy to be chaperoning the kids."

"And what about you? Are you happy?"

Alice considered Jane's question for a moment. "Actually, I am. Next to nursing, the most rewarding thing I do is work with these young people. Besides, my classmates have things planned throughout the reunion. I'll barely miss a thing."

"It's settled then," Louise said unexpectedly. There was an impish glint in her eye that her sisters rarely saw. "Jane will represent the family as the beautiful, successful one." She turned an eye to Jane. "You will, won't you?"

Jane had heard that tone in Louise's voice before. Louise had made up her mind and nothing was going to change it.

"I can't. ..."

"You most certainly can. Let's go upstairs and look through your wardrobe."

"I don't have a handsome man in there."

"Then I will make a call. Is Ned Arnold handsome enough for you?"

Louise, who had not "sprawled" on anything for a number of years, had done so, in a ladylike fashion, of course, across Jane's bed. Alice was perched beside her, eyes bright. How on earth she had gotten into this Jane would never know. *This was like the years her sisters had called conferences to decide what Jane should wear on dates*, she thought as she modeled yet another evening dress for her sisters. In San Francisco, she had gone regularly to dressy occasions, gallery openings and the like. Here, her formal clothes had been in retirement—until now, the most unlikely of circumstances, a blind date set up by Louise and Alice.

"This reminds me of you two playing 'dress up' with me as a child," Jane complained as Louise spun a finger in the air, telling her to twirl around for them again.

"You always looked like a little doll," Alice said mistily. "Remember how we used to braid her hair, Louise?"

Jane's heart melted. They were having fun. This reminded them of their youth, when the most important thing was making sure their baby sister was as pretty as she could be. It was harmless. Why not let them have that fun again?

Besides, Jane admitted to herself, maybe she would feel a little more comfortable wearing a dynamite dress when facing her nemesis for the first time.

They settled on a graceful, sophisticated, white-beaded dress with a dipping back. It was Jane's favorite dress. It fit her like a glove and the shiny flecks of beads danced in the light when she moved. The dress had been a hit at several parties and, Jane had to admit, it made her feel confident and poised.

"I think you should wear your hair up," Louise was saying.

"But not too severe," Alice said, "you know, something messy but elegant. Like those women in magazine ads."

Jane grabbed her thick hair, twisted it at the back of her head and secured it with the nearest thing she could find, a pencil.

"That's it!" Alice said delightedly. "Except, of course, it can't be a pencil."

"You and Ned will make a lovely couple," Louise said with a note of satisfaction in her voice. It had been she who had reached Ned at the pharmacy and had explained the situation. Ned graciously told her that he would *love* to escort Jane to her party. (Jane didn't want to know exactly what Louise had told him. The whole thing was far too humiliating already.)

Louise's eyes twinkled. "I think he likes you, you know."

Jane, as she had as a youngster, clapped her hands over her ears. "Louie, don't even go there."

Louise settled in with an enigmatic smile. Jane thought that was almost worse than her saying something. Louise's prediction for the reunion had come true—everyone *had* gone mad—including Louise.

⌒

Jane met Mr. Enrich in the hall. He had struck up a bit of a friendship with Joe and had been advising him on certain issues with rosebushes and mulch. He had a little color in his face although a smile was still missing.

"I believe you're getting a tan," she said by way of greeting.

He put his hand to his cheek. "Well, that's a change." He tipped his head and entered the library.

One of many, Jane thought. Mr. Enrich was eating more and talking more at breakfast. She had heard him out on the porch in an involved conversation with Josie about the state of health of some of her dolls, and he had begun opening doors for people and performing other small civilities around the inn. And he had moved into the library, made his own bed and settled in to read even more of her father's books.

She couldn't imagine how many of them he had already read. Jane had noticed that most of those he carried with him to the porch or garden were spiritual in nature.

Alice always had extra Bibles on hand, and Jane reminded herself to give one to Mr. Enrich when he decided to leave. He still had not mentioned his departure date. That was very strange since initially he had promised, "I won't be here much longer." Oh well. He had become part of the fabric of the household now and whenever he did leave, he would be missed.

Lloyd and Ethel were both on the verge of heart attacks.

It might appear, Jane thought, that her aunt and the mayor were in total charge of all aspects of the reunion and were run ragged by it when, in reality, they were primarily spectators who were wearing themselves out cheering on the home team.

Lloyd had taken to wearing bow ties in red, white and blue or those of Acorn Hill's school colors, yellow and burgundy. They were not colors meant for a bow tie. They made Lloyd's corpulent chins appear to be tied in gift wrap. Ethel, meanwhile, recently had had her hair dyed and the vivid red "Titian Dreams" color hadn't had time to soften or fade. She could be seen coming from a block away.

The mayor had also begun carrying a little red notebook in which he scribbled at intervals. Sylvia had told Jane that no one on the reunion committee had appointed Lloyd record keeper, judge or jury. He had taken the task on himself.

"Cars are pouring into this little town like maple syrup onto pancakes," Lloyd announced. His similes were colorful but inspired odd mental images. "We've got people out parking them in fields. I've just been to Fred's Hardware and bought every flashlight so our parking attendants can direct people out of the fields at night."

"And tell him about the bug spray, Lloyd," Ethel instructed.

"He's already sold out and he ordered two extra cases. We're fogging the town, but I gave him strict orders to get more spray in here tomorrow. We can't have people going home bitten up and complaining about Acorn Hill."

I'll bet Fred loved that, Jane thought. Aloud, she said, "Everyone coming to the reunion once lived here, Lloyd. They're probably well acquainted with the hometown bugs."

Ignoring her, Lloyd continued. "Ethel and I did a check of every store in town to see that they were well-stocked. Joseph had threatened to close the antique store for the reunion, but I told him he'd be crazy to do it. He'd lose a lot of money not being open on the busiest days of the decade."

"He is on the reunion committee," Jane reminded Lloyd. "Maybe he has too much to do."

"That's why *I* found someone to work for him," Ethel said proudly.

Jane did a double take. Ethel? Temporary employment agency?

"Josie and her mother Justine were in the Coffee Shop. She told me she had the reunion days off from work and I hired her on the spot."

"You did? For Joseph?"

"I did." Ethel snapped her slightly pudgy fingers. "Just like that."

"And Joseph was delighted," Lloyd added. "He's going to pay her a commission on everything she sells, besides an hourly rate."

"Good for her," Jane said. Justine struggled financially as a single mom and extra income would make life easier for her.

"If she works out," Ethel confided, "he might hire her to work for him full-time."

Jane smiled. Things were going swimmingly.

The inn was hopping. Alice had checked in all but one guest—Shirley Taylor—and Louise was busy keeping the fruit bowl full and giving directions.

Today Jane would see if this Shirley Taylor was the same woman with whom she had attended school.

A knock on the door made Jane spin around. A handsome man with dark hair stood in the doorway.

"Yes? May I help you?"

"I'm looking for Jane Howard. Is she here?"

"I'm Jane." She had an odd feeling in the pit of her stomach.

"I'm Ray Cottrell, Clarissa's son from South Dakota. My mother's had some bad news, I'm afraid, and she wondered if you'd mind coming over."

Without a second thought, Jane grabbed her wide-brimmed straw hat and headed out the door.

Chapter Nine

"What's happened?" Jane's long legs could barely keep up with Ray's even longer ones.

"Mom just got a call from an old friend. It seems her sister, an even closer friend of my mother's, has had a stroke. They aren't sure how much damage has been done, although they do believe it's not life-threatening. Mom always handles things like this so well, but this time she just fell apart. Livvy—who isn't great at a big show of emotion—is beside herself. My brother Kent is a pastor, but apparently it's more difficult to comfort one's own mother—too close and too concerned, I suppose, to be of much help. Anyway, it was you that Mom asked for."

He grinned and Jane saw Clarissa's playfulness in him. "She said she needed someone with a 'good head on her shoulders' and she didn't mean any of her children."

"I'm sorry. . . ."

"Don't be. We all know that Livvy has a heart of gold. It's just hard to find it, sometimes, especially when she's upset. The more worried she is, the more she wants to be in charge of everything, as if when she's directing traffic nothing will crash. And my brother's heart is almost too big for him. It hurts for everyone. I'm the practical one in the family." He held out his work-worn hands, and Jane could see dirt and grease imbedded so firmly beneath his fingernails that nothing would get it out. "I'm an auto mechanic. It breaks and I fix it. That makes sense to me. Livvy and Kent are always trying to change the world. I'm just trying to make it easier and more pleasant for people, one person at a time."

He grinned again, and Jane was smitten. "And I've got a good business and loyal customers too."

"I'll bet you do." She looked at him as they walked. "You're the most like your mother, aren't you?"

"So they say." He stopped and stared at her somberly. "I have a gut feeling it's not my mother's sick friend that is causing Mom's distress, but something has triggered this and I'd be very grateful if you could help us figure it out."

Jane took a deep breath. Mind reader. One more skill for her résumé.

When they arrived at the house, the air crackled with tension. Livvy was pacing the floor. Kent, who looked much like Livvy but with soft brown hair, jumped to his feet.

Jane introduced herself to Kent and inquired, "What's happening?"

"Mom lost it. Her friend's sister said she believed things would be okay but that she thought Mom would want to know about the stroke. Mom really took it hard."

"It's because of that bakery." Livvy pointed out. "She's working too hard. No wonder she doesn't have any emotional reserves left."

Clarissa had more "emotional reserves" left than most people had ever had, Jane thought as she climbed the stairs to Clarissa's room.

"It's about time someone sane came to see me," Clarissa said. She put the Bible she had been reading on the table next to her easy chair.

Jane chuckled and walked in. "What's this about you being so terribly upset because of a friend? Is it serious?"

"For Mimi? I doubt it. Not according to her sister, at least. They wanted my prayers for her, not to tell me she was dying."

"I'm glad to hear that. Then what's the fuss about? Your children said you 'lost it.' Livvy says your 'emotional reserves' are low because of how hard you work at the bakery."

"Educated mumbo-jumbo," Clarissa muttered. "I thought I taught that girl to speak English."

"Don't be too hard on her. She loves you and she's worried about you."

"No need to be. I'm fine when no one is telling me I'm an old, weak, incompetent woman."

"Then why did you react so strongly?"

Jane sat down on the edge of the bed across from Clarissa's chair.

"That could have been me. I could've been the one who had a stroke."

"It could've been any of us, for that matter."

Clarissa's eyes bored into Jane's. "This age thing is getting to me, Jane. I don't feel old up here," she pointed to her head, "but here," Clarissa rubbed her hip, "it's not looking so good. When that young Colwin couple came in and started helping me, I realized just how much I've slowed down. Do you think Livvy and her brothers are right? *Am* I too old for this?"

"What do you think?"

"I'm not willing to give it all up, Jane, but I'm not sure I can keep it all either." She chuckled humorlessly. "I guess what the baker in me is saying is that I can't have my cake and eat it too. If I give up the Good Apple, what would I do? Livvy thinks I'd be happy crocheting doilies and doing crossword puzzles. Where's the meaning in that?"

"It sounds like it's not the bakery that you don't want to give up as much as it is the meaning and purpose in your life."

Clarissa chewed on that a bit and then nodded. "You're right. I'm needed at the Good Apple. People come and visit and take baked goods home to their families. Through the bakery I can make people's lives a little more pleasant and easy. When I feel like it, I can bake extra and give it away."

Jane didn't say anything, but she did know that Clarissa had been more than generous to Justine and her daughter as they struggled to make ends meet. Justine had told Jane that some nights Clarissa made the difference in whether they had something to eat for supper.

"I need to have some meaning in my life, Jane. I want to have the ability to contribute. And Livvy doesn't see that."

"She's not here every day, how could she? I feel a little guilty for the predicament you're in right now," Jane confessed. "If I hadn't snared you into doing all the work for the reunion, Livvy wouldn't be so concerned and you wouldn't be so frustrated." She reached out and took her friend's hand.

"Livvy is just like her father. He'd keep coming at a problem from the same angle until he wore himself out." Clarissa looked misty. "And I loved him for it. I knew he'd never give up on us or stop working for his family."

"So when it's good, it's very good and when it's bad …"

"It's one big nuisance." Clarissa was smiling again.

"Why don't we turn it over to God and let Him figure it out."

Together, they bowed their heads.

"Dear Heavenly Father, one of Your children has a problem. Help Clarissa to know what You want her to do. She's been Your steward in the Good Apple all these years and now things are changing. What's the meaning of this, Lord, and what do You want her to do about it? Her children want to help her, her friends want to support her and her customers love her. Unfold the answers for Clarissa that only You can provide. And, Lord, let her children see what their mother really needs—freedom to make her own decisions, support, not force, and love, not lectures."

"And take care of my friend who's ill and get us through this reunion, please," Clarissa added.

"Amen," they chorused together.

Clarissa squeezed Jane's hand. "*Whew*. I feel better. But how do I go downstairs and explain to my family that I took a temporary leave of my sanity?" Clarissa wondered out loud.

"No explanations necessary. You get to feel what you feel. You were upset and now you've turned it all over to God. You're trusting Him to deal with it now."

"That's exactly what I'm going to say." Clarissa looked at Jane. "I'm glad God brought you back to Acorn Hill. I think He did it just for me."

"And just for me. Otherwise, I'd still be in San Francisco, estranged from my home and family."

"Mysterious ways. Definitely mysterious ways." Then Clarissa's eyebrows shot upward. "Before we go downstairs, I have something I'd like to show you." She went to her closet and pulled out a large, flat box. "You got me thinking, out there at Fairy Pond." She opened the top flaps of the box and Jane gasped. There inside, was a startlingly realistic portrait of Livvy, showing the fire, the compassion and the stern set of her lips—beautiful, complex and sweet.

"I've done the boys too." She lifted the portrait of Livvy to reveal portraits of her two sons.

Jane almost laughed out loud at the twinkle in Ray's eyes and the commonsense set of his jaw. In Kent's sketch, Clarissa had captured the empathetic good-heartedness he wore like a garment. He looked a little puzzled too, as if he were baffled and perplexed at all the negativity in the world. "These are amazing!"

"You think so?" Clarissa studied the visual renderings critically.

"Absolutely. Your talent is remarkable—and so is finding it so late in life."

"A regular Grandma Moses, huh?"

"Do your children know about this?"

"No, and I'm not going to tell them right now. When they boss me around, I escape to my room to 'nap,' because that's what they expect of me. That's when I draw. I think

Ray is on to me because he's the one who sees me most clearly, but even he has no idea what I'm up to. I'm planning to give them their portraits on their way out the door after the reunion." Clarissa's eye twinkled. "That'll teach 'em to think I need all those naps."

As Jane accompanied Clarissa downstairs, she could feel Livvy's eyes on her.

When Clarissa had made her declaration that she was "just fine," Jane tried to take her leave. Livvy caught her as she said her good-byes.

"What do you think?" Livvy asked breathlessly.

"About what?"

"Mother, of course. Is she ... you know ... losing it?"

"Livvy, your mother hasn't lost a thing. She's smart, clear-headed, talented and wise. She's remarkable. I count her as a dear friend. She might be twenty-five years older than I, but her mind is as good as mine. Better, maybe."

Livvy looked as though she and Jane were discussing two different people. "That can't be ... not at her age."

"Why? I know people twenty-five years old who act as old as the hills. Your mother's mind is barely twenty-five now." Jane took Livvy's hand. "I know how much you love your mom and want to take care of her. She loves you that much in return. But if you love her, then empower her. Let her make her own choices as long as she's able."

"But is she able now?" Livvy wondered, her trepidation clear.

"More than most, Livvy. More than most."

♍

"You can't see past your own nose, Zack Colwin."

"Aw, Nancy, I'm just being practical. You've got this goofy idea about picket fences, a dog in the front yard and some quaint little diner, but diners are history. Blue-plate specials are passé. Inventiveness and creativity are in."

The voices came from the dining room. Jane winced as she passed through the hall. This was the same old argument. Nancy had fallen head over heels in love with Acorn Hill—its size, its ambiance, its people.

"I want to live in a place like this," she had told Jane. "Of course, you've got all the food establishments you really need, with Potterston so close and all, but there's got to be somewhere similar, a place that needs a good restaurant."

"What does Zack say about this?" Jane had asked. She had not liked the troubled expression the question had brought to Nancy's face.

"Zack has got his head in the clouds. He wants to be a famous chef someday. He thinks you were crazy to leave San Francisco. He's heard of the Blue Fish Grille. He'd give almost anything to have the job that you walked away from."

Jane could have told Zack that she rarely thought of the Blue Fish anymore. When she did, it was with fond memories—and no desire to go back. He wouldn't believe her, of course. There were certain things about life that one had to learn for oneself.

Now Jane heard Louise come in the back door. She had been practicing at the church, judging from the music she was carrying. The two sisters could hear the pair in the dining room in intent discussion. Casting her eyes heavenward, she asked, "Not again?"

"Why don't you start playing some of that music you're carrying," Jane suggested softly. "We need a change of pace around here."

"If you think it will work." Louise went into the parlor and over to the piano. She put her books on the piano bench and slid in beside them. With more gusto than she usually displayed, she began an enthusiastic rendition of "Jesus Loves Me." Then she began to sing. "Jesus loves me, this I know, for the Bible tells me so. Little ones to Him belong, they are weak but He is strong. *Yessssss*, Jesus loves me! *Yessssss*, Jesus loves me. *Yessssss* . . ."

Louise's voice was nearly as good as her piano playing. Jane, however, had been absent when that particular talent had been handed out. Still, she sang along, knowing that if pretty music might not cause some interest, her off-key vocalizations always would.

The bickering stopped almost immediately, partially drowned out by the performance. Jane smiled and kept singing. Louise shook her head at her and played on.

Soon, two curious faces peered around the doorjamb.

Jane waved them in and invited them to sing. Nancy looked at Zack and smiled. They stepped into the room and, standing next to Jane, began to sing.

After several choruses of "Jesus Loves Me," Louise switched to another old favorite with a catchy chorus. "I've got a home in glory land that outshines the sun, oh, I've got a home in glory land that outshines the sun . . ." and they all chimed in again.

Then, surprisingly, another voice joined the group. This voice was low and on key. Mr. Enrich had entered the room and was standing behind them, singing, his face stiff and somber, his eyes intent. Zack impulsively threw his arm around the older man and invited him into the fold.

"Do, Lord, oh do, Lord, oh do remember me . . . Michael row the boat ashore . . ." Alice had now joined them and they were all smiling—even Mr. Enrich—when they finished.

Nancy clapped her hands and Zack gave her a hug. "That was fun."

Jane watched them exchange a fond glance. These two were so in love with each other and so at odds about their futures. At least for the moment, the quibbling was forgotten.

"You have a wonderful voice, Mr. Enrich," Alice said. "As good as Jane's is bad."

"Hey, are you complaining about my singing?" Jane teased.

"Just the tune, dear, not the volume."

Mr. Enrich blushed and escaped from the room.

Later, when the sisters were alone, they discussed what had happened.

"It was a miracle, really," Louise commented, "Mr. Enrich *singing.*"

"And smiling," Alice added. "Or at least trying to. The gentleman has come a long way since he arrived." She looked at Jane. "In no little part, thanks to you."

"We've all been praying," Jane pointed out. "And it looks as if God is answering."

"I wonder," Louise mused, "what it is that Mr. Enrich needs to hear."

⌐

The countdown was over. This was the day of blast-off. The reunion was about to begin.

Walking through the streets of Acorn Hill, Jane marveled at the number of cars in the streets and people milling on the sidewalks. Many were hugging and laughing, and a few were already on overload, sporting glazed expressions even though the party had not yet begun.

She ran into Sylvia coming out of the Coffee Shop.

"Well, the big day is here."

Sylvia bobbed her head and dabbed at the corner of her mouth. "I just had a piece of pie to fortify myself. Are you ready for the formal gathering tonight?"

"My sisters will have me ready. They've been fussing over me like mother hens. They picked out my clothing and even found me a date."

"No kidding?" Sylvia's eyes grew wide. "Louise and Alice? Or do you have other sisters hidden away somewhere?"

"They have it in their heads that since Shirley Taylor is coming to the reunion—and staying at the inn—I should look pretty and successful." Jane grinned widely. "It's fun. I'm seeing them as they used to be—always hovering over me, trying to make sure that everything was right. I didn't appreciate it then, but now I realize just how sweet they were trying to be."

"And you don't mind?"

"Actually, I'm pleased to have a place to wear some of my old clothes. There are not many occasions for sparkles in Acorn Hill."

"And the date?"

"Ned Arnold. He's being such a good sport about it. Besides, he says it gives him the opportunity to enjoy the reunion as a participant rather than as an observer. He's looking forward to it."

"And that's it?" Sylvia looked intently quizzical. Then she waggled her eyebrows.

"That's it. No romance. Just friendship. But, if you can believe this, Louise told him to be very attentive to me this evening. She told him that an old boyfriend of mine would be there and the woman who tried to 'steal' him away. Isn't that hilarious?"

"I've known Alice a long time, and Louise as long as I've known you, Jane, and I must say, when you arrived, you brought some new excitement into their lives."

Jane thought back to their first difficult days. Back then, she had wondered if she represented too much excitement. Now, it seemed, Louise and Alice had turned the tables and were giving her a run for her money. "Like Louise says, it's all in good fun. I appreciate the fact that they don't want an old rival to get me down, but they do seem to forget that I can handle myself."

"Enjoy," Sylvia advised. "Are they coming to the reunion too?"

"Louise is coming later with Viola. Alice will come as soon as all the guests are checked in and her responsibilities with the car wash are finished. Even Nancy and Zack said they might stop by and peek in. I heard them ask Mr. Enrich if he'd like to come along."

"You're getting to be quite a cozy little family over there, aren't you?"

Jane hadn't thought about it in quite that way, but she supposed Sylvia was right. Since they had opened the inn, their family had grown to encompass everyone who passed through their doors. Right now, it seemed that some of their more needy family members were in residence.

"Where have you been?" Louise demanded when Jane walked through the front door. "You have to start getting ready."

"I've got over an hour before I meet Ned."

"*Humph*. Ned will pick you up. We discussed it this morning."

Jane opened her mouth to protest and then shut it again. "Enjoy," Sylvia had said. And she would.

"You had better go upstairs and shower," Louise instructed.

"Are you bossing her around?" Alice asked as she came from the kitchen. "You know how she disliked that as a child."

Jane laughed inwardly. Then she noticed the serious expression in Alice's eyes.

"What's wrong?"

"Shirley Taylor checked in," Alice said in a whisper. "I had Justine watch the inn for an hour while I went to check on the kids' schedule for the car wash and she came while I was gone."

A little flutter of butterflies waved their wings in Jane's stomach.

"I'm sure we'll all have a wonderful time," Jane said cheerfully. "Louise is right. I'd better get ready."

For once, her hair did exactly what she wanted it to do. She had lost a few pounds since the last time she had worn the dress, a result of all the hard work she had been doing at the inn, no doubt. So it glided over her slender hips like a dream. Louise insisted that she wear the diamond drop earrings that Eliot had given her for their twenty-fifth wedding anniversary. Alice surprised her with a small, silver-mesh evening bag that had been Madeleine's.

Jane returned the favors by giving both Louise and Alice brooches she had made especially for them, commemorating the years of their own high-school graduations and color-coordinated to the dresses they planned to wear. Both were delighted.

Mr. Enrich came out of the library and into the kitchen as Jane stood there doing one last check of her catering list before Ned arrived. Mr. Enrich had obviously had his suit dry-cleaned and his shoes polished. She wasn't sure, but she thought he had also had his hair trimmed.

"Don't you look nice."

"I feel like a fool," he growled. "Look at me, dressed up for a party I'm not invited to."

"Nonsense. This is a party for anyone who's ever lived in or loved Acorn Hill. That means you. Besides, Nancy and Zack are thrilled that you've agreed to go with them. They won't know anyone else either so you'll be able to converse with each other—and me and my sisters, of course. I even think Joe Morales might make a showing. Perhaps you can befriend him if he comes."

Mr. Enrich looked at her oddly. "You watch out for everyone, don't you? You care. Why?"

Jane was taken aback. "Why not? We're all God's children. It's only right that we care about one another."

"This is the strangest place I've ever been," Mr. Enrich mumbled in bewilderment. "Extraordinary."

Jane took that as a compliment.

Ned was prompt, ringing the doorbell at the appointed time. Jane heard her sisters go to answer the door. How many potential suitors had those two scared off when she was in high school? Who knew? And if they weren't intimidating enough, Daniel Howard would emerge from his study to question those young boys about their plans and the hour they would have her home. Jane marveled that she had ever had a male friend at all.

Jeremy Patterson had been the one boy who hadn't seemed intimidated by her family. Football player, all-around athlete, honor student and genuinely nice guy, Jeremy had been a high-school heartthrob as well as Jane's boyfriend. It was the word *friend* that defined their relationship. Both Jane and Jeremy had their eyes on dreams in the future and, because of their similar aspirations, had become united in their desire to hurry through high school and to get on with their lives.

It was a concept not shared with most of their classmates, who had been more interested in the here and now—dates, social status and popularity. So, while everyone saw Jane and Jeremy as a "couple," they viewed themselves as collaborators on their futures.

But that was the past and this was the present. Ned, looking incredibly handsome in a dark suit, a crisp white shirt and a red tie, was standing in the front hall waiting for her.

Jane said good-bye to her sisters and got Ned out the door before Louise or Alice could suggest taking a photo. She had enough of those stored in a shoebox somewhere. In each one, she and her date at the time stood stiff and uncomfortable posing for the Kodak moment.

"Sorry about the abrupt departure. My sisters are acting as if I'm going to the prom. I was afraid they'd bring out the camera."

Ned threw back his head and laughed. "No teenager ever looked as good as you do tonight. You're absolutely lovely, Jane."

"And I might say the same about you."

He chuckled. "It's a pleasant change to wear something other than a white lab coat for a few hours."

"Is it busy at the pharmacy?"

"Surprisingly, yes. Treatments for poison ivy, sunburn and stomachache, mostly." He gestured toward his silver sports car. "Here we are."

As they pulled up in front of the high school gymnasium, which had been transformed by the reunion committee into something that resembled a silk purse more than the sow's ear it actually was, she felt a thrill of excitement. She also noticed that what seemed to be the entire male population was hanging around the school's entrance and was now focused on Ned's car. The whistles of admiration, she knew, were not for her.

Okay, Lord, here we go. Whatever goes on tonight, let me be a representative of You.

In the gymnasium, there was much squealing going on as old classmates recognized one another. For a moment, Jane couldn't pick out a single person she knew.

"All friends of yours, I presume?" Ned breathed into her ear.

"I have no idea. I don't recognize a soul. It appears that everyone has gotten old but me."

Ned laughed out loud. "You have that problem too? I went to my own reunion and wondered where all these old folks had come from. For a moment I forgot that I was the one with totally gray hair." His eyes twinkled. "Prematurely gray, of course."

"I wonder if I look as old as everyone else," Jane mused, more to herself than to Ned.

"Not a chance," he whispered.

Slightly comforted, Jane ventured forth, grabbing Ned by the hand and pulling him with her.

Suddenly faces were becoming recognizable. "Martie?" Jane ventured as she walked toward a cheerfully round-faced woman with pink cheeks and bottle-blonde hair.

"Jane?" There was dumbfounded amazement in the voice. "Jane Howard? What time warp did you get caught in? You don't look a day older."

Jane only smiled and reached out to give her old classmate a hug. Martie did look days, months and years older, but her ebullient personality was still intact. "Have you seen Sarah and Jean? They're over by the refreshment table.

And wait until you see Mr. Longer. Remember him? Our math teacher. When we were in school I thought he was ancient, but now I realize that he was only about six years older than his students. He looks great. Not, of course, as great as you. . . ."

They wound their way through the crowd, Ned's hand firmly planted in the small of Jane's back, greeting friends and neighbors. Music was playing on the stage, a string quartet. There would be an oldies group coming later.

"Jane? Martie told me you were over here and she said you were beautiful. I had to come and check it out for myself." Linda Watson and her husband Glen, both classmates, were looking at Jane with studied awe. Glen, who had had a full head of black hair as a youth, was bald as an egg. Linda's own beautiful red hair was giving way to gray.

"What have you been up to?" Linda asked.

"I'm a chef and have been for several years. I also paint and design jewelry. And you?"

"We own a photography studio in Kentucky. I love it there, but there's something about Acorn Hill that always makes me nostalgic." Linda leaned toward Jane confidentially. "What's your secret?"

"Do I have one?" Jane puzzled.

"You're thin, you're lovely, your dress is amazing and you are being escorted by a man that could be a model. I want to know how you managed all that."

"I've trained myself not to eat much of my own cooking, and my sisters pulled the dress out of my closet and fixed me up with the handsome man, that's all."

"You're holding back on me," Linda accused cheerfully, "but the reunion isn't over yet. I'll learn how you found the fountain of youth."

Jane and Ned laughed and then moved on with the flow of people.

"You're a hit," Ned whispered in Jane's ear.

"Thanks, I think."

"You aren't sure?"

"All everyone is looking at is the outside, the appearance, the shell. What really counts is what is inside people—how they think, where they hurt, what they believe. I may look fine, but I've had my trials just like everyone else in the room. This doesn't feel quite real."

"That's only because you are so real, Jane, so down-to-earth and unpretentious. And for tonight, at least, before they all let down their guards and become the people who aren't trying to impress anyone anymore, you may have to grin and bear it."

She squeezed his hand in appreciation and he smiled down at her as if she were the only woman in the room.

They were not alone, however. Jane could feel a gaze drawing her like a magnet. She glanced around, but couldn't locate the source of the feeling. Who was here that she was missing?

Then a pleasant-faced man approached. He was portly, a little jowly, but his eyes gave him away. They were startlingly blue and intent and, as always, seemed to be looking almost past her into the future.

"Jeremy!" Unthinking, Jane threw her arms around her old boyfriend and gave him a hug. Then she stepped back, embarrassed. That quickly faded, however, when she saw the delight in his eyes.

"I can't tell you how many times over the years I've thought of you, Janie. I've wondered where you were, what you were doing and if you'd accomplished any of those big dreams we used to spend so much time discussing."

"I've managed a few. I'm a chef and an artist. How about you?"

"I made some money in technology before it hit the skids. Now I have a company that manufactures medical equipment. It keeps food on the table."

"I'll bet." Jane smiled at him, delighted that all their hopes for him had come to fruition. "Jeremy, I'd like you to meet my friend Ned. Ned, this is Jeremy."

Graciously, the two men greeted each other and a bond was set. Before Jane knew what was happening, they were discussing the medical field, pharmacy, pacemakers, implants and the like. She chuckled to herself. Ned and Jeremy had more to discuss with each other than she did with either.

She turned to glance around the room and saw Ethel and Lloyd bearing down upon them. Ethel had outdone herself. She wore a bright pink dress that clashed with not only her own hair but with nearly every other garment in the room. On the dress she wore a corsage. It was long, curving at least ten inches down from her shoulder, and incorporated flowers in every shade of pink and burgundy. Greenery sprouted every which way and a reddish-purple ribbon decorated the stems.

"Great flowers, Aunt Ethel." Jane gave her aunt a hug, being careful not to crush the spray on her chest.

Ethel beamed. "Lloyd gave them to me. Aren't they wonderful? Oh my, I can't even think how many years it's been since ..." Her eyes grew misty.

Touched, Jane reached out and hugged Lloyd too. "How sweet of you," she whispered in his ear. He blushed the same color as Ethel's dress.

"And the dress matches perfectly," Ned offered politely.

"Thank you so much for noticing. Why, I feel like a schoolgirl tonight," Ethel practically giggled. "Come, Lloyd, I think they're serving cranberry punch at that table over there. It's your favorite, you know."

And off they went in a happy haze.

"Well, well," Ned said politely. "Isn't that nice?"

"They are just too cute. And they do a beautiful job of keeping each other entertained."

Chapter Ten

Before long, Jane and Ned were caught up again in a throng of people and memories. From the corner of her eyes, she saw Nancy, Zack, Joe and Mr. Enrich enter through the front door. Zack, taking charge, steered the little group toward the music and refreshments. Jane was pleased to see a flicker of interest in the usually blank expression of Mr. Enrich. Joe was utterly wide-eyed and amazed.

Jane noticed a couple near the band, swaying to the music. Both had long gray ponytails snaking down their backs. She quickly looked around for Vera, but couldn't see her. The couple was Betty and Bill Paige, the "flower children" that Vera had wondered about. Jane laughed to herself. Some things just never changed.

Louise and Viola came in later. Louise looked elegant in a steel-blue silk dress from Nellie's shop, one Jane had insisted she buy because "it didn't make her look like a piano teacher."

Viola, of course, was swathed in a long scarf and made her entrance like an opera diva coming onstage.

Alice, in a smart black evening suit, arrived with Rev. Thompson shortly after. Both were smiling, which meant all had gone well that evening with the car wash. Jane hoped that her sister was enjoying her moment of respite, because she knew that once the business started again tomorrow, Alice would have her hands full.

"Do you know everyone here?" Ned finally asked, after being introduced to dozens more people than he could possibly remember.

He was the ultimate escort, Jane decided, courteous, thoughtful, never forward or pushy and handsome besides. Her sisters had outdone themselves this time.

She saw Louise edging toward her through the crowd and affection welled up within her. Who would have thought it? Louise was set on having her baby sister the prettiest girl at the ball—and with the most hand-some man too. Jane knew why she and Alice had done it and loved them for it.

"You look fabulous, Louie," Jane said when her sister drew nearer.

"Vera said that until tonight she thought I owned nothing but skirts and sweaters."

"Well, the way you look in this dress proves that you should vary your 'uniform' more often."

Louise smiled and gave Jane a hug. "Are you having fun?"

"More than I expected. As I talk to people the years simply fall away and it's like we'd been apart months instead of decades."

"Good. Have you seen ..."

There was a commotion near the punch table. One of the waiters had spilled the sticky red drink down his white shirt and onto the floor. The ensuing fuss created by several people trying to clean up the mess with paper napkins drew Jane's attention to the far side of the room. As she turned in that direction, the tiny hairs at the back of her neck began to tingle eerily. Jane scanned the room for what—or who—was causing this strange sensation.

On the far side of the room, Fred and Vera Humbert were laughing together with a pair of classmates. Over to the left side, Viola had found a listening ear in a gentleman who was struggling not to yawn, and on the right side, Lloyd and Ethel were moving clockwise, slowly making the rounds as unofficial greeters. It occurred to Jane that those two had made this entire event their own personal party.

As she continued to look over the crowd, she finally found the person whose eyes were boring into her. It was a woman who looked to be in her late fifties. She was quite beautiful, but hers was a hard-edged beauty, a kind with which Jane was familiar. Many of her patrons at the

Blue Fish were women her own age who had started in business thirty years ago when the work climate was much less welcoming to females. Many had had to work doubly hard for their success, often developing a tough veneer. They had paved the way for younger women of today—often at a personal cost. Jane had a hunch that the person staring at her was probably younger than she looked. Her hair was artificially dark with streaks of paler highlights. The effect was formidable rather than soft. It was cut and styled close to her head with dramatic wisps of hair framing her face. Even these had been tamed into perfection with plenty of gel and hairspray. *Literally*, Jane thought, *not a hair out of place*. The woman wore a tight-fitting sequined top over black tuxedo pants with the jacket studiously arranged over one arm. And her eyes never left Jane.

"What's wrong?" Ned leaned close to Jane's ear and whispered the question. "I just felt you stiffen."

She put her hand on his arm gratefully. "There's someone staring at me."

"Everyone is staring at you, Jane. Everyone we've talked to says you look just like you did in high school, but prettier, and no one can get over it. Frankly, if you could bottle whatever your secret is, I could quit being a pharmacist and retire on commission selling it for you."

She beamed up at him. Another point for Ned and his charm. "Let me rephrase: She's not staring, she's *glaring*."

Ned gave a low whistle as he turned to look at the woman. "Wow. Ice wouldn't melt in her hands, would it? Who is it?" Their heads were close together and Ned had put his arm around her waist to lean in and hear her over the din.

"I have no idea. She doesn't look like anyone I remember."

"Shall we go over and talk with her?"

Jane had turned her back to the woman but felt the antagonistic gaze burn through her shoulder blades. "I'm not sure." Then curiosity got the best of her. "Let's casually move in that direction. Maybe we'll run into someone who can tell me who it is."

Nonchalantly but methodically, Jane and Ned wound their way through the crowd. When the woman began to talk to one of Jane's classmates, Jane nudged Ned. "Let's go. She's talking to Wenda Carson. Maybe we can get close enough to hear something that will tell us who she is. If she's someone I should know, I don't want to make a fool of myself by failing to know her name."

Deftly Ned steered her through the crowd. Jane was thankful for him because, for some reason, the single unfriendly stare in the room had unnerved her. *Silly*, she thought. *It's probably that her shoes are uncomfortable. If my feet hurt, I'd probably be frowning too.*

As they neared, Wenda caught sight of Jane, put her hand in the air, and waved. "Jane! Jane Howard. Over here."

"Here goes," Jane muttered to Ned, who was still faithfully sticking to her side.

"You look twenty years younger than the rest of us," Wenda said in greeting. "Everyone from our class is raving about you. It is so good to see you." Wenda wrapped Jane in a warm embrace. Then she set Jane back a bit and turned to Ned. "And who is this good-looking man you have with you?"

Ned, as if on cue, said smoothly. "I'm Ned Arnold. I'm a pharmacist here in Acorn Hill."

"Lucky you," Wenda said slyly. Then she turned to Jane. "And lucky *you*."

Before Jane could open her mouth, Ned smoothly turned to the smaller woman watching the exchange. "Hello, I'm Ned." He reached out to shake her hand, and she laid a well-manicured hand in his. "It is so nice to meet Jane's old friends."

"I'm sorry, where are my manners?" Wenda apologized. "This is another classmate of mine and Jane's, Shirley Taylor. Jane, of course you know Shirley."

"Of course." The words nearly stuck in Jane's throat. "Hello, Shirley." This was Shirley? Up close, Jane realized that Shirley was wearing a skillfully applied but substantial layer of makeup, kohl eyeliner and heavy blush, as if she were going onstage.

Shirley was beautiful and glamorous, but unapproachable.

Shocked, Jane took a step backward and ran into Ned's solid warm chest. He caught her by the upper arms to steady her. Shirley's gaze did not miss a thing.

"I had just asked Shirley what she was doing now. Go ahead, Shirley, tell us about your life," Wenda encouraged, oblivious to Jane's discomfort. "What have you been up to these past few years?"

"I run my own company." Now Jane recognized her— by the sound of her voice, which was familiar though lower and more studied.

"Really?" Wenda sounded impressed. "What kind of company?"

"Real estate."

"Oh, that sounds wonderful. I'd love to go through homes all day. I must say you didn't seem the business type in school." Wenda was having the time of her life reuniting with two old classmates. The two old classmates, however, were not enjoying it all that much.

"I've changed since school, and there were a few things that you most likely didn't know about me," Shirley said abruptly. "Probably no one did."

"Is your business successful?" Wenda probed.

"Very. Actually, I deal in commercial real estate. There's more profit in that."

Ned suddenly became Jane's cheerleader. "Jane and her sisters own some valuable real estate right here in Acorn Hill, the Grace Chapel Inn. In addition to being the chef for the inn, Jane does amazing oils and watercolors and designs jewelry as well."

Jane noticed Shirley's jaw tighten. Otherwise her face was completely passive and expressionless.

"I've heard about the inn and how wonderful it is, but an artist…" Wenda was impressed. "Tell me more."

Although Jane's mouth was stuck in neutral, Ned's was not. As he spoke, he made her sound like some sort of female Van Gogh, but she was too preoccupied to correct him.

This was Shirley Taylor? She made Jane, who wore light make-up and the classic beaded gown, feel almost underdressed. Shirley's commanding, almost aggressive, presence made Jane feel somehow out of the race. Then Jane smiled inwardly. That was exactly how she wanted it. She was done with making an impression for business, always being "on." For a moment, she had nearly been drawn into what Shirley seemed to represent. Jane had been there, done that and was no longer interested.

"…And that is, of course, why she's had so much success as a chef. I eat at the inn a lot and the presentation is always beautiful."

"A chef too? Jane, you're a Renaissance woman. I had no idea of all your interests." Wenda was still carrying the conversation and was oblivious to the undercurrents.

"I noticed a little placard on the table over there filled with those beautiful candies. 'Chocolates donated by Madeleine and Daughters Candy Company.' I never knew her, of course, but your mother's name was Madeleine, wasn't it? When I'd stop at your house, your father would often mention her."

Again, Ned picked up the slack in the conversation. "That's Jane's company, named after her mother."

Wenda appeared delighted. "Both you and Shirley run businesses! My goodness, and I was excited to tell everyone about my little gardening service. Compared to the two of you, I haven't done a thing."

When Shirley didn't speak, Jane jumped in. "There's nothing more delightful than a garden, Wenda. The one at the inn has been a big challenge for us. We aren't sure what truly old-fashioned plants would be appropriate for a place like that. Maybe I could hire you to consult."

"Why don't we get some punch, Jane?" Ned suggested. He asked the others, "Would either of you ladies care for some? No? Then if you'll excuse us . . ." and he spirited Jane away.

"Thank you," Jane breathed as they approached the punch table. "I was about to babble, wasn't I? Seeing Shirley Taylor blew me away."

"Me too," Ned said with a chuckle. "I stood there comparing the two of you and wondered if two successful women could possibly be more different."

"Back in high school there was some bad blood between us, more than her jealousy over my boyfriend," Jane began. "I should tell you…"

"No need to explain. Your sisters told me all about it."

"They did?"

"Aren't you glad they did?"

"Well … yes." Jane blushed. "Always taking care of me, those two. Whether I need it or not." She looked up gratefully at Ned. "And tonight I needed it. I don't know what I expected, but Shirley certainly didn't fit any image I'd had in my mind."

"Want to talk about it?"

Actually, Jane did. They found a table for two at the far corner of the room, and Jane told him the whole story, and that Shirley was one of the motivating factors that led her to leave Acorn Hill. Ned listened attentively.

They both turned to look at Shirley. Her face was animated now, softer and more pleasing. "Look at them," Jane marveled, nodding her head to where Shirley stood talking with Jeremy Patterson, middle-aged, stout, pleasant Jeremy. His equally nice, mild-looking wife was at his side.

"It's funny, isn't it?" she mused. "At certain ages how tender and impressionable one is. When I was seventeen, what Shirley did to me seemed unforgivable. And now ..."

Ned raised an eyebrow questioningly.

"And now I realize that I foolishly allowed it to affect the choices I made about my life." Jane suddenly felt very, very tired. Was there ever a time in one's life when one stopped learning? Evidently not. God was sculpting and cultivating her life every day, now more than ever.

"She's an intimidating presence," Ned commented. "Are you feeling okay about all this?"

"Do you mean am I jealous or wishing I was more like her after all these years? Not on your life."

"Then you don't want to leave?" Ned asked, concern written on his handsome face.

"Leave?" Jane considered the irony of the question. "No way. I allowed Shirley to chase me away from something wonderful once, Acorn Hill. I'm not letting it happen again."

"Good." Ned looked delighted. Suddenly Jane noticed that she was delighted too.

Jane was late getting breakfast started the next morning, but everyone else was even later coming down for it.

The festivities had gone on well into the wee hours and, if last night had been the only event planned, the reunion still would have been considered a complete success.

Jane had just returned to the kitchen from arranging fruit, breads, yogurts and cereal on the sideboard when Sylvia called softly through the back screen door, "Is the coffee pot on?"

"Sure is."

"I'm sorry to barge in when the inn is full of guests, but I wanted to chat and I figured they wouldn't be up yet."

"I'm glad you dropped by. No one is stirring yet. Sit down and I'll get you some coffee. It's strong this morning, but I'm not sure anything is strong enough for you right now. You look exhausted."

"I ran between Potterston and here last night, so I took in two reunions rather than one. If I make it to the end of this weekend, I'm checking in here and having you and your sisters pamper me until I'm rested."

"That should only take a month or two," Jane said. She put two steaming mugs and a pitcher of cream on the table between them. "So far so good?"

"It seems like it. What did you think of last night? You looked like you were having a wonderful time."

"Ned is an absolute gem." Jane told Sylvia about more of her sisters' machinations.

"What a hoot! I'm seeing an entirely new side of Louise and Alice."

"And which side might that be?" Louise's slightly haughty voice came from the kitchen door.

Jane crossed the kitchen and threw her arms around her sister. "The side we knew was there but that you wouldn't let out."

Sylvia moved over so Louise could join them. Alice soon followed.

The guests were obviously sleeping late as no one else had yet ventured down the stairs. The conversation had covered almost everyone at the party when Shirley's name came up.

"I wouldn't have recognized her," Louise said.

"Nor I," Alice admitted.

Then they both remained silent. Gossiping had not been approved in Daniel Howard's household when he was alive—and it was not condoned now that he was gone.

Sylvia, however, had not grown up with the Howard's rules of good behavior. "All I have to say is that I felt as though I were in the presence of an ice queen. Whatever her appeal is, I don't see it. And Jane, well, you were stunning I loved it."

Jane glanced at her sisters and was amused to notice that they were both bobbing their heads in agreement. "I'm just sorry," Alice blurted, "that Shirley isn't fat and dumpy."

Sylvia's jaw dropped. This was so unlike Alice.

"It doesn't matter," Louise said. "Jane is more beautiful—and more real." Then Louise touched her lips with her perennial hankie. "Oh dear, we shouldn't be talking like this."

Gloating hadn't been allowed in their household either, but Jane knew that Louise and Alice were not so much putting Shirley down as being protective of their sister. The conversation ended when some of the guests entered the dining room. Sylvia left for reunion duties and Louise and Alice served the guests while Jane stayed in the kitchen making phone calls and assuring herself that her catering plans were all on track.

It was almost too easy, she decided, after everyone had assured her there were "no problems" and that she didn't even have to come around to check on them. Zack and Nancy had taken over most of the responsibilities, and right now they were spearheading the community breakfast. They had even told her to stay home as long as she wanted, that they would handle everything. They were a pair of hard workers. Jane heartily wished they could somehow reconcile their differences.

When breakfast was over, Louise and Alice left—rather hastily, Jane thought—Louise to help Viola at the book tent and Alice to organize the first crew of car washers. Jane went into the dining room to collect the breakfast remnants.

She was startled to see Shirley Taylor at the table, sipping a cup of coffee.

"Oh, I thought everyone had left. I'm sorry." Jane moved toward the kitchen.

"Go ahead and clean up, don't bother about me." Shirley's eyes narrowed. "I never thought I'd get to see you in the role of waitress." She said it so derogatorily that Jane frowned.

She seemed to want to pick a fight, but Jane was not going to oblige her. "You looked as if you were pondering something. I don't want to interrupt."

This morning Shirley was again painted with makeup. She was dressed smartly in slim white slacks and a black-and-white patterned silk-knit sweater. Jane recognized that her black, quilted handbag must have cost a fortune.

Jane, in slim-fitting jeans, a trim T-shirt and no makeup, felt like her polar opposite. *Oh well,* Jane told herself, *I look like me—and I'm comfortable.*

"You look very nice," Jane offered.

"And you look so casual."

"I know, but I'll get myself pulled together for ..."

"I meant it as a compliment." She didn't sound very happy about it.

It was a strange compliment, Jane thought. Where was Shirley going with this? And why had Louise and Alice left so early? They would have been useful in this odd conversation.

"I watched you last night."

So I noticed, Jane wanted to say. Instead she tipped her head inquiringly.

"You're very popular here."

"It's my home," Jane said and realized how very true that was for her now. "What's going on, Shirley?"

"You're an easy person to hate."

Jane felt the breath leak out of her and an emptiness in her chest.

"Frankly, I was disappointed when I saw you. I wanted to find you fat and dumpy, miserable maybe." Shirley talked calmly, as if they were discussing the weather. "You've always had it all and you never even seemed to realize it. Everything was so easy for you back when we were young."

"Easy?" *Things had looked easy?* That was not how Jane had felt as a teenager. And this woman sitting across from her had not helped one bit. Nor was she helping now. Then it occurred to Jane that there was a second message that Shirley was sending. It was unsaid but was as loud as the first.

"Are you trying to say that you've been spending your life trying to catch up?"

The shock on Shirley's face told Jane she was exactly right. That didn't make Jane feel any better, however, for no matter what Shirley had in mind, it had never been Jane's intention to hurt anyone. All these years, Shirley had been smarting with jealousy.

"Did you see Jeremy Patterson last night?" Jane grasped for something to say and immediately realized that was perhaps the worst topic she could have chosen.

No amount of makeup in the world could have hidden the scowl on Shirley's face. "Yes. He's aged."

"Haven't we all?"

"Everyone but you, it seems."

Jane felt as though she had fallen into an alien universe in which whatever she said was wrong, twisted into meanings she didn't intend.

"I should have known," Shirley added with a bitter laugh.

"Jeremy was a nice boy in high school," Jane stammered lamely.

"You knew him better than I did."

And apparently that was at least part of the problem.

Jane sat down at the table. She was tempted to take Shirley's hand, but resisted. She wasn't sure this woman would allow her to be so personal. "Shirley, I know you hated me back then, although I'm not sure of the reasons why. I know my friendship with Jeremy played a big part in it. But we're grown women, and we're dredging up old feelings that have no place in our lives now. Whatever was between us should be buried. I don't want to be someone whose life's most pivotal events occurred before they were eighteen years old."

She *had* been one of those people for a long time, and it had prevented her from coming home to Acorn Hill for years. She wasn't like that anymore.

"We all know about the former football stars or cheer-leaders for whom the most important events of their lives, the ones they revisit and relive, are from a time that is really part of their childhoods. The big touchdown that saved the game. Being chosen homecoming queen. Silly, but impor-tant nevertheless because those are the only things from which those people have taken their identity. We are so much more than our pasts."

Jane kept talking, feeling a little desperate since Shirley didn't respond. "I am so grateful I have a God who erases our pasts when we ask for forgiveness. If He can forget our mistakes, surely we can. If I've learned any-thing since I returned to Acorn Hill, it's that all I can do with the past is learn from it—and move forward with my life. That's what I've done. That's what I want for every-one to do—to start looking forward instead of back."

The chill in Shirley's eyes didn't soften. She reached down, picked up her designer handbag and stood up. "That was most interesting, Jane. Something to think about, I'm sure." And she walked out.

Jane sagged in her chair and felt a flood of weariness wash over her. She said a quick prayer for Shirley, who'd struggled more than she had. Jane leaned back in her chair and looked up to the ceiling. She thought of Shirley, of Zack and Nancy, of Mr. Enrich and of the numerous other guests who had come through the doors of the inn needing help and comfort. Then she prayed, *After the reunion, Lord, could You send us a few easy visitors? Just so we can rest up.*

"Look at all the candy I've got." Josie held open a bag filled with wrapped candies, small toys and an occasional coin. "They're just throwing them off the floats. Isn't that *silly?*"

"Is this your first parade, Josie?" Jane asked.

"Uh-huh. Momma said I've been to others but not for a long, long time."

"Well, the people on the floats are throwing the candy to you, Josie, because they want you to have it. It's part of the fun."

Just then a big flatbed truck hauling a community band drove by. Josie dropped her bag and covered her ears. "They sound funny."

"That doesn't tell the half of it," Louise muttered in Jane's ear. "I thought they would practice before they got on that float."

"I think they did. Sylvia told me I should have heard them before."

"Here come some clowns!" Josie clapped her hands with pleasure. "The clowns always have lots of candy." And she darted off, her eye on an orange-haired fellow in a purple-and-red striped suit.

"She's having fun."

"I'm happy for her, but I will be glad when all these antique cars go by. Is every single year and make of car since the Model T represented here?"

"Sylvia requested a few extras when she thought the parade wouldn't be long enough. Looks like she overdid it." The procession did look more like a traffic jam than a parade at the moment. "You will have to wait to see the horses, Louise. You can't give up now."

Louise sighed. "I wish I had worn tennis shoes and borrowed a baseball cap to shield my eyes from the sun. And a stool, I should have brought a stool."

Jane grinned through the rest of the parade, all the way to the last clown who had cleanup duty behind the horses, just imagining Louise perched on a stool wearing jogging shoes and a hat advertising John Deere tractors.

"Like clockwork."

"Easy as pie."

"Not a hitch."

"More fun than anyone had had in years."

"We must do this again in five years. With the same committee, of course."

Jane had been collecting comments and compliments about the reunion to share with Sylvia and Joseph, who were not only busy making sure the reunion was on course but also staving off their personal nervous breakdowns.

Things *were* moving as smoothly as oiled gears. The makeshift catering was a hit. The programs were entertaining. The marketplace was booming and food was being consumed by the truckload. Even Viola was happy.

"I cannot believe how many books I have sold," she gushed to Louise and Jane as they stood in the now sparsely inventoried Nine Lives book tent. "Not only have they practically emptied me out here, but the store has been busy too. And I've been selling *history* books, isn't that wonderful?"

Jane did not point out that some of the "history" books were *The History of Disco*, *When Swing Was the Thing* and *Collecting Muscle Cars of the 1950s*.

"I'm so glad I did this."

Jane blinked. Hadn't the committee dragged Viola kicking and screaming into this venture? Hadn't she been the one to predict certain doom for the effort? Apparently, Viola was one among a number of people with conveniently selective memories.

Lloyd and Ethel approached the tent beaming. They had spent the morning at the breakfast tent telling everyone that all the food was lovingly prepared and served by Acorn Hill residents just for them. They added that, if they had not stepped in and saved the day, Acorn Hill alumni might have been eating rolls and Danish shipped in from who-knows-where. Jane had listened to them for a while, amused. She was happy that at least the Good Apple and the church ladies were getting credit for their efforts.

"They are outrageous," Louise said to Jane. "You were the one who pulled the food together."

"Oh, let them have their fun. I'm used to it. Caterers sneak in the back door of the house, provide a banquet and sneak out as if they've never been there and the hostess get the credit for being wise enough to employ them. It works for me."

"You are certainly laid back about things," Louise commented.

"'Laid back?' I don't believe I've heard you use that term before, Louie."

Louise reddened. "I've been listening to Alice too much. She's picked up the vernacular of those young people she works with and it is catching."

"Speaking of Alice, do you want to wander over to the car wash and see how business is?"

For two days, no matter that there was a program, a concert or even the parade, the parking lot of Grace Chapel had been full to overflowing with cars to be washed. To expedite the process, Rev. Thompson and Joe had developed a sort of car valet service. Rev. Thompson would park cleaned cars on the back side of the church, and Joe would hand out keys to the owners as they came to collect their vehicles.

Alice, who had been up early every morning and to bed late every night, was exhausted and beaming. "We've made over fifteen hundred dollars," she said to her sisters. "People have been amazingly generous. The kids say people have handed them twenty-dollar bills and said, 'Keep the change.' Now we're trying to decide what to do with all the money. The Youth Group's mission trip is paid for. With their share, the ANGELs want to buy toys for underprivileged children at Christmas and to set up a visitation program for the children's ward at the hospital in Potterston." Alice's face was glowing. "God is so good. The kids are learning to enjoy working for the good of others, and their faith is growing."

"Amazing, absolutely amazing," Louise said. "The car wash, the bookstore . . . this entire event is a huge success."

Well, almost, Jane thought. She had not been able to get Shirley out of her mind. The woman came and went from the inn as if it were an onerous duty to attend the reunion functions. Even poor Alice had given up trying to draw her out. She wore an entirely different face when with the public. She was . . . networking. Jane could describe it no other way. Even at the reunion, she was offering business cards. There was something mechanical, robotic about the way she approached people. There were exceptions, of course, mostly men who had aged well and were obviously successful.

Jane, however, couldn't forget their conversation at breakfast. What if God had given up on her before she returned home? She had no idea how she could get through to Shirley, but she knew she couldn't give up either.

Josie, her mother Justine and Joe converged on the sisters at once.

Justine was all smiles. "Josie's never had so much fun," she said. "It's the biggest parade she's ever seen in her life, and Clarissa gave her cookies for free. Miss Viola even gave her a book on turtles. You know how much Josie loves turtles."

Good will was everywhere, Jane mused. She turned to Joe. "How about you, Joe, are you having fun?"

"It's like a festival. It's wonderful."

"I'm sad it's going to end soon," Josie said. "I'll practically be a grown-up by the time there's another one."

"It hardly seems possible that this is the last day," Louise agreed with Josie. "That means we have to make the most of it. If you, your mother and Joe would care for some, I would like to buy ice cream for all of you."

The trio assented happily and disappeared into the crowd with Louise.

"She's loosened up," Jane commented to Alice.

"It's good for her. She gets lonely sometimes with Cynthia so far away. I'm glad Josie has captured her heart."

"Josie is a real blessing," Jane agreed. "Well, I'll leave you to your work. I think I will walk down to the Good Apple and see how my favorite bakers are doing."

Jane felt her step lighten as she approached the shop. Clarissa, Zack and Nancy had saved the day. Clarissa had even been able to spend time with her family thanks to the Colwins' efficiency.

The bakery was fairly quiet. Jane walked around the counter and toward the swinging doors that separated the front from the kitchen. Nancy and Zack were talking in low tones on the other side of the door.

"But I love it here."

"I like it too, Nancy, but it's not for us. If we opened a place like this, we'd be struggling...."

"Clarissa raised a family."

"We'll have to do it my way. We'll never make it otherwise."

"Maybe we won't 'make' it at all if we do it your way, Zack. Your attitude is pretty selfish. Can't you at least consider my idea?"

"'Selfish?'"

"Time out, guys," Jane said as she walked through the doorway. "There's an answer to your problem. We just haven't found it yet."

Chapter Eleven

Monday morning. It was over. The reunion was history. Sunday had flown by with the all-faiths church service and the final good-byes. Cars had started pulling out of town in the afternoon, and by the next morning Acorn Hill was back to its former size. Although there would be visitors and families who lingered for a few more days, by next week the only tangible reminder of all that had happened would be the brass plaque that had been hung at the school to commemorate the first all-school reunion.

Those who hadn't served on any committees were already proposing that the reunion-planning group be retained to do another in five years. Those who *had* served on the aforementioned committees were hiding out and making plans to leave town if anyone so much as dared to mention a reprise of the event any time in the next hundred years.

The Antique Store and Sylvia's Buttons were closed and their owners were sleeping late. Fred Humbert was reordering bug spray, umbrellas, fold-up stools and numerous other items that had sold out. Viola was walking dreamily from shelf to shelf in the bookstore admiring all the gaping holes where books had been only last week. All seemed well in Acorn Hill.

But the tug of war between Zack and Nancy had been hanging heavy on Jane's spirit. So had the chill emanating from Shirley Taylor. Odd, Jane mused, since she was the one who had been hurt. Or did Shirley have pain of her own?

Jane, reminding herself that she was a glutton for punishment, poured coffee into a carafe and freshly squeezed orange juice into a chilled glass, put them on a tray, squared her shoulders and marched up the stairs to Shirley's room.

She would make one more try with Shirley. She would not give up. Shirley would have to be the one who ended the conversation. If God wanted Jane to talk to Shirley, then she would, and trust that He would give her something to say.

Jane tapped on the door with her toe and to her surprise, it swung open. "Excuse me, the door just opened. I thought I'd bring you some..."

Shirley was seated at the small dressing table applying mascara. The open closet across the room revealed a spectacular selection of clothing and the floor was cluttered with shoes.

"Oh!" Shirley said. "I'm not quite ready."

"I thought you might like some coffee while you were dressing."

"You might as well leave it on the table." Shirley sounded put upon.

"Are you sure? I could come back with it later."

"I'm sure." Shirley said flatly and rotated on the bench to face Jane.

Ooookay. So that was the way it would be. Jane came into the room, set down the tray and started toward the door.

"Wait."

Jane turned.

"Why don't you join me? I have a cup here from my tea last night. I'll use that."

"I ... ah ... *er* ... okay." Jane walked toward the table and sat down on one of the two chairs. *Now what?*

In agonizingly slow motion, Shirley finished straightening her makeup and then poured the coffee.

"So this is how it is to be waited on by Jane Howard. It's rather fun, but why are you trying so hard? I'm sure you think that *I* should be trying to make amends. I'm the one who hurt you."

So she did remember.

"I don't want you to leave here without knowing that everything is forgiven—on my side, at least."

The other woman studied Jane. "You have no idea what I'm thinking."

"It doesn't matter. I just want you to know that although I'm not sure exactly why you did what you did, it doesn't matter anymore."

"Making that comment about you and your mother, you mean?" Shirley reddened. "I suppose that was a cruel thing to do."

Jane gaped at her. *Suppose?*

"I wanted to hurt you, but you looked *so* injured. I didn't know how to take it back, so I just let it go. I suppose I should have apologized but I was young and angry."

She saw Jane's questioning gaze and continued. "You still don't get it, do you? I hated you." Shirley gave a small sound. "I thought nothing could bother you. You were smart, pretty and popular. You had lots of friends, a boyfriend ... everything I wanted ..." her voice trailed off. "And I was so in love with Jeremy Patterson that I thought I'd die of it—and he wouldn't look at anyone but you."

Shirley paused, as if remembering her long-ago feelings. "When I saw Jeremy for the first time this weekend, I nearly fainted. He certainly wasn't the superhero I'd made him out to be."

"Jeremy is a nice, pleasant man with a normal job and a normal family," Jane pointed out, fascinated by what

Shirley was revealing and by the cold, calculating tone of her voice.

"Back then, I thought that if Jeremy and I could be together, everything would be perfect." Shirley's eyes narrowed. "Of course, that never came about, but I've spent my life trying to make things perfect for myself.

"I suppose I should thank you, really," Shirley commented.

Startled, Jane asked, "What for?"

"For standing in the way, for drawing his attention away from me." Shirley shuddered lightly. "Imagine! If I'd been stuck with him, I might still be living in a one-horse town like this." She eyed Jane's casual attire. "Like you."

Jane read between the lines. *How pathetic to end up here. How pathetic that this is the best place that you can find to live.* Why this woman could still get to her, Jane didn't understand. She and Shirley had been tied together for a lifetime in a relationship that was miserable for both of them.

What is your will, Father? What kind of role is Shirley supposed to play in my life now? Or I in hers?

The idea that this encounter was of God's design comforted her. It also reminded Jane that her discomfort was not important, especially if there was something she should say to Shirley or do for her.

"So how has it worked out, the 'perfect' life, I mean?" Jane asked.

Shirley contemplated the question, and as she did so, Jane thought about how much Shirley's words had changed them both.

"My jealousy gave me drive and ambition," she said frankly. "I wouldn't be where I am businesswise if not for that." She looked around the room and gave a brittle laugh. "I have a lot of money and I'm not still trapped in this town."

"Oh, I'm not trapped," Jane said softly. "When I left, I thought it was because of you. Now I think it was also because of *me*. I felt like a pariah, thinking that my mother might have lived if it hadn't been for me. I suppose it was so shocking because I hadn't known that before...."

"You mean I was the first to tell you?" Shirley put her hands to her lips, rattled for the first time. "I had no idea...."

"It's worked out," Jane said, feeling peace settle at her core. "I didn't realize it for a long time, but returning to Acorn Hill and knowing my life has come full circle here has been a joyous experience. Interesting, isn't it, that we both wasted our energy on that single incident," Jane concluded. "I don't want either one of us to waste any more." She reached out a hand. "All is forgiven?" She sensed Shirley hesitating.

How sad. Even now, Jane realized, Shirley didn't see that she had other options, that life could be lived in gratitude and joy, not driven by jealousy or greed.

"You don't have to forgive me for anything, if you don't want to," Jane added. "There doesn't need to be a truce between us now, if it's not genuine. I don't want anything but the truth in my life anymore. It's all right."

"What's the deal with you, Jane?" Shirley asked.

"I've found God, the most significant Forgiver of all."

"Now you sound like your father's daughter." The way Shirley said it made it hard to tell whether the statement was praise or condemnation.

"Good!" Jane beamed. "I'll take that as a compliment, and it's the nicest one I've had all weekend."

"Take it as you like." Frustrated, Shirley simply turned back to the mirror to finish her makeup.

"How did you mean it then?" Jane wanted nothing more than to get away from the unpleasantness Shirley was radiating, but something compelled her to stay. Was it one of God's nudges? Or something curious in her that was fascinated by what Shirley had become?

Shirley spun around so quickly that Jane took a step backward, startled. "Jane, I don't buy your faith or your holier-than-thou attitude or whatever your church is trying to preach today. The bottom line is that if I can't be successful at something, I don't do it. And I was never very successful at being a churchgoer, so why bother? I don't think that God is the only one who can do good things for us." She gestured at the closet full of clothing and the jewelry scattered on the dresser top. "I've done pretty well for myself, don't you think?"

Jane felt her heart sinking. It was as though Shirley had doused her with a bucket of cold water.

"No . . ."

"*Yes*. That's how I feel, Jane. You've followed God and look where it's gotten you."

"He's provided me with everything I want."

Shirley's expression was pitying. "And I got everything I wanted all by myself." She looked Jane over again. "And I think I did a better job."

Jane left the room, stunned.

⸺

"Well?" Alice asked after Shirley had checked out.

"What happened?" Louise said almost at the same time.

"Not what I'd hoped."

"Oh my," Alice murmured.

"What do you mean?" Louise asked.

Jane repeated the conversation she had had with Shirley.

"She's like . . . like ice . . . where God's concerned. She thinks He's incompetent, ineffective and maybe not even real." Jane sank into a chair and rubbed her forehead with her hand. "Where did I go wrong?"

"Where did *you* go wrong?" Louise echoed. "Whatever makes *you* think that *you* went wrong?"

"I should've been able to say something to get through to her, but it was like a child throwing a dart at a castle wall. Nothing I said had an effect. She was impenetrable."

"*Hmm.*" Alice sat down at the table across from Jane. "What's wrong with this picture?"

Jane looked up and Louise's expression showed her curiosity.

"What do you mean? Everything's wrong with this picture. Shirley..."

"Not about Shirley, about you, Jane."

"Me? I failed to get through to her. I feel partly responsible for the way she is. I ..."

"You're not giving God any credit whatsoever, are you?" Alice asked gently.

"What do you mean?"

"Here you are, bewailing the fact that you, personally, didn't turn Shirley's life around. Now you're thinking you're ineffective and a poor witness."

"Yes, so?"

"My, what a big ego you have."

"Alice," Louise began, "Jane's feeling bad because ..."

"Because God didn't choose hers to be the message that got through to Shirley Taylor?"

Louise and Jane stared at their sister.

"Is that what I'm saying?" Jane asked.

"Sounds a bit like it to me," Alice said. "Who knows how God will use this conversation between you and Shirley? Obviously, she's not ready or willing to turn the reins of her life over to anyone, even God, right now. I have a strong feeling that whatever happened today wasn't even about you, Jane. It was all about Shirley."

"It's true," Louise admitted, "that I often forget that sometimes I'm just a tool in God's hands and not the target of God's attention. I suppose we are just being human when we are always so concerned about ourselves and how we feel."

"You're exactly right, Alice," Jane said. "All I was thinking of was how I had failed Shirley, not how God might be using me in a way I don't understand."

Jane slipped down in her chair and rested her head against the chair back. "What a wake-up call." She sat up again. "You're absolutely right. The Lord *does* work in mysterious ways. What I should be praying is that I moved His plan forward and didn't interfere with it."

"God still has much work to do with Shirley," Louise commented.

Jane jumped up and knelt between the chairs in which her sisters sat. Then she reached over and took her sisters' hands. "I love you two so much," Jane said. "I wouldn't trade you for all the jewelry in the world."

"*Harrumph*. I should hope not," Louise said.

Jane smiled and then reached over to give Alice a hug. "Thanks for reminding me that I'm not shouldering the problems of the world alone." Then she opened her hands as if to release the burdens she had been carrying. "I've got God helping me."

"And that's the good news," Alice said. "We know He is helping. We'll just trust Him to speak to Shirley in His own time."

"'God's time—'" Louise murmured, "it's not always our time, but it's always best."

Feeling more at ease but oddly exhausted, Jane went to her room. She needed to sit down with her Bible for a bit. Scripture was her rudder, the thing that kept her in line, and she was very hungry for that right now. She lay down on the bed and reached for her Bible. She felt humbled by what she had discussed with her sisters.

A slight smile touched her lips. Alice often had commented about the less mature teenagers with whom she sometimes worked at church. "Everything is all about them," Alice would say. "If only I could get them to turn their eyes outward and see the rest of us for a change."

That's me, Jane thought, *suffering from an elevated sense of self-importance.* She picked up the Bible and opened it to the book of Matthew, but before she could read more than a few words, her eyes drifted shut and she was asleep.

She was standing in a vast warehouse. It was something, she imagined, like a furniture distributor might use. As she stood in the middle of one long row, it was virtually impossible to see either end. On the endless shelves were rows of brightly wrapped boxes stenciled with the contents of each. Jewelry. Money. Influence. Accolades. Bonds. Savings Accounts. Beauty. Prestige. Silver. Gold. On the side of each box were photos of the contents of the boxes.

Curious and completely unafraid, Jane moved toward the nearest box. On it was a photo of what looked like a jeweler's display case. There were rings pictured, with multi-carat diamonds; tennis bracelets; and bejeweled brooches. Fascinated as she had always been by jewelry and for new ideas about making her own, Jane did not resist the urge to lift the top of the box and peek inside. A small puff of dust appeared from the interior of the box and Jane sneezed. Carefully, she pulled the box closer and slid the lid away from her until it fell off the back of the box. As she stared inside, a small gasp escaped her lips.

The lovely jewelry pictured on the outside of the box was not there. Instead, in its place, there was a tangle of rusting necklaces and crumbling bits of fake colored glass. Much of the box's contents were covered with greenish-blue mold.

Quickly, she pushed the box away and turned to another marked "Investments." Instead of important looking documents and certificates, this box held nothing more than bits of ashy paper and mouse droppings. Most of whatever had been inside had been consumed by rodents. Shuddering, Jane pushed the box into place and looked around. A pervading mustiness offended her nostrils. As she walked down the aisle, she rapped on the boxes she passed. Most seemed empty and some had foul odors emanating from them. What was this place? Whose things were these? Then, as if in response to her question, wavering bits of light appeared on each box spelling out names of the owners. Only one name leaped out at her, one recognizable name—*Shirley Taylor*. Horrified, Jane took a step backward and screamed.

"Wake up. Wake up. You're having a nightmare, dear." Alice's calm voice broke Jane's dream. "My, my, but you can scream. I thought someone had stepped on Wendell's tail."

Blinking hard against the light, Jane pulled herself upright to find that Alice and Louise were peering down at her. "I was dreaming. . . ."

"You certainly were. And thrashing around like, oh, I don't know, like there were mice running up and down your legs."

Jane shuddered and closed her eyes, recalling the images that had passed through her dream. "I was in a warehouse," she stammered, "and it was full of boxes. There were supposed to be beautiful things in the boxes, but they were all rotted, rusted or foul in some way. I don't know what I was doing there, but . . . that was the weirdest dream . . ." Jane's brow furrowed. "It was all so familiar. Like I knew who all of the worthless trash belonged to. . . . "

"Maybe I do," Louise said. She picked up the Bible that lay open at the place where Jane had fallen asleep and began to read, "Matthew 6:19. 'Do not store up for yourselves treasures here on earth, where moths and rust destroy, and where thieves break in. But store up for yourselves treasures in heaven, where moth and rust do not destroy, and where thieves do not break in and steal . . .'"

Jane took the glass of water Alice offered. It was still warm, for Alice hadn't taken time to run cold water in Jane's bathroom sink. Still it tasted good sliding down her throat. She thought about what Louise had read. "That was Shirley Taylor's warehouse I dreamed I was in. All the things she's so proud of were worthless. . . ." Jane closed her eyes as if her head had begun to ache. "And all those material things are so important to her. I should have . . ."

"Remember what we were talking about, Jane," Alice said sternly. "You aren't capable of changing the world or every person in it. You did what you could and Shirley ignored you. That's all."

"'All?' But I should . . ."

". . . trust God with this one. He still has His eye on her, Jane, even if you don't." Louise's voice was compassionate but firm.

"You're right, Louie. This is between Shirley and God."

"And you did your best. Now you can pray for Shirley, but you'll have to leave the rest to Him." Alice pointed heavenward. "Now throw some water on your face and finish your grocery list. I'm going shopping."

Nancy and Zack were hardly speaking when they returned to the inn that afternoon from the walk they had taken. Zack loped up the stairs two at a time. Jane touched Nancy on the arm before she too went to their room.

"It's none of my affair and you can tell me to mind my business, but I still have to ask. What's happening between you two? You seem to be more miserable by the minute."

The young woman stared until Jane feared that she had gone too far and intruded too much. Then Nancy burst into tears and threw herself into Jane's arms.

"I love it here," she wailed. "I want to live in a place just like this one. I could work for Clarissa forever, but Zack says he needs to 'try out' his dream."

She pulled back from Jane to wipe her eyes on the edge of her sleeve. "This is tearing apart our marriage. He doesn't feel I appreciate him, and I think he's being selfish. What are we going to do?"

Jane patted the young woman on the back. "I don't know, honey. I don't know."

By dinnertime that evening, Jane's faith in miracles was restored: Mr. Enrich had offered to cook dinner.

"No, I insist." He carried two grocery bags into the house from the General Store. "I want to do this as my way of saying 'thank you.'"

"For which part?" Louise inquired. "For sending you to sleep in the library? Or for completely forgetting to give you clean towels? Or would it be..."

"Maybe it's that we quit treating him like a guest." Alice gave a quick little shrug of her shoulders. "What's that old saying about treating family like guests and guests like family? That seems to be what happened here."

"And that's what I'm trying to say thank you for." Mr. Enrich said, shaking his head as if he thought the sisters would never figure it out.

Jane happily relinquished control of the kitchen. Even she, who loved to cook, was feeling burnt out.

"Right now I don't care if I see the inside of a kitchen for a month," she announced to her sisters. The inn had emptied of all its guests but Mr. Enrich and the Colwins, and they were all tired.

"Think about poor Clarissa," Alice said. "I daresay she would have had to sleep at the Good Apple if it hadn't been for Nancy and Zack."

"I noticed Livvy, Kent and Raymond taking turns there too." Louise smiled. "Livvy was a little rusty on the cash register."

"Have they left yet?"

Neither Louise nor Alice knew the answer.

"If she's home alone, I'm going to invite her for dinner too."

"But it's Mr. Enrich's party tonight and he's already invited Nancy and Zack," said Alice.

"If he says there's enough for one more, I'm going to call her."

When Clarissa answered the phone, Jane could hear the strain in her voice. Before Jane could even finish explaining the dinner plans, Clarissa said, "I'll be right over."

"So your children have left then?"

"Left? Of course not. If they'd left already, I could stay home. They're trying to browbeat me into going to live with one of them. They say then they won't have to worry about me. Hah! I don't want to be treated like an old lady until I consider myself old and I can assure you that won't be any time in the near future. My hip may hurt and my hair might be gray, but neither of these things has affected my mind. They're talking to me like I'm senile, for goodness sake. I'm old, not deaf and dumb." She sounded thoroughly disgusted. "They've all wandered off for the moment. I'll leave them a note and be right over."

It wasn't more than fifteen minutes before they heard Clarissa's voice at the screen door. Jane walked to answer it.

"Hi. I'm so glad you could come . . . what's that?"

Clarissa carried a big flat leather case in her hand. "Something I wanted to show you. I found this case in the attic." She patted the large folder. "Something Ray had when he took a drafting class years ago. I didn't know how else to sneak these things out without having them be seen."

"Did you tell them where you were going?"

"Nope. Just left a note. That was supposed to be good enough for me when they were teenagers. Let's see how they like it." Clarissa was already in a much cheerier mood.

As Clarissa sat down, Jane said, "The cake you made for the reunion was a masterpiece. You could have a full-time job just decorating cakes."

"Now that would be fun." Clarissa looked dreamy. "My idea of the perfect job."

Then she snapped back to her businesslike self. "And, thanks to you, I found something else I like to do. Is there any place to lay this out?"

"Mr. Enrich is cooking supper, and it won't be ready for a while yet. We can spread things out on the dining room table."

"Getting pretty friendly with the guests, I see," Clarissa said, referring to Mr. Enrich.

Jane nodded pensively. "It's odd. I can't explain it, but all three of us have been praying for him ever since he arrived. We're attributing it to a nudge from God and trusting He'll work it out when the time is right."

"He could get involved in a few things right now," Clarissa murmured. "My kids and their insistence that I'm too old to work, that nice young couple trying to figure out what to do with their lives. God could be busy here for a long time."

"Or," Jane said, "He could wrap it up in a single night."

"What have we here?" Louise entered the dining room, and Alice trailed behind her. Mr. Enrich had banished them from the kitchen.

"Jane gave me something to play with the other day," Clarissa explained as she unzipped the large folder. "I wanted to show her what I've done."

As Clarissa pulled the contents from the folder, three jaws went slack with incredulity.

"You did these?" Jane heard the crack in her own voice—joy, admiration, awe.

"Are they bad?" Clarissa frowned. "I thought they looked pretty good at home but now . . ."

"'Pretty good'? They're fantastic!"

Jane picked up the sketch on top.

Fairy Pond shimmered in all its natural glory. Every hue of green was there, the feathering fronds of fern, the canopy of trees above, the lily pads and even the ripples in the water. And there, so delicately and faintly that they were difficult to see at first, were the fairies. They were interwoven throughout the drawing. Green ones were tucked into the ferns. Blue fairies seemed to swim just below the surface of the water, and a pink blossoming flower along the bank was really a cluster of crimson fairies curled into tight balls, each with its wings tucked neatly around them. These were far more sophisticated than the first sketches Clarissa had drawn.

In fact, Jane realized, Clarissa had in effect drawn a picture in a picture. The fairies' limbs and wings made up the leaves and blades of grass. The ripples of the water, if one looked deep enough, were made of faint fairies doing the backstroke.

Jane had seen work like this before, a picture within a picture, one dominant and the other receding into the background of the other, but she had never done it herself. It was painstaking work to accomplish the effect. And Clarissa, in less than a week, had created several of these pieces.

She had sketched Jane leaning against a tree. In the bark of the tree were tiny faces smiling. And Josie! Clarissa had drawn her perched on a large flat stone at the edge of the pond, peering into its depths. Josie, in bright yellow like her curls, was a magical creature herself who, owing to Clarissa's talented hand, seemed to hover slightly above the rock to study a tiny reflection of herself sitting on a lily pad.

"You did these all since we were at the pond?" Jane asked.

"I know they were done fast, but I couldn't stop myself. I'd come home from the Good Apple exhausted and see the art supplies you gave me and I couldn't help myself. I'd find myself yawning three hours later, with one of these almost done. I'm sure if I'd had time I could have made them better."

"I don't think you can get better than this," Alice said.

Louise nodded her agreement.

"No wonder your family thought you were tired. You were running on only a couple hours of sleep a night," said Jane.

"But it's like a compulsion, Jane. Now that I've tried this, I don't want to stop. I have so many more ideas...."

Suddenly there was a knock at the front door and a voice called through the screen, "Mother? Mother? Are you here?"

Clarissa groaned. "The posse found me," she muttered. "In here, Livvy," she said aloud.

Livvy walked in with Kent and Ray in tow. Her beautiful black eyes were flashing. Kent looked concerned and Ray had an amused grin playing around his lips, as if he were enjoying his sister's theatrics.

"What's the idea of that note, Mother? It isn't funny. We were worried about you running out like that. It will be dark soon and . . ."

"And my old blind eyes won't function properly, I'll get lost on the way home, fall into a swamp and be eaten by an alligator? Well, Livvy, we don't have alligators here, so I suppose I'd have to be nibbled to death by bunny rabbits or carried into the trees by owls that make me sit on their eggs while they go hunting or . . ."

Jane covered her smile. Clarissa was very imaginative.

"*Motherrrrr*," Livvy protested.

Ray burst out laughing. "I told you not to run after her like she's a child, Liv. She's been here all her life. Why are you getting so worked up about her living here now?"

"She's not as young as she used to be. . . ."

"But I'm not as old as I'm going to be either, honey." Clarissa put her arms around her daughter. "I know you feel guilty that you're way out west and I'm here by myself, but it's okay." She stepped back and eyed her beautiful daughter at arm's length. "I do declare, Livvy, that if I had to be bossed around by you every day, I'd be *much* older than I am right now."

Livvy's displeasure turned to distress. "But you're so alone out here."

"I have more friends than you can shake a stick at." Clarissa gestured at the three Howard women. "Here are some of them."

"But all you do is work. You need hobbies, something more."

"She has this." Jane pointed to the fan of sketches on the table.

"Yes, but . . ." Livvy did a double take as she looked at the pictures. Kent stepped nearer. Ray whistled.

"You didn't do these . . . did you? Are they Jane's?"

"I wish I could take credit for something so beautiful, Livvy, but these are your mom's."

"But when . . ."

"After she got home from the Good Apple," Louise said proudly. "While all of you thought she was resting."

"You are amazing, Clarissa," Alice chimed in. "Working all day and staying up all night to draw. Why, people *half your age* couldn't do that."

"You did these this weekend?" Kent gasped.

"After we went to bed?" Ray whistled again. "You don't need anyone taking care of you." He glanced at Livvy. "I think it's your children who need the help."

Livvy didn't speak. She moved forward as if in a trance to touch the delicate artwork. Her eyes blurred with tears as she reached out to touch one of the creatures Clarissa had so deftly drawn into the foliage. "Fairies."

When she looked up, the tears were running down her cheeks. "When I was little, Mom used to take me to Fairy Pond. We'd make up stories about the animals living there and imagined a community so tiny and fragile that we could only see glimpses of its inhabitants, the fairies."

"Remember the Butcher and the Baker fairies?" Clarissa prodded. "And the Preacher fairy who looked a lot like Pastor Howard?"

"And the Teacher fairy who never made her students stay after school to clean the blackboard." Livvy looked up, her eyes shining. "Mom and I solved a lot of problems at Fairy Pond. She'd tell me to practice talking to the Teacher fairy so I knew what to say when I had to apologize for misbehavior. And the Manners fairy—well, no book of etiquette had anything on her."

Livvy looked at her mother with so much love in her eyes that Jane wanted to put her hands to her heart.

"I'm sorry, Mom. I grew up and thought I had all the answers." She looked ashamed.

Clarissa opened her arms and Livvy flew into them.

"Now that that's settled," Ray said, sounding relieved, "we can . . ."

The screen door slammed.

"You do whatever you want, Zachary," Nancy's voice trembled with frustration. "Start 'Zachary's' restaurant. Cook a scallop, decorate it with pâté and call it gourmet, if you like. I'm more interested in real food. And a real life. I'm going to ask Clarissa if she'll hire me and if she will, I'm staying here."

Nancy flounced past the dining room and was startled to find it full of people. And Clarissa.

"Oh, hi, I didn't mean . . . it's not that you have to hire me . . . I was just going to ask . . ."

Zack stomped after her to see to whom she was talking. His eyes widened.

"What's the problem here?" Kent asked. "What were you going to ask my mother?"

"I just wanted to know if she'd like an employee." Nancy turned to glare at Zack. "I'm available."

"But I thought when we were working together at the Good Apple, Zack told me that you were going to start a nightspot," Livvy said. Her arm was still around her mother.

"That's what he's going to do. That's always been his dream, not mine." Nancy smiled through her tears. "I just want to run a little place like the Good Apple."

"Oh, for goodness sake," Clarissa muttered.

Louise was clucking her tongue like a mother hen, and Alice started murmuring, "Oh dear, oh dear, oh dear."

"Well, I could use a little help," Clarissa admitted, "because I found a new hobby I'd like to take up, but I won't hire a wife away from her husband, so I guess you can't count on me for a job."

"But . . ." Nancy looked devastated. She obviously had not planned any course beyond this one.

"Come on, Nance, we'll work this out. When I get my place started and it starts paying for itself, then we can find you something," Zack pleaded.

"Why can't we start *my* place first?"

"Oh, good grief," Livvy suddenly sputtered. "You two sound just like the kids on the playground of my school. Have you listened to yourselves? You're both being terribly childish. If you were my students, I'd make you sit down and write a compromise. What good is having your dreams realized if you don't have anyone to share them with? And since when did marriage become such a throw-away commodity?"

Nancy took a step back, her eyes wide. "But he said …"

"But she said …"

"That's it," Livvy pointed out calmly. "But what do 'we' say?"

Jane could see why Livvy was such a good teacher. She wouldn't let any student get by with less than his or her best, if this showdown with the Colwins was any indication. It was a very odd scenario being played out at the inn, but Jane had no inclination to put a stop to it. In fact, she was relieved to have someone else asking the hard questions for a change.

"'We' say we need to get a place where we can do *both* a supper club and a diner," Zack stammered. "But where would we go to find that?"

"'Find' it?" Louise asked calmly. "Why don't you *create* it?"

Everyone turned to look at her.

"How would we do that?"

"You would have to buy a versatile building that could be used as a diner by day and a supper club at night. Something with either two stories or two large spaces with a kitchen in the middle," Livvy suggested, as if it were the simplest solution in the world.

"Or a bakery and supper club," Nancy said. "I've really enjoyed the work at the Good Apple."

Zack looked at Nancy, the idea taking hold in his mind. "It could have separate entrances but we'd be able to use the same kitchen. That's what's so expensive. Neither business would have to be big if we were running them simultaneously because we'd be open eighteen hours a day. It's a great idea."

"I suppose," Nancy said doubtfully, "but even one building is going to be expensive if it must be large enough for two businesses, isn't it?"

"Not if you can rent it inexpensively enough." Clarissa spoke calmly as well. "Maybe you could go into partnership with someone and add on a second eating area."

"How would that work?"

"Take the Good Apple, for example. If you left the bakery just like it is and built a supper club addition off the back, you could have your main entrance there. Homey in front, classy in back."

The entire room was silent as Clarissa's words sunk in.

"That's a great idea," Zack said. "But where are we going to find someone who wants to do that?"

"Seems like there'd be others besides me who'd consider it. I like the idea myself. If a young couple like you were to do that and let me stay on in the bakery to supervise and decorate cakes, why, I believe I'd be happy as a mouse in a cheese factory."

Livvy's eyes grew large at Clarissa's words.

"Yes, sir, then someone like me could do what she enjoys doing and leave the rest to someone else. And, since they'd be in partnership with this young couple, there would be some revenue coming in every month. Why, it sounds like a perfect deal to me."

"You mean you'd consider . . ." Zack began as everyone in the room held their breaths.

Just then, Mr. Enrich came through the kitchen door holding a large spoon. His white chef's apron was spattered with spaghetti sauce.

"Dinner's done. Time for you to sit down and eat."

Chapter Twelve

Mr. Enrich's eyes grew wide as he took in the crowded dining room.

Jane could practically hear him wondering where all these people had come from, calculating the amount of food on the stove and dividing it by the ten people present. The mathematics of it must have worked, because Mr. Enrich turned to her. "You haven't set the table yet."

Suddenly, everyone started to scurry. Clarissa and Livvy whisked the sketches off the table and propped them lovingly on the sideboard so everyone could look at them during supper.

Louise scooped a bowl of Swedish mints from the middle of the table; Alice whipped a tablecloth from a nearby drawer and snapped it into place.

Ray and Kent hustled for the extra chairs stationed around the room.

And Zack and Nancy stood in the middle of the melee crying and hugging.

Jane walked up to Mr. Enrich. "Do you have enough food?"

"I learned to cook in the Army. I'm not very good at cooking for any less than twenty-five. We should be fine." Then he frowned. "Except I forgot Caesar salad dressing. I remembered the anchovies but forgot the dressing."

"No problem," Jane said. "I have some in the refrigerator that I made this morning. I was planning on not making anything but salads for dinner for the rest of the week."

"Perfect." Mr. Enrich looked as pleased as one could be —one who was unaccustomed to smiling, that is.

The enormous tossed salad was rich with bite-sized romaine and crumbly croutons. Mr. Enrich had purchased loaves of Italian bread. He had heated them, and then basted them with butter and garlic, and heated them again so that the tops glistened and the bread was chewy on the outside, soft and white on the inside.

He had also cut carrots, celery, broccoli and cauliflower, arranged them on a bed of lettuce and decorated them with radish roses and cherry tomatoes. He had found vegetable dip at the General Store and a crystal bowl to serve it in. There was a fresh fruit platter, sparkling water and the largest pot of spaghetti Jane had ever seen.

Mushrooms, beef, Italian sausage—the sauce had it all. After everyone had been served, Mr. Enrich went around the table with a chunk of fresh Parmesan and grated it for each guest.

When he grated the cheese over Zack's plate with a flourish, Zack turned to him and said, "If you ever decide you want to work in the restaurant business, I'll hire you. You'd be a great maître d'."

Mr. Enrich, Jane noticed, scowled but flushed with pleasure.

When Mr. Enrich returned to the table at his place, Alice folded her hands and bowed her head. "Lord, we thank You for this marvelous gift of food and the cook who made it for us. Mr. Enrich has been a blessing and we thank You for bringing him into our lives as well as all the people at this table. Work Your will and let us experience the wisdom of Your ways. Amen."

When Jane raised her head, she realized that Mr. Enrich had tears running down his cheeks.

"You actually would consider something like that?" Zack asked, leaning forward. The Colwins and all the Cottrells were gathered around the table eating dessert and having a high-level planning meeting. Dessert, flaming cherries jubilee, had been a rousing success even though Louise feared the tablecloth would go up in flames and Alice eyed the chandelier for smoke smudges.

Jane, Alice, Louise and Mr. Enrich sat in a huddle in the corner of the room drinking coffee, too polite to pull up to the table and too curious to leave the room.

"If you and Nancy ran the Good Apple as it is," Zack went on enthusiastically, "and we managed to build an addition without shutting the kitchen down for too long…"

"And that way, our business wouldn't compete with that of the Coffee Shop," Nancy continued happily. "I'd be happy to do what Clarissa's always done during the day and open the restaurant after the Coffee Shop closes for the night."

Clarissa nodded emphatically, liking the idea.

"Then," Zack said excitedly, "when that's done, we'll build Clarissa her own cake decorating room."

"My 'studio,'" Clarissa corrected impishly.

"And we can put in a glass wall so everyone can watch her work," Nancy finished.

Clarissa frowned. "Does that mean I have to start dressing up? I don't want to feel like I'm on television or anything."

Nancy laid a comforting hand on the older woman's arm. "You get to do exactly what you please from now on."

"*Humph.*" Clarissa eyed her daughter. "I can manage that."

Livvy had been alternately laughing and crying all evening. Laughing every time her mother came up with a new idea or a quick retort. And crying, Jane guessed, every time she thought about how little credit she had given her mother for being the clearheaded independent woman that she was.

"And when you're ready, or," Livvy corrected herself, "when you *feel* like it, you can come and stay with any of us."

Clarissa eyed her family. "Now that's what I like to hear. You could've put it that way in the first place."

"You're never going to quit teaching us lessons, are you, Mom?" Kent rubbed his mother's shoulder.

"Now's the time you could ask me what I'd like to do," Clarissa hinted.

"And that is?" Ray said.

"I'm looking forward to the idea of doing only cake decorating and helping these two get their feet on the ground. I'd love to visit each of you for a month or so out of the year. Maybe more, depending on how it goes with my new hobby." She gestured toward the pictures. "Jane thinks that if I had these made into note cards, they'd sell well here at the inn and probably around town. Wilhelm could supply gift cards in Time for Tea and Viola wouldn't say no to selling them at Nine Lives."

"So you'll be starting a new business," Alice exclaimed. "How exciting."

"I guess it isn't true that you can't teach an old dog new tricks," Clarissa commented. "This old dog still has plenty of tricks up her sleeve."

෨

"I thought they'd talk all night," Alice said after the Cottrells had left and Nancy and Zack had gone upstairs. "I've never seen such an excited group."

"With good reason." Louise cleared plates from the table. "By the way, has anyone seen Mr. Enrich in the last hour?"

"Is he in the kitchen?" Jane jumped to her feet. "I forgot all about him."

Mr. Enrich was buffing the butcher-block counter to a high gleam when Jane entered. Foamy warm water bubbled in the sink and the dishwasher door was open for the last of the dishes. Otherwise, the kitchen was immaculate.

"Wow. You're good. Zack was right. You'd be great in the restaurant business."

"Yeah? It sounds kind of fun. Maybe I could work with Zack. But, of course, we'd have to call the place 'Enrich's.'"

Both burst out laughing as Louise carried a tray of cups and saucers into the room.

෨

"What are they doing here so late in the evening?" Alice wondered. She had stood to look out the window and had seen Ethel and Lloyd trotting down the driveway to the inn. Only the three sisters and Mr. Enrich remained on the first floor. Louise, Alice and Jane liked to have a quiet moment at the end of the day whenever they could to reflect and give thanks. Mr. Enrich, who was usually the first to disappear, seemed reluctant to do so tonight.

"They're probably still on 'reunion hours.' I bet those two were the last to leave every event they attended. I wouldn't be surprised if Lloyd swept the floor and Ethel turned out the lights before they left." Jane had her feet up, still enjoying her night off from the kitchen. "If nothing else, the reunion was memory-making for them."

"*Yoo-hoo!* Is anybody home?" As usual, Ethel didn't wait for an answer but came right in, towing Lloyd with her.

They were both bursting with enthusiasm. Lloyd's pink cheeks were even ruddier than usual and Ethel's bottle-red hair was in surprisingly attractive disarray. Ethel was getting all the mileage she could from her corsage even though it looked more out of place than ever on the orange jacket and slacks set she wore.

"Our little town did itself proud!" Lloyd announced pompously. "'Course I knew it would all along. I just came from the football field. I checked up on those Boy Scouts and they did a fine job picking up after the fireworks. Clean as a whistle, it was. I knew that they would be the best choice for a cleanup crew. You can't beat the Boy Scouts."

Jane marveled at the selective memories Lloyd and her aunt sometimes possessed. Before long, in Lloyd's memory, Sylvia would be demoted from the one who planned the reunion to the one who did her best to foul it up by not hiring the Boy Scouts for cleanup duty.

"We ran into Nellie," Ethel said. "She's pleased as punch with the way things turned out for her. She sold every one of those 'Countywide Reunion' T-shirts she ordered, as well as so many gift items she could barely count. Even your jewelry went, Jane. Nellie ran out and needs some more."

"*Even* your jewelry?" Alice whispered into Jane's ear. "My, my, the tourists must have been desperate for things to take home."

"Very funny, Alice. You know she tried to make that a compliment."

"She's not very good at it, is she?"

"Out of practice, that's all."

Lloyd waved his arm to catch Jane and Alice's attention. "And," he said with some amazement in his voice, "the rumor is that Joseph sold that ugly statue he's had in the antique shop since he opened it. Whoever bought it paid good money for it too. Can you imagine? For something so ugly?"

Jane tried to recall which of the statues in the antique shop might be billed as ugly. Joseph and his wife had excellent taste and chose wisely for their store. She had a hunch that Lloyd and Ethel dismissed the place only because much of what Joseph considered "antique" had been new and modern when they were young. It was, Jane thought, a little like the time she had visited the Smithsonian and found toys from the fifties and sixties on display behind protective glass.

"We stopped at the Coffee Shop for breakfast this morning," Ethel continued. "Hope said her feet are about to fall off from standing on them, but they had a steady stream of customers throughout the weekend. She wondered if we should have these reunions more often for all the business they brought to town."

Louise, Alice and Jane all sighed.

"But I have saved the best news for last," Ethel announced. She turned to Louise. "Have you talked to Viola?"

"Not in the past few hours. Why?"

"Because she earned so much from her sale of books that she's going to be able to fulfill a lifelong dream of hers."

"What's that?" Jane mentally explored the possibilities —an addition to the store for selling rare first editions? A basement where the popular fiction could be stored in an even *lower* spot at Nine Lives? Or perhaps a little boutique that sold only scarves and boas in every color under the sun?

"A rescue shelter for stray cats." Ethel looked enormously pleased with the announcement. "You know how much Viola loves cats, so she's going to convert that little house she owns on the south side of the fire hall for that purpose. It's practically kitty-corner from the store."

"'*Kitty*-corner?' How convenient." Jane couldn't resist.

Ethel, of course, didn't catch the pun and rolled on with her story. "You know that she inherited that house from an old aunt and has been wondering what on earth to do with the place. Although it's very sweet from the outside, it needs a lot of interior work to be rental property and Viola's not made of money. But," Ethel said gleefully, "the cats won't care."

"Let me get this straight," Louise managed in a strangled voice. "Viola is going to fill her house with stray cats?"

Lloyd, who had been unusually silent until now, stepped in. "That was my first question too. Being the mayor, I didn't want anything strange or foolish happening in town, but Viola's got it all figured out. It's going to be a rescue and adoption center. She has promised to limit the number of cats and make sure that they're being adopted out to good homes nearly as fast as they come in. Why, Viola's goal is for every house in Acorn Hill to own a cat."

Jane glanced at Wendell, so relaxed that he appeared boneless on his pillow. "I've heard of worse things, I guess."

"And best of all," Lloyd said, "people who come to pick out a cat will do a little shopping here, maybe have pie and coffee and then leave." Lloyd loved it when people had reason to visit Acorn Hill but had no excuse to stay.

Wacky as it was, the idea was harmless and rather sweet, Jane decided. Besides, it would give Viola something to do other than trying to talk people out of buying the books of which she didn't approve.

"Indeed," Louise said to no one in particular.

Jane had no doubt her sister would be discussing the idea with Viola at the first opportunity.

"I don't know about the rest of you," Alice suddenly announced, "but I'm exhausted. Sorry I can't stay up to visit, Aunt Ethel, Lloyd, but that car wash wore me out."

"Another big success," Lloyd said delightedly. "Only positive comments, and the kids set a lot of people's minds to thinking." He patted his shirt pocket. "I've been carrying around that little message of faith they handed out."

"Come, Lloyd," Ethel tugged on Lloyd's hand. "I want to stop in and see how Sylvia's doing, too. And these girls need to get their beauty sleep."

After the pair left, the three women collapsed into laughter.

"'These *girls* need to get their *beauty sleep*'?" Alice wiped a tear of laughter from her eye. "Then I'd better get to bed right now and not get up till a week from Wednesday. I do love Aunt Ethel. She makes me feel so young."

Shortly it was only Jane and Mr. Enrich left downstairs. She eyed him speculatively. "I'm going to make a cup of herbal tea to take upstairs. Would you like one?"

Even though she had asked, she was surprised when he nodded and followed her to the kitchen.

"We all appreciated your supper very much," Jane said as she put water on to boil. "It was very generous of you to do that. And you even had enough for our unexpected guests."

"My pleasure—and it's you and your family that I appreciate."

"A mutual admiration society of sorts, then," Jane said as she put the steaming brew in front of him.

"I don't understand." Mr. Enrich looked genuinely mystified.

Jane gave a little huff of frustration. "Maybe that's the problem. You put people off because you don't believe you're likable."

"*Likable?* That's a word I haven't heard in a long time."

"You were likable tonight, serving dinner."

"It's different here. You people are very ... accepting."

"And other places you've been are not?"

Mr. Enrich was silent so long that Jane began to grow uncomfortable. Maybe she had overstepped the limits.

When he spoke, there was heaviness in his words that wrenched at her heart. "This is the only place I've been in several years where I began to think it might be all right just to be myself."

Jane waited.

He looked at her and their gazes locked. "May I tell you something? I'll understand if you're tired and . . ."

"Tell away." She settled deeper in her chair.

"I made a complete mess of my marriage," he began softly. "It might not have been perfect to begin with, but I did nothing to help. I thought that a man had to be a good provider for his family. It really never occurred to me that financial support was only a fraction of what was expected of me.

"My wife was always angry when I was never home for meals or gatherings—sometimes I wasn't even home for holidays. I chased that almighty dollar as hard as I could and it still got away from me. That, and everything else."

He raked his fingers through his dark hair and Jane saw pain etched in his features. "When the baby came, my son Mitchell, I guess I thought she'd be entertained by him and would quit nagging me, but it only got worse. I missed the baby's first tooth, his first word, his first step, and I didn't understand why she was so furious about it. I was giving them what I thought I was suppose to give—debt-free living, nice clothes, food and shelter. And it was as if she hated me for it.

"Pretty soon we were so angry with each other that we just quit talking. I suppose Mitch was nine or ten by then. Sometimes he'd try to get us together as a 'family,' but my wife wasn't interested in being with me anymore. 'You go with your father,' she'd say." He uttered a bitter sound. "And I had little idea what to do with him when we were together. I got expensive tickets to football games and learned later that he liked hockey. I took him camping once as a surprise and it wasn't until the second night when I found him in tears that I discovered he hated camping. And what did I do? I scolded him about it. I told him that camping would help to make him a man."

Jane winced inwardly.

"You get the idea. I blew it completely, all the while telling myself what a good provider I was. That's what my own father was, a provider. My mother was the one I went to for everything that was important to me." He looked at Jane with tortured eyes. "You'd have thought, with my own experience, that I would have figured out that I hadn't liked or respected my father because he was so absent and distant. I was determined to be a 'good' husband and father and proceeded to imitate him. I didn't really know any other way to be, I suppose, since my own dad was the only role model I'd ever had." Regret seemed to fill the air around him. "By the time my wife left me, Mitch was fourteen. We asked him who he wanted to stay with and he laughed. 'Mom, of course. I'm too young to live alone.'"

Mr. Enrich sunk deeper into his chair looking dispirited. "But it gets worse. That business I slaved for? It went belly-up during the technology tumble. I lost everything I had, even the house."

"Where have you been living?" Jane murmured.

"In a one-bedroom efficiency apartment over the offices from which I used to run my business. It is a constant reminder of my failure."

"Where are they now?" Jane asked softly. "Where is your family?"

"Pittsburgh."

"Did you go to see them?"

He looked at her disconsolately. "I was in Pittsburgh for two days before I came here. I'm ashamed to say I never talked to them." He trailed a spoon through his tea. "The first day I was there, I was parked across the street from their house when I saw my wife drive up. I was about to jump out of my car to meet her when I realized that she wasn't alone. There was a good-looking guy, younger than I, with her."

"A friend?"

"I thought so at first. Then he kissed her before they went inside. After that, I kept coming back to the house and parking out of sight so I could watch the house. It was as if I was compelled to be there. People came in and out. She had a party. I could see people laughing and talking inside. Nothing like that happened when we were living together. Or if it did, I wasn't there to see it. When I was home, I wanted it to be quiet because I'd been working hard all day."

"And your son?"

"I didn't see him at first. I thought maybe I could catch him separately. I don't know what good I thought it would do. He hasn't shown much interest in talking to me for three years, so why should he start now?"

"Did you talk with him?"

"The first time I saw him leave the house, I followed him."

This was as truly pathetic a story as Jane could imagine— a man who didn't know how to communicate with his wife or son, a man who skulked around to spy on them instead.

"He went to the library," Mr. Enrich continued. "I thought that was perfect. I could find him there, and we'd have some privacy in which to talk." He took a deep breath. "But he wasn't alone there. He'd met several of his friends. I overheard them say they were working on a project together."

He looked at Jane. "Yes, I spied on him too."

"Did you talk to him anyway?"

"No. Not after what I overheard."

Jane tipped her head questioningly but didn't speak.

"I guess it serves me right for eavesdropping. They were all talking about going to a hockey game. One of the boys said to Mitch, 'You're going with us, aren't you?'

"'Of course he's going with you,' one of his other friends retorted. 'Everyone knows how much he likes hockey.'

"Then Mitch said, 'Everyone but my father,' and went on to tell them about the football incident. I knew I couldn't seek Mitch out then—not in that group and probably not at all. I could hear in Mitch's voice that he had no interest in or feeling for me. I'd doused that like water douses a flame. So I slunk out of my place behind the wall of books and went back to my car."

He looked at Jane oddly. "And I came here." A disconcerting silence hung in the air between them. "To hide. I wanted to . . ." He let his voice trail off.

The bottom seemed to drop out of Jane's stomach. "You weren't going to injure yourself?"

He shrugged.

Jane took a deep breath and looked him in the eye. "What stopped you?"

"Cowardice, at first. I didn't want to live, but I didn't want to die either. But I know I could have done it if it hadn't been for," he drew a breath, "that apple pie."

Jane's eyes widened.

"All the time I was working myself up to end my life, you and your sisters were being kind to me, acting as if I actually *mattered* to you."

"Of course you matter," Jane said softly, remembering how all three sisters had been nudged to pray for their cantankerous guest.

"I saw that. I didn't believe it at first. I was as cold and as self-pitying as a human could be, and you just kept on being kind." He looked at her intently. "I didn't plan to be here for more than a night or two. Then I planned to be … gone."

The thought sickened Jane.

"I tried to build myself up to it, but it was odd, I couldn't bear to turn my light off at night. The darkness terrified me. So I slept with every light in the room burning.

"And two days became three, and three turned into four." He spread his hands in helpless amazement. "Then you all began to treat me less like a guest and more like, I don't know, family. I haven't had much experience with 'family,' but I guessed perhaps that was how it felt."

He continued more quickly now, as if relieved to talk about it. "This might sound silly to you, but the cat would come up to me and wrap himself around my legs just when I was feeling my lowest. And he started sitting with me while I read, so I began taking all those books of your father's out of the library. They're amazing books, really. I've never read anything like them."

Jane was not surprised that Mr. Enrich hadn't taken the opportunity to read anything about biblical history or the Christian faith before.

"And you noticed that Belgian waffles are my favorite."

How simple the act, Jane thought, *but how profound the effect*.

"And that tea party. If you'd told me a week earlier that I'd be sitting at someone's table drinking tea with my pinkie finger in the air … well …"

Jane could have hugged Josie at that moment.

"The day I ran into you at the pond was one of my most difficult times. If you hadn't been there then, well, I just don't know.

"But it was when you agreed to let me sleep in the library …"

Jane drew a breath, afraid that they could have pushed him over the edge somehow.

"... that I knew I didn't want to do it. That's when I realized you thought of me as kin." A smile flashed on his features. What a difference that smile made.

"You could have kicked me out. You'd never promised me a room during the reunion. I had no reason to anticipate you'd let me stay. I'm ashamed to say it now, but I was testing you, expecting that I already knew the answer—that your concern hadn't been sincere. And then you said 'yes.' I couldn't believe my ears. You didn't brush me off. Instead, you accommodated me as best you could."

What a small thing to bring about such an enormous result.

"Crazy as it sounds, everything you and your sisters did after that seemed to snowball. You even let me help you with some chores for the reunion." He peered at her. "Do you know how long it's been since I've felt useful to anyone?

"And the vase ..." His tone changed. "You saw that it mattered to me and you gave it to me," he snapped his fingers, "just like that."

He grew pensive. "My wife came back before our divorce and cleaned out our house." His voice was soft. "She took everything. *Everything.* Including a vase similar to yours that my mother had given to me. It had been my grandmother's. It was the one family memento that meant something to me." He shrugged. "I've never really blamed my ex-wife for that. If I didn't seem to care about anything but my work, I suppose she thought I wouldn't even remember something as insignificant as a cheap vase."

"I am so, so sorry," Jane said.

"It's okay, because that's when I was really sure that things were different here."

"Have you figured out what that difference is?" Jane asked.

"At first I thought maybe you three, being pastor's daughters and all, just didn't know any better."

Jane, somber as she felt, couldn't help but smile. "Like we were too dumb to figure it out?"

Mr. Enrich reddened. "Something like that."

"I see."

"But it became obvious that none of you was 'dumb.' You're the savviest group I've ever met—professional, wise, realistic and unerringly kind. After a while I guess I decided to 'hang around' to see what you'd do next."

Hang around?

"And?"

"It's like you're in partnership with God, or something." His brow furrowed. "I've seen you all praying at one time or another when you thought no one was watching. I've seen people pray in church, but alone? Just because they want to?

And when no one's looking? What good is that, I asked myself, unless there really is Somebody up there to talk to?"

Suddenly he looked ashamed. "I'm sorry. I sound like all I do is spy on people."

"No apology necessary. I'm happy to be caught praying."

"Then the reunion rolled around, and it was as if I couldn't help myself. Joe invited me to go with him to some of the activities so he wouldn't be alone. I understand more than anyone how hard that can be, so I said 'yes.'"

He appeared pensive. "I'd forgotten about parties and music. I'd forgotten about fun."

Now he blushed outright. "I even volunteered to help with the ANGELs' car wash."

"Alice never told me."

"She doesn't know. Pastor Thompson was there."

"So how was it?"

Mr. Enrich looked puzzled again. "Odd. Very odd. Hymns were playing and all those young people were talking among themselves about why they believed in Jesus. Yet, at other times they laughed and joked and acted so normal."

"Christians can be normal," Jane commented wryly. "I know several who are."

"Pastor Thompson was watching me, and he came up to ask me if I wanted to talk to him."

Good for you, Ken. God works in mysterious ways.

"He said he'd been compelled to pray for me for days and that when that happens, he always liked to ... how'd he say it? 'Follow through and see what God was up to now.'"

So God had the entire Acorn Hill team praying for Mr. Enrich, not just Grace Chapel Inn? Jane thought.

"I don't know what came over me, but I spilled it all, just like I did now."

"And what did he say?" Jane asked.

"'God loves you.' Then he gave me the little Bible out of his pocket and some pamphlets. He said, 'I have a sense that you need time to read this and formulate some questions.' We've set up a time to meet tomorrow."

"Ahh."

"And then I decided to cook a meal for you and your family to show you how grateful I am. I believe you saved my life."

"We may have been instruments in the process," Jane said, "but we were guided by Someone much greater than ourselves. Someone who loves us all equally."

"Mind-boggling," Mr. Enrich muttered. "I've been reading that material Pastor Thompson gave me. I have lots of questions."

"I bet you do," Jane said with a smile. "But first I have one for you. Mr. Enrich, what is your first name?"

He smiled, really smiled, and a softness settled over him. "Warren. My name is Warren."

"Warren, would you pray with me?"

"I've been trying that on my own, but I'm not very good at it. I'm not sure I'm getting through."

"I know you are," Jane assured him. "God is always listening. It's we who don't pay proper attention."

After Mr. Enrich thanked Jane for any- and everything he could think of and said good night, he went upstairs to the bedroom he had reclaimed after the other guests had left. Before Jane put out the lights, she went into her father's library. What she wanted to do most was to scream for joy. Instead, out of courtesy for her sleeping sisters, she hugged her arms around herself in delight.

Oh, there was surely a party in heaven tonight.

Chapter Thirteen

I've never seen such a big fuss in my life," Clarissa raised her voice to be heard over the hammering and sawing behind her bakery wall. "I've had to come in early to get my bread and cakes done before these workmen arrive. I can't bake anything but cookies during the day because they're already flat and there's no danger of them caving in."

A rat-a-tat-tat shook the building.

"Plumbers," she said sorrowfully. "Digging holes all over the place. This noise has been going on for weeks."

"Zack showed me the plans your architect drew up." Jane had a giant molasses cookie with white frosting on her plate and a bag of Good Apple pecan sticky buns at her side. "The restaurant and the kitchen will be wonderful."

"That Zack has some fine ideas. He's spent a lot of time thinking about this and he's got his opinions, all right."

"Most chefs do. I didn't settle down at the inn until I could rearrange everything in the cupboards. That put Louise and Alice in a spin for a few days."

"I'll bet."

"And, since we're on the topic of families, how is Livvy handling this new life of yours?"

Someone dropped something very heavy on the far side of the bakery and started yelling. Both women jumped, then laughed.

"It's taking her a while to switch gears. She was so convinced that there was a certain birthday at which one becomes 'old' that letting go of the idea is difficult. Realizing that 'old' can also be an attitude is an eye-opener for my daughter. Frankly, it's been good for Livvy. She's had tunnel vision all her life, believing her way is the best way. Now she's working hard to release some of the control she thought she had to have over her family and her life."

Clarissa smiled mischievously and that endearing web of wrinkles creased her face. Jane thought of them as wisdom-wrinkles now. "My son-in-law called to say it was a welcome change. Oh, and I almost forgot, I have something to show you." Clarissa rose and bent to dig underneath the counter beneath the cash register. "Here it is."

She gave Jane a small square box made of recycled cardboard wrapped in a raffia bow. "Livvy said I should surprise you with this. It's something she had made up when she got home from Acorn Hill."

Carefully Jane untied the bow. "Is this for me?"

"And there's lots more where that came from."

Curious, Jane lifted the lid from the box and gave a tiny gasp. "Oh, Clarissa, how beautiful."

"There's more than one, so keep looking." Clarissa leaned over Jane's shoulder and beamed. "They turned out pretty well, don't you think?"

Gently Jane laid her new gifts on the table. Note cards. Each made from one of Clarissa's sketches at Fairy Pond.

"Even the people who printed them asked if they could buy some, according to Livvy. She's been stopping at gift stores and little boutiques and says several people have already placed orders and asked for a wider selection." Clarissa looked baffled by the very idea. "Now what do you think of that?"

"I think it's fabulous. Is Livvy sending more?"

"Soon, I think."

"Then I'd like to buy two dozen boxes to sell at the inn. No, make that three."

"You don't have to baby me, Jane. I'll understand if you don't want any. They're just little old sketches of a puddle and some imaginary pixies."

"Just a puddle and some pixies? Don't sell yourself short. These are truly remarkable. What is your next subject?"

Her friend brightened. "I've decided to do a few more drawings of Ed. You do remember Ed, don't you?"

Jane recalled the elegant frog Clarissa had first sketched at the pond. "Of course. How could I forget such a handsome fellow?"

"Something you said that day at the pond put an idea in my head," Clarissa confessed. "You said that my pictures of Ed were as good as the illustrations in some children's books."

"I did, and they are."

"Well, I've been thinking about Ed a lot lately. I've decided I want to leave something special for my grandchildren, something they know I made especially for them. So," and Clarissa grinned broadly, "I'm going to start writing and illustrating books for them about Ed and Fairy Pond."

Jane clapped her hands together in delight. "Oh, what a wonderful idea. I hope you'll share them with more than your grandchildren."

"I guess that depends on how the stories turn out. I'm thinking that Ed is the mayor of a little town called Lily Pad Landing, which is populated by not only frogs and fairies but also by gossipy birds and talking flowers. Maybe there will even be a little girl in my story, a girl with golden curls and cornflower blue eyes. I'll call her Cornflower. She and Ed will have adventures together and learn so many things, all the things I want my grandchildren to know about growing up. Maybe Ed will go to school with Cornflower one day . . . ."

Jane burst out laughing. "Why are you in here when you could be sitting in the sun making sketches for your books?"

"Come to think about it, I don't know. Nancy has already learned every trick about baking that I ever had. I'm just waiting for the cake decorating area to be done so I can feel useful around here again. And," Clarissa said, waggling her eyebrows playfully, "I'd like to report that our young couple is getting along much better now. Why, they're so sweet to each other, I've thought about not ordering sugar anymore."

At that moment, Zack appeared in the front door covered with sawdust. "Hi, Jane. Boy, am I glad to see you. I wanted to ask you what length counters you'd recommend for . . ."

Jane and Zack, heads together, went in the back for a consultation, and Clarissa happily leaned back in her chair to watch Nancy package the buns the Coffee Shop had ordered.

In the kitchen, or what would be a kitchen when it was finished, Jane gasped at the progress that had been made. The bakery equipment had been set up temporarily in what had been Clarissa's storage room, so that the bakery could remain open while construction was being done. In what would be the expanded kitchen, the walls and ceiling were in, the floor had been tiled, and overhead lighting had been installed.

Through the window, Jane could see a large tarp covering a mound of something outside. "What's that?" she asked pointing at the tarp.

"Oh, Clarissa didn't tell you? That's all the kitchen equipment we bought. We had an incredible stroke of luck, thanks to June Carter," Zack replied. "She has an acquaintance who owned a small restaurant and decided to close it. Her partner wanted out of the business, and she didn't want to try to run it herself. So, she was selling everything. June told her about us, and she gave us first shot at buying her stuff."

"Wow, that *is* good luck. I know from the inn that equipment always costs more than you estimate."

"Yeah, in fact, if June hadn't been so thoughtful, we might have been in trouble. Nancy and I had put away a fair amount of money, but it was starting to look as if it wouldn't be enough for all the kitchen stuff, not to mention the furniture and dinnerware for the dining room."

"So what did you buy?"

"Nearly everything we needed. The restaurant hadn't been in business all that long, so the ovens, refrigerators, freezers and all were in good shape. The pots and pans aren't all shiny and new, but they're serviceable and the china is simple but modern and fits into my plans for the dining-room décor. We're a little short on glassware, but I'm sure we can get some more that matches or comes close to what we bought."

Jane smiled and shook her head slowly. "When you and Nancy first came here, it seemed that your dreams would never materialize, and now..." She gave him a one-armed hug. "Now it seems that doors are being opened for you everywhere."

"Yep," he agreed with a smile. "I can't imagine all this happening in any other place than Acorn Hill. Though I am a city boy, the idea of going back to live in one has absolutely no appeal for me anymore."

"I'm glad to hear that, Zack. I know Nancy loves small-town life, but it's important that you are happy here as well."

Just then, near the doorway they heard a familiar "*Yoo hoo!*" and saw the flash of scarlet that signaled Ethel's approach.

"Living in a small town can require some adjustment," Jane said with a chuckle, "and some patience."

Viola had taken on the cat rescue project with her typical vigor.

When Jane, who had just come out of the pharmacy, saw her toting an enormous bag of cat food out of the General Store, she ran down the street to Viola and offered to help her carry it to the shelter.

"Perhaps I should be buying smaller bags of food, but this is so much more economical," Viola panted.

"It is unless you give yourself a heart attack trying to get it home to the cats."

"Perhaps I could borrow Josie's wagon from now on. Oh dear, I think I have to rest."

"Need some help, ladies?" Ned Arnold pulled up beside them on the corner of Chapel Road and Berry Lane. He jumped out, slung the enormous bag into the passenger seat of his car and drove it to Viola's door. The words *Cat Rescue Shelter* were printed on cardboard and thumbtacked to the siding.

"On your way home?" Viola wheezed as Ned carried the bag into the house and back to the kitchen.

"Until the Palmers' next vacation." He looked at her with concern. "Are you having difficulty catching your breath?"

"It's nothing. Nothing at all. It will pass." Viola walked with him to the front door. "Drive carefully."

Ned backed toward his car looking doubtful about leaving the woman gasping for breath. Jane, however, gave him a reassuring wave. She and Viola returned to the kitchen where they scooped the cat food into a large, clean, lidded garbage can to keep it dry. *There shouldn't be any danger of rodents getting into it,* Jane thought. *No rodent in the world would be dumb enough to try to dine in a place like this one.*

Cats peered from every flat surface. A sleek ebony tom with huge golden eyes stared at her accusingly, as if she had tried to break and enter rather than to deliver dinner. Several tabbies, none of them as healthy as Wendell, were curled into fur puddles on the furniture. A dirty white cat with one blue eye and one brown nursed two equally dirty kittens.

"Pastor Ley brought in that poor mama cat. She's nearly starved to death and nursing her two kittens besides. I took the entire batch to the veterinarian in Potterston yesterday and made sure they were all healthy and gave them their shots. I have purchased vitamins for all." Viola looked pleased. "Now I have to begin the next level of my little project."

Jane glanced around the room. Though not fancy, it had soft, comfy-looking old furniture. It was nothing she would want at the inn, but it was perfect for cats. "And what is that?"

"Adopting them out, of course." Viola eyed her speculatively. "How do you think Wendell would react to a kitten in the house?"

"About as well as if I brought a Doberman home. Not well at all."

"He is rather spoiled," Viola agreed kindly. "My own cats aren't interested in having any more at my house either."

How, Jane wondered, *did she know? Had she asked them?*

Viola suddenly broke into an alarming fit of coughing.

"Are you coming down with something?"

"I certainly hope not. I don't have time to be sick. My cats need me. Here kitty, kitty." She picked up the nearest feline, buried her nose in its fur and came up coughing and wheezing so hard her eyes watered.

"If you hear of anyone who wants a cat, let me know, will you, Jane? In fact, let me know about people who don't have any pets. They might not realize that they want a cat. Let's see, I have a pen and paper around here somewhere. I think I'll start a list."

When Jane slipped out some moments later, she could hear Viola start hacking again. If she sounded the same tomorrow, Jane decided she would encourage Louise to insist that Viola see a doctor.

Ethel was at the inn when Jane arrived. She and Louise were looking over photos Lloyd had taken at the reunion.

"Come see these, dear," she greeted Jane. "I'm sending these to my children. There's a lovely photo of you in here."

Ethel clucked like a broody hen. "I hadn't realized quite how thin you are, Jane. Perhaps you should join Lloyd and me at the Coffee Shop for blackberry pie later."

Jane grinned at Louise over Ethel's head. "Thanks, but I think I'll pass this time."

"Then I'll make you some of my peach tarts. They'll fatten you up in no time."

So I'm not the only one to blame for Lloyd's figure, Jane thought.

On her way up the stairs, she met Alice coming down with an armful of laundry. "Are things quieting down out there?" Alice inquired.

"It's actually rather boring. I'm like Josie, waiting for the next party to begin."

"I know what you mean." Alice leaned against the banister and looked pensive. "It was nice to have so much activity. But who knows what will turn up next around here?"

"Alice, is there something going around, a flu or cough?"

"Not much of anything that we've seen at the hospital. Why?"

"Because I just came from Viola's new shelter and she sounds terrible. Her throat gurgles and she coughs like she's going to detach her head from her body. I'm a little worried about her."

"Have you talked to Louise? She and Viola spend the most time together."

"Not yet. Aunt Ethel is here and I don't want the word to get around town that Viola is ill."

"I'm going to put this laundry in the washer, and then I'll walk down to Nine Lives and see her for myself."

"Thanks, Alice. Now I can breathe a sigh of relief."

"Not so fast," Alice advised. "We don't know what's wrong with her yet."

After Jane had retrieved what she had wanted from her room, she came down the stairs and saw Lloyd coming up the front walk. Jane noticed that he looked a little hangdog as he walked up the sidewalk to the porch.

"Is Ethel here?" he inquired.

"Yes, she is. She's looking at the reunion photos in the parlor with Louise. Is there something wrong, Lloyd? You don't look very happy."

"Oh, it's nothing really. At least I don't think it is. I certainly hope it isn't. We don't need a problem or anything. I can't see that it would be much of a problem. Of course, Ethel might have other ideas...."

He would have kept on for a long time with this one-sided conversation if Jane hadn't broken in to ask, "What is this potential problem we're discussing?"

Lloyd looked alarmed. "Do you think it *will* be a problem?"

"Not yet. I have no idea what you're talking about."

Lloyd blushed all the way to his scalp. "It's just that I ran into Viola a few minutes ago . . . she's got a nasty cough, by the way . . . but somehow she managed to get me to agree to . . . Oh, I'll bet Ethel will be upset. . . ."

"Let me guess. She got you to agree to adopt a cat."

Lloyd's shoulders slumped. "Yes. It happened so quickly that I hardly knew what hit me. First she was discussing my bachelor status and how quiet it must be in my house. The next thing you know, she had me agreeing that it was fairly quiet most of the time. Then, before I could tell her that sometimes I *liked* it that way, she got me to agree to take a cat home for company. When I think about it, I'm still not quite sure what happened. I must have been listening to that cough of hers and she caught me unawares."

Viola, Jane thought, *could sell ice to an Eskimo.*

"Do you like cats, Lloyd?"

"Yes. I suppose I do. I like Wendell very much."

"Would you mind taking care of one?"

"They can't be so hard, can they? Food, water, a warm dry bed and a litter box, I suppose. Not much to that."

"Would you pet a cat if you had one?"

Lloyd pondered that for a moment. "Yes. I certainly would. I think it would be calming to my nerves."

"Then it sounds like it's just fine that you agreed to adopt a cat."

"But Ethel..."

"It's your home, Lloyd. Shouldn't you get to decide whether you want a pet there or not?"

It appeared that that sort of independent thinking hadn't gone on for quite a while in Lloyd's head. He rolled the idea over in his mind. "Yes, yes, indeed." He squared his shoulders and raised his chin. "Excuse me, Jane, I have to go in and tell your aunt that I adopted a cat."

A week later, Louise peeked into her sister's room and found Jane doing an uncomfortable looking calf-stretch. "Jane?"

"Yes?" She shook out her arms and legs and bounced a bit on her toes, ready to go for a run.

"Do you have a minute? I would like to discuss something with you."

"Sure. Come in."

"Alice is waiting downstairs. I would like the three of us to talk."

"Okay." Jane followed her sister downstairs. She couldn't remember the last time Louise had called for a "family conference."

Alice was sitting at the kitchen table looking every bit as somber as Louise.

"Alice and I have been visiting," Louise began, "and she's brought up something unsettling."

"Something to do with the inn?"

"No. It's Viola. We feel that she may be quite ill."

"I know she has that cough, and it worried me too, but she's been running all over town convincing people they need a cat or two. She can't be too bad if she has the energy to do that."

"But have you *heard* her?"

"Well, not lately, but when I did she sounded like a baby with croup."

"It's been getting worse," Alice said. "I told Louise that I thought Viola should go to the hospital and have it checked out."

"And?"

"And she won't do it," Louise said. "The woman is stubborn. I'm afraid she may have a lung infection or pneumonia and she keeps saying that it's 'nothing' and that 'it will pass.' She says she doesn't have time for doctors' appointments right now. She's all booked up with the vet."

"Ride with her on her next trip to Potterston and on the way home, convince her to stop at the urgent care center at the hospital," Jane suggested. "Obviously telling her to plan the appointment herself isn't working. Maybe she'll do it on impulse if you encourage her."

"It's a good idea," Alice added. "Especially if she starts coughing in front of the emergency room."

⌒

It was an uneasy day. Jane found herself looking at the clock every few minutes, wondering how things were going with Louise and Viola. They had gone together to deliver a kitten to its new family, and Louise left determined to have Viola see a doctor before they returned. None of this would have seemed so important if Alice had not reminded them that Viola's father had suffered from emphysema and died at a young age. Louise had not rested since.

Jane walked down to Sylvia's Buttons just to wear off a little energy. Sylvia was buried in new fabric.

"Fall fabrics are in, I see." Jane peered over a stack of bolts at her friend.

"It's amazing how quickly time passes. Seems like it was spring only yesterday."

"Are we getting old, Sylvia?"

A chuckle emanated from behind the heap. "I hope I get old the way Clarissa is. With Nancy and Zack there, it's like she's had a breath of fresh air. She's been getting more energy every day. Just knowing she doesn't *have* to do all the work makes her work harder."

It was true. Clarissa was blooming.

"You don't look very happy," Sylvia commented as she wedged a few more bolts of fabric onto her already overstuffed shelves.

"Louise is going to try to get Viola to see the doctor in Potterston today about that cough."

"Good. I thought she was going to choke to death in church on Sunday. And she keeps saying 'Oh, it's nothing,' like she just cleared her throat instead of turning her own face bright red."

"Alice thinks it might be serious. We've been praying for her."

"I think several have. As much as we might shake our heads and chuckle behind her back, Viola is an important part of this town. The way she's thrown herself into that rescue place is remarkable. They did an article about her in the *Acorn Nutshell*."

"She feels such affection for those animals and loves placing them in good homes. She's as determined to put a cat in every household as she is to keep best sellers out," Jane said.

Sylvia looked at Jane, compassion in her face. "Hang in there. Louise and Viola will be back soon. Sometimes waiting is the worst."

In this case, however, waiting was not the worst. The facts were.

Later that day Louise came into the inn leading a sobbing Viola by the arm. Jane leaped to her feet and pulled out a chair while Alice ran for iced tea. Viola's wails seemed to pierce the walls. They certainly pierced Jane's heart.

"Is it serious?" Alice ventured.

Viola increased the volume of her sobbing.

"Surely there's something that can be done about this…."

Viola shook her head and wailed.

"Louise, what did the doctor say? You're frightening us."

Before Louise could convey the information, Viola hiccupped and imparted the doctor's awful diagnosis. "He thinks I'm allergic to cats."

"She has had cats around before this, of course," Louise told them later. "It is just that now she is around so many cats all at once. It seems a bit odd, but that is the only thing the doctor can imagine might be wrong with her. Otherwise, Viola is healthy as the proverbial horse."

"But the rescue center," Alice stammered.

"That's why she's so upset," Louise said. "She loves what she's doing there. The doctor told her that she should either find someone to handle the cats for her or get rid of them. Viola is beside herself. What is she going to do?"

Chapter Fourteen

*I*t was not only Viola who was upset by the turn of events, but also most of Acorn Hill.

"Who's going to take the rescue center over if Viola can't do it?" Lloyd fretted.

"And this happened just after that lovely article came out about the cat shelter in the *Acorn Nutshell* too," Ethel added in dismay.

"It was a great commentary on our little village," Lloyd said. "That Viola may not be able to continue is a terrible shame."

"What are Lloyd and Ethel worried about?" Sylvia whispered to Jane as they sat in the Coffee Shop. They couldn't help overhearing the pair complaining to Hope Collins as she waited on them in the next booth. "Viola's health or the city's reputation?"

"A little of both, I think. Now Viola may have to hire someone to take care of the cats, which could be costly. I'm not sure she can afford that. And," Jane added, "Louise thinks Viola is in denial over this whole thing.

Viola still insists that she's not allergic to the cats. She goes to the shelter to care for them and comes out red-faced and sounding like she's coughing up a hairball herself."

"*Ewww.*" Sylvia made a face.

"Louise also says that Viola has made appointments with other doctors and an allergist, hoping they'll tell her she's *not* allergic to cats. As if that's going to make a difference in how she feels."

"I feel sorry for her," Sylvia said. "She was so pleased with her idea. It seems a shame that she might have to close the place so soon."

"It 'casts a pall on our otherwise happy community,'" Jane intoned, quoting her sister Louise.

"Other than this, however, the entire county seems to be smiling since the reunion." Sylvia looked half pleased and half relieved. "It went well, didn't it?"

"Thanks to you and your committee. Everyone loved the idea of having community reunions plus a countywide gathering. So," Jane asked, "did you take notes for the next one?"

"There'll be no 'next one' as far as I'm concerned. Somebody else is going to have to throw the next big party."

"Someone already is."

"Really?" Sylvia perked up. "Who?"

"Nancy, Zack and Clarissa. They're having their grand opening soon. Clarissa said that they're waiting for the furniture to arrive. You'll read all about it in the *Acorn Nutshell*."

"That should be quite an event."

"Clarissa's children are returning for it. They told their mother that they wouldn't miss it for the world. She's shining with happiness. And," Jane took a deep breath, "Warren Enrich called last night."

Sylvia's eyebrow arched with surprise. Jane had told her Mr. Enrich's story. "No kidding? What did he have to say?"

"He wants to come back for the grand opening. He says he feels 'connected' here and wants to see his friends again."

"Remarkable."

"He also said he was going to attempt to contact his son."

"I hope it works out for him," Sylvia said.

So do I, Jane thought. *More than you can imagine.*

Several weeks later, as she worked in the garden, Jane heard a voice call, "Look who's here." Wiping her hands on the back of her jeans—a habit Ethel called "deplorable"—Jane walked to the front porch where Clarissa and Livvy were standing. "Welcome, Livvy. How nice to see you." Jane gestured toward the wicker porch chairs. "Can you sit for a minute?"

"We've got nothing to do but sit," Clarissa said. "Nancy and Zack kicked me out of my own place of business. Said I needed to be home visiting with my daughter."

"What do you think of that, Livvy?" Jane asked.

"Music to my ears. I can't help worrying about Mom even if she insists she's fine, so knowing that those two are making sure she gets a break is a real relief for me." Livvy smiled tenderly at her mother. "And now that I'm not nagging her about it, she's actually taking time off."

"Are you saying that all of your stubbornness didn't come from your father's side of the family after all?" Jane asked.

Both Livvy and Clarissa burst out laughing.

"The child was doomed to be contrary from the start," Clarissa admitted.

Livvy took her mother's hand and gave it a squeeze—quite a difference from the first time Jane had seen them together during the reunion weekend.

"Are you ready for the grand opening this evening?"

"Ready as I'll ever be. Ray and Kent are down at Zachary's helping out. Livvy made me go to Nellie's and buy a new dress. I'll be gussied up like a Thanksgiving turkey tonight."

"Good. We only have one guest this evening and he'll be coming with us to the party. Warren Enrich said he'd be here before five."

"Pretty nice of him to travel all this way for us."

"He says he's happy to have such a special place to go."

"Well, we're all happy as ducks in water then, except, of course, poor Viola."

"Have you talked to her today?"

"She came in for doughnuts early this morning. Said she was on her way to another doctor. She's still looking for someone who will tell her she's not allergic to cats. The woman is persistent, no doubt about that."

Well, Jane thought after the Cottrells had left, *at least most of the people at the party would be happy.*

"Are you coming or not?" Louise asked at five minutes to six.

"I'm just writing a note for Warren Enrich telling him to come to the restaurant when he gets here."

"I thought he said he would be here by now."

"Something must have held him up. I hope he didn't have car trouble."

"Well, he knows the way. We should get going."

When they arrived at the restaurant, Alice glanced wide-eyed around the room. "Oh my."

"Indeed," Louise intoned.

Even Jane was surprised. She had been here several times a week during the construction of the dining room, but this was the first time that she had seen it as it was supposed to be. The walls were painted a creamy white. On them hung original art that was illuminated by small halogen spotlights. Many of the works were Jane's, some were Sylvia's quilt art and the rest were done by Clarissa. In fact, several people, including Ethel, Lloyd, the Humberts and Rev. Thompson, were gathered at the head of the room beneath a large painting in an ornate frame.

"Look," Alice said happily, "Clarissa's fairies."

It had been quite a project to help Clarissa turn her small sketch into a full-fledged painting, but size only made the picture more delightful. Jane noticed that people were beginning to discover the artwork within the artwork and were trying to count how many pixies Clarissa had hidden in the picture.

In the softly lit room, the crisp white linen contrasted with the thick wine-colored carpet and the brushed steel chairs upholstered in gray velour. Silver candles in crystal holders and exotic, brilliant-colored fresh flowers decorated every table. At each place was a brushed steel charger that held a service plate decorated with one of Clarissa's scenes from Fairy Pond. These had been a surprise gift to the restaurant from Livvy.

Waiters in white shirts, black ties and black trousers passed the first course. They offered petite chevre tarts, miniature lamb kabobs, tiny meatballs in brandied apricot sauce and flutes of bubbling champagne. According to Alice, competition to work at the new nightspot had been keen among the young men in the area. Zack and Nancy had put them through an intense training program. Clearly the program had been effective, for the waiters were moving expertly through the crowded room making sure everyone was served.

"I simply can't believe it," Vera whispered to Alice after being served by an impeccably groomed young waiter. "That was Billy Hull. I had him in fifth grade. He always had his shirttails out. He'd spill his lunch on himself nearly every day, and now look at him."

Alice smiled. She, too, remembered Billy as a sweet but clumsy boy. "Yes, he looks like a Hollywood version of a waiter."

Ray and Kent Cottrell were acting as hosts along with Nancy and Zack while Clarissa, looking lovely in her new dress, held Livvy's hand and greeted her friends as they came through the doors.

Jane walked across the room to give her a hug.

"It can't get much better than this, can it, Jane?" Clarissa beamed. "I'm a blessed woman. Frankly, I've spent most of the day just saying 'Thanks, Lord' as the sweet,

God-given gifts in my life come by. Livvy, Kent, Ray, Nancy, Zack, you … and, of course, there's new life for both me and the Good Apple."

"God is awesome," Jane agreed. "In fact . . ." her voice trailed away.

A good-looking, dark-haired man in a navy blazer and gray slacks strode across the room to where Jane was standing. In his wake followed a younger man of similar coloring and a stocky build. Although the younger man was quite serious, the older wore a wide smile.

"Warren?" Jane was afraid her eyes might be deceiving her. "Mr. Enrich?"

"Hello, Jane. Sorry we're late. Hello, Clarissa. Congratulations on your new venture."

"Mighty nice of you to come," Clarissa said.

Before they could chat, Sylvia Songer and Craig Tracy walked up to Clarissa to greet her. Jane and Mr. Enrich stepped aside.

"It *is* you. You look so different, so happy."

Mr. Enrich's dark eyes twinkled and Jane observed that he looked ten years younger than when he had first stayed with them at the inn.

"I *am* happy." Mr. Enrich turned to the young man standing behind him. "Mitch, I'd like you to meet Jane. Jane, this is my son Mitchell."

Now it was Jane's turn to be surprised.

"Mitch and I have been getting together occasionally, just to talk. When I told him I was coming for the grand opening, he decided to ride along so we could get to know each other again. I called Zack and he told me that it was fine to bring him."

"Welcome to Acorn Hill." Jane extended her hand.

"Hi," Mitch said as he took her hand shyly.

Another man of few words, she thought.

"Jane, good things have started to happen to me. One of my former clients approached me with a job. You know, I always thought that working for myself was the only way to go, but I really like being an employee. Oh, I work hard, but when I leave the office, I leave my work there. Mitch has seen the change in me," Mr. Enrich said. "I told him that I learned a lot when I was here and that I'd like to introduce him to some of the people who made a difference in my life. I've been telling him a little about my new relationship with God too."

Mr. Enrich, Jane could tell, was hopeful. It had taken a long time to ruin the connection with his son, but at least he was getting a chance to try to mend it.

Suddenly there was the sound of an accented voice from behind them and Joe Morales greeted his friend with pleasure, pounding him heartily on the back. "Mr. Enrich, you've come back. How is my amigo? I'm working here part-time now. Mr. Fred says that if I don't quit accepting jobs I'm going to be the richest man in Acorn Hill." Joe's laughter was musical. "But I don't need more money. I'm already the happiest man here."

"I'm afraid that you will have to share that title with me," Mr. Enrich replied.

It was nice for a change, Jane thought, *to have that kind of contest going on.*

Soon the guests were asked to be seated and Rev. Thompson offered grace. The salad course—butter lettuce with slices of ripe pears, crumbled blue cheese and toasted pine nuts—was being served when Louise leaned toward Jane. "I am getting worried about Viola. It's not like her to be late."

"Sylvia told me she was going to another doctor today. Maybe she was delayed there."

"I wish she would just accept the fact that she cannot run the shelter. Apparently a cat or two is fine, but twenty..."

At that moment Viola appeared in the doorway. She was smiling widely and seemed to be full of energy.

Louise rose and went over to her. "We saved a spot for you. Come sit down. How are you feeling?"

"I have never in my life felt better. I am fit as a fiddle."

"You are?" Louise tried to hide her surprise. "Well, let's go over to our table so you can tell all of us about it. I thought you were going to see a doctor today. You must have had good news."

When they were seated, Viola greeted the others and then announced, "I found a competent doctor, finally. One who didn't just tell me to get rid of my cats. It took some research, but I finally discovered a *brilliant* doctor."

"But your allergy . . . it can't have disappeared just like that," Louise said.

"Oh no, my allergy is fully present and accounted for," Viola said with satisfaction.

"Then what are you so happy about?" Jane asked.

"Because my new doctor found out what I am really allergic to: *kitty litter*."

Every head at the table swiveled to look at her.

"But you have always used kitty litter for your own cats, Viola," Alice said.

"Yes, of course, but at home I use unscented, dust free, top-of-the-line kitty litter. For the shelter, I've been buying whatever is cheapest on the shelves to save money. I'm not allergic to cats at all. I'm allergic to dusty, scented litter. Isn't that wonderful?"

"So you don't have to get rid of the cats? Just change the brand of litter?" Jane made sure she was hearing this correctly.

"That's all there is to it. In fact, my new allergist is a cat lover himself. He liked my idea of a rescue shelter so much that he volunteered to donate two hundred pounds of scent-free, dust-free litter to the cause. Now what do you think about that?"

Jane could not remember when she had been so happy to discuss kitty litter.

Conversation ebbed as everyone concentrated on the entreé. Zack had poached wild salmon, topped it with *duxelles* and then wrapped it in puff pastry. The result was a golden flaky mound that sat on each plate surrounded by a creamy mushroom sauce. Accompanying the salmon were thin French green beans tied into bundles with strips of cooked red pepper.

As the waiters cleared the tables for dessert, Zack rapped a spoon against a crystal goblet to get the room's attention. Nancy stood at his side and Clarissa next to her.

Zack, who had been so bold and confident about this restaurant suddenly looked shy. "The three of us have so many people here to thank that it might take all evening and, if you'll bear with us, we would like to do it individually. But Clarissa told me I had to get my priorities straight and do first things first."

He grinned boyishly. "So before I tell you how much it means to us to be a part of this community and to be so welcomed into your lives and into the community of Acorn Hill and, of course, into Clarissa's own business, we wanted to thank you for all that you've done for us."

Nancy's eyes glistened with happiness.

"You've made Acorn Hill feel like home—a home we can both love." Zack smiled at his wife.

Jane leaned back in her chair as the applause began. Zack was one hundred percent right. There really was no better place to live.

"God is good," Louise murmured.

"The very best," Jane said as she started clapping.

The Way We Were

In memory of Ann Fox. And for Casey, Sarah, Erin,
Amber and Ashley Fox. She will be remembered.

Chapter One

"Where do you think she is?" asked Louise Howard Smith from her seat on the porch of Grace Chapel Inn. She peered down Chapel Road, and then leaned back in her white wicker rocker. Picking up a frosted glass, she took a sip of icy lemonade. "It's not like Alice to be late."

"Something must have held her up at the hospital," her sister Jane said. Jane crossed her khaki-clad legs and wiggled her toes, revealed by a pair of rubber flip-flops, admiring her freshly painted toenails. "Frankly, I'm enjoying the chance to put my feet up. I don't mind having dinner a bit late."

Louise nodded, her perfectly coiffed silver hair gleaming in the sun. Her blue eyes matched the sky blue of her blouse, which had a lace hankie peeking daintily from its pocket.

They gazed languidly at the quiet street, relishing their idleness. A peaceful hour on the porch during a summer afternoon was a luxury ever since they'd made their childhood home in Acorn Hill, Pennsylvania, into a popular bed-and-breakfast. Usually they would be engaged in the care of the inn's guests.

"It's been busy at the inn, hasn't it?" Louise said, sighing. Grace Chapel Inn had been full nearly every day for the past several weeks. "I'm not complaining, mind you, but I am a little tired. Sometimes I don't know how Alice does it, working at the hospital in Potterston and helping out here as well."

"She loves it." Jane gave her older sister a heavy-lidded glance. "You know she does. And I do too. Coming home to Acorn Hill to be with you and Alice at the inn is one of the best decisions I've ever made. I can hardly wait to introduce my friends to this wonderful place."

Louise was about to respond when Alice's car turned the corner and came up the driveway at an unusually fast clip.

"Who lit a fire under her?" Jane murmured.

Alice turned her small blue Toyota into the inn's parking lot and stepped out, pushing the door closed behind her. Her red brown hair shone in the sunlight, and her brown eyes were aglow with excitement. Louise and Jane glanced at each other, then back at Alice.

Alice hurried to the porch and up the steps.

"Hi, dear. Pull up a chair and relax," Jane said. She leaned forward and patted the padded rocker next to hers.

"You look as though you've heard exciting news. Tell us what it is."

"Exciting? Well, I'm not sure I'd say that ... except in a medical sense, I suppose. In all my years of nursing, I've seen so little of this that it is, well ..." Alice flushed and put her hands to her cheeks, "stimulating."

"Maybe I should get you a glass of lemonade," Jane suggested.

"That would be wonderful." Alice fluttered a hand in front of her face. "It really is warm this afternoon."

Jane glanced at Louise, who was smiling. Alice was normally a very composed woman. It wasn't often that she was so keyed up. Jane disappeared into the house and returned with a glass and a pitcher, which she set on a low table in front of her sister.

Alice sipped her lemonade. "I don't believe I've ever worked with a patient with this diagnosis before."

"What is it?" Louise asked. "Are you allowed to tell us?"

"Oh yes. This patient wants *everyone* to know what her difficulty is. She is encouraging us to share her story."

"Just what is this remarkable condition?" Jane asked, urging her sister along.

"Amnesia."

"You have a patient with amnesia?" Jane sat forward in her chair.

"I didn't know that actually happened," Louise said.

"It's quite rare, I imagine," Jane said.

"That's what makes it so interesting." Alice nodded. "This is a textbook case." She took a sip of lemonade and continued. "There are two basic kinds of amnesia—anterograde and retrograde. Anterograde amnesia is the inability to remember events *after* the trauma or disease that caused it. New events in the immediate memory aren't transferred to the permanent, long-term memory. It's why so many people, after an accident, say that they can't remember a thing about what happened to them when they were hurt.

"Retrograde amnesia causes people to be unable to recall events that occurred *before* the onset of the amnesia. Sometimes both can occur in the same patient."

"Trent Vescio, my old boss in San Francisco, had a motorcycle accident," Jane said. "He woke up at the hospital unable to remember that he'd even been driving his bike. I went to see him, as did several other people from the Blue Fish Grille, but when he came back to work, he admitted that he couldn't remember any of us being there."

"He recovered, didn't he?" Louise asked.

"Oh yes," Jane said, smiling. "He still doesn't remember anything surrounding the accident, but everything else is there."

Alice frowned. "What's troubling about this woman is that she is exhibiting total memory loss about her past and everything leading up to and just after the accident. It's as if she never had a childhood, a family or a history of any kind. She doesn't know if she's married or has children. She doesn't even know her own name."

"Oh dear." Louise put on the wire-rimmed glasses that hung from a chain around her neck. Though her sisters teased her about it, Louise felt that she could hear better when she wore her glasses. "That poor woman."

"I'm concerned that if the amnesia continues much longer it might be a sign that it's going to be permanent." Alice took a sip of her lemonade. "I know Mary—that's what we're calling her—would appreciate your prayers."

"You know she'll have them," Louise said.

"Yes, of course," Jane added. "How frightening it must be to wake up and not know who you are."

"For some reason, it feels as if God has placed me in Mary's life. I want to do what I can."

"Do you know about what happened to her?" Jane asked.

"It's the strangest thing. She was found on the side of a rural road not far from Acorn Hill, just past Fairy Pond. There was no car around and no sign of how she got there. She had a very nasty bruise on her head, a black eye, and numerous contusions, cuts and abrasions. Her shoulder was dislocated and she had a lot of dirt and gravel embedded in her arm and leg. The doctor said she could have been in a car accident, or maybe she had been hiking and had taken a serious fall. Of course we have no real idea what happened."

Louise practically clucked with dismay.

"If it hadn't been for the dog, no one knows how long she might have lain by the side of the road."

Both Louise and Jane looked at her in surprise. "What dog?" they asked nearly in unison.

"Finnias, an Irish setter. He's called Finn for short. Apparently Finn discovered Mary and sat down by her side. I think you know his owner, Kieran Morgan. When Kieran noticed that Finn hadn't come home, he went out looking for him. Kieran called Finn when he saw him up ahead on the road, but Finn refused to come. So Mr. Morgan went to the dog to lead him to his truck and found Mary lying unconscious in the grass," Alice said. "The dog is a real hero."

"Amazing," Jane said in a whisper, caught up in Alice's story. "To be saved by a dog. It's hard to imagine."

"What will happen to her?" Louise wondered out loud. "What if she *doesn't* remember who she is?"

"Right now she has to stay in the hospital. The doctor is worried about a concussion. But when she's ready to leave, I'm not sure where she'll go, especially if she has no idea where she belongs."

"No wonder you were so agitated when you arrived, Alice. You've had quite an extraordinary day."

"I've been praying that Mary's memory returns quickly." Alice always prayed for her patients, believing that the Great Physician was the One who could heal the soul and the body. "And I've been trying to think of ways to get her story out."

"Why does she want everyone to know her problem?" Louise asked.

"She's hoping someone will come forward and tell her who she is," Alice said, her voice sad.

"Of course," Louise said. "Well, it's too late for this week's *Acorn Nutshell*. I'm sure Carlene has the edition all laid out. But perhaps you can check with Mary and see if she'd like the idea of an article in the newspaper next week."

"Yes, I'll do that."

"Why don't you put Ethel and Florence on the case? Those two are better than television for spreading the news." Jane smiled. "That's how Lloyd does it when he wants lots of people at a city council meeting. He tells Ethel, who tells Florence, who tells everyone she knows, who tell everyone they know."

Louise laughed. "And the town hall is bursting at the seams by seven in the evening."

Ethel Buckley was their much-loved aunt, the half sister of Daniel Howard, the sisters' late father. Widowed, Ethel lived next door in the inn's carriage house and popped in to visit almost as regularly as a clock reads noon and midnight. She and her friend Florence Simpson, a well-to-do woman in the community, were, for the most part, benevolent gossips. Getting to know everything about everyone had become a hobby for them, like stamp collecting. Of course neither Ethel nor Florence was wired for a sedate leisure pursuit like philately.

"Perhaps you should go upstairs and take a shower to relax you before dinner, Alice," Jane suggested gently. "You've had a difficult day. We're having a cold supper: ham, rolls, broccoli-and-cauliflower salad, and fresh tomatoes with mozzarella and basil. I'll put it out, and we'll eat when you're ready."

Tenderly, Alice put her hand on Jane's cheek. "You are such a blessing. Thanks for taking such good care of me."

Jane rose from her chair to gather her sister in her arms. "You have so much compassion for people that sometimes I'm afraid you'll simply wear out from giving of yourself."

"I'm just passing it along," Alice said with a smile. "God gives generously to me, and I hand it on to someone else."

"And it appears that Mary may be the next lucky recipient of your gifts."

Alice laughed. "God did practically toss her into my lap."

After Alice had gone upstairs, Louise helped Jane set the table in the kitchen.

"It sounds as though Alice has a new project on her hands," Louise said as she laid out napkins.

"No doubt this woman will need someone on her side," Jane said as she sliced a tomato. "I can't think of anyone better than our sister."

Chapter Two

*L*ouise had gone upstairs to freshen up before dinner, and as Jane waited for her sisters to join her, she sampled the salad she'd made, savoring the creamy taste of the dressing. There was just enough vinegar, the merest hint of dry mustard—perfect. One of the things she was most grateful for about running the inn was that she could use her culinary abilities to please others. A professional chef, she'd turned her formidable talent toward the kitchen at Grace Chapel Inn, making their bed-and-breakfast a favored destination for travelers in that part of Pennsylvania. She'd become an expert at creating delicious breakfasts, and guests rarely missed that meal. In addition to traditional fare, Jane offered things such as pannekuken, chili con huevos, crème brûlée, Scandinavian fruit soup, brioches and chocolate pecan strudel.

Jane looked around her professional-grade kitchen. Being a chef in a country inn wasn't the life she'd envisioned for herself early in her career. She wasn't presiding over the kitchen in her own trendy restaurant or living in a sleek, contemporary apartment with a view of San Francisco. And she wasn't wearing designer clothing and jewelry—unless you considered that she had designed much of her clothing and costume jewelry herself. Nor was she supporting herself with her art. How did she measure up to the vision she'd had for herself when she left art school to tackle the world?

She was happy, contented and sure that God had put her in this place for a reason. That is what counted most, even if she didn't appear outwardly successful, not, at least, by the standards of her former college roommates.

A flutter of anticipation went through her. Her old college friends were due at the inn the next afternoon for a five-night stay. It would be the first reunion the four of them had had together in far too many years.

Jane recalled the little yellow house they'd rented during their second year of art school. It was an old, tiny place in a semirun-down part of town that was slowly being gentrified. The girls had loved the ethnic atmosphere of the area with wonderful little mom-and-pop shops and great family restaurants. They'd all been so proud to be completely independent and on their own.

"You're daydreaming again," Louise said as she and Alice entered the kitchen. "You've been particularly pensive lately. Are you excited about this reunion of yours?"

Louise was right, Jane decided as she waved to her sisters to take a seat at the table. Jane had been giving the visit a great deal of thought. It was normal, Jane suspected, to be a bit uneasy when it had been so many years—and miles—since she and her friends had been together. Would they be strangers or would they fall easily into old patterns of friendship?

"Refresh my memory. It's been a long time since we've talked about your friends. Tell us again about them when you were all in school," Alice said as she sat down in one of the wooden chairs. "You were always so busy back then that we had a difficult time keeping up with you.

"First, let's say grace," Louise suggested, placing her napkin in her lap.

The sisters bowed their heads, and Louise began. "Dear Heavenly Father, thank You for this food and for the person who cooked it. Jane is so special to us, so generous, loving and creative. We ask that You particularly bless her this week and that the reunion will be an opportunity to glorify You. And we pray for Mary, that she find not only her health but her identity. Keep her from being afraid. In Your name we pray."

"Amen," the three sisters chorused.

Alice enthusiastically spooned a helping of salad onto her plate.

Louise split open a fragrant dinner roll and looked expectantly at Jane. "Now let's hear those stories."

"Stella, Patty, Becky and I are four distinct personalities. Sometimes I'm surprised we got along at all. Other times I realize that our differences are what made us so close." Jane took a sip of water before continuing.

"Patty and Becky tended to be more reserved—in crowds, at least—while Stella and I were always up for a party."

"Some things just never change," Louise murmured.

"Hey!" Jane nudged her sister's arm. "You aren't averse to parties yourself."

Jane glanced out the window toward the carriage house as if seeing something from the past. "Soon after we all moved into the little house we rented off campus, Stella and I gave a party, and, oh what a party it was! Patty and Becky told us we could never have another—at least of that magnitude."

"Do tell," Louise encouraged.

"We decided to have a housewarming. We'd known each other the year before, but hung out in different crowds. Becky and I had a lot of mutual friends, and Stella and Patty knew each other from several classes they'd shared. Becky and I had discussed rooming together, as had Stella and Patty. Two of us couldn't afford anything very nice, but together we were able to rent the house. We thought a party would give all our friends a chance to meet one another. Besides, considering the tiny dorm rooms we'd been living in the year before, our place seemed like a mansion, and we were eager to show it off."

Jane cleared her throat. "Turns out it was not quite big enough for the party we gave. Becky and Patty thought we should each plan a guest list so we knew how many would be coming, but Stella and I figured that no matter how many people we invited, a number of them wouldn't be able to come. We decided it would be safer, like the airlines, to 'overbook' the guests rather than have an empty house."

"Oh dear," Alice murmured. "I'm glad you got over that idea before you came back to help run the inn."

"I learned my lesson, believe me. The grocery store was advertising ridiculously cheap frozen pizzas as a loss leader, so I bought twenty of them, figuring that what we didn't eat at the party, we would finish later."

"Twenty pizzas?" Louise said in mock sternness. "No wonder you were always so pleased when one of us sent you a bit of extra money. Even then you were spending it on food."

Jane laughed. "Yes, I guess so. Well, anyway, we went out and invited everyone we knew. Becky, Patty and I didn't know it, but Stella also told everyone she invited to bring a friend. That night our little house was full by the time the party was to start and people were in the basement, on the porch and spilling into the yard. My twenty pizzas were gone in half an hour and I had to run to the store for twenty more."

"How many people came to this party? Forty pizzas?" Alice marveled.

"We lost count at one hundred and fifty."

Jane's sisters both set down their forks on the table and stared at her.

She shrugged cheerfully. "Stella took a collection for the next round of pizzas. Everyone was happy to contribute because we were having such a good time. Stella collected so much that I had enough left over to buy ice cream and chocolate syrup. Anyone with a sweet tooth had to take a turn having dessert, of course, because we had only a limited number of bowls and glasses. Patty stood at the sink washing used glassware and dishes while Becky dried them and Stella and I filled them up again. We felt like the lunch ladies at school by the time the evening was over."

"But what happened? With all those people, I mean?"

"They all had a great time, played volleyball in the backyard, got to know each other and eventually—in the middle of the night—went home. The next week one of the guests sent us a coupon for a free pizza and said it was the best party she'd ever attended."

"So you pulled it off?"

"We did. Stella and I got into some trouble with our roommates, however. They said no more parties of more than fifty people, and I got strict instructions that if I was ever going to serve ice cream again, I'd have to provide disposable bowls."

"We knew you loved people, Jane, but a hundred and fifty…" Louise shook her head.

"It was a great way to start the year," Jane said. "I knew a lot more people on campus after that."

Louise stood up to refill their water glasses, and when she sat down, she said, "I'm surprised you didn't get into trouble with your landlord over that one."

"Actually, we'd invited his daughter to the party, and she had a wonderful time."

Jane leaned back in her chair and an impish smile graced her features. "We did have a problem with our landlord concerning something else, though."

Her sisters leaned forward, waiting for what she would say next.

"It served the landlord right, actually. He had no business sneaking around the house after dark."

"What?" Louise and Alice said in unison.

Jane put down her fork. "Not 'sneaking,' exactly, but how were the rest of us to know that Patty had called him to report a leak in the outside faucet? Becky, who was in the bedroom studying, heard something scratching outside her window. She was very excitable in those days anyway, and there had been a cat burglar reported only a couple of miles away, so she decided the noise was the burglar. She got on her hands and knees and crawled out the bedroom door, found Stella and me in the living room and told us we had to do something."

"Did you call the police?" Alice asked.

"I did, but Stella has a real creative streak. While I was on the telephone, she talked Becky into helping her. They took a big blanket and tiptoed outside. They saw a man kneeling on the ground, head down, looking into our basement window. They got close enough to throw the blanket over him and they were still struggling with him when the police arrived."

Alice put her hand to her heart.

"*That's* when we got in trouble with our landlord. He was just trying to fix the faucet and, since Patty had called him, he didn't think it necessary to warn us that he was coming."

Jane's eyes twinkled at the memory. "When they threw the blanket over him, he bumped his eye on the faucet handle, and it had started turning black and blue. It took the police quite a while to straighten out the mess. It wasn't until Patty came home and told them she was the one who'd called our landlord and identified him that they decided not to arrest him."

"I would have had a heart attack if I'd known all this was going on!" Louise exclaimed.

"It was just good college fun," Jane said. "He threatened to raise our rent but finally had to admit he should have alerted us before he came over."

"Well, as disturbing as that little story was, I'm beginning to get a picture of your friends," Louise commented.

Jane imagined Stella as she'd last seen her. It had been at Stella's wedding, a lavish affair. She'd married a man much older than herself, Al Leftner, an art gallery owner who, over the years, had featured and sold much of Stella's work. She'd known Al as a business collaborator for many years, but it wasn't until she was in her late thirties that they had realized they'd fallen in love.

"Stella is a wealthy woman," Jane commented aloud. "Her artwork has received a lot of recognition, much of it thanks to her husband's gallery. He's a very prosperous man. They've never had children, so her husband and her work have always been her main concerns."

"Is he the one with the sailboat and the small island?" Louise asked. "The one in the photo you received in a Christmas card one year?"

"That's Al."

"Oh my, do you think the inn will be good enough for her?" Alice's forehead creased in a frown.

"I know it will be. Although Stella has money, she's not a snob. She's more impressed by warmth and coziness than she is with cold elegance." Jane took a bite of salad, then continued. "Stella studied abroad during high school and summered with her aunt and uncle in their beach home in West Hampton, New York. Her relatives were 'very proper and very distant' she always said. The warmth and charm of the inn will be perfect. Stella will enjoy it here. Despite her upbringing—or Al's status—she's not likely to be critical or fussy." Jane laid down her fork. "About her surroundings, anyway."

"But she *is* critical and fussy about something, I take it?" Louise asked.

"Herself."

Louise's and Alice's eyebrows arched in surprise.

"When she was in college, Stella was very concerned about her weight and her looks, though she was slender and beautiful. I remember telling her once that I'd tallied up all she'd eaten one semester and it amounted to three bunches of celery, two bags of radishes and a crate of lettuce. She'd watch the rest of us eat fried chicken or mounds of take-out Chinese food and then tell us how fat she felt. We'd eat with gusto, going through a huge order of shrimp fried rice while she'd nibble on bok choy and bean sprouts. The rest of us would have loved to have looked as beautiful and put together as she, but none of us cared to put in as much effort as she did."

"That's probably for the best," Alice said.

"Becky was always *planning* to go on a diet, but she never actually got around to it. She was always bemoaning her round face and chubby cheeks, but she'd still have had those no matter how little she ate."

"Did Becky come from a wealthy family too?"

"No. Becky's father left the family when she was young, and she had to take on a lot of responsibility for her younger siblings at an early age."

Jane chuckled. "Becky was in an earth-mother stage in college and claimed that anything uncomfortable was unnatural. She threw out all her shoes except for a pair of clogs and some tennis shoes. As for clothing, if it wasn't pajamas, jeans or some dreadful granny dress, she wouldn't wear it."

"What about Patty?" Louise had forgotten about eating now, and was completely immersed in Jane's stories.

"She is an interior decorator and runs her own company. Her parents were in their forties when she was born. She also married a man several years older than herself. She has one stepchild, a boy."

"Such different personalities and lives," Louise murmured. "This will be a very interesting visit."

"I wonder if Stella still needs to be in control of everything," Jane mused.

"I imagine it was rather difficult to control you," Alice, the voice of experience, said. "I recall your having a very strong mind of your own."

A faint smile lit Jane's features. "Poor Stella. It was difficult to manage us. I remember the time she decided that we were all going to follow her beauty regimen for a month. We nearly drove her crazy. Becky would get up, throw on a long raincoat over her pajamas and go to class. I'd use all of Stella's products in the wrong order, and she'd lecture me about clogging my pores. Patty tried to follow Stella's instructions but never quite succeeded. Pretty soon Stella gave up on us and found projects that were more manageable."

"Stella sounds like an interesting character," Alice said.

"Stella was…is…complicated. Despite her talent and beauty, she was never very self-confident. Because she was always unsure of how things might turn out or what might happen, she wanted to be in control of every situation—and that included us."

"I wonder what she's like now," Louise buttered another roll as she spoke.

"So do I," Jane murmured.

"It sounds as though you all got along despite your differences," Louise said.

"For the most part. It wasn't always smooth sailing though."

"Why do you say that?" Alice asked.

"There was nothing big, but sometimes we got under each other's skin. Becky was a night owl who liked to sleep in. Patty was an up-with-the-birds sort of person. More than once, Becky sneaked into Patty's room after she'd gone to bed and turned off her alarm clock so that Patty wouldn't be up rustling around at five in the morning and wake her up."

"I suppose that didn't go over well," Louise said with a chuckle.

"The only thing that got everyone upset was the month or two that Stella decided that smoking was not only sophisticated, but also a great diet aid. She smelled up our house until a guy she was dating convinced her that the habit wasn't at all appealing. Thanks to him, she quit and never took it up again."

The kitchen door swung open and Aunt Ethel chugged purposefully into the room. Her face was flushed with excitement, and her Titian red hair looked as though she'd combed it in a hurry.

"Did you hear?" she blurted.

"Hear what?" Alice asked. Ethel had a tendency to be overly dramatic. She could just as easily be about to announce the news of an airplane landing on Hill Street as to report a new food item at the Good Apple Bakery.

"Alma Streeter, the Acorn Hill postmistress, has been called away to an emergency in her family."

"I hope nothing serious," Alice said.

"An ailing parent, I understand. Open-heart surgery, maybe, or a broken leg. I'm not sure which."

There was a difference between Ethel's diagnoses, but Jane and her sisters didn't point that out. Sometimes facts only got in the way of Ethel's fun.

Jane noticed her aunt eyeing the dinner table. "Would you like some dinner?"

Ethel pulled out a chair and sat down. "Just some of your wonderful salad, please. Oh, and a tiny bit of ham. Are those homemade rolls?"

Jane got up to get Ethel a plate and silverware, then rejoined her sisters at the table.

"Who'll be running the post office?" Louise asked as she handed the basket of rolls to her aunt.

"Someone from Pittsburgh or Philadelphia." Ethel cut her slice of ham. "She's starting tomorrow."

"That will be quite a change," Jane said, "from the big city to the little burg of Acorn Hill."

"She will, of course, need friends." Ethel practically beamed with purpose and goodwill.

"And that's where you come in?"

"Florence and I have already decided we should act as Acorn Hill's unofficial welcoming committee. Won't that be nice?"

"What inspired this idea?" Jane asked. *Why should Aunt Ethel be so interested in a substitute postal worker?* she wondered. Ethel had never been interested in the post office before except for what news and gossip she could learn in the lobby.

"A couple of things, really. Lloyd has been so busy with his mayoral duties that I thought I could help him out a bit by welcoming our new postmistress to the town."

That meant that because Lloyd was busy, Ethel had extra time on her hands. Ethel and Mayor Tynan ordinarily spent a lot of time together, and she often depended upon him to entertain her.

"My other inspiration is a Bible study Florence and I have been doing together."

"How nice." Alice said. "I didn't know you were doing that." Their aunt, despite her proclivity to gossip, was a sweet, sweet soul.

Ethel looked pleased with herself. "It's very good for us. We're applying what we're studying, making it real, you might say."

"We were just talking about Jane's college roommates who are coming tomorrow for a stay at the inn," Alice explained as they ate. "I'd like to hear more about the one who illustrates children's books. What fun that must be."

"Becky? You'll love her. She's such a sweetheart and so good-natured. I can't remember her ever being anything but kind, compassionate and generous. She's always adored children and she is wonderful with them. She was the oldest of five, and she spent many hours reading stories to her siblings. That experience might have influenced her decision to use her talent for children's illustrations."

"Does she have any children of her own?"

"Two girls and two boys. They're grown, of course, and out of the house." Jane laughed. "I remember when the last one went off to college. Becky said that, much as she loved him, it was rather nice not to compete with loud music in the house and to find food still in the refrigerator at the end of the day."

"I know exactly what she means," Ethel pronounced, "not on that scale, of course, but I have been inviting Lloyd for dinner since he's been so busy. I can't keep food in the house. He keeps telling me he has to eat to keep up his strength, that he's just a 'growing boy.'" She smiled fondly as if she could see him standing in front of her patting his ample tummy.

"Growing out, maybe, not up," Jane mumbled. Alice gave her a warning look.

All three sisters were glad that Lloyd Tynan was in their aunt's life. He kept her company, enriched her involvement in the community and made her laugh.

Ethel glanced at her watch. "I'd better go. I thought I might stop by the post office and say hello to the new post-mistress. Thanks for the wonderful meal, Jane. I wish so often that you could have cooked for your mother. You remind me so much of her."

After she'd bustled out the door, Louise and Jane began to clear away the dishes.

"Aunt Ethel certainly has a lot of zeal for getting to know the new person in town," Louise murmured. "Did I detect even more enthusiasm than usual?"

"Although I'm not crazy about Ethel's love of gossip, I'd be more uncomfortable if she weren't curious," Jane observed. "It's in her blood. You know how much she loves to be invited to any function we're having here."

"She likes the food."

"Maybe, but she's even more eager to meet our guests, particularly those she thinks are 'important.'"

"Then, considering her interest, our newcomer must be very important." Alice picked up a book that was lying on the kitchen counter and tucked it beneath her arm. "If you will excuse me, I think I'll go to bed now."

"So early?" Jane looked at her wristwatch. "It's only nine."

"Oh, I don't plan to go to sleep. I brought home some reading material on amnesia. I'm finding Mary's case quite fascinating."

"I'll be along shortly," Louise said. "I'm tired. I spent a lot of time practicing the organ today, and my back aches."

"Don't expect me to turn in early," Jane said. "I'd never be able to sleep anyway. I can't quit thinking about tomorrow."

Jane stayed up long after her sisters had gone to bed, looking at recipe books and listening to jazz.

Finally she laid one of Julia Child's tomes across her lap and stared out the window toward the garden in which she spent so much time. Her thoughts drifted again to her art school days and to the friends with whom she'd shared so much.

Slender and high-strung Stella with her model-perfect figure and long, dark hair had been popular with men. But despite all the flattery, the flowers and the dates, Stella had been dreadfully hard on herself. Jane recalled her staring into the mirror on a hunt for imaginary imperfections.

She'd change clothes a half-dozen times before a date and still leave frowning, sure she didn't look good enough. As Jane had told her sisters, Stella didn't like anything she couldn't control, and a flare-up of acne or an extra pound could upset her terribly. Jane suspected that Stella had battled with eating disorders back then.

"So lovely and so unhappy about it," Jane murmured to herself.

Patty had struggled, too, in her own way. She was obsessive about her class work. Stella did well in school without much effort. She was a true, natural talent and was always one of the professors' favorites. Patty, on the other hand, worked hard for every accomplishment. Tall, big-boned, slow-moving, meticulous, never-to-be-rushed Patty. Like Stella, she was also a beauty, but in a more natural, voluptuous way. She'd grown up in Texas and wore her blonde hair full and fluffy. Jeans and boots were her favorite default clothing.

Patty was doggedly persistent, and her projects were often notable in their creativity and beauty. Patty worked steadily until she achieved success while Stella sprinted ahead, claimed her accomplishments and went on to something else.

A memory flickered in Jane's mind, a shopping trip: Stella, in a bright blue wool pantsuit, her hair teased into a poufy bouffant and held back with a red, blue and yellow scarf, had herded them into a department store.

"We've got two hours to find each of you a new outfit. We'll have to hurry."

"I don't need anything new," Becky groused.

"I'm sorry, but something purchased at Goodwill is not appropriate for an art gallery. This is an opening! We have to be elegant, refined."

"Then you'll have to do more than buy me some new clothes," Patty said. "You're the elegant, refined one in this group. Besides, no matter what I wear I still have size eleven feet. The most beautiful shoes in the world look like canoes on me. I'd rather wear boots."

"Help me here, Jane, will you?" Stella had pleaded. "The four of us have been invited to a gallery opening by my art professor. There will be other artists there. And buyers! Not to mention a string quartet and canapés. I know you'll look perfect, but these two can't come looking like Ma Kettle and Calamity Jane."

It had been like pulling teeth but Stella had managed to convince them all that sequins were the *perfect* thing for an opening. As far as Jane could recall, they'd ended up at the gallery opening looking more like Diana Ross and the Supremes than aspiring art students.

Tall, curvy Patty was stunning, Jane remembered, but she told everyone she met that high heels were instruments of torture and Stella was abusing her by making her wear them.

Jane had enjoyed dressing up almost as much as Stella. All in all, the night had been a success even though Becky and Patty refused, for many years, to admit it.

Grinning at the memory, Jane made herself a cup of tea and grabbed a handful of almonds. It was past her bedtime, but she found the quiet moments thinking about her friends to be soothing, a preparation for their arrival the following day.

Crunching on an almond, she returned to her post and continued to stare out the window.

It was Becky to whom Jane had been closest. She was so sweet-natured, compassionate and generous that Jane had been immediately attracted to her. Becky was born to mother and loved to take care of people, to comfort them and to tend to their needs. If anyone in the house caught a cold, it was Becky who made chicken soup and doled out cough drops.

Since Jane's own mother had died giving birth to her, those maternal qualities in Becky had drawn Jane to her. The roommates had always assumed that Becky would have the largest family and find a career that involved children.

The scenario would be perfect for her patient, nurturing personality.

Jane popped another almond into her mouth. She couldn't, in fact, remember Becky ever being very upset about anything.

When Jane finally went to bed, she hoped her brain would simply turn off and go to sleep, but she had no such luck. Instead, it whirred with even more thoughts and memories of her old friends and curious questions about what the next day would bring.

Chapter Three

*J*ane awoke early on Tuesday morning. She showered, then pulled on a pair of jeans and a flowing top and headed for the kitchen. In the hallway, Jane met Louise, who looked crisp and proper as she always did.

"How do you do it, Louise?" Jane asked with a yawn. "Never a hair out of place, never a wrinkle in your clothes."

"I used to love to see you come to the breakfast table when you were a child," Louise said. "A sleepy little whirlwind. You always looked as if, rather than drifting off to sleep, you had simply dropped in your tracks, then woke up and just started moving again, giving no mind to your hair or your clothes. Although we all tried to be firm, you were the funniest little thing. Sometimes it was nearly noon before Alice or I could snare you and put you in the bathtub."

Louise put her hand on Jane's arm. "I don't tell you this nearly often enough, Jane, but I love you. The three of us being back home has been delightful for me."

Louise smiled fondly, and Jane was surprised at her older sister's uncharacteristic show of emotion. "Living with you and Alice again, here, has made me … oh, I don't know … younger, maybe."

Jane threw her arms around Louise and kissed her on the cheek. "You'll never be old to me. When I was small, I thought you had to be at least a million years old, but now that's been whittled down to a reasonable amount."

Louise waved her hand across her face in a sign of relief, and they laughed together.

A rapping sound made them turn to stare at each other.

"Is that someone knocking on the front door?" Jane inquired. "At this time of morning?"

They opened the door to see a woman in her early thirties standing there, a suitcase at her feet. She was slender and of medium height, with dark hair and eyes.

"Hello, I was hoping you would have a room available," she said. Her face was flushed and she seemed a bit out of breath. "I know it's early, but I just had to get away."

Louise stepped forward, put her hand on the woman's arm and ushered her inside. Jane picked up the suitcase, which was heavy. She wondered how long their guest was hoping to stay.

"You are *most* welcome here, my dear," Louise said comfortingly. "As it turns out, we have one room free. I'm Louise Smith, and this is my sister Jane Howard."

"I'm Claire. Claire Jenkins."

"Have you come a long way?" Louise walked toward the registration desk and began to check in their new guest.

"Just from Potterston," Claire said, smiling a little guiltily.

Louise tried to conceal her surprise at the fact that her guest lived so nearby. "Jane is about to make breakfast. You can register and freshen up, if you like. Then please join us in the dining room. We'd be happy to treat you to this breakfast. How does that sound?"

"Perfect," Claire said gratefully. "Thank you so much. Just show me what I need to sign."

Sun streamed through the windows as Jane ground coffee beans and filled the coffee pot with cold water. Fortunately, she'd made a breakfast casserole the night before. All she had to do was bake and serve it with sticky buns and fruit.

"Are you making what I think you're making?" Louise asked hopefully as she entered the kitchen and eyed the baking dish on the counter. "My favorite?"

"*One* of your favorites," Jane retorted with a laugh. "It seems to me that you walk in here and say that every morning."

Louise poured the fresh brewed coffee into a carafe that Jane had warmed with hot water. "Can I help it if you're a wonderful cook? Claire's getting settled in her room right now." Louise frowned. "Our new guest is lovely, but she was very distracted as she registered."

"I noticed you took her under your wing immediately."

"Odd, isn't it, how we react to people. I liked her at once. In fact, I almost feel the need to take care of her." Louise put a hand to her cheek. "I'd better get over that right away. Mothering the guests won't go over very well."

"A delicious breakfast is what she needs," Jane said. "When in doubt, feed someone. I'd better get busy."

"I tried to start a conversation with her, but I think I put my foot in my mouth."

"You, Louie? I'm not sure that's possible. You never make a blunder." Jane sliced into a cantaloupe and laid the sections in a pretty blue bowl.

"I saw that she was wearing a wedding ring and made some vague reference to her husband, and it changed her whole demeanor. She was looking around the room, saying how much she loved it. Then I misspoke and she grew very silent."

"Maybe that explains why she came here alone. Something may be awry at home."

"Maybe." Louise shrugged. "She wanted to know if we put chocolates on the pillows every night and if we kept fresh ice water in the pitcher. I think perhaps she's a bit spoiled."

"You don't seem to mind."

"She also seems sweet." Louise watched Jane work for a moment. "I'll go bring the coffee and fruit into the dining room and wait for her there."

Jane was busy at the stove when Louise returned to the kitchen some time later.

"Claire is enjoying her melon," she said. "And Alice has just come downstairs."

"Great. The timing is perfect." Jane bent to pull the pan from the oven and cut a generous piece for Claire and added a gooey sticky bun, then prepared three more plates. She and Louise carried the plates into the dining room where Alice and their guest were waiting.

"How magnificent," Claire murmured. "Surely you didn't do all that for me?"

"Of course I did. When we don't have guests, I make my sisters eat cold cereal. Right, ladies?"

"Don't believe her for a moment." Louise put the plates down carefully. "Enjoy."

Claire picked up her fork, then put it down again and burst into tears.

Jane regarded her with surprise. She had seen a lot of responses to her cooking but she couldn't remember the last time someone had erupted in sobs.

"Are you okay, dear?" Alice asked immediately. "Is something wrong?"

"It...it's...wonderful. I feel so pampered here."

"That's what we want. But we don't want to make you cry," Jane said.

Claire gave a wobbly smile and rubbed at her eye with the back of her hand. "I'm not usually so emotional, but I didn't sleep much last night. Let's just say I've been a little upset."

The sisters waited, but Claire didn't elaborate. Instead she seemed to shake off for the moment whatever was troubling her and started to eat her breakfast.

"How did you discover Grace Chapel Inn?" Alice asked.

"I've heard from friends how nice it is. My girlfriend spent two or three days here just decompressing after a big project at work." Claire smiled faintly. "I needed a peaceful place that would offer me time to think."

"You've come to the right spot," Louise assured her. "We'll be sure not to disturb you."

"Oh, I don't want to be alone with my thoughts 24–7. I may need someone to talk to." A shadow crossed her pretty features. "I might as well be frank with you. My husband did something that hurt me and I needed to have some space..." Her voice trailed away.

"If there is anything we can do, please let us know," Louise said gently.

Claire rose from her chair, "I plan to take you up on that. Thank you so much. I already know I made a good choice coming here. But if you'll excuse me, I think I'll go to my room and lie down. I suddenly feel like taking a nap. The charm of this place must already be working." Blushing slightly, she hurried from the room.

"God's just tossing us people who seem to need us, isn't He?" Jane said wryly.

Alice glanced at her wristwatch. "I'd love to stay and chat but unfortunately I have to go to work. I'd like to spend some time with Claire, too, but I'll have to put that off until later. Jane, have you seen my sweater? Even though it's nearly July, I get chilled in the air-conditioning at the hospital."

Jane pointed to the back of a chair from which Alice's tan sweater hung. "Over there."

"I'll visit with Claire later," Louise offered. "If she wants to talk, that is. You have enough on your plate, Alice. And Jane certainly can't take on any more, not with her friends coming in a few hours. Let me deal with Claire."

"Gladly," Jane and Alice said in unison. Claire was secure in Louise's capable hands.

After breakfast, Jane put together everything she'd need for an easy dinner of red pepper tostadas with sirloin steak, a strawberry and spinach salad and, for a fun and un- expected dessert, caramel apples dipped in chopped pecans, dried cherries and crushed candy bars. She recalled that all three of her friends had been particularly fond of caramel apples in the fall. While autumn was a long way off, this would be a nostalgic surprise for them.

Then, since there was no more preparation to be done for her friends' arrival, Jane took a couple of small packages that had to be mailed from the desk and walked toward the post office.

As usual, her path was not a straight one. She strolled by the Coffee Shop and waved at the patrons enjoying their morning coffee, poked her head in at the Good Apple Bakery to say hello and take a deep whiff of the delicious aroma of baking bread, and then veered off toward Sylvia's Buttons, a fabric and craft shop owned by her good friend Sylvia Songer.

"Hey, lady, what's up?"

Sylvia looked up from the table where she was meticulously cutting fabric for quilt kits that she sold at the store. In a vivid purple smock and appliquéd jeans, she was as bright as the multitude of prints and florals surrounding her. She pushed back a strand of her strawberry blonde hair and smiled.

"Oh, good. An excuse to quit cutting for a while. My back is killing me." Sylvia kneaded her lower back and gave a long sigh. "Sometimes I lose track of time, and when I finally remember to take a break, I'm so stiff that I wonder if I'll have to spend the rest of my life bent at an eighty-degree angle."

Jane put an arm around Sylvia's shoulders and gave her a quick hug. "You work too hard."

"That's the pot calling the kettle black," Sylvia retorted cheerfully. She laid her scissors on top of the material.

Jane moved toward the stacks of cloth. "You truly are an artist, Sylvia. These combinations are fabulous."

"Let's hope my customers think so." She sounded a little wistful.

"Business slow these days?"

"More so than usual. I know it will pick up again, but you know me. I get bored if there's not something to keep me busy."

"Then you should be working for us at the inn," Jane murmured. "It's hopping there right now. One of our guests arrived at just after six this morning."

"Isn't this the day of the big reunion?" Sylvia sat down on a stool behind the counter. Jane pulled up a second stool and faced her.

"Yes. Why don't you come over for dinner tonight and meet my friends?"

"Don't you want to spend time alone with them?"

"Alice and Louise will be there, and Aunt Ethel will probably appear on the doorstep with some minor errand just as I'm taking the food out of the oven. Besides, we haven't been together, not all four of us, at least, in many years. It might be nice to have you there in case we can't think of anything to talk about."

Sylvia burst out laughing. "Four women who can't think of a thing to say? This I've got to see."

"Great. Be at the inn by six thirty."

"Formal attire?"

Jane eyed her friend. "Pick the thread off your clothes."

"It *is* formal then."

"I'd better get going. I'm actually on my way to the post office. Do you have anything you need mailed? As long as I'm going there, I'd be happy to take it with me."

"I have a couple of small boxes." Sylvia flipped the sign from OPEN to CLOSED on the shop window and took off her smock. "A few mail orders. I'll walk with you."

They crossed the street and peeked into the window of Wild Things, the town's flower shop. Craig Tracy, the owner, was inside placing moss into a container. He waved and gestured for them to come in.

"Out for a walk?" Craig dusted off his hands and moved aside a large bucket of long-stemmed roses ready to go into the cooler.

"To as exotic a place as the post office," Sylvia said with a laugh.

"I hear it *is* a bit more exotic there these days. It's been a long time since we had a new postmistress." Craig ran his fingers through his hair, and his cowlick became endearingly unruly.

"Aunt Ethel and Florence think it's thrilling. They're eager to befriend her—for a variety of reasons."

Craig looked curious.

"Well, Acorn Hill doesn't get that many new residents. Even a temporary one is quite fascinating, something—and someone—new to be curious about. And the second reason is really quite sweet." Jane told them what Ethel had shared about the Bible study she and Florence were doing. "She wants to put her faith into action. Granted, she'll think it's a coup to be the first one to get to know the newcomer, but I can't argue with that motivation. I only hope this woman is up to their kindness.

Craig grinned knowingly. "Not to mention that they'll probably get more information from her than they could from Alma."

"What do you mean?"

"Alma has always been quite tight-lipped about the doings in *her* post office. A certified or registered letter is treated like information passed between international spies."

Sylvia giggled. "That's true. Alma has always handled the mail like every piece is marked 'Top Secret.'"

"She always lays the mail face down on the counter when she hands it to you," Craig said. "It probably drives Florence crazy. She seems to feel she has the absolute right to know everything that happens in Acorn Hill."

Jane chuckled. "True. Maybe we should pray for the new postmistress."

Craig smiled and lifted the bucket of roses, then began walking toward the cooler.

"We'd better get going," Sylvia said. "You have a busy afternoon ahead."

She stepped away from the counter, and Jane followed her toward the door.

"Wait, I have something for you." Craig put the roses in the cooler and then reached into another bucket and pulled out two pink Gerbera daisies. "Enjoy."

Jane tucked her flower behind her ear, and Sylvia put hers in the buttonhole of her white blouse.

"What a nice man," Sylvia said as soon as they were out on the street. "I'm glad his business is good. Acorn Hill is fortunate to have him and his store."

As they strolled down Acorn Avenue, Jane told Sylvia about Alice's patient with amnesia.

"No kidding?" Sylvia said as they passed Time for Tea. "I thought that only happened on television and in the movies."

"It happens in real life too."

"And the dog found and saved her? What a great story. It seems as though some major paper should come in and cover this. It might help this woman find out who she is too."

"National coverage might help her find her family even if they aren't from around here," Jane said, nodding. "That's something to think about."

Sylvia gasped. Jane looked at her, but didn't see anything amiss.

"What is it?"

Sylvia pointed down the block. "Is that a *line* forming at the post office?"

"Oh my," Jane said. "And everyone is holding just one letter, I notice. I suppose they all had to write one and bring it here to buy a stamp and mail it just to get a look at the new postmistress."

"People around here need more hobbies," Sylvia muttered under her breath. "They should all take up quilting. That would solve my problem *and* theirs."

The Acorn Hill post office was close and warm, and Jane could smell the faint scent of newsprint and ink. The building had not been modernized in many years and was much like it had been when she was a little girl.

Jane recalled that as a child, holding on to her father's hand as they waited in line to post a letter, she had thought that the little locked mail cubbies contained untold treasures. Right, left, right, her father would turn the knob and she would hear the gear click into place and see the small brass door with its thick peek-a-boo window open. Sometimes he pulled out what seemed like an enormous amount of mail. The scene reminded Jane of clowns tumbling out of a Volkswagen at the circus—just how much could that tiny space hold? Her father would methodically place the letters inside the newspaper that he received from Potterston and then lead her to the window to purchase stamps or, if the woman wasn't busy, to chat with the postmistress behind the grated window.

Jane always hoped that there would be no one else in the post office because when there were no other patrons, the postmistress would rummage in her stamp drawer and magically produce butterscotch disks wrapped in gold cellophane or red-and-white striped peppermints that she handed out to good little girls and boys.

Jane recalled the spittoon, which had sat inside the front door, and the thick sheaf of wanted posters and community announcements on the bulletin board. It had all seemed very exotic and exciting, and she'd longed to learn more about the places from which the letters and packages arrived.

Maybe I had itchy feet even then, she thought. *And it's taken this long for me to realize that Acorn Hill is my favorite place to be.*

This small post office would no doubt be modernized and enlarged as the rural areas around Acorn Hill became more densely populated and the volume of the mail increased, but for now it remained a trip down memory lane for Jane.

A mild-looking woman dressed in a pale blue regulation shirt and navy sweater was behind the counter. She wore no makeup and her faded blonde hair was pulled severely away from her face. A worried crease between her eyebrows punctuated her features.

"She looks like she could use a friend," Sylvia murmured. "I'm glad Ethel and Florence are going to take her under their wings."

"If she can stand their enthusiasm," Jane said. "Being someone's project can be rather tiring." Jane had been Ethel's pet project more than once and knew the pitfalls.

When it was their turn, Sylvia plopped her packages onto the counter. "Priority Mail for these, please."

The woman looked with interest at the return address. "Sylvia's Buttons. You have a very pretty display in your window, I've noticed." She thrust out her hand. "My name is LeAnn."

"LeAnn, I'm Sylvia Songer. It's so nice to meet you. Welcome to Acorn Hill."

"Thank you. It's a very nice town. I'm looking forward to learning all about it." LeAnn smiled. "Nothing like handling everyone's mail to learn about people, you know."

Jane was struck by the odd comment, but her friend didn't seem to notice. Sylvia was still thinking about LeAnn's compliment about her store.

"Are you a quilter?"

"No, but I'd like to be."

"I'm teaching a beginner's class starting next week. You should come."

"I don't have a sewing machine. I'm renting a room while I'm here."

"I have one at the shop you can use on class night, if you like. It's there for demonstrations, so I can't let you take it home with you, but it would help a little. I'm sure we could get a quilt pieced for you while you're here."

"Thank you. I'll consider it. It's difficult to be a stranger in a new place. I appreciate your invitation."

LeAnn would be receptive to Ethel's proffered friendship. She was a regular at the post office—often studying the posters on the walls to see if pictures of any new hard-boiled criminals had arrived. She'd no doubt be even more of a regular now that she'd set her sights on befriending LeAnn.

Chapter Four

The door to the hospital room was partially closed, and through the crack Alice could see that the curtain had been pulled around the bed. Alice tapped softly on the door.

Nothing.

She tapped again, a little more firmly this time. She pushed the door open a bit and murmured, "Hello, anyone home?"

Alice heard the rustle of sheets and took that as enough encouragement to walk in. "Hello, Mary? Are you . . ."

"I'm not Mary," a strangled-sounding voice whispered from the other side of the divider. "I don't know who I am, but I know I'm not Mary."

Alice stepped around the curtain. "I'm sorry to barge in, but I thought you might like some company. I'm a nurse here. We met yesterday." Alice wasn't attending to Mary today, but she wanted to check in on the ailing woman.

"Yes, I remember. I recall everything from the time I woke up with that dog licking my face. You were very kind to me. Thank you." The woman's eyes welled with tears. "I hope I was as kind to others in the past."

Mary was in her midforties, slender, with shoulder-length brown hair. Her eyes, a faded blue, were wary. Alice could see that her body trembled, as if the anxiety she felt couldn't be contained.

"I'm praying that your memory will come back very soon," Alice said gently. "And until then, I just wanted you to know that if there is anything...anything," she repeated for emphasis, "that I can do, please let me know."

"Thank you, Alice. And despite what I just said, until I learn my real name, you may call me Mary."

"Fine...Mary." Alice sat down on the chair next to the bed.

"When you have time, maybe you could help me get some clothing. All I have are the things I was wearing when I was brought into the hospital and they're in pretty bad shape."

Alice put her hand to the woman's cheek. "Of course I'll find you clothing. I'll bring you some of mine. I think my things might fit, or at least not be too big on you. I also have two sisters. I'll bring some of their garments too so that you can try them on and see what fits you best and what colors are most flattering. I tend to wear rusts, browns and greens. My sister Louise wears a lot of blue and beige, but my sister Jane, well, her closet looks like a rainbow exploded in it."

A smile graced Mary's features, revealing how pretty she could be if the unhappiness was erased. "I guess I talked to the right person."

"I should say so," Alice said emphatically. "God's been pushing me in your direction ever since you were brought into the emergency room, so ..." Alice spread her hands as if accepting whatever responsibility might be placed in them, "here I am."

"'Here I am. Send me,'" Mary murmured softly and looked immediately startled by her own words.

"Isaiah 6:8," Alice said. "So you know the Bible?"

"I must." Mary looked at Alice intently. "This is the first thing I've recalled and it's because of you." Tears skated down her cheeks. "Will you help me find myself again?"

Mary's request did something so poignant, so powerful, to Alice's heart that she needed time to regroup.

She laid a hand on Mary's arm. "I'll do all I can. In fact, it's just about time for my lunch break. Let me run to the mall and pick up a few things for you right now. You'll need a gown and robe, slippers, toothpaste ..."

"I've got this," Mary pulled ruefully on the faded hospital gown she was wearing.

"Well, you aren't going to be in the hospital forever, you know."

Mary looked at Alice, stricken. "But where will I go?"

Alice patted the woman on the arm. "I don't know yet. I know the hospital has a social worker who will probably try to find you temporary housing, but—"

At the sight of Mary's scared face, Alice paused. "But we'll figure it out together. I promise."

Alice was relieved to escape the hospital to go shopping. Where *would* Mary go? She was so alone in the world right now. There was no one to help her.

Except you.

Alice started. It was as if a voice had spoken in her head, a sudden knowing. God. He did that sometimes, making it apparent in which direction she was to go. She'd suspected that God had placed her in this lost, confused woman's life, and now she was sure that Mary was hers to deal with. She would persuade the social worker to let her take Mary home.

"Then I'd better get started," she murmured, and strode purposefully to her car.

When Alice came back from the mall, Mary had another visitor.

"Hello, Kieran," Alice said, her face breaking into a smile. Kieran Morgan lived on the outskirts of Acorn Hill, near Riverton, and though Alice didn't know him well, she'd met him several times. "How's the hero dog?"

"Finn is doing just great," the tall Irishman said, his pale skin turning a little pink. He ran his hand through a shock of red hair. "He's been getting an extra treat at dinner every night, and he sure seems to like that."

Alice laughed, then laid her shopping bags down on the padded chair next to Mary's bed.

"I'd better get going," Kieran said, giving Mary a little salute.

"Thank you so much for coming," Mary said, her voice faltering. "And as for Finn. I … I don't know what would have happened if he hadn't found me."

Kieran waved her words away.

"Feel better soon, Mary." Kieran turned, his rubber sole squeaking on the linoleum floor, and walked out into the hallway.

"It was nice of him to visit," Alice said as she moved some of the packages to the foot of Mary's bed. She began to rummage around in the largest shopping bag.

"He's a nice man. I'm so glad I got to meet him," Mary said, watching Alice carefully. "And I hope to meet Finn someday—"

Mary gasped as Alice pulled a soft pink robe from its white tissue paper wrapping.

"Oh, you shouldn't have!" Alice handed it to her, and she put it against her face to feel the velvety fabric. "It's too beautiful."

"Too beautiful for what? You? Hardly." Alice lifted out another box and handed it to her Mary. "Here are the matching nightgown and slippers."

Mary opened the package and held up the contents in admiration. The floral gown was fresh and springy and the pink slippers had a matching bloom attached to each toe. "Lovely!" she exclaimed.

"And I stopped at the drugstore." Alice put a large plastic bag on the bed.

She watched as Mary sorted through nail files, polish, facial cleansing products, scented powder, toothbrushes and a variety of other items. Alice had shopped until her basket was nearly overflowing, taking things off the shelves until all Mary's needs were met. Although Alice was always careful with money, she felt strongly that these purchases were necessary.

"How did you know?" Mary asked quietly.

"Know what?"

"That lavender is my favorite scent and that..." Mary paused. "How do *I* know it's my favorite scent?"

"It's coming back," Alice said gently. "Be patient, give it time."

Mary sighed and lay back against her pillows. "So now we know I've read the Bible and like lavender. That should get me far in the world."

Alice didn't say it aloud, but she was confident that the Bible would get Mary a lot further than she might imagine.

While they were looking through magazines that Alice had purchased hoping that an image in one of them might spark Mary's memory, a physician strolled in.

"Did you go on a shopping spree, Alice?" Dr. Broadmoor said with a smile, eyeing the packages. "Or have you adopted Mary?"

"A little of both, I suppose." Alice glanced at Mary. "Would you like me to leave so you can visit with the doctor?"

Mary clutched Alice's arm. "Please stay?"

Alice sat down on a chair and tried to stay discreetly out of the way while Dr. Broadmoor looked into Mary's eyes with a light and checked her reflexes. Then he referred to the chart, and a frown creased his brow.

The twenty-third Psalm came into Alice's mind.

The Lord is my shepherd . . . I shall not be in want . . . I will fear no evil for you are with me . . . I will dwell in the house of the Lord forever.

That was the promise Mary had, whether she knew it or not, remembered it or not.

"Anything?" the doctor finally asked.

They both knew what he meant. *Do you remember anything?*

"I've read the Bible and I like the scent of lavender," Mary said quietly. "That's all."

"That's something," he said encouragingly.

"But not enough." She looked at him appraisingly. "And now you're going to tell me that I can't stay in the hospital much longer."

"You are improving rapidly. We have to consider your leaving sooner or later."

A frantic look crossed Mary's face, and Alice could feel Mary's fear. What would it be like to be alone, to have no idea who you are, where you came from or why you were found lying injured by the side of a road? It was almost beyond imagining, Alice thought. It was the stuff of which nightmares are made. How, for instance, had Mary ended up hidden in the grass rather than on the road? A chill passed through Alice. If Mary's injuries had been inflicted *intentionally*, perhaps she was *still* in danger.

Mary clung to Alice's hand after the doctor left, but said nothing. Finally she seemed to doze, and Alice slipped away and went back to her assigned duties. When her shift ended, Alice did not immediately leave for home. She needed to think, so she went to the tiny chapel on the first floor of the hospital. It was a square room scarcely twenty feet wide with three rows of pews on each side of a wide aisle, which led to a small altar. Behind the altar was a painting of Christ feeding lambs. One tiny creature nestled in the crook of His arm.

For a long time, Alice sat in the peaceful silence before pulling her compact Bible from her purse. Mary knew the Bible. What, in here, would speak to her? What was it that God wanted Mary to know? What, Alice wondered, did He want her to know? She flipped it open to one of her favorite verses. "Under his wings you will find refuge; his faithfulness will be your shield" (Psalm 91:4). Alice smiled. It was comforting to remember that as bad as it all seemed God would deal with it. He was Mary's refuge and her shield just as He was for Alice and her sisters. Alice said a prayer for Mary—for her mental, physical and spiritual safety, as well as for a quick return of her memory.

Renewed, Alice replaced her Bible in her purse, tucked her purse under her arm and left the chapel. Then she headed for her car in the parking lot.

She was driving toward Acorn Hill when she impulsively stopped outside the Potterston police station. Feeling a little silly, she went inside. She approached a thickset man in a pair of khakis and a navy jacket that strained across his shoulders.

"I was wondering if I could speak to whoever is working on the 'Jane Doe' case at the hospital."

"The woman with amnesia? I'm Detective Cahill. I've been on that case."

"I'm a nurse at the hospital, and Mary and I have become friendly. I know this might seem silly of me, but I can't get it out of my mind that she might be in danger from someone."

"It's something we've considered," Detective Cahill said. "We have to deal with the possibility that someone left her injured on the side of the road since no vehicle was found with her."

Alice was relieved that the police were protecting Mary. "I was almost sure you would have considered that scenario, but I thought I should ask, just in case."

"You were right to come." The detective shook Alice's hand. "Thank you."

When Alice returned to her car, she was much consoled and glanced absently at her wristwatch. Was it so late already? Jane's guests would be arriving soon and Alice wanted to help as much as she could so that Jane could enjoy her friends.

She pulled away from the police station and turned her car toward Acorn Hill.

Chapter Five

*L*ouise and Jane were in the living room Tuesday afternoon, awaiting the arrival of Jane's friends.

"You're nervous as a cat," Louise said as Jane flitted from one part of the room to another, straightening things that weren't crooked, dusting off items that were already immaculate and peeking out of the window every few minutes.

"As that cat?" Jane asked with a laugh as she pointed to Wendell, their tabby, who was nearly comatose on the floor. "That cat doesn't seem particularly nervous."

"Wendell is a special case. I'm sure many cats would give the tip of their tails to have it as good as he does. You know perfectly well what I mean."

"I'm excited, not nervous," Jane informed her sister. "It seems as if it's taking forever for my friends to arrive. I thought they'd be here by now. They'd planned to meet and rent a car at the airport."

"Perhaps someone's plane was late," Louise suggested.

"That's possible, I guess." Jane smoothed her long, dark hair, which she'd pulled back from her face in an elaborate clip she'd made. She wore trim-fitting jeans and a coral colored silk shirt. She was lovely in a natural, unaffected way.

"Are you concerned that this reunion might be awkward?" Louise asked. "You haven't seen one another for a long time."

Jane considered the question. "No, we've talked and e-mailed for years. Some of us have met for dinner when traveling in other parts of the country. The four of us have just never all been together at once."

"Surely this isn't the first time you've ever tried to meet as a group?"

"No, but Patty was never free when the rest of us were. She not only runs her own company but she also does much of the painting. There was always an employee crisis or a pressing deadline that couldn't be ignored."

"From your stories, it sounds like you all got along well in school."

Jane stared out the window and over the yard. "Usually, yes, but even though we love one another, there's always been friendly competition among us. It's probably natural with four smart, spirited women in the same field. At one time each of us thought she was going to be the next Picasso or Georgia O'Keefe. It wasn't always art that had us competing, though. Sometimes it was clothes or academics ... or men."

Louise raised one eyebrow. "Indeed."

Jane laughed at her sister's reaction. "Think of it, Louie. We all had an eye for symmetry and beauty. Is it any wonder that sometimes we liked the same guys? Not everyone can stand up to those standards."

"When you put it that way ..."

"Although now we've found ourselves, so to speak, when we were younger, we all had big dreams about being the artist who made it to the top, the one who became famous."

"And did any of them reach that goal?"

Jane smiled. "Yes and no. None of us is famous, but we have done well in our chosen fields. Becky, for example, has won several prestigious awards for her illustration of children's books."

"That's impressive."

"She says that it's not a big deal to be able to draw a bunny or a wagon better than anyone else, but she always plays down her accomplishments. I know that established writers *ask* to have Becky work on their books. And the best thing for Becky is knowing that parents and children cuddle together to look at her pictures. It's always been her dream to do something that would make children feel safe and happy."

"She sounds like a lovely person," Louise said, smiling at Jane, who was making another trip to the window.

"I can hardly wait for you to meet her—all of them. They're all interesting. Patty, for example, was recently featured in a national decorating magazine. They recognized her for her faux painting and trompe l'oeil business. She works with the most fashionable interior designers and does specialty painting in some amazing homes. Sometimes a decorator will have some pretty fantastic ideas. Not only does Patty have to execute the ideas, but she also has to reassure the nervous home owners that they haven't made any huge, expensive mistakes."

"And you were well known as a chef on the West Coast."

"And now I make breakfasts. Quite a switch from the art world. Stella, of course, is the most celebrated in that venue. There's no getting around the fact that she is good."

"Well, I hope everything goes as planned and that everyone has a good time. It sounds like the perfect opportunity to renew old friendships."

Lord, I pray that this reunion will be a wonderful one. Bless us with Your presence, Jane petitioned. She now sat on the front porch to await her guests. Her eagerness to see her friends was growing. The conversation with Louise had whetted her excitement even further. She felt just as she had when she was a small girl, waiting for her friends to arrive so her birthday party could begin.

It was probably Becky's fault that they weren't here yet, Jane mused. Becky once said that she'd been late for her own birthday by being nearly two weeks overdue. Her excuse for her tardiness was always that she'd started out behind and still hadn't caught up.

It wasn't long before a white minivan with Pennsylvania rental plates slowly drove up Chapel Road toward the inn. Jane could see the shadows of three faces peering out the windows as they neared.

The inn was an impressive sight from the road, and Jane could imagine the threesome chattering like magpies about it. A three-story Victorian built in the late nineteenth century, the house had a large porch decorated with plants and flowers and many comfortable chairs that beckoned to weary travelers. The colors that they had selected for the inn, cocoa, with eggplant, green and creamy white trim, were historically correct and a delight to the eye. Coming to Grace Chapel Inn was rather like stepping back in time, a feeling the Howard sisters encouraged. What better way to get away than to leave the hustle and bustle of the contemporary world behind for a few days? Many of their guests told them that they'd come for that very reason.

Jane stood up and ran down the path to the curb, her heart beating a little faster in anticipation. The van pulled up to the front of the inn and three doors opened at once to a chorus of gleeful calls.

Becky, wearing a wide-brimmed hat that she held on her head with one hand, exited first. Her pretty round face fairly shone with delight and her wide blue eyes danced. "Jane, this is fabulous!"

She flung herself into Jane's open arms, and they both burst out laughing. "You look as wonderful as ever," Becky said cheerfully. "Why don't you age like the rest of the world?"

Before Jane could respond, Stella, dressed in a lime green tunic and white linen slacks that had somehow managed to remain unwrinkled during her long trip, spoke up. "What a great place you have. This is something out of a storybook. And the garden, it's perfect. I'm sure that's thanks to you. I remember your trying to grow tomatoes in the bedroom in college. And you had chives and basil on the windowsill." Stella paused for a breath. "Becky's right. You look the same as you did years ago—gorgeous."

"When do we eat?" Patty called. "I'm starved and I've been thinking about your cooking for two days." Patty was wearing blue jeans and a white shirt. Around her neck she wore a red, white and blue scarf. With her blonde hair and dazzling smile, she looked as wholesome and American as the Fourth of July. "Do you still make that weird apple pie recipe?" she asked wistfully. "I love your pie."

"The one she cooks in a paper bag, you mean?" Becky, who was pulling suitcases out of the back, asked. "I thought you were crazy the first time you made it. I was sure you'd burn down the house."

"You're the one who nearly burned down the house," Stella pointed out. "Remember that candle fixation you had?"

"It wasn't a *fixation* exactly."

"You had them all over the house."

"It was a phase. You had a few quirks too, you know. Remember the time…"

Jane listened to her friends chatter giddily and a pleasing warmth spread through her. Things hadn't changed much, even after all these years.

"Jane, darling, this is a wonderful idea. I've been looking forward to it for weeks." Stella Leftner threw her arms around Jane's neck and pecked her on the cheek. Stella still wore her signature Gucci scent. She was even thinner than she had been in college and more fit and athletic looking as well. Her arms in her sleeveless silk tunic were shapely in a way that suggested regular work-outs, and her makeup was flawless, applied, one could accurately say, by a true artist. Jane noticed that Stella had capped her teeth to hide the small overlap of her two front teeth, which Stella had always hated. After nearly thirty years, Stella actually looked better than she had in college. She was more edgy, however. A tense energy radiated from her.

While Stella was dark, tense and sophisticated, Patty was fair, laid-back and down-to-earth. Her green eyes glistened with unspoken emotion. "I can't believe you did it, Jane. You got us all here at once. I never dreamed it would happen."

"We're all busy, but not that busy." Jane gave Patty an extra squeeze.

Jane might have said more had not Becky taken another turn at hugging her. Her hat fell off her head, revealing luxuriant, wavy, chestnut-colored hair, which always looked slightly unruly.

Dear, sweet Becky looked the role of an illustrator of children's books with her wide-eyed but gentle expression and embracing, comforting manner.

Then Jane looked down and saw something quite remarkable—Becky's shoes, which looked like something Aladdin might wear. The brocade flats with turned-up toes were not the perfect complement to Becky's denim dress.

Becky saw Jane staring at her feet. "Don't you dare say a word. The gentleman at the shoe store said that this look is popular in Europe and very 'cutting edge.' I really do need to get out of my studio more often. I know how to dress bunnies, teddy bears and even penguins, but myself? My son calls me a 'benevolent fashion disaster.'"

"Well, he's wrong. You are a sight for sore eyes."

"You still know how to say all the right things, Jane." Becky said, clearly pleased.

"And how is that son of yours, the oldest boy Blaine? He was the most beautiful baby and toddler I'd ever seen. I suppose he's an old man by now."

Becky's first baby had been quite a novelty for all of them, who considered him their very own real, live doll. Becky had dated the man she would ultimately marry while they were still in art school. Jane, Stella and Patty had been her bridesmaids and less than twelve months after that, hostesses for her baby shower. Jane had only seen her other children in annual Christmas photos.

"He's twenty-seven now."

Jane was surprised not to hear the usual delight in Becky's voice when she talked about one of her children. She sounded almost...peeved...instead.

"And how are the other kids?"

"Carl, Joy and Sonja are just fine. They have good jobs, and I'm pleased with the lives they've made for themselves. Carl is getting his master's degree. Joy is engaged to be married. And Sonja is teaching first grade. She reads my books to the children."

"And Blaine?"

Becky seemed not to hear Jane. Instead she pulled a particularly unwieldy duffle bag from the vehicle.

All the chatter had brought Louise from the house. After introductions had been made, she helped them remove all the suitcases from the back of the van—enough to outfit six people on an expedition to the North Pole. Most of the luggage seemed to belong to Stella.

"We don't need to stand outside and visit," Jane said. "You can park the van in our lot later on. Louise and I will help you get these things inside. I've got lemonade and iced tea in the refrigerator."

Patty sighed blissfully. "Now I feel like I've come home. Does it get any better than this?"

Laughing, they toted their bags inside but didn't get any farther than the foyer before they forgot about the suitcases and began to ooh and aah about the house.

The front hall was warm and inviting, decorated with gold and cream wallpaper. An impressive staircase in the foyer led to the second floor.

"This place is incredible!" Stella pronounced.

"I'll show you around after we take your luggage to your rooms," Jane said. "Stella, I hadn't realized you'd planned to move in permanently."

"You know how I am, Jane. I'm just never sure what I'm going to want to wear until I know what I feel like, what the weather is, what I'm going to do—"

"Until she goes outside, licks her finger and sticks it in the air to see what direction the wind is blowing," Becky added.

"Reads the barometer and the *Wall Street Journal*—" Patty chimed in.

"And sees if it's going to be a good or a bad hair day—" Becky continued the litany.

"What do you mean? Stella never has a bad hair day," Jane said with a chuckle.

Laughing, Stella held up her hands. "Okay, I can say for sure that you guys haven't changed a bit."

"And neither have you," Becky pointed out.

They all struggled upstairs with the luggage and arrived at the second floor hall.

"This is your room, Stella," Louise said as she opened the door to the Sunset Room. "Jane says you are partial to the Impressionist painters, so we thought you'd enjoy this one." The room had terra cotta colored walls, creamy painted furniture and artfully hung Impressionist prints.

Stella lay a garment bag across the bed and stood, hands on slender hips, in the middle of the room, admiring it.

"It couldn't be better," Stella said, delighted. "You've thought of everything."

"We'll be downstairs when you're ready for that cool drink," Jane said, giving her friend a hug. "Make yourself at home."

They ushered Becky into the Sunrise Room. She was charmed with the blue walls and bright yellow and white accents.

That left the Garden Room for Patty, who had had a green thumb and loved the floral border and rosewood furniture.

"You couldn't have chosen better for us," Becky told Jane, "but whose room is that?" She pointed toward a closed door.

"We have one more guest. She's in the Symphony Room."

"I'd hoped we'd have the place to ourselves," Stella said, overhearing Jane's comment.

"It's a big place, believe me, you haven't seen the half of it yet. Besides, the other guest will be very quiet, I think."

At that moment, their topic of conversation popped her head out the door of her room to see what was going on. Her hair was tousled and she looked sleepy.

"Did we wake you? I'm sorry," Jane said.

"Don't be. All I've done since I got here is nap. The quiet ambiance of this place is as good as a sedative." Claire gave them a bright smile and disappeared once again into her room.

"She seems nice," Becky observed. "I hope we'll get to visit later."

"Stella's looking good, isn't she?" Patty said.

"No better than you, my dear." Jane took her friend's hand. "Right now I feel like I'm looking at the three most beautiful faces on the planet."

They hugged again and Stella and Becky fell upon them too. Soon they were laughing like the giddy schoolgirls they'd once been.

"You three can settle in and freshen up," Jane instructed. "I'll be downstairs whenever you're ready."

They regrouped later in the dining room around the big mahogany table. Patty, who loved good food and good candy, was already popping Swedish mints into her mouth from the dish on the table and eagerly eyeing the plate of cookies.

They chatted with Louise as they drank iced tea and ate homemade gingersnaps, telling her stories about Jane at school.

"...She was always the cook," Patty said, still eating mints. "Do you remember the time she spent our grocery money for the month to buy a rib roast and jumbo shrimp?"

"It was the most fabulous meal," Becky said wistfully. "My mouth still waters when I think about it."

"But we were all so sick of Ramen noodles, peanut butter and tuna fish by the end of the month," Stella added, "that Jane wasn't allowed to go shopping alone after that."

"Do you think you ladies could find something more interesting to talk about than my culinary adventures?" Jane suggested. "How about the time Becky brought home a litter of puppies that were being given away? Do any of you remember how much of our grocery money went to puppy chow before we gave those babies to new owners?"

"Oh, the landlord was upset about that one."

"I really don't know why he should have been," Becky defended. "Our place wasn't all that nice to begin with. Remember the wallpaper? It hadn't been changed since the thirties. There were cabbage roses on my walls so large they gave me nightmares."

"At least you had flowers. Remember the color of my walls?" Patty shuddered. "What do they call that?

Bottle green? It was so glaring that I often wished I were color-blind."

"Not a good thing for an artist," Jane said.

"I wonder if that carpet in the living room is still there," Stella said. "It looked like brown and beige worms all tangled together. It never showed any wear—no matter what we did to it, hoping to get rid of it."

"I think it will exist in a landfill somewhere until the end of time," Becky sighed. "Too bad they can't make panty hose as durable as that ugly thing."

"Decorating aside," Jane said, addressing Louise, "it was a cute little place. The living room ran across the front of the house. The dining room was just behind the living room and led into the kitchen. Our bedrooms were off to one side and we shared the one bathroom."

"There are stories we could tell you about that," Patty said laughing. "Four women and one bath the size of a postage stamp!"

"I liked that place," Becky said. "It was full of good memories. Remember how, when we moved out, we filled all the nail holes in the place with our foundation makeup?"

"But we left the place clean," Stella said. "The landlord said it was 'immaculate.'"

"It should have been. I cleaned the floor registers for the furnace with a toothbrush," Patty recalled.

"My toothbrush, if I remember correctly," Becky said. "The least you could have done was warn me before I used it that night."

"You didn't use it," Jane corrected. "You asked us why it smelled like lemons and disinfectant, remember?"

"It was a very close call."

Laughing, Louise dabbed her eyes with a handkerchief. Eventually they all sank into a companionable silence.

The tense lines around Stella's mouth softened, the worry line in Becky's brow relaxed and Patty's uncharacteristic frown lessened.

It was high time they all became reacquainted, Jane mused. No matter how celebrated Stella or Becky became, no matter how successful Patty's business was, they were still much like the girls they used to be. This reunion was just what the doctor ordered.

Chapter Six

Oh, I'm so sorry I'm late, Jane," Alice said as she entered the dining room. "I got delayed by an errand." She smiled at the group around the table. "And who have we here? The famous Stella, Becky and Patty, I presume."

The chatter exploded after Jane made the introductions. The women gathered around Alice as if they had known her forever.

"We've heard so much about you," Stella said after they were seated again. Then her eyes began to twinkle. "Is it all true? That strict big sister stuff?"

"That must have been Louise that Jane was talking about." Alice answered so quickly and with so much assurance that everyone laughed.

"Don't pay any attention to her," Louise advised them, getting into the spirit of things. "I was Jane's favorite sister."

"You were?" Jane and Alice said together, creating even more mirth around the table.

"I don't think you look much like your sisters, Jane," Patty commented. "You are all so different in appearance."

"And in personality, they say," Louise interjected wryly. "Or maybe you haven't noticed."

That comment inspired another round of laughter.

"Alice has something very interesting going on in her life right now," Louise continued. "Alice, tell them about Mary."

For the next twenty minutes, Alice recounted the story of Mary, Finn and the terrifying circumstances in which the woman found herself.

"It concerns me that someone might have intentionally hurt this woman." Alice told the group. "If someone did, and Mary can't remember who injured her, how will she protect herself?"

"You're right," Patty breathed. "How could she?"

"Of course that is only speculation, but I stopped at the Potterston police station on my way home and had a talk with a detective on the case. They'd already thought of the possibility."

"You are really getting into this, aren't you?" Jane commented.

"I suppose, but I feel better now. I was very impressed with the detective I talked to. Even though they're stymied so far, the outlook of the police is optimistic."

"Isn't there something more that they...or you...can do?" Sympathetic Becky was just as inclined as Alice to pick up a cause or to champion an underdog.

"Trust me, I've been asking myself that, but so far I have no answers."

Shortly after Alice's arrival, Ethel hurried into the house and made a beeline for the dining room, talking all the while.

"Guess who I'm having lunch with tomorrow? The new postmistress! We're going to meet at the Coffee Shop at noon. She seems very personable and open to—" Ethel stopped in midsentence when she became aware of the group around the table.

"And this must be your Aunt Ethel," Stella said, amusement playing on her features.

"Jane's college friends, of course. Welcome to Grace Chapel Inn. Jane has been looking forward to your arrival for days. The inn is lovely, isn't it?"

The guests agreed, and Jane made the necessary introductions.

"Don't let us stop you from telling your nieces whatever it was you were going to say," Patty said. "Treat us like family too. We'd like that very much."

"We almost feel like family already," Becky added. "We've heard so much about all of you from Jane."

Alice and Jane exchanged a glance. Patty and Becky had just given Ethel an open-ended invitation to regale them with gossip from Acorn Hill. Ethel embraced the opportunity.

"I've been worried about that sweet little couple from church—Mr. and Mrs. Billings. He was a friend of my brother Daniel's, you know. I've always wondered how they manage to survive financially. I know they're very careful, good stewards, certainly, but sometimes that's just not enough. Today, when I was in the post office talking to LeAnn, that's our new postmistress, I saw—" Ethel stopped again in midsentence, seemingly thinking better of finishing her statement. "Oh well, maybe I'm over-reacting. There just seem to be so many people who need so much."

Becky lifted her fingers to her mouth to hide a smile.

Jane stood up, hoping to divert her aunt's current missionary zeal. "I'm going to start dinner now. If anyone wants to take a catnap or to freshen up, now is the time."

"Sounds good to me," Patty said. "I barely slept last night, thinking about today."

"Me too," Becky echoed. "A shower would feel great."

The guests disappeared upstairs one by one, and when they had all gone to their rooms, Ethel followed Jane, Alice and Louise into the kitchen.

"Brotherly love is such an important thing, don't you think?" Ethel asked no one in particular. "We really should all show more of it." She looked as if she was going to say more, but her eye caught the time on the wall clock.

"So late already? I'd better freshen up too, and come back for dinner." Ethel always assumed she was invited to every event at Grace Chapel Inn. "You have such lovely friends, Jane. See you later."

She left the room waving backward over her shoulder.

"What do you think that post office business was all about?" Alice asked when Ethel had gone.

"Who knows?" Louise shrugged.

"She has a nose for news," Jane said, tying an apron around her waist. "Sometimes it's just best not to ask what she's up to."

Alice nodded. "What can we do to help you with dinner, dear?"

"The spinach needs to be washed and dried. Then you can prepare the salad. The strawberries are in the refrigerator. Here's the recipe." Jane handed Alice a recipe card. "Oh, and the caramel apples should be put on a tray. I'll start to sauté the steak for tostadas."

"By the way, Jane, have you seen Claire since the ladies checked in?" Louise asked.

"Not since we awakened her from her nap. But she did say she needed time to think," Jane said.

"It always disturbs me when I hear of a marriage in trouble," Louise admitted. "My own marriage was very fulfilling. I wish that for everyone."

"You and Eliot had something special," Alice agreed.

"Maybe I'll just check on her," Louise said.

"I'll stay here and help Jane," Alice said and busied herself with the spinach.

Louise mounted the stairs and knocked on Claire's door. "Mrs. Jenkins?"

There was no answer.

Louise inclined her ear toward the heavy wood door and listened.

Inside she heard a faint rustle, so she knocked again.

After a few moments, footsteps crossed the floor and the door opened a crack.

"Yes?" Claire said. Her voice was strong but her eyes were red and watery.

"We don't normally invite inn guests to join us for dinner but tonight is a special occasion," Louise said impulsively. "My sister's college friends have come for a few days, so we're having a little celebration. Would you like to join us?"

"That's lovely of you but I don't want to intrude. You have quite a group here already."

"You wouldn't be intruding. Alice and I are just getting to know Jane's friends ourselves."

"I don't feel much like partying at the moment, but thank you for asking. I packed some things so that I wouldn't have to go out to eat if I didn't feel like it.

"The invitation still stands if you change your mind."

"You are so thoughtful and caring. If only everyone could be that way. I'm sure *you* would never forget…" She stopped herself from adding more.

Another impulse came over Louise. She heard herself saying, "If there's anything you'd like to talk about, I'm here."

Claire smiled. "Thank you so much. I'll keep that in mind."

What, Louise wondered, *had happened between Claire and her husband that would send Claire off like this?* Then she shrugged, reminding herself that this brand of curiosity was Aunt Ethel's domain, not her own.

Louise decided to go to her room to freshen up as well and when she returned to the first floor, a party was in full swing.

Stella had changed clothes and was now dressed for dinner in a bright red sheath that showed the angular ath-leticism of her body. Patty wore a sparkling sweater and had fluffed her hair to its full height. Becky, ever-practical Becky, was still in her traveling clothes.

Ethel had returned. She had changed into an eye-grabbing pink dress, which made quite a fashion statement with her bottle-red hair. She was, as she loved to be, the center of attention.

"Did I tell you about the time Lloyd, my friend Mayor Tynan, had to relocate a family of baby raccoons from the attic of town hall? The city council wanted the janitor to do it but the janitor wanted the police to do it. The police, of course, said it was the job of animal rescue and they couldn't send anyone out until the following Monday. Monday! Can you imagine? And Lloyd was scheduled to give a tour of his office on Monday to some people who worked for the governor." Her cheeks reddened until they were nearly the hue of her hair.

Stella, who obviously thought Ethel was hilarious, wiped her eyes. "What did he do?"

"He had to keep them quiet—the raccoons, I mean, not the officials," Ethel said. "He couldn't have animals scratching around up there. It would never do to have state officials think we had rodents in town hall, so Lloyd took a ladder, got up there and opened a loaf of bread, which he put beside a pan of water, hoping they'd eat and settle down for a nap."

"You're kidding!" Patty practically hooted with glee.

"It worked fairly well, but the guests were a little late in arriving, and the raccoons started to move around before everyone was ready to depart."

"Then what?"

"Lloyd's secretary started playing patriotic tunes on her CD player to drown out the scratching. When the noises got louder, she turned up the music." Ethel chuckled until she started to quiver. "Lloyd said that by the time the officials left, they were all practically marching to the music. Later he got a letter saying that the visiting group had enjoyed Acorn Hill the most of all their stops and they were very impressed with the community's patriotism."

The doorbell rang, but could barely be heard over the din of laughter.

"That must be Sylvia," Jane said.

"Why did she ring the bell?" Louise wondered out loud. "She always just walks right in."

"Her hands might be full," Jane said. "I asked her to bring over some of her sample quilts. I thought everyone might enjoy looking at them. Sylvia is also an artist. Her medium is fabric and thread."

When Jane opened the door, Sylvia's hands were indeed occupied. She carried a large plastic tub into the foyer. She even wore her quilting, an elaborate, meticulously made patchwork jacket in teals, jade green and oranges.

"Sorry I'm late. I got carried away packing my samples for show and tell."

"No problem. Come, meet my friends." One by one, Jane introduced them to Sylvia.

"So you are the amazing person Jane mentions so often," Stella said, grasping Sylvia's hand in both hers. "I'm delighted to meet you."

"You talk about me?" Sylvia looked at Jane in surprise.

"Of course. You're a good part of the reason I've enjoyed Acorn Hill so much since I moved back here. Don't you know that?"

Sylvia flushed pink.

When it was her turn to meet Becky, Sylvia surprised her by saying, "I have to admit that I went to the library and checked out a couple of your books. I'm fascinated by illustrations, and yours are extraordinary."

Now it was Becky's turn to blush. "Thank you for going to the trouble. I'm flattered."

"I looked at them for a long while," Sylvia said. "I could imagine some of your pictures made into patterns for quilts."

Becky's eyes grew wide. "Really? What a wonderful idea. I've often imagined one of my characters re-created as a toy or in a coloring book, but a quilt. Wouldn't that be clever? Do you actually think it's possible?"

"You'd have to enlarge a character or scene in order to make a pattern, but I've done that several times. You'll see some of the things I've made."

Within minutes they were discussing the complexity of transforming one of Becky's illustrations into a quilt pattern, talking as if they'd been friends forever.

Jane sat back and watched the interactions with delight. Sylvia and Becky had their heads together. Stella and Patty were listening with rapt attention to Aunt Ethel telling a story about Jane's father, and Louise and Alice were joining in. This was exactly what she'd hoped the reunion would be.

♦

Some minutes late, Jane announced dinner. "Please sit down, ladies," Jane said, knowing the women would keep talking all evening if she didn't interrupt.

After they were settled around the dining table, Jane turned to Louise. "Would you please lead us in prayer?"

"I'd be delighted." She bowed her silver head. "Dear Heavenly Father, thank You for gathering us here today. Bless our food, our conversation and our fellowship. If there is anyone in this house who can use Your curing touch, please administer Your healing. I pray that this weekend will be a blessing of friendship and fellowship. And bless Jane as she prepares our food. Amen."

A murmur of *Amens* echoed around the table.

As the guests ate their salads, Jane served the tostadas. When she got to Louise, she leaned forward and whispered in her ear. "That wasn't exactly the prayer I expected."

Louise glanced up at her. "It wasn't the prayer I'd planned to pray either. It just came out."

"Well, it was lovely."

"Perhaps I was thinking of Claire."

"I'll go up later and invite her for dessert."

"She may not want to be disturbed."

"Anyone should want to be disturbed for my caramel apples," Jane said cheerfully and continued to serve dinner.

As the food was passed, Ethel, who had been so gregarious before dinner, grew silent, as if her thoughts were miles away.

"You're quiet, Aunt Ethel," Alice observed. "Have you had a busy day?"

Ethel looked up from her salad. "I was just thinking of something else. Did you know that Fred and Vera Humbert's daughter Jean is planning to spend time in Australia?" Ethel asked.

"I had no idea." Louise was curious. "I saw Vera yesterday and she didn't say a thing about that."

"She has a friend there—a *special* friend." Ethel nodded sagely. "I do hope she doesn't decide to move there. It would break Fred and Vera's hearts to have her so far away."

"Vera didn't mention anything about that the last time I spoke with her," Alice said. "I'm sure that she would have told me. Although Jean was with her, so maybe she didn't feel free to talk about it."

"I don't think Vera knows how serious this is," Ethel said primly.

And you do? All three sisters' expressions said. *How?*

Ethel, however, was more interested in imparting gossip than explaining where it came from.

"Oh, to be young again," Stella sighed. "Romance, travel, first love..."

"What do you mean 'to be young again'?" Jane spluttered. "You *are* young. We're only as old as we think, I say. I'm not a day over twenty-nine, myself."

Stella looked at her doubtfully. "The mirror doesn't lie, Jane."

"Jane looks great," Patty responded. "And so do you and Becky."

"And you too, Patty," Becky added. "We aren't old. We're just becoming what we once dreamed we would be— especially you, Stella. Your reputation as a watercolorist is growing, your marriage is happy, you look like a model...."

Stella stared sadly at Becky as if to say, *Oh, you deluded darling . . .*

"Well, it's true."

It was apparent that Stella didn't agree with her friends' comments, but she didn't say more.

"How is your family, Becky?" Patty inquired, changing the subject. "You've hardly said a thing about them."

Becky shrugged as if she were uninterested in the subject.

"What about Blaine? He's just finishing his master's degree, isn't he?"

Becky nodded shortly.

Sensing it was time for a diversion, Jane slipped out of her chair and quietly mounted the stairs to Claire's room. She rapped on the door.

"Yes?"

"It's Jane Howard. I know you didn't want to have dinner, but I thought you might enjoy having dessert with us. Nothing fancy. Caramel apples, actually. My friends have a particular fondness for them so I made some just to surprise them. Interested?"

The door opened, and the light from a small lamp framed Claire in the doorway.

"Caramel apples? Seriously?" She appeared amused. "I haven't had one of those in years."

"Then it's time. And feel free to tell me if I'm being a pest. We don't want to intrude."

"You aren't. Funny, but if I'm alone, I want company. And if I'm with people, I feel like being alone. I don't quite know what I want these days." Claire studied Jane. "Have you ever been married?"

"Once. It didn't work out the way I'd hoped."

"I'm sorry. I shouldn't have pried, but my husband did something that's troubling me a great deal. That's why I needed to get away." Her eyes flashed and Jane saw in her expression that she didn't like to be crossed. Then Claire smiled a little and her features softened. "Or maybe I just need to drown my sorrows in a caramel apple."

"It's worth a try. Come on."

A smile spread across Louise's face when Jane and Claire walked into the dining room together. She made introductions while Jane presented her playful dessert.

"Well, Jane, you haven't lost your touch," Becky said as she dabbed the corners of her lips with a napkin. "Your cooking is even better than it used to be. This is all so lovely that I think I could stay here forever. Maybe I will. It's better than going back to all the work at home." She sounded very serious when she said it.

"Or perhaps we could take Jane back with us," Patty mused. "Can anyone figure out how to do that?"

"We've been hearing all sorts of stories about Jane and her friends when they were in college," Louise told Claire. "Had I known what my little sister was up to, I might have worried more about her."

"We were practically angels," Jane informed her sister. "Why, even the one time I thought we might have gone too far turned out for the best in the end."

"Whatever do you mean?" Ethel frowned. "The time you 'might have gone too far'?"

Suddenly Becky began to blush to the roots of her hair.

"It started out innocently enough. Becky had broken up with a boyfriend—one we didn't much approve of anyway," Patty said. "And she moped around the house like Eeyore from *Winnie the Pooh*."

"It wasn't *that* bad!" Becky hesitated. "Was it?"

"You actually *said* the words 'Woe is me,' Becky," Stella reminded her. "That's bad. I thought people only said that in B-movies."

"Anyway," Patty picked up the story, "we decided we needed to help her out. You know, give her something to distract her, to cheer her up."

"What was that?" Sylvia asked.

"We thought she needed a new date." Patty flushed. "But maybe we did go a little overboard in getting one for her."

"What did you do?" Alice asked warily.

"We took out a personal ad for her in the local paper," Patty said.

"You didn't!" Alice exclaimed, horrified.

"I'm afraid we did," Jane said with a sigh. "Thinking back on it, it was a crazy idea, but at the time..."

"I hope you told any man who called that you weren't interested," Alice said.

"Not exactly." Becky flushed scarlet. "I married one of them instead."

She burst out laughing at Alice and Louise's horrified expressions.

"He called while my conniving roommates were out. They hadn't told me what they'd done, so by the time Jack explained to me where he'd gotten my number and I'd told him who I suspected had put the ad in the paper, we'd had a good laugh. It turned out that his own roommates had dared him to call, and he'd done it just to quiet them." Becky's blue eyes twinkled merrily. "We showed them all, didn't we?"

"You can't believe how scared we were when we heard that someone had actually answered the ad," Patty admitted. "It was a silly lark. We hadn't considered the possible consequences."

"We were even more upset when Becky said she was going to date him. Just to get even with us she made him sound mysterious and creepy. We were terrified for her."

"Served you right," Becky said smugly.

"She didn't tell us that he went to the same school or that they'd discovered his father and Becky's uncle were old friends," Patty said.

"It's a small world," Becky said with a shrug.

"But we didn't know anything about him," Stella said. "And Becky was so mysterious. She was just trying to scare us for what we'd done."

"It worked too. You quit playing tricks on me after that."

"I should hope so." Louise leaned back in her chair. "If I'd known all you were up to Jane, my hair would have turned gray years earlier."

Chapter Seven

S ylvia, may we see the quilts you brought?" Stella asked, settling into the couch in the parlor.

"Sure. I'll get them." Sylvia jumped up and returned with the large container she'd carried from the shop.

While Jane and Alice cleared dishes from the dining room, Louise served coffee to the group in the parlor.

Sylvia took the lid off the container and lifted a folded piece from the top of a mound of fabric.

"Here's a little farmyard scene I did. I based it on a photo a friend sent me."

She unfolded a quilted wall hanging about three feet square and held it up, revealing a charming, primitive rendition of a red barn, white house and a yard filled with chickens, horses and cows.

"This represents my friend's home. I'm going to send it to her for Christmas."

"It's remarkable," Becky breathed. "It reminds me of my grandparents' place in Minnesota."

"And here's a quilt I just finished as a baby gift," she said, reaching into the pile. "I didn't have the time to work on it before the baby was born so I thought I'd take a stab at the baby's portrait. It took forever but it's worth it, don't you think?" She unfurled a soft blanket with a portrait of a baby's face done in various flesh-toned fabrics. The child's bright blue eyes and rosy lips smiled out at them.

"It looks so difficult to make."

"I like the challenge. If she decided to pursue it, this is what Becky's artwork would look like when the quilt was done."

"You *are* an artist," Stella said, "an amazing one. How many people can actually re-create a photo from bits of fabric?"

Claire, who had been quietly sipping coffee, spoke up. "I'd give anything to be able to make something as beautiful as that. It's like a fabric mosaic."

"You ladies flatter me," Sylvia responded modestly. She pulled out samples of some of the things she was currently working on, beautiful compositions of rich greens, deep blues and warm reds.

"I wish I'd taken up a sensible hobby like this when I was young," Becky said, running her hand over the surface of a pastel baby quilt.

"Me too," Patty said. "After that candle phase passed, you got into macramé, remember?"

"She macraméd all sorts of things—hanging plant holders and purses," Jane shook her head in amazement at Becky's productivity, "and even curtains."

"Just one curtain. Granted, it was large, but I thought it looked nice as a divider between the kitchen and dining room."

Patty stirred a sugar cube into her coffee. "Those were the days."

"I have an idea," Stella announced. She turned to Sylvia. "Would you consider working for me? We're going to be here until Monday morning. I'd like to hire you to help us each start a quilt while we're here. Then, even though we can't stay at Grace Chapel Inn permanently, we can take a bit of it home with us, as a memory."

Patty brightened. "That would be fun. Could you, Sylvia?"

Sylvia glanced at Jane who smiled encouragingly. "Well, the shop has been slow lately. I suppose I could have Justine Gilmore watch the store. She's done it before."

"And I want to buy the fabrics for all the quilts," Stella said. "It will be my gift to each one of you." She looked at Claire. "And you too, if you haven't got other plans. I can't think of a more pleasant way to spend the week. It's good to chat and be busy with our hands. A lot of problems can be solved when women share as they work." Stella grinned. "In fact, maybe I'll start a quilting group on Friday nights when I get home. I'll call it Quilt Therapy."

"This all sounds wonderful," Ethel said, "and I wish I could join you, but I have plans with LeAnn. Maybe I'll stop by tomorrow and check on your progress."

She didn't say it, but all three Howard sisters knew enough to add "*And eat dinner with you.*"

"Please join us, Claire." Louise's eyes were intent.

"But you don't even know me," Claire said, taken aback by the offer. Still, she looked interested. "You ladies are very generous. I could take a lesson or two from you."

"Yes, a *quilting* lesson," Louise said with a laugh. "It's settled then."

"Come to the store tomorrow morning, and we'll start putting together ideas and picking out fabric," Sylvia said. "A quilt retreat—this will be fun."

"What do you think of Stella's idea to make quilts?" Alice asked Jane later in the evening as they cleared up in the kitchen. Louise sat at the table looking over the registration book for the following week.

"I think it's wonderful." Jane industriously polished the sink. "It's great to see my friends, and they all appear very happy to be here, but they seem to have a lot on their minds. I know them well enough to see the signs. Stella appears to be nervous. Patty is a tad sour when she and Stella are together. Becky ... well, she's the most puzzling."

"What do you mean?"

"The 'old' Becky would never have made a reference to not wanting to go home to her family, even in jest. Something's bothering her."

"She is older now and has had more life experiences," Alice said gently. "People's personalities do change."

"That's not what I'm talking about. Becky's *spirit* seems heavy. Everyone is putting on a happy face, but I sense that there are lots of things not being said." Jane carefully put her feelings into words. "That's why I like the idea of our quilting together. As Stella said, it's easy to talk and share when one's hands are busy. Once we all relax, the barriers may come down."

"It is also an opportunity for us to get to know your friends better." Louise paused to look up from what she was doing. "And I think it was lovely that Stella included Claire. I'm glad she agreed to join us."

Jane walked over and hugged her sister. "I think that you have a special fondness for Claire."

"She seems to have the weight of the world on her shoulders right now."

"I know what you mean about that weight on one's shoulders." Alice put away the dish towel she'd been using and took a seat across from Louise. "That's exactly how Mary, the woman at the hospital, looks. Heavily burdened."

"What's going to happen to her, Alice?"

"No one knows. She's recalled a couple of things, like some bits of Scripture, but it's not enough to help her locate her family or discover something about her past."

"If she knows Scripture, maybe she attended a church somewhere. Could you start there?" Jane suggested.

"It's a thought. I'll mention it to Rev. Thompson or Pastor Ley," Louise said. "They have a list of every congregation in the area. They could give that to the police. Perhaps they could send out a photo of Mary to see if anyone recognizes her."

Alice frowned. "On the other hand, she could have come by car from quite a distance."

"God seems to be directing you to help Mary," Louise said. "He knows what He's doing."

"Don't forget about Aunt Ethel. She'll spread the news." Jane joined them at the table.

"If she's not too busy with the poor woman she's determined to befriend," Alice said. Jane laughed, but Louise gave them both a stern look.

"Extra prayers tonight," Louise said, nodding. Her sisters nodded in agreement.

◦

The door to Stella's room was slightly ajar as Jane passed. She stopped and rapped softly.

"Come in," Stella called from the bathroom.

"You didn't even ask who it was."

"It had to be someone I like. Those are the only people here, you know." Stella's face was covered in an aqua facial masque and when she spoke her lips barely moved. She'd pulled her hair back from her face with a terry-cloth band.

"You would scare off a bad guy with that gunk on your face anyway. What's it supposed to do for you?"

"It's drawing out impurities. I've become a bit of a fanatic about my skin. I wish I'd started doing this years ago, before I was a lifeguard and thought of a tan as beautifying, not sun damage." She looked worried even beneath the concealing masque. "There are so many things I wish I'd done differently. Moisturizer, sunblock, organic foods . . ."

"But you're doing all that now." Jane sat down on the bed and made herself at home. "So what's the point of looking back?"

"Hold on a minute. I've got to chip this thing off." Stella disappeared and water began to run in the bathroom.

Two minutes later Stella emerged maskless, with ruddy cheeks.

"Don't you have regrets, Jane?" She picked up the conversation right where they'd left off. "I would look so much better now if I'd listened to my mother. 'Stella, wear a hat in the sun,' 'don't lie on the deck and bake like a pan of cookies ...' you get the idea."

"You're always hard on yourself."

"You think I'm hard on myself now? You should have known me at fourteen."

"What were you like back then?" Jane took one of Stella's pillows, laid it across her lap and put her elbows on it, propping her chin in her hands, just like she'd done a hundred times when they'd roomed together.

"About forty pounds heavier, for one thing."

Stella appeared amused by the startled expression on Jane's face. "That's right. I was a roly-poly teenager."

"It's difficult to believe, looking at you now." Jane cocked her head a bit and studied her friend. "You never mentioned a weight problem."

"It was too close to me back then. I didn't want to talk about it. Later it just didn't seem relevant." Stella curled up on a chair across from Jane. There was no hint of a chubby teenager in the lithe woman of today. "I allowed my feelings about my looks to run my life. In some ways I'm afraid I still do."

"You look fabulous for your age."

Stella groaned. "*For my age?* I don't want to look my age, Jane. I want to look younger."

Stella, with her feet curled under her on the chair, her hair damp and tousled and her face glowing from the cleansing, looked just fine to Jane. "What's this about, Stella? Fighting World War Wrinkle? I've noticed you staring at yourself in the mirrors around the inn."

"Sometimes I still feel like I can't keep up," Stella said softly. "You should see some of the beautiful young women who come through my husband's gallery. Sometimes I don't feel fifty, I feel a *thousand*! I don't like the idea of being an old lady doddering around the edges of this glamorous crowd any more than I enjoyed having the nickname 'Chub' in junior high."

"You are talented, beautiful and stylish. Who could hope to compete with that—at any age?"

"That's what my husband Al says." She sighed. "He's a wonderful man." Stella began to look at her finely polished finger nails, and her next question was not as casual as she tried to make it sound.

"Have you noticed that when a woman turns fifty she disappears?"

Jane held out her arm and looked at it. Then she waggled her fingers. "Nope. Still here."

"Not literally, of course, but figuratively. People don't *notice* women our age. We become...inconsequential."

"It's not other people we need to be noticed by, Stella, it's God, and He's fully aware of our presence."

Stella smiled a little wanly at Jane. "Oh, never mind. You're so unaffected and natural that these types of things never enter your mind."

"And they shouldn't enter yours." Jane stood up and embraced her friend. "If you worried less, you could smile more, and everyone would notice that. But I know that you can't turn off old feelings and memories like a light switch. Just don't let them keep you from recognizing the person you really are."

Stella put her hand on Jane's cheek. "I'm so glad we're here. It does me good to be around someone calm and centered like you."

Jane didn't dispute Stella's statement. While no one was ever "calm and centered" all the time, as long as she stayed close to God, Jane did a better job of keeping on an even keel.

Chapter Eight

*A*lice hummed along with the radio as she drove toward Potterston Wednesday morning. The day before had been full with the arrival of their guests at the inn, but she didn't feel tired. She was, in fact, invigorated. It was early in the morning, and the sky was growing incrementally lighter as the sun rose in the sky. Dawn was a bit of God's most artistic handiwork, she mused.

She was more eager to get to work today than she had been in a long time, and it wasn't because she had only a four-hour shift this morning. She was brimming with curiosity about how Mary was doing. Had she remembered anything? Had the police discovered something new?

She parked in her usual spot in employee parking and entered the building through a side door. She changed into the practical, heavy-soled shoes she preferred to wear on the unyielding hospital tile floors, ran a comb through her hair and began her day.

Alice was swept into her duties and didn't find time to visit Mary's room until her shift was complete. The door was closed, and she could hear voices inside. Then she heard Mary wail loudly, "But what am I going to do?"

Impulsively, Alice rapped on the door and stepped into the room. One of the physicians on staff was there, his nurse and, to her surprise, Rev. Kenneth Thompson.

Mary turned frightened eyes toward Alice. "Help me. Please." Her external bruises were fading rapidly, but she seemed as wounded as ever on the inside.

Alice looked from the doctor to Rev. Thompson and back to Mary.

"Hello, Alice. Louise passed on the suggestion about faxing area churches with Mary's photo. I did that early this morning, but we've not received any responses yet," Rev. Thompson said. He was, as always, immaculately dressed, wearing a white button-down shirt and a navy blazer with a small gold cross in his lapel. "I asked that they include Mary in their prayer chains."

"The doctor says I'm ready to leave the hospital." Mary's voice quivered. "But I don't have anywhere to go."

"We'll call the social worker and—" the doctor began, but Mary cut him off.

"I don't want a social worker. I want my life back. You're a doctor—do something!"

"Our church, Grace Chapel, has a fund for emergencies. This definitely falls into that category. We can provide you funds for a hotel room and meals," Rev. Thompson said.

Mary turned to Alice. Now there was terror in her eyes.

Alice's heart, which was tender in any circumstance, melted completely. A single verse came into her mind. *"Religion . . . is this: to look after orphans and widows in their distress"* (James 1:27).

"Mary, you'll come home with me," Alice said.

That left them all speechless.

"But you don't know me," Mary finally said. *"I* don't even know me."

"I know you need help. I also know that the Good Samaritan who found the injured man by the side of the road didn't know him either, but he stopped anyway."

What Alice didn't add was that those words of invitation had come out of her mouth practically unbidden. She hadn't had time to think it through and obviously hadn't consulted her sisters. The inn was completely full, and every bed was taken, yet she knew that God was prodding her to help this woman. If God wanted something to happen, He'd help her get it done. All she had to be was obedient.

Mary stared at her puzzled, until Rev. Thompson asked Mary gently, "Do you *know* the story of the Good Samaritan?"

Mary's brow furrowed. "It sounds as though I should know it, but..."

Rev. Thompson opened the Bible he was holding to the book of Luke. "In Scripture, a lawyer once asked Jesus whom he might consider his neighbor," Rev. Thompson said. "Jesus told a story about a man beaten and left for dead on the side of the road. Three men walked past him as he lay on the ground. Two moved to the far side of the road but the third stopped to help, bound his wounds and paid an innkeeper to care for him. '"Which of these three,"' Rev. Thompson read, "'do you think was a neighbor to the man who fell into the hands of the robbers?"' Jesus asked. The lawyer responded, '"The one who had mercy on him"' (Luke 10:36).

Mary stared at Alice. "You'd do that for me?"

"Of course I would. Acorn Hill isn't far from here. You can stay in touch with both the doctor and the police."

"Are you sure you have room? I don't need much space, but taking me into your home . . ."

Alice exchanged a glance with Rev. Thompson. "Let's just say that somehow, I'll find you room at the inn."

It wasn't until Mary was checked out of the hospital and sitting in the waiting room that Alice began to get nervous.

"I hope my sisters won't be upset with me," she said in an aside to Rev. Thompson, who was helping her with the discharge paperwork.

"You three are a household of Good Samaritans." His smile warmed his expression. "I believe they will be glad to help."

"Oh, I have no doubt of that. The problem is that we don't have an empty bed in the place. Every room is occupied. I didn't stop to consider that. The invitation just spilled out. We do have ways of squeezing another person or two into the house, but it means sharing bedrooms."

"If God extended the invitation then He'll find the space for her. And, don't forget, our Helping Hands ministry will help with the cost of Mary's board and room."

"It'll be interesting to see how God works things out this time," Alice said with a worried smile before she motioned for Mary to go with her to the car.

On the way to Acorn Hill, Alice told Mary about her sisters and how they had come together to turn their old childhood home into a bed-and-breakfast. She entertained her with stories about Louise and Jane and how she and Louise had taken on the role of mothering their little sister.

"We tease Jane about giving us gray hairs, but of course it isn't true. Jane is such a blessing, and her talent in the kitchen is a good part of the reason Grace Chapel Inn is so successful."

Mary looked interested, so Alice continued. "Even when she was tiny, Jane had a flair for cooking. One day I was making oatmeal raisin cookies and discovered that the box of raisins was missing. First I blamed Louise for eating them, then went to my father to see if he'd been snacking on them. It wasn't until I found Jane in the sandbox 'cooking' up a storm with sand, dirt, water and my entire box of raisins that I realized that we should channel her talent into something that was more edible."

"I can't tell you how much you've lifted my spirits. My appetite is coming back. Even raisin mud pies sound good to me right now." Mary patted her concave tummy. "It certainly appears I need nutrition."

"You may be a little thin right now, but Jane'll have you back to your normal weight soon."

"I don't know what my normal weight is. Maybe this is it."

The clothes that Mary had worn when they found her were those of a larger woman than the person seated next to Alice. Either Mary was wearing someone else's clothes, or she had lost weight, as well as her memory, in the recent past.

"What are your favorite foods?" Alice asked. "I'm sure my sister will want to know."

"I'm not sure. In the hospital, I didn't like much of anything."

"You aren't the first, nor will you be the last, to say that. Fortunately, Jane's cooking is light-years beyond that of the hospital."

"They served mashed potatoes one night, but they tasted like the inside of a cardboard box. And the peas might have been good, but they'd cooked all the color out of them."

"I don't know what Jane is fixing tonight, but it will be delicious. Her three best friends from her college years are at Grace Chapel Inn for a reunion, and she's going all out for them."

"I wonder if I went to college," Mary said. "It's hard to guess because right now my mind is mostly blank."

"Your memory will come back. You just have to give it time."

"And what if it doesn't?"

"Then we'll cross that bridge. There's no use worrying about something that probably won't happen."

When they arrived at Grace Chapel Inn, Alice hustled Mary through the kitchen and up the stairs to her own bedroom before anyone saw them. Alice heard laughter in the dining room but didn't want to spring

Mary upon her sisters while their guests were present. They might be upset that she'd offered shelter at a time when the inn was so busy. Yet, she suspected that they would understand.

"This is a beautiful house," Mary said, awe in her voice, as they walked down the hall to Alice's room.

"It's brought us a lot of joy," Alice said. "God is good. Now I want you to lie down while I go downstairs and tell my sisters that you are here."

"They'll be upset."

"Now why would you say that?"

"Because people don't just drag strays home off the streets. That's what I am, a stray. Maybe I'm dangerous or crazy or a thief. Have you thought of that?"

"Not likely. Rest a few minutes and I'll be back for you."

"Do you have a Bible I could look at while you're gone? I want to read that Samaritan story."

"Of course." Alice retrieved the Bible and opened it to the appropriate chapter in Luke. Handing the book to Mary, she patted her hand and then left the room.

Alice took a deep breath as she marched downstairs resolutely to where her sisters and the guests were visiting.

"Hello, everyone . . ." Alice stared at the dining room table, which was now piled high with fabric and shopping bags.

"We went shopping at Sylvia's Buttons while you were gone and got the materials we'll be needing to begin our quilts. Beautiful, aren't they?"

Stella picked up a piece of royal blue fabric with small purple flowers and waved it in the air. "Come see what we've chosen."

Stella's fabric choices were all jewel-toned—sapphire, emerald, ruby, topaz and aquamarine. Becky had chosen pastels and prints with flowers, bunnies, ducks and fish in the patterns.

Patty's colors were a strange mishmash. It was as if she couldn't quite make up her mind what to choose, so she'd chosen a little of everything. The quilt was not unlike what Alice had seen of Patty herself, a seeming conflict of moods.

"Jane, since you are going to help the others, would you set up cutting and ironing stations for us so we aren't tripping over each other? I brought an iron and I know you have one." Sylvia, her strawberry blonde bun sprouting pencils, had to raise her voice to be heard above the noise in the room. "The rest of you will have to be very careful to cut the fabric accurately according to your pattern. No gabbing and forgetting what you're doing now."

Discreetly Alice beckoned Louise and Jane into the kitchen. No one else noticed their leaving.

"What's up?" Jane asked. "Are you planning to sew, or would you like to help the others as I am? You'll have to get your fabric if you're going to join the fun."

"I'm looking forward to quilting lessons with Claire," Louise said.

"Sylvia said today was the best sale day she's had in her shop in weeks," Jane said. "Stella went wild buying gizmos and gadgets for cutting and sewing. We've got rulers, rotary cutters, quilting pins, threads, you name it, Stella bought it. We also borrowed more machines and two tables, one from Aunt Ethel and another from Vera."

Jane paused, finally noticing her sister's silence. "Alice? Is something wrong? You aren't saying a word."

"I have a confession to make. I hope the two of you aren't going to be angry with me."

That got her sisters' full attention.

"Mary, the patient I've been talking about, was released from the hospital today."

"She got her memory back? How wonderful," Louise said.

"No, she didn't, unfortunately, and the doctor said she wasn't a candidate for hospitalization any longer."

"But what will she do?" Jane frowned. "They can't put her out onto the street."

"That's what I said." Alice sounded relieved.

"But they did it anyway?" Louise asked.

"Well, they discharged her. That's why I had to bring her home with me."

Jane did a double take. "What did you say?"

"I brought her to stay with us. What else could I do? She's so fragile right now. She *needs* us."

"Where will we put her?" Louise asked, ever practical. "The inn is packed to its eaves right now. You see what's going on in the other room."

Alice chewed on her lip. "I know, but I thought . . ."

"I'll ask Patty if I can bunk with her tonight. I'd rather enjoy it—for old times' sake," Jane said. "Mary can have my bed. We'll figure out the rest of the week later."

The relief on Alice's face was clear. "You'd do that?"

"You don't do things frivolously, Alice. You were led to do this. We'll try it for tonight. Maybe one of us can stay at Aunt Ethel's tomorrow night if need be. I think Patty and I will enjoy bunking together. We'll work it out."

Alice flung her arms around Jane. "I'd hoped you'd say that."

She turned to Louise. "You don't mind?"

"Of course not," Louise said. "Who am I to second-guess God?"

"Bless you both." Alice placed a kiss on the cheek of each of her sisters. "Maybe Sylvia will take Mary and me to her shop, and I can buy fabric for her and help her make a quilt as well."

Alice's expression radiated determination. "We also have to figure out some way to jog that sleepy memory of hers."

Chapter Nine

*P*lease don't feel obligated to include me in your party. It's awfully kind of you but…" Claire looked at Louise pensively.

"Nonsense." Louise eyed the younger woman. She had brought a selection of Sylvia's fabrics to Claire's room, determined to help the woman. "If I've ever seen anyone in need of a party, it's you." She paused. "Unless all the noise and chatter is too much for you. If you'd like, I can show you how to cut and stitch the top of your quilt right here in your room. I have made a few quilts in my day."

Claire's eyes widened. "You're too kind, but that's not necessary." Her expression hardened for a moment. "I wish everyone were so thoughtful." She ran her hand over the different fabrics, her eyes resting on the darker shades.

Louise sat down in one of the chairs in the room and gestured for Claire to take the other. "Please tell me if I should mind my own business, but I have to ask if there is any way I can help you. We try to treat our guests as family here at Grace Chapel Inn."

Claire stared at the tips of her shoes for a long time. It was almost as though she'd forgotten Louise was there. Then she spoke hesitantly. "I'm not sure anyone can help. Maybe we've blown it already and it's too late."

"Too late? I'm not much of a believer in 'too late.'"

"I don't know about that, especially in relationships," Claire said. "Sometimes they become irreparably broken."

"And you have a relationship like that?"

"I didn't think so until this week." An expression of irritation crossed her features. "I can't believe he forgot."

"Forgot what?"

"My birthday. He knows how important birthdays are to me. While I was growing up, my sister and I looked forward to our birthdays more than any other day of the year. It was 'our' day. Once my parents even rented a pony for my party. The least my own husband could do is give me a *card*, don't you think?"

Louise hid a smile. *All this over a birthday?*

"He forgot the anniversary of our very first date, too, but I forgave him for that. Once I can handle. Twice..." Claire lowered her head. "Frankly, he hurt my feelings."

"Did you tell him?"

"Oh, I told him—in the letter I left for him on the kitchen counter." She scowled. "I told him that if he loved me—really loved me—he'd know how important things like this are to me."

"Indeed," Louise said.

"I suppose I've been spoiled. My parents always made sure that every holiday was a celebration—May baskets, little flags on the Fourth of July, that sort of thing—but I'm not asking him to remember Groundhog Day or anything, just my birthday."

Claire drew a deep breath. "Then I got here and had some time to think. Maybe I have been pouting a little, but we're practically newlyweds. Don't you think the least he could have done was remember my birthday? He was so sweet and considerate before the wedding. Do you think that was all an act?" Claire lifted her eyes to look at Louise. "Were you ever married?"

"Oh yes. My husband's name was Eliot. We married one year after I graduated from college."

"Did you meet him there?"

"Yes. He was my music theory teacher. He was a dear man, fifteen years older than I. We had one daughter. Cynthia is thirty-four now." She shook her head in wonderment. "My, how time flies. I can still see her as a little girl. Eliot was so proud of her."

"What happened to him, if I may ask?"

"He died of cancer."

"I'm sorry," Claire said. "That must have been awful. I know how terrible it would be if I lost Ben." She hesitated a moment, as if recognizing the irony in her own words.

Louise ignored the confusion on Claire's face. "It's been several years since I lost him. I think of him every day, but now I recall the good times we had, not the bad ones."

"Tell me about him." Claire leaned forward and flipped through swatches on the bed in front of her.

No one had asked Louise about Eliot in a long time. He had died four years before her father had gone to heaven. It was difficult for Louise to believe she'd been widowed so long.

"When we first married, we lived in Philadelphia. Those were wonderful years. We worked together to restore a nineteenth-century Greek-revival house. Eliot liked the classics in everything, houses as well as music."

"A musician," Claire murmured. "My husband is a carpenter. At least he started out that way. Now he's a contractor and builds homes. That is very different from being a musician."

"Not as different as you might think," Louise said. "Musicians and carpenters both create things with their hands. A musician starts with standard notes and creates a composition. A carpenter starts with wood and nails and creates a home, a cradle or a chair."

"I never thought about it that way," Claire admitted. "But I think of musicians as sensitive. If Ben were sensitive, he would have remembered something so important to me, don't you think?"

Louise waited quietly, amused by this young woman's annoyance and exasperation over something so trivial, yet knowing that her husband's oversight truly troubled her.

"Did you ever have a problem like this with Eliot?" Claire asked. A quick, wry smile graced her features. "I can't imagine you running off in a snit as I did. Being here, with all of you gracious people, makes me feel a little...well... ashamed of myself."

Louise pondered for a moment. "Eliot and I did have a similar problem once."

Claire leaned forward, ready to hear Louise's story. Misery, after all, does love company.

"The second year we were married, our anniversary fell on the day his students were supposed to give a concert," Louise said, taking a deep breath. "They'd given many concerts before but this was to be something special. A benefactor was considering donating a lot of money to the music department, and there was pressure on Eliot to make sure that his students made a good impression. I, of course, wasn't the least bit worried about it because I knew with every fiber of my being that Eliot was the finest teacher in the world."

Claire's lips turned up in a smile. "You *were* in love, weren't you?" She pulled a piece of brown calico out and set it in its own pile.

"Completely." Louise smiled back. "Anyway, while Eliot was fussing over the concert, I was daydreaming about the lovely meal I'd have ready for him when he returned from the college. I certainly was never as good a cook as my sister Jane, but I tried, and I figured I could cook a roast. I set the table with candles and a white linen tablecloth we had gotten for our wedding. I even put on the dress that I wore only on special occasions."

"And what happened?" Claire was smiling along with Louise now, imagining the romantic setting and the effort to which Louise had gone. "Did he love it?"

"My dear, he didn't even *see* it."

"What?" Claire looked horrified, and Louise could imagine how she'd appeared when she'd discovered her husband had overlooked her birthday.

"He came home while I was in the kitchen and went straight upstairs to bed. He had a headache, he told me later, and didn't want to disturb me with his problems. He'd been disappointed in the concert and was sure that the department wouldn't receive the donation."

"What did you do?"

"Unfortunately I hadn't heard him come in so I sat up waiting until nearly midnight. Then I put my overdone roast in the refrigerator, blew out my guttering candles and went to bed. Imagine my shock when I saw him lying there, sound asleep."

"I would have been furious," Claire admitted. "Headache or not, he should have talked to you."

"I agree. And what added insult to injury was that he hadn't recalled for even a moment that it was our anniversary. Worse yet, the next morning he was up and gone before I awakened. He'd left me a note saying that he had an important meeting and that he'd decided to let me sleep." Louise pursed her lips. "That didn't sit very well with me either, I'll tell you."

"That's even worse then having him forget your birthday," Claire said. "Of course, he did have a good excuse." She selected a robin's egg blue swatch and laid it with the brown piece.

"He did, but I didn't quite see it that way at the time. I was so upset that I called my father to talk about it."

Louise smiled at Claire's curious expression. "My father was pastor of Grace Chapel, the church you can see out the window of the inn. What a wise, kind man he was. We—his daughters and the community—still miss him."

"What did he have to say about Eliot's behavior?"

"That was a surprise, I'll tell you." Louise shook her head as she recalled the conversation. "I was sure that my father would take my side."

"He didn't?" Claire looked aghast. "Not that of his own daughter?"

"Oh, he didn't take sides at all. Instead of commiserating with me, my father began to challenge me about my response to Eliot's behavior."

"But you weren't the one who forgot the anniversary," Claire said, flushing in indignation.

"That's true, but my father reminded me that to love like Christ loves us means that *no matter* how someone treats us, it is our responsibility to love them. We aren't supposed to love someone when he is good to us and hate him when he is bad. We are to love him as Jesus loves us—in spite of flaws, mistakes and missteps. We are to respond with the same love Christ gives to us."

Claire looked down at the piles of fabric in front of her. Louise waited silently.

"What did you do when Eliot got home from work?" she finally said.

Emotion played on Louise's face, and her blue eyes seemed to be looking into the past.

"I talked with him about the night before. The poor man had no idea what trouble he'd been in or even that, due to my father's wisdom, he'd gotten out of it. He had been innocently going about his work, absorbed in the duties of the day. In fact, when he realized he'd missed our anniversary, he excused himself to get something out of his bedroom closet. He came back with a lovely gold necklace he'd purchased for the occasion."

"So he hadn't forgotten after all, at least not completely."

Louise smiled with satisfaction. "My father was a very wise man."

Claire was silent for a long time. "You've given me a lot to think about, Louise."

$\backsim$

"You're sure this is okay with you?" Jane asked Wednesday night as she and Patty sat on Patty's bed in their pajamas. They'd done this a hundred times as young women, but now that they were adults she was afraid Patty would be less thrilled about sharing her room.

"I think it's great. I have you all to myself." Patty looked pleased about the prospect. "It's hard for me to get a word in edgewise with Stella around."

Jane smiled but didn't say anything.

"Sometimes I just don't know about that woman," Patty said. "I *love* Stella. I just don't like her very much at times. She grates on my nerves."

"Why do you think that is?" Jane leaned back against her pillows and stretched her legs out in front of her.

"The first time I saw Stella she was strolling across a parking lot on campus. All the other students looked pretty normal, but Stella was so . . . exotic. Her dark hair was pulled back from her face, and she wore the most amazing sunglasses. She was about a size two. I could tell, even from a distance, that her purse was a real designer bag. I felt like a big clunky oaf just being near her."

"You? A clunky oaf? What parallel universe were you living in?"

"Stella made me feel inferior from the moment we met," Patty admitted ruefully.

Jane shook her head in disbelief. "Amazing," she murmured.

"What?"

"Here you are, talking about how inferior Stella made you feel. If only you'd heard our conversation earlier, when Stella told me how she'd struggled with self-esteem as a chubby teenager."

"You're kidding, right?" Patty's expressive eyes were doubtful.

"I'm afraid not. You and Stella have more in common than you have differences." Jane told her a little of what she and Stella had discussed.

"I never knew." Patty smoothed the leg of her pajamas with the palm of her hand. "I liked her, of course, when I got to know her. I couldn't help it. She's generous and funny and very kind. It might have been different if we hadn't shared so many art classes. Stella is quick. She's sure of her work and gets right down to business. I'm always second-guessing myself. I just felt like I could never keep up."

"And now?"

"I'm satisfied with what I do. I have a good business. My name isn't on the lips of the art critics, but I do have a lot of decorators who think I can do magic with paint and brushes. It's just that some . . . things . . . have flooded back." Her expression was pained. "And now that I know how mistaken I was, I feel even worse."

"Things?" Jane was quick to pick up on Patty's elusive statement. "What things?"

"Stuff that happened between Stella and me. That's all." Patty's expression darkened. "I was a stupid kid."

"What happened between the two of you that was so important that you'd carry it forward all these years?"

Patty sighed and shifted on the bed. "Remember Barry Handgrove?"

"I do. Cute guy. Nice too. I seem to remember . . ." Jane paused and her eyes widened. "You and Stella had a crush on him at the same time, right?"

"I never had a chance. What guy wouldn't prefer Stella to gangly old me?"

"Several, I imagine."

"Not Barry. He was crazy about her. And I was crazy about him. Not a nice situation to be in."

"Stella liked him a lot, too, I remember."

"Yes. He gave her a necklace with a real diamond in it."

"I recall that. It was an item of gossip for a long time. Everyone thought an engagement ring might be next, but it never happened. There was something about that necklace . . . didn't they break up over it eventually? I can't quite remember."

"The necklace disappeared. Barry was very hurt and angry. Stella said she was sure she'd put it in her drawer and just didn't know what happened to it. Barry said that if the necklace had really meant something to her, she would have taken better care of it. The argument turned bitter, and they decided not to go with each other anymore."

"But what does that have to do with you and Stella? It happened almost thirty years ago."

"Sometimes it feels like just yesterday that we were in school." Patty looked dreamily into the distance. "Do you ever get that feeling?"

"I suppose so, but I still don't understand what this has to do with you and Stella."

Patty reached for her purse at the foot of the bed and pulled it toward her. She dug in the side pocket for a moment and then pulled out a single fine strand of gold with a diamond dangling from it. "Stella didn't lose the necklace. I took it."

Jane stared at the glittering chain, dumbfounded.

"I was sick with jealousy," Patty said sadly. "I wasn't going to keep it, but I wanted to give her a scare. She didn't notice it was gone right away. I went away for a long week-end with my folks, and when I came back she and Barry had had their big blowup. I didn't dare tell her what happened after that."

"So you kept it?"

"I should have confessed to what I'd done. Maybe Stella and Barry would have made up, married even, but I was scared. I didn't confess. I let it go." Patty stared at the fine gauge necklace and sparkling diamond in her palm. "And it's haunted me ever since."

"You mean that is why you and Stella never seemed to get along as well as the rest of us?"

"She was—is—the living reminder of how stupid I'd been. Instead of being mad at myself, I turned it around in my head and was angry with Stella."

Patty's porcelain skin looked gray beneath her eyes. "I've been able to forget about this necklace for long periods of time, but the memory keeps coming back. This reunion made that whole muddle feel like yesterday. I don't know what to do. I messed up a lot of things for her, Jane. I'm sure she doesn't think about this necklace anymore, but I do. Maybe she and Barry would have married if I'd come clean right away. Her life might have been so different."

She shifted restlessly. "And now you tell me all this about Stella's insecurities. It's just getting worse and worse."

"You could still give it back," Jane said. "Ask for forgiveness and move on. You have been punishing yourself for a lot of years, Patty. And it's kept a wedge in your friendship with Stella. Perhaps we'd have all gotten together more often if it weren't for—"

"I know, I know. I intentionally found excuses not to get together with the rest of you when you tried to meet. We've missed a lot of opportunities to enjoy each other's company as a group. I knew I'd hurt both her and Barry. I was simply a coward. By waiting, I made everything worse."

"I still say give it back." Jane put her hand on Patty's arm. "You'll never feel whole until you do."

"What will she think of me?"

"Perhaps you've underestimated her."

Patty looked unconvinced. "Me? Underestimate Stella? I don't think so."

"We're not kids anymore. Give her some credit."

"I don't know...I just don't know."

"Have you prayed about it?"

Patty looked at Jane with an expression filled with pain. "No, I haven't. This guilt makes me feel like God probably doesn't want to talk to me. I guess I've kind of...drifted away...from Him."

"Patty, He's the *Master* of forgiveness. Don't let this keep the two of you apart."

"Can we change the subject, Jane?"

Disappointed, but knowing more conversation right now wouldn't help, Jane nodded.

They didn't say much more as they slipped into bed.

Jane's mind raced as she lay in the darkness and she wondered if she'd ever get to sleep. She knew Patty wasn't sleeping either.

Finally Patty spoke out of the darkness. "Becky seems different somehow. I've seen her several times in the past few years when she's been traveling through my area. She's usually so lighthearted."

"She's a little more serious and quiet than she used to be." Jane had noticed the change, of course, especially when she'd tried to ask questions about Becky's family.

"She didn't say a lot in the van on the trip over here. Every time Stella or I tried to get her to talk by asking her questions about her family, she'd change the subject. I've

never known her not to want to talk about her children."
Patty punched her pillow. "Maybe someone else is messed
up besides me. Pathetic, isn't it? Grown women who can't
manage their own lives?"

"You're managing your lives just fine," Jane said gently.
"There are *elements* that are problematic right now, that's all.
Everyone's life is like that—ups and downs."

"How do you do it, Jane? How do you manage?"

"I've had help."

"Your sisters?"

"Partly. But these days I leave the heavy lifting to God."

"I miss Him," Patty murmured. "Maybe He'd forgive
me if I could only forgive myself."

Chapter Ten

*J*ane left Patty sleeping soundly on Thursday morning. Dawn was just breaking when she tiptoed downstairs.

She was surprised to see that she was not the first one up. Mary was sitting at the dining room table, wearing the robe and slippers that Alice had given her.

"Good morning," Jane murmured.

Mary looked up. "I didn't make too much noise, did I?"

"No. I didn't hear you at all. I'm just an early riser." Jane beckoned to her. "Come with me into the kitchen. I'll put on coffee and pour some juice and we can chat."

The kitchen glowed with the first rosy rays of the sun. Flowers from the garden sat on the counter looking as fresh this morning as they had when Jane brought them in the night before. Jane took two glasses from the cupboard and set them on the counter, then she went to the refrigerator for juice.

"How did you sleep?"

"Better than I did in the hospital. For the first time in days, I actually feel rested."

"Excellent. We pride ourselves on comfortable beds and a good night's sleep around here."

"I'm feeling guilty, though. I've ousted you from your bed. I feel terrible that you have to share a room."

"Don't." Jane smiled at Mary. "I should thank you. Patty and I had a wonderful heart-to-heart that we might not have had if we'd been in separate rooms. It's like old times. When we lived together in our little house during college, we would have thought our accommodations last night were luxurious."

"If you're sure..."

"Are you hungry?" Jane moved easily around the kitchen, making coffee and setting dishes on the counter.

Mary pondered the question. "I am unless you're going to have tasteless oatmeal, watery juice, egg substitute and cold toast."

Jane laughed. "Will you settle for homemade granola, baked eggs with wild rice and homemade breads and muffins? Of course, if you really *want* egg substitute I do have some in the freezer."

"I'll settle for your menu, thank you." Mary looked pleased. "You ladies are being so kind to me."

"We're treating you like we treat anyone who comes through our door. It's our privilege to have you here."

Mary bowed her head and sipped at the orange juice Jane had handed her.

"I hope that's true," she finally said. "Unfortunately I'm a complete stranger ... to both you and me."

Jane, who always approached things head on, didn't dance around the topic of Mary's amnesia. "Nothing has come back yet, then?"

"A couple of things. I was reading the Bible last night, and there were some stories that were familiar. And when I went to brush my teeth, I realized that Alice had purchased my brand of toothpaste. That's not much progress, I'm afraid."

"It's only been a few days. Whatever happened must have traumatized you a great deal."

"That's the other thing that worries me. What did happen? If I'd been in a car accident, shouldn't the car have been there? And if someone did this to me and then dumped me ..." She shuddered. "I just can't think about that."

"Then don't. Take advantage of the time here to rest your mind. Let your body heal. I fully believe that, in time, everything will be revealed."

"How can I ever repay you?" Mary asked, her voice strangled with emotion.

Jane eyed her. "You could start by putting dollops of the batter I mixed up last night into muffin cups. I'll bake them later so that they'll be fresh and hot when the others get up."

Relieved to have something useful to do, Mary nodded eagerly and rose to her feet. She put muffin papers in the bottoms of a pan and then began to spoon the batter into the individual cups.

"It's nice working here with you," Mary said as she rinsed out the bowl and spoon she'd been using. "You have a lovely kitchen."

"We remodeled it before opening the inn. I must say, it's the one time I got everything I asked for. Alice and Louise let me plan it entirely."

The muffins were just going into the oven and the eggs, in individual ramekins, were ready to follow when Alice and Louise entered the kitchen.

"The early birds are already at work, I see," Alice said and yawned. "I heard stirrings in the guest rooms. I'd say everyone will be down for breakfast soon."

"Mary has been helping me. We've decided that in her past, she knew her way around a kitchen. She even mixed up a banana bread batter—from memory."

Alice clapped her hands, delighted.

Mary flushed but looked pleased. "At least now we know that if all else fails, I can get a job in a bakery," she joked.

$\backsim$

Patty was first to arrive at the breakfast table. Dressed in jeans and a white T-shirt under a blue chambray blouse, her hair pulled into a tousled knot on the top of her head, she looked ready to get to work. She gave Jane a warning glance that Jane took to mean that their conversation last night was off limits in the light of day.

Jane would never utter a word about Patty's secret to anyone, but she hoped Patty would do the right thing. Confession, Jane knew, was good for the soul.

Stella breezed in next, in a scarlet blouse and black silk trousers. She wore her hair in a French knot held in place with what looked like a pair of black, patent leather chopsticks. The diamond ring on her finger had to be at least three carats, Jane decided. Stella didn't "do" costume jewelry. She was also the only one who'd taken time to put on makeup and jewelry.

"Good morning, all. Did you have a glorious night's sleep? I did. Where do you get your mattresses? I want to take mine home with me. My word, look at the food on this table. Jane strikes again. Hello, Louise, don't you look lovely today. And Alice . . ."

Stella prattled on cheerfully, blissfully ignorant of the miserable look on Patty's face.

"Where's Becky?" Stella finally asked.

"I'll go find her," Jane offered. "Louise, why don't you and Alice lead everyone in a prayer and begin to eat? Becky and I will catch up."

Sun shone on the meticulously polished hallway floor as Jane approached Becky's room. She rapped on the door.

"Just a minute, I'm not ready..." The door flew open to reveal Becky, still in her nightgown. "Oh, Jane. Sorry. I couldn't sleep last night, and I was so exhausted that just about the time I should have been getting up, I dozed off." Her blue eyes were red-rimmed from lack of sleep. "Is breakfast ready? I'll pull on some clothes and be right down. I'll shower after breakfast."

"That's a plan," Jane said.

Becky left the door open, disappeared into her bathroom and popped out again dressed in a hot pink velour jogging suit. She plucked ruefully at the waistband.

"Elastic. That's all I brought this trip. I remembered the way you cook and knew I wouldn't be able to fit into anything else on the return trip." She peered into the mirror. "How do I look?"

"Lovely. Pink becomes you."

"I look like an Easter egg, actually, an Easter egg with wrinkles and gray hair."

"You don't have either wrinkles or gray hair."

"Not yet, maybe, but they're coming. I can feel it." She looked in the mirror again. "You and Stella didn't have children and look at you. You aren't all that different from our school days. Me? Bags beneath my eyes, crow's-feet. Bags on my crow's-feet and crow's-feet on my bags ..."

Jane burst out laughing at Becky's cheerful and entirely fictitious description.

"I've discovered what causes aging, you know."

"And what, pray tell, is that? When this gets out, you'll probably be a wealthy woman." Jane leaned casually against the door jamb and crossed her arms over her chest.

"Children. They're what do it. The cause of gray hair, frown and worry lines and bags beneath the eyes. I'd still look twenty-five if I hadn't had children."

"You adore your children. Even if that notion about the gray hair and wrinkles were true, and it's not, you'd say they're worth it."

"Don't jump to conclusions so quickly, Jane." Becky said this lightly, but there was a hint of conviction in her voice.

By the time Jane and Becky arrived, Claire was also seated at the table.

Breakfast was a festive affair. How could it be otherwise with the three friends telling every tale they could think of about Jane? They passed around stories as easily as they passed dishes from one to another, and Alice and Louise were in their element, hearing about their much-loved sister.

"I'll never forget the night that the cat walked on Jane's painting," Stella said as she helped herself to a muffin. "That was the most upset I've ever seen her. I felt bad for her, of course, but I still couldn't keep from laughing."

"Fine friend you were," Jane retorted. "It had been my most ambitious project up to then—ruined."

"It wasn't ruined, it was just abstracted, that's all," Stella said.

"I blame you for that, Becky," Jane said. "You're the one who brought the cat home."

Louise and Alice were looking more confused by the moment.

"Slow down, please. What cat?" asked Louise.

"Becky volunteered to cat-sit for a friend without telling any of us," Patty began. "She took it into the bedroom with its litter box. No one was home to tell about the kitten, so she just closed the door, planning to inform us later."

"How was I to know the cat was a Houdini?" Becky asked. "My friend didn't warn me that he could open doors."

"Jane had been working for two weeks on a still-life oil painting that she was supposed to turn in as part of a class project," Stella continued. "She took it off her easel and laid it on the dining room table so that she could work on another piece. Meanwhile, Becky's cat managed to open the door and escape into the other part of the house."

"Imagine how I felt," Jane said, picking up the story, "when I turned around to see a kitten walking across my wet oil painting, his little paws covered with paint. Then, before I could stop him, the little thing *sat down* on the canvas. I thought I'd die."

"She yelled so loudly, she scared the cat. It jumped off the table and left colorful little footprints all the way back to the bedroom."

Louise and Alice laughed merrily. Mary and Claire grinned, as much at the way the friends were telling it as the story itself.

No one even noticed that Ethel had come in, until she arrived at Louise's side at the table.

"Good morning, everyone. It sounds as though you all are having a lovely time." Ethel poured a cup of coffee at the sideboard and joined the group at the table.

"I haven't had this much fun in ages," Louise admitted. "I wish you ladies could stay until you've told us all your stories about Jane."

"We'd be here a long time," Stella said cheerfully. "Jane was an entertaining roommate to have."

"Would you like something to eat, Aunt Ethel?" Jane asked.

"Just a muffin, dear. I haven't time for more." Ethel took a seat and accepted the basket of muffins Jane passed to her.

"You're very busy these days," Alice observed. "How was your lunch with the new postmistress?"

Ethel frowned. "Fine, but I was a little disappointed that I wasn't the first to show her hospitality."

"Someone beat you to it?" Jane asked, amused.

"Florence took her a homemade pie." Ethel looked frustrated. "I could have been first, if only I'd thought of it."

"I think it's wonderful that you are both being so welcoming."

"I did so want to be the first..."

Jane hoped LeAnn wasn't shy. She couldn't think of anything worse for a shy person than to have her be introduced to society by Florence and Ethel, two whirlwinds.

"What else is new with you, Aunt Ethel? We haven't seen much of you the past couple days," Alice asked.

"Oh, there's nothing new with me, but I have been worried sick about poor Mr. and Mrs. Billings." Ethel lowered her voice conspiratorially. "LeAnn told me that they've received several letters from the IRS."

"Should she be doing that?" Becky whispered to Jane, who sighed and shrugged. It probably wasn't against the law, but it was an unusual confidence to share.

"They've got financial troubles, I'm sure of it." Ethel shook her head and clucked sympathetically, the picture of concern.

She finished her muffin and pushed away from the table. "I really must go. Do you girls have anything you want mailed?"

After they assured her that they didn't, she left, and Louise, Alice and Jane gathered in the kitchen.

"Aunt Ethel was in top form today. She was such a wealth of information." Jane filled the carafe with more coffee.

"Yes, she was. I do feel bad about the Billingses," Alice said.

"I'm handy with numbers," Louise said. "Perhaps next time I see them I should discreetly offer to help them if they have anything they're concerned about. They were friends of Father's, after all. I remember his telling me what a kind, dear couple he thought they were. I believe he'd like it if he knew we were watching out for them."

"It would be a nice gesture if you can do it tactfully," Jane said.

"Don't worry about that," Alice replied. "Louise is always the soul of tact."

"Well, we don't have any time to worry right now," Jane said as she walked toward the dining room with the coffee. "Sylvia will be here soon to help us start quilting."

Almost as she spoke, Sylvia walked into the house and handed a package to Alice. "Here's what you called for."

"What's that, Alice?" Jane asked.

"I asked Sylvia to bring a quilt kit for Mary."

"We'll do a log cabin pattern," Sylvia announced to the ladies gathered in the dining room after she had greeted them all. "Even though we'll all be cutting our fabrics in the same sized blocks, you will be amazed at how different they will look." She picked up a pattern book. "First I need to tell you about darks and lights. When we make quilt squares, one side of each log cabin quilt block will be composed of the lighter shades of fabric. When we sew the squares together, it will add dimension to our quilt." Sylvia opened the book to a page of pictures. "Like this."

"I'm in over my head already," Patty moaned. "Did I ever tell you I was born with ten thumbs when it comes to sewing?"

"I can't believe that," Sylvia said. "You're an *artist*."

"Maybe you should believe it," Becky said as she picked up her fabric and headed for the kitchen to spread out her project. "The week before the Founders' Day banquet at college, we all decided we needed new dresses. We were all broke, of course, and Patty had the brilliant idea that we should design and sew our own new outfits."

Stella smiled fondly in Patty's direction. "It was more difficult than you expected, wasn't it?"

Patty turned pink. "I had no idea that my machine was set on a basting stitch."

"The threads holding the skirt to the top of Patty's dress started to snap before we got half way across campus," Jane told her sisters. "It was all we could do to keep the dress from falling apart and dropping off as we walked."

"We borrowed safety pins from everyone we met and kept the thing together through the meal, but Patty had to slip out and go home before the speaker began because she was afraid her dress would disintegrate."

Sylvia waited for the laughter to die down. "I see what you mean. The good news is that if your quilt falls apart, it won't be a public embarrassment." She waggled a finger at Jane. "You're in charge of Patty's sewing machine. Don't let her touch any settings."

Before long, every woman had spread out her work, taking over much of the first floor of the inn.

Jane and Becky shared the kitchen table while they were cutting cloth into squares.

"When I was little I used to consider quilting a rather strange concept," Jane said as they arranged cutting boards and put new blades in the cutters Sylvia had provided. "First, you buy beautiful fabric. Then you cut it into pieces. Next you sew it all back together again. I wondered if it would be easier to make blankets out of the whole pieces of cloth in the first place?"

"That's a little like your saying, let's buy groceries—broccoli, chicken and rice—and cook and eat them each separately rather than making a tasty casserole in which they are all mixed together," Becky said. "It's still good food, but combinations are definitely more interesting." She examined her growing stack of fabric blocks. "If this turns out at all, I think I'll give it to my daughter as a wedding present. That will certainly be a surprise."

"Have you done much planning for the wedding?" Jane asked as she sliced the rotary cutter through one of Becky's fabrics.

"We're getting ideas." Becky began to measure fabric. "I never imagined how complicated it was to plan a wedding. The details are getting to me. That reminds me, I'd like to place an order for your famous truffles as table favors at dinner."

"What are your daughter's favorite flavors? I can make a raspberry truffle that is out of this world. I want it to be my gift to you."

"We couldn't let you do that. It's going to be a big wedding."

"It's my gift to the bride and groom then. I insist."

As they worked, Jane and Becky talked more about the upcoming wedding, but much of the time they were silent, concentrating on the shapes and patterns that were emerging from the fabric.

Finally Jane worked up the nerve to ask what had been gnawing at her all morning. "What's wrong, Becky? You've had something on your mind ever since you arrived."

Becky looked up, her cheeks pink and eyes bright. "Wrong? Who says anything is wrong?"

"It's written all over your face and in your demeanor. You're dressed like a rainbow," Jane said, gesturing at Becky's outfit of blue denim overalls with a yellow shirt and pink sneakers. Becky laughed good-naturedly. "But you seem down. Every time I've mentioned your children you've diverted the conversation to something else. That's completely unlike you. What's up?"

"Nothing anyone here can do anything about," Becky said, setting down her fabric.

"Would talking about it help?"

Becky sighed. "It's my son Blaine." Tears welled in her eyes. "I'm so disappointed in him, Jane. I just don't understand what he's doing."

Blaine was her oldest son, the one for whom Becky had always had such high hopes.

"What *is* he doing?"

Becky's face reddened. "Nothing. Absolutely nothing. Nada. Zip. Nothing."

"Excuse me?" Jane looked up from her work and turned to Becky, trying to read her face.

"Blaine quit his job, dropped out of graduate school, moved back home and spends twenty hours a day in his basement bedroom watching television, reading books and sleeping."

Jane recalled that Becky's son had been an excellent student, had made the dean's list at college and graduated magna cum laude. When he'd begun a master's degree in history, Becky was incredibly proud. What had happened to *that* Blaine?

"He has no ambition whatsoever. He's made no mention of moving on or getting a job. Instead he borrows money from his siblings, mooches off his dad and me, and spends half the night watching infomercials. Jane, I don't think I even know this kid anymore."

"But that's so unlike Blaine..." Jane said, unsure of how else to respond.

"It's as though a switch turned off." Becky shrugged. "And the light that was inside Blaine went out."

"Will he talk to you about it?"

"Are you kidding? He communicates in grunts, caveman style. We told him that if he was going to live under our roof, he would have to pay rent. We didn't realize until this past week that he was taking the money out of an account he'd set up to finish school. Now he's depleting the fund that could help him most."

Becky sat down on a stool and put her head into her hands. "It is so frustrating. He absolutely refuses to admit anything is wrong. He says he just doesn't 'feel' like working or going to school right now. He says he needs a 'break.' I'll tell you the truth, Jane, it's his dad and I who need a break—from him."

"What, do you suppose, is he hiding from?"

Becky stared at Jane. "'Hiding?'"

"A bird who loves to soar doesn't just stop flying, dig a hole, crawl in and begin acting like a mole, you know. Something has to happen to a bird to keep it on the ground." Jane picked up her scissors and lined them up with the pattern.

"Lately I've been too upset and angry to think," Becky admitted. "I was married and had a child when I was his age. I don't understand how he can be content with his life as it is now. I certainly wouldn't be."

"What does he say about it?" The satisfying swish of the scissors cutting through the fabric was comforting.

"He says he's 'on sabbatical.'" Becky rolled her eyes. "A sabbatical from life. I can't believe I raised such a lazy son."

"Who is this about, Becky," Jane asked, raising her eyebrows. "You or him?"

"Him, of course. I want him to be successful and productive and…and…" Her face reddened. Becky slowly shook her head. "I never believed for a moment that my children would turn out less than perfect. I illustrate children's books, for goodness sake. If anyone knows how to make a world look perfect, it would be me."

"So it's not all Blaine. You're embarrassed by his behavior."

Becky flushed. "When you put it that way…yes, and I'm ashamed of being embarrassed. I love Blaine but I dislike his behavior."

There were tears in Becky's eyes. "What happened to that unconditional motherly love I thought I had? Why can't I seem to give it to Blaine now?"

"You are human, after all."

"I feel like I'm walking around with a brick in my stomach. I almost called to tell you that I couldn't come to our get-together. I knew I'd be a wet blanket on the party. As it is, you're the first I've told about this. Now I suppose I've thrown my wet blanket over you too."

Jane smiled and shook her head. "I'm glad you didn't cancel. We'd have been horribly disappointed. Besides, we're just what you need right now, people to cheer you up."

"I do feel better." Becky admitted. "I guess I deluded myself into thinking that if I were a good enough mother, my children wouldn't run into the snags and detours that others do."

"Pretty proud of your mothering capabilities, aren't you?" Jane said softly.

"I am. I'm a good mother. I ..." Becky hesitated, "and 'pride goes before a fall.'" She leaned back in her chair. "I guess I set myself up for that one, huh?"

Jane hugged her friend. "Blaine isn't a lazy guy. Something must have happened that he's not telling you about."

"You don't think it's just pure laziness like his father does?"

"That's one of the *last* conclusions I'd jump to. Maybe being here with us will give you a new perspective about him."

Becky stood up. "Maybe you're right. I've been stewing about Blaine's behavior until I'm so furious with him that I've lost sight of the amazing person he is. As always, you helped me clear my head."

"Be careful. Once we start sewing these quilts together your head might become all muddled again."

"At least," Becky muttered, "it will be a problem that, with enough time and ingenuity, I'll be able to figure out for myself."

Chapter Eleven

"You're all making wonderful progress," Sylvia announced to the women at Grace Chapel Inn as Thursday morning marched toward noon. "I don't believe I've ever had a beginners' class so full of quick studies."

Alice glanced at her watch. "Jane, do you want me to help you start lunch?"

Jane looked up from her work with surprise. The inn had been turned upside down as she and the others had taken over every available surface for their quilting projects. Stella had the lapel of her blouse covered with pins. Patty had put her hands to her head in frustration so many times that she had mussed her hair until it looked like a blonde cloud around her face. Claire and Mary were sitting side by side, quietly doing their work, but taking in every word that was said. A cozy, convivial atmosphere prevailed.

Wendell, who'd hidden in the study for most of the friends' visit, had come out to play with the thread and fabric scraps decorating the floor. He purred loudly as he batted an empty thread spool around the room.

"It can't be that late already," Jane protested. Then she looked at her watch. "But it *is*. . Where did the time go?"

Becky stretched, catlike. She'd been at a sewing machine for the last hour, stitching fabric pieces into blocks. She held up the block she'd just completed. "Isn't it grand? I haven't felt so relaxed in ages."

"I can see why our grandmothers and great-grandmothers used to gather to quilt," Stella said. "Chatting, listening, being busy like we are today. It's nice. A circle of friends."

"But I've dropped the ball," Jane said. "I should have had lunch ready by now. I got so involved I forgot about time."

"Why don't you keep working?" Alice said as she stood up. "Mary and I will take care of lunch today."

"There's plenty of stuff in the refrigerator. You could make—"

Alice interrupted Jane's suggestions. "Mary and I will find something. In fact, I think we should go to town and pick up a few things. Who knows what might be fresh at the Good Apple? And perhaps there is an extra blackberry pie at the Coffee Shop we can buy."

Before Jane could protest, Alice beckoned Mary to follow her. "Besides, it might be good to stretch our legs. What do you think, Mary?"

"I haven't been out in the 'real' world since I lost my memory." Mary stood up to follow Alice. "Maybe something I see will nudge it along."

"It's settled then. Mary and I will forage for food and bring home what we find."

"Don't go to a lot of bother," Becky suggested. "I'm still full to my ears from breakfast."

As Alice and Mary prepared to leave the house, the others returned to what they were doing, and the conversation, which had so far that morning covered everything from the best make of automobile to fertilizing tomato plants turned to books.

"What a fascinating group of women they are," Mary said when they stepped out onto the front porch and into the sunshine. "So diverse and intelligent."

"Did any of the talk jog memories for you?" Alice asked as they started to walk toward the Good Apple.

"Much of it sounded familiar, but there was no *aha* moment for me like the scent of lavender was."

"Keep your eyes and ears open, maybe it will happen again." Alice inhaled a deep breath of fresh summer air, and the two women chatted as they walked the peaceful road into town.

When they turned into the Good Apple, they found Clarissa Cottrell frosting a gigantic wedding cake.

"Somebody over in Potterston ordered this. They must be inviting the entire county to the wedding," she said as she finished a delicate piece of frosting latticework.

"You do beautiful work, Clarissa. What would we do without you?"

"Oh, someone else would decorate cakes. I'm not indispensable." The older woman put a bit of frosting on the cake with a flourish. "But you won't see me leaving any time soon, I don't think."

"Clarissa, forgive my manners. I'd like you to meet my friend Mary."

When she turned to Mary, Alice saw that the woman was staring intently at the cake.

"Nice to meet you, Mary," Clarissa said. "If you'll excuse me just a minute, I have to check something in the oven."

"Is something coming to you, dear?" Alice whispered as Clarissa went into the back of the store.

"I wonder if I'm married," Mary said, her voice wistful. She looked down at her hands. "I don't have a wedding ring." She sighed. "If I am married, why isn't my husband looking for me?"

That question had troubled Alice as well. She simply hugged Mary, then smiled as Clarissa returned and put in her order for some fresh-from-the-oven buns for sandwiches and some dainty sugar cookies for afternoon tea. Thanking Clarissa, they took their purchases and headed toward the Coffee Shop.

"I love it in here," Mary said when they entered the building. She looked at the red faux-leather booths with silver piping. The bakery case was filled with pies, cookies and doughnuts, displayed to entice customers to order something to go with their morning or afternoon coffee. The lunch hour was in progress, and the place smelled of roast beef, mashed potatoes and gravy. Three people were just finishing their coffee and pie, including Vera and her pretty college-aged daughter Jean.

"Let's sit down and have a cup of tea," Alice suggested. "Everyone back at the house is so engrossed in her own project that another few minutes isn't going to matter a bit. It will only take a moment to assemble the sandwiches when we get home. Maybe this place will jog your memory."

Hope Collins came to their table carrying two menus. "You ladies want lunch? There's some mighty good split pea and ham soup if you're interested."

"Just tea for me. Is all your blackberry pie sold? I'd like to get a whole pie to take back to the house."

"You're in luck, Alice. We made extra today. There are two in the back."

"Good. We'll take one."

"Done." Hope turned to Mary. "Can I get you anything?"

Mary's face screwed up in concentration. "I'd like ... I'd like ... a chocolate malt. With plenty of malt powder. Extra thick." She looked at Alice and blushed. "It's a memory worth ruining my appetite for, don't you think?"

"One chocolate malt, coming right up."

Hope turned away and Mary grabbed both of Alice's hands in her own.

"I used to order those all the time as a child, I'm sure of it. Maybe in a little restaurant like this." Mary looked excited. "If I can remember that, I'll remember more."

Mary released Alice's hands and held out her own hand, her thumb and forefinger about an inch apart. "I feel like I'm this close to remembering and then it slips away again. It's so frustrating I could scream." She smiled before Alice could say anything. "Patience is a virtue, right? I remember that too. Apparently it's one virtue I'm going to get to polish before I come through this."

She fingered the silverware in front of her. "I wish I could think of a way to say 'thank you' properly. Not only to you but to Finn and his owner. I've thought a lot about how different things might have been if the dog hadn't found and stayed beside me. It took a while to revive me. If I'd lain there overnight ..." She shuddered. "That dog is a real hero."

"Maybe we could think of something," Alice offered. "A basket full of bones and doggie chews, perhaps? Surely there is something nice we can do for Finn."

The Coffee Shop gradually emptied, and Hope had just refilled Alice's teacup when Ethel, Florence and LeAnn, in her uniform, entered.

"Hello, ladies," Alice greeted them. Florence and Ethel both had determined smiles on their faces. Alice felt a quick wave of sympathy. She hoped LeAnn had enough stamina to be befriended by these two. "Out for lunch?"

"LeAnn has help today so she could take a few minutes off." They sat down in the booth behind Mary and Alice so that Alice's back was to them.

Alice, intrigued by Mary's idea of saying "thank you" to Finn, began to doodle on a napkin. What would a trophy for a dog look like, anyway? A retriever in a noble pose, head up, appearing to sniff the scent of the air? Or like a big bone? Mary, seeing what Alice was sketching, playfully started to offer suggestions about the dog.

"A fuller tail, I think. And smaller ears. Your dog looks like Bugs Bunny. No, not that small. Now he doesn't appear to have ears at all."

Distracted by the sketching, at first Alice paid no attention to the booth behind theirs. Then, almost subconsciously, she caught the drift of the conversation behind her.

"More letters from Australia? You don't say. Someone is very interested in Jean down there on the other side of the world."

"I was in the post office this morning when Mr. Billings picked up his mail," Florence said to LeAnn. "Poor man dropped it all over the floor in the foyer, so I helped him pick it up. It looked as though he had some very important letters." Florence lowered her voice. "*From the government.*"

"Oh yes, he gets a lot of that, I've noticed," LeAnn said. "I try to remember the types of mail people get. Sometimes it tells me a lot about them, especially the catalogs they receive. For example, there's a gentleman in town who gets only catalogs containing sports equipment. His magazines are about sports too."

"Really?" Ethel sounded interested.

"Oh yes. Of course Mrs. Ley, the pastor's wife, gets lovely magazines. Inspirational ones. And there's a lady with new twins who always has baby magazines coming in the mail...."

"I noticed that Clarissa Cottrell had a magazine from a retirement community on the counter in the bakery the other day," Florence said, obviously fishing for more information.

"She gets a lot of those. All from the same place." She laughed. "They must really want her to move there."

Now Alice was listening more closely. Her aunt and Florence were grilling poor LeAnn. She glanced at Mary, who looked questioningly at the clock.

Reluctantly, Alice scooted herself out of the booth. She was more than curious about what else the pair would squeeze out of LeAnn.

As she paid the bill, she heard Florence's voice float to the front of the room. "South America? What on earth kind of business does Wilhelm have in *South America*?

"Did you overhear the conversation going on behind us?" Alice asked Mary, as they walked into the bright sunlight.

"They are very curious, aren't they?"

"That is the understatement of the year. Where gossip is concerned, Florence and Ethel can be like sharks when there's blood in the water."

"The postmistress appears able to take care of herself." Mary giggled. "I hope I have a relative like your aunt. She must make life interesting."

Alice considered what she'd overheard for a moment. "It's probably all harmless. I know that Ethel and Florence are simply intent on befriending the woman. How they do it is their business."

"You befriended me, and I'll never be able to express how much I appreciate it," Mary said as they walked down the street. The sun shining on the picturesque buildings made Acorn Hill look like a postcard or magazine ad for the idyllic life.

She looked at her watch. "I think we'll just walk by Craig Tracy's shop before we head home. I know you'd enjoy seeing it."

Craig was whistling as he put together eight elaborate floral centerpieces. When Alice and Mary came in he glanced up and smiled. "Hello, ladies. What can I do for you today?"

"I wanted to show your shop to my friend here, Mary." Alice closed the door softly behind them.

"Well, I'm glad you stopped by. It's nice to meet you, Mary." Craig slipped a red tulip into the vase and leaned back to take an appraising look. "I'm afraid the shop is a bit of a mess right now. I'm working on a very large order for a wedding."

"Those arrangements are beautiful. I love tulips," Mary murmured.

She and Alice exchanged a glance. One more memory in place.

"You must be helping to prepare for the same wedding in Potterston for which Clarissa at the Good Apple is decorating a cake." Alice leaned in to smell the fragrant bouquet.

"One and the same." He looked pleased. "I've been getting very good business from weddings lately. Word must be getting out about my work."

"You know Clarissa well, don't you?" Alice watched him carefully.

"We've consulted on a lot of weddings, if that's what you mean." Craig nodded. "Sometimes brides want real flowers on their cakes."

"You don't think she's considering retiring, do you?"

"No. She's never even hinted at that." Craig laid down a flower on the counter. "Why, has she said something to you?"

"Just the opposite, actually. But I overheard something in the Coffee Shop that made me wonder."

"Well, you know, sometimes people talk without having all the facts." He stepped back to look at what he was doing. Alice watched Craig work, while Mary peered into the refrigerated cases.

"Craig, you and Wilhelm Wood are friends." Her voice went up a little at the end, making her statement sound more like a question.

Craig nodded.

"Has he mentioned going to South America to you?"

Craig looked surprised. "Wilhelm travels a lot, but he's never mentioned South America."

Alice and Mary exchanged a glance as they headed for the door.

Craig put a perfect yellow tulip and some baby's breath in a piece of green florist tissue and handed it to Mary. "There you are. My welcoming gift. Enjoy."

"Oh, thank you, Craig," Mary said, her face lighting up.

"You ladies have a nice day."

They waved, then stepped onto Hill Street.

"I'm going to make an easy lunch," Alice said on the way home. "There's sliced turkey in the refrigerator, which will go nicely with the multigrain buns we bought. We'll make sandwiches and have blackberry pie. Jane no doubt has a big supper planned, so something quick and simple will be just right."

"I'm full from that malted milk, but it was worth it," Mary said as they strolled down Acorn Avenue. "Memories are swirling beneath the surface, and something I try will make them pop into view, I just know it. Thank you for taking me out today." Mary stopped and looked at Alice with true gratitude in her eyes. "Now that I remember malt shops and tulips, it gives me hope that the rest will return as well."

"Time, patience and prayer," Alice said. "That's my prescription for your healing."

When they returned to Grace Chapel Inn, everyone was sitting on the front porch. Small, brightly colored quilt tops were hung over the porch rail like cheerful flags.

"What's this?" Alice asked. "I thought you'd all be inside working your fingers to the bone, and here you are. Don't tell me that all the quilts are done."

"These aren't quite finished, but they looked so pretty I thought we'd sit outside and enjoy them," Jane said. "Claire is still inside sewing. She'll have hers completed soon. She's been sewing while the rest of us talked."

Mary squirmed beside Alice. "I've been thinking. You've got all these guests. Maybe I should find another—"

"Nonsense!" Louise looked appalled. "We wouldn't think of it."

"Are you absolutely sure?"

"The least you can do is let us try to help you settle the mystery of your identity," Alice teased gently.

Mary laughed. "So I'd be like a parlor game? That might be fun. Maybe I'm a millionaire, and when we discover that, I can take you all on a cruise in the Mediterranean."

"I'd like the Caribbean better," Jane said.

"I vote for a trip to Hawaii myself," Louise said primly. "I've always wanted to go there."

"Mexico for me," Alice added. "I can hardly wait."

"Sylvia and I are taking Stella, Patty and Becky to Fairy Pond," Jane announced after lunch. "Anyone else want to go along?" She looked around the room. "No takers? Off we go then."

After they'd left, the house grew very quiet. Alice and Mary took advantage of the unused machines and began to sew.

Claire approached Louise cautiously.

"Is everything okay?" Louise asked.

"More 'okay' than it was when I first came here," Claire admitted. "I was so angry and upset that I never thought I'd ever laugh again, and now I've laughed dozens of times already. This is a healing place." She sighed. "My husband Ben calls me a 'drama queen.'" She shifted from foot to foot. "I hope you don't mind my asking you something."

"Please do."

"I've been thinking a lot about our last conversation, the one about my husband."

Louise nodded. "Let's go into the sunroom where we can talk privately."

Claire followed Louise into the room, and they seated themselves in the comfortable chairs. Wendell, who was sleeping in a bright patch of sun, opened one eye, blinked and closed it again.

"I came here feeling so...so...righteous. I was sure I was the one who was wronged and that my husband was an inconsiderate jerk."

Louise's eyes widened a bit but she didn't speak.

"Then I met Mary, you and your sisters and it was like a splash of cold water in my face. As I've been with all of you, I've begun to realize that I came here thinking I was the center of the universe, that everything had to revolve around me. Ben was in trouble because he didn't live up to my expectations."

Her expression turned thoughtful. "I suppose, if I'd wanted a birthday card so badly, I could have reminded him or dropped a hint or two. He's a hard worker. It shouldn't be such a surprise to me that it slipped his mind. He even forgot his *own* birthday once while we were dating." She looked contrite. "But I conveniently forgot all about that."

Louse sat quietly, waiting for her to go on.

"My older brother tells me I was a spoiled child and haven't outgrown it yet. For the first time in my life, I've begun to wonder if there might be some truth to that."

Claire squirmed, misery written on her face. "I started listening to and thinking about Mary. Suddenly not only did my little problem seem like just that—a *little* problem—but it's embarrassing that I made such a mountain out of a molehill. The poor woman has no memory, no money, no idea where her family is and no way of knowing when her memory will come back. And I'm upset with my husband over a *birthday card*." She rolled her eyes. "What a baby I've been."

"What made you fall in love with Ben in the first place?" Louise asked gently.

Claire looked startled. Her brow furrowed in thought. "Well, he's very handsome. At least *I* think so. He has a beautiful smile."

"What else made you love him?"

"He's so funny, always joking around. I'm too serious much of the time, and he makes me laugh. Sometimes I think he'd forget his own head if it weren't attached. I call him my Absentminded Professor..." A light dawned in her eyes. "And now I'm angry with him for the very thing that made me fall in love with him." She put the heel of her hand to her forehead.

Louise smiled.

"If you don't mind, I'm going to my room to think. I only hope I haven't messed up things too badly. I need to apologize to my husband." She put her arms around Louise and gave her a quick hug before disappearing up the stairs.

Chapter Twelve

I can't remember feeling this relaxed in an eon," Stella said as they walked toward Fairy Pond.

"'An eon'? That covers a lot of years and territory." Becky picked up a broken branch to use as a walking stick.

"Okay, maybe not 'an eon,'" Stella said, laughing, "but the times have been rare. It's not easy to control the entire world, you know." She let out a slow breath.

Patty raised her eyebrows.

"I know I can be bossy," Stella said, looking at her friends. "I must have been impossible to live with in school."

"It was difficult sometimes," Becky admitted. "I never felt as if I lived up to your expectations."

Stella grabbed Becky's hand. "I was always envious of the fact that you were all so much at ease in your own skin. I wasn't. Being a perfectionist was my way of trying to get comfortable."

They were all quiet after that as they hiked toward the pond. Stella had just unveiled a portion of herself they'd never seen before.

"Thank you for telling us that," Jane murmured finally. "I know it isn't easy for a perfectionist to admit a flaw."

When they reached the pond, Stella stood by the water, her head tipped back, sunshine caressing her face. The innumerable shades of green that surrounded the pond shimmered in the light. "This is beautiful."

Patty sat down on a log, broke off a wide blade of grass, held it between her thumbs and tried to make a whistling sound through it.

"What a wonderful place it would be to capture in a painting," Becky added. "Look at the frogs over here!" She squatted close to the ground to get eye to eye with one. "I have a manuscript about frogs to illustrate soon. I think I'll sketch some of these big guys. I can see it already. Watercolors, I think. Pale green ferns, translucent blue water in the pond, these guys on the bank, on a log..."

Becky had transported herself from the real Fairy Pond into an imaginary one. "Water lilies, birds...what kind of birds are native to this place, Jane?" She looked up to see her friends laughing.

Becky stood up and dusted off her hands. "Did I go into illustrator zone there? I couldn't help it. This is such a beautiful place."

"I come here a lot," Jane acknowledged. "It's so peaceful. Sylvia comes here a lot too." Jane turned to her. "Don't you?"

"Love it," Sylvia agreed. "I once designed a quilt based on what I've seen here. I used batiks mostly, and made my own rendition of Fairy Pond. It won first place at a local fair."

"And I see Wilhelm Wood, who owns the tea shop, here occasionally. He likes solitude sometimes, and this is the perfect place for that. I also run into Craig Tracy out here. He's a student of plant life, of course, and lately he's been taking photos. He told me once that his first dream was to become a florist and his second was to be a photographer."

"Oh, thanks for reminding me. I've got my digital camera in my pocket." Becky pulled out a camera no bigger than a deck of cards. "I'll take photos so I can paint at home. I'll e-mail them to all of you."

She squatted down near the water in an attempt to get a portrait of a frog. Her brow was unlined and her expression relaxed. For the moment, at least, she'd forgotten to worry about Blaine.

Patty still sat on the log, making faint whistling sounds through her blade of grass. She looked up as Jane watched her.

"Old trick my daddy taught me."

"I never knew much about your parents. You didn't talk about them a lot when we lived together."

Patty shrugged. "Not much to say. They were quiet people, at least at the age they had me." She smiled at Jane's curious look.

"I was born when they were in their forties. I was pampered and protected, as you might imagine. My parents would have been happy if I hadn't dated a boy or driven a car until I was forty-five years old."

She picked up a stick and stirred it in the dirt. "I think that's part of why I married my husband. He's older than I am, you know. I was always comfortable with people not my own age. We are the product of our upbringings, aren't we?"

"I'm certainly beginning to see that in our little group."

"I know I am," Becky said. "My father left when I was a baby. I always vowed to have a *whole* family, a perfect one, because mine was so fragmented." She looked dreamily over the pond. "When I was young I was sure I was going to have sixteen children."

Patty nearly choked on her blade of grass. "Sixteen?"

"If I remember correctly, when you were young you couldn't even handle two," Jane said.

Recollection dawned in Becky's eyes. "I'd almost forgotten. You're talking about the time my cousin's children came to stay with us for the weekend."

"Came to take us apart from limb to limb, you mean." Stella perched on a tree stump, sunning herself. "Those were the most undisciplined children I've ever seen. To this day I believe they are the reason I never had children of my own."

"You just weren't accustomed to kids, that's all," Becky said weakly, a smile playing at the corners of her lips.

"Not all children lock themselves in the bathroom for two hours and use *other people's* makeup," Stella said.

"It washed off."

"And I had to replace everything I owned," Stella grumbled. "I never did find another tube of *Radiant Rose* lipstick. It was discontinued."

"They were cute, though, weren't they?" Becky asked. "Connie and Bonnie. They are all grown up now and have children of their own."

"I hope their children wet the bed," Stella said, "like Connie and Bonnie did mine."

Jane and Patty, sitting side by side on the downed tree, burst out laughing. "You did get the raw end of that deal, Stella, but those kids hung on you like burrs on a dog. They adored you."

"Remember how they answered the door and told my date to go away, that I didn't like him anymore? It took a lot of talking to convince him that the girls hadn't heard that from me."

Stella rose from the stump and stretched. "Who wants to walk to the other side of the pond?"

Sylvia and Becky stood up. Jane and Patty stayed where they were.

"We'll look for more amphibians for Becky," Sylvia said as they wandered off.

Jane waited until they were out of earshot to say to Patty, "You look like you have something serious on your mind."

"I've been thinking about our conversation last night, Jane. I'm going to be miserable no matter what I do. If I don't give the necklace back, I won't forgive myself, but if I do, I don't know what kind of fireworks I'll set a match to."

"Are you so sure there'll be fireworks?"

Patty's lips turned down at the corners. "I don't want to be the one to break up the old gang, especially now that we've all reconnected and are having so much fun. I've *missed* you guys."

"You've certainly made up your mind about Stella's response."

"I ruined her relationship, and even though I never meant to actually steal the necklace, I did choose not to give it back. After all this time I've finally begun to understand Stella. I don't want her furious with me now."

"How do you know that she will be?"

"I just know. . . ." Patty's jaw set stubbornly.

"When did you become a mind reader?" Jane chided.

Patty started to reply, but their attention was diverted by someone crashing noisily through the trees.

Craig Tracy erupted into the clearing, red faced and puffing. He had a walking stick in his hand and looked ready to use it as a machete. He looked surprised to see them in the clearing.

"I didn't know anyone was out here. Sorry. I made a lot of noise and probably frightened all the birds away."

"You were thrashing along, that's for sure," Jane said, "but you didn't frighten the frogs, and that's our primary focus at the moment."

Craig looked puzzled.

Jane gestured toward the opposite side of the pond where the other group was walking. "My friend Becky is going to use Fairy Pond's frogs as models for the next children's book she illustrates."

"Oh, I see." Craig looked pleased. "It's high time Fairy Pond was immortalized."

"Craig, this is Patty, another of my roommates from college. We're here to enjoy the serenity of the pond and to work up an appetite for dinner. What brings you here?"

"Nice to meet you, Patty. Jane has been telling me all about her college friends. To answer your question, Jane,

I'm walking off my embarrassment mostly. I had the craziest thing happen to me today."

"We're all ears. Tell us what happened."

He took off his sunglasses and shook his head. "Your Aunt Ethel came into the shop today looking for a plant to give to the new postmistress. She said she wanted her to have it so that when she saw it on her window ledge, she would be reminded that she has friends in Acorn Hill."

"That's sweet," Patty commented.

Craig continued. "Ethel was full of news, as usual. She surprised me by telling me that Carmen Olander was expecting a baby. She said she'd overheard it at the post office. She was delighted because she said she'd wondered if Carmen would ever take time away from the horses she raises to start a family."

"My aunt concerns herself with a lot of things that aren't her business," Jane said.

"It wasn't even twenty minutes later that Carmen walked into my shop and asked for a mixed bouquet to give to her neighbor. She looked around the shop while I put it together. When she paid for the flowers, I handed her a rose."

"That was thoughtful of you," Jane said.

"When Carmen asked me what it was for, I said 'I hear congratulations are in order. There's going to be a new baby.' I told her how pleased I was for her and her husband."

Craig reddened. "Imagine how I felt when Carmen told me that she wasn't going to have a baby but that her new mare was going to have a colt!"

Patty covered her mouth with her hand, but Jane burst out laughing.

"It was a completely innocent mistake," Craig blurted, "but I can't remember the last time I've been so embarrassed."

"I'm sorry I'm laughing," Jane said as she wiped her eyes, "but you have to admit it's funny."

"Not so funny if you are the one putting your foot in your mouth." Craig looked grim. "You'd better tell your aunt Ethel to get her facts straight, Jane. Granted, all that happened was that Carmen and I had a good laugh, but what if Carmen was trying to have a baby and was sensitive about the subject?"

Jane had a sinking feeling in the pit of her stomach. Ethel would feel awful about embarrassing Craig. She would never intentionally hurt a fly. Unfortunately putting a curb on Ethel's gossip was a little like herding cats—nearly impossible.

"I'll wait for the right moment to mention it to her. Maybe if I tell her what happened without making a big deal of it, she'll get the idea."

"Thanks, Jane." Craig smiled at the women. "At least I feel a *little* better now."

"Don't beat up any more trees with your walking stick on the way out," Jane suggested pleasantly.

"No. I won't." Craig nodded to Patty. "Nice to meet you." He took a few steps and disappeared into the woods in the direction of Acorn Hill.

"I'd almost forgotten how small town life could be," Patty said. "But I think you made him feel better."

The others came into sight as they rounded a stand of trees. Becky waved her digital camera over her head. "I got some great photos. Just wait until you see them."

On the way home from Fairy Pond, the group took a detour to Time for Tea.

"What a darling shop." Patty inhaled deeply as she stepped in the door. The scents of various teas blended together like a perfume. Displays of tea services and china cups decorated the room.

"Maybe I'll get some green tea," Stella announced, examining the different blends for sale. "I drink it all the time. It's very good for you, full of antioxidants that prevent aging."

"They must work," Becky commented. "You certainly don't look as if you've aged."

Stella turned a grateful look on her friend. "Do you mean it?"

"I wouldn't have said it if I didn't mean it."

"It's true, Stella," Patty added. "You look great."

Before anyone could comment further, Wilhelm moved forward to introduce himself. "Welcome to Time for Tea. Jane, who are these lovely ladies?"

Jane introduced her friends, and Wilhelm turned on his considerable charm. "I've got hot water in the back. Would you like to sample some teas?" The women nodded, and Wilhelm began to set out dainty cups and saucers on the counter.

$\backsim$

"You should have brought us here right away," Stella said to Jane over a steaming cup of oolong. "I have to buy some of this to take home."

"I want this." Becky held up a teapot that looked like a yellow duck with a spout for a beak and a handle in its tail feathers.

As Jane watched the shopping frenzy in progress, she leaned across the counter to Wilhelm. "I think it's your charm that's sold them."

Wilhelm chuckled as he wrapped the packages the others had purchased.

"Thank you, Jane," Wilhelm said. "I haven't had this many sales in a single hour in a long time."

"Glad to help. I hope business improves."

"Fortunately, my mail-order business for my china has picked up considerably lately. I've been busy searching for replacement cups, saucers and plates for some of my customers. It takes a good deal of time, communicating with other dealers."

"I hear you're going to be doing some traveling too. South America, isn't it?" Jane recalled Alice telling her about Florence's comment in the Coffee Shop earlier.

Much to Jane's astonishment, Wilhelm's eyes widened and he looked surreptitiously from right to left, as though he were afraid someone might have heard her comment.

"How do you know that?"

"Alice heard it in town."

Suddenly Wilhelm looked very worried. "In town?"

"What's the problem? You travel all the time."

"That is the price you pay for living in a little place like this. People think they know your business better than you do."

"I'm sorry. I can see you're upset." Jane glanced over her shoulder. Her friends were busy admiring a wicker table and chair in the window, set with items for a formal tea.

"I *am* planning to go to South America," Wilhelm said quietly, "but nothing is finalized yet. I haven't shared the news with my mother." Wilhelm and his elderly mother lived together and he was very solicitous of her. "Mother is more nervous about my traveling than she used to be. Too much twenty-four-hour-a-day television news, I think. She's especially down on South America right now. She's been reading about drug cartels and who knows what else in news magazines. Her worries are unfounded, of course. I'm a very cautious and experienced traveler. Still, I don't want her to know I'm going yet. I want to break the news to her gently."

Wilhelm looked pleadingly at Jane. "You do understand, don't you? If Mother were to hear this from someone else, it would upset her terribly. I can't understand how it even got out. Only a few people know about my plans."

Not anymore, Jane thought to herself. *Plenty of people already know if Ethel and Florence were privy to the information.*

"I'm sorry you're worried. Maybe you should speak with your mother soon—just in case." Jane grimaced. "And I'll try to squelch the rumor in town," she added.

I'll speak to Aunt Ethel, she thought. *This is one time seemingly harmless gossip could actually cause some trouble.* Wilhelm's elderly mother was fragile. The last thing she needed was to worry more about her son's safety.

By the time Jane and the others got home late Thursday afternoon, Alice and Mary had Mary's quilt blocks completed and Claire was helping them to lay out the pieces on the floor in the sunroom in an appealing pattern.

"Next time I'm going to make something larger. This will be great as a wall hanging, but now I want to make something bed-sized," Mary said as she surveyed her creation proudly.

"You put us to shame," Stella said, obviously delighted with how popular her idea to make quilts had been.

"Claire, you're almost done too," Sylvia said. "Shall I help you finish it up? Let's take it into the sunroom."

"I'm going to lie down for a few minutes," Patty said with a yawn and mounted the stairs to her room. Becky trailed into the sunroom to help Claire.

That left Jane and Stella alone in the dining room.

"Jane, does Patty seem … different … to you?" Stella asked. "She's much quieter than she used to be, don't you think?"

"Maybe she's got something on her mind."

"Surely she could tell us what it was. We are her best friends, after all." Stella hesitated. "Or at least we *were*. I'd like us to be close again—like old times."

Jane watched Stella, sure that Stella had never known the extent of Patty's resentment or jealousy. And now she didn't know about the guilt Patty carried either.

"'O, what a tangled web we weave, When first we practice to deceive...'" Jane murmured to herself, remembering the words of Sir Walter Scott that her father often quoted.

Stella pulled out a chair and sat down. "I remember how beautiful I always thought Patty was when we were in school. Here I was, dark-haired and angular and she, so blonde, curvy and lovely. I hate to admit it, but I was jealous of her." Jane tried not to let the astonishment show on her face.

Stella stared out the window at a bird perched on a feeder. "Why do you think I try so hard at everything, Jane? My husband says it's because I'm afraid of not measuring up."

"If that's the case, none of us had any idea. You're a great actress."

Stella looked at Jane with fondness. "But being with you guys for even a few hours makes me feel—real. It's not much fun pretending all the time. It doesn't seem so important to have to measure up here." Stella stood and wrapped her arms around Jane. "You are a good friend. Thank you for listening." She pulled back and flushed, as if embarrassed to have shared so much. "I think it's time for me to start sewing again."

Late in the afternoon Claire found Louise in the kitchen enjoying a cup of tea.

"Could we talk a little?" The young woman asked nervously. "I have something to tell you."

"Of course." Louise placed her cup down on the table and gestured to the empty chair.

"I've come to realize that I acted like a spoiled brat," Claire said. She took a deep breath. "It's time I grew up and apologized to my husband. I'm going to call him. I'm ready to go home."

Chapter Thirteen

inner is served."

"It's about time," Becky said. "We're dying in here. It's cruel and unusual punishment to keep us away from the food, Jane."

"Whatever you're serving, it smells divine," Stella declared.

Stella, Patty and Becky were playfully pouting about being told to stay in the sunroom and out of the dining room for a half hour before dinner. Mary and Claire were more content, having started to work a jigsaw puzzle.

"I'm glad you stayed for dinner," Becky said to Claire as she put a hand on her shoulder. "Louise said you were going home."

"I'd planned to, but I called Ben's office and they told me he'd left for the day. I called home, but he wasn't there. Wouldn't you know it? Now, when I *want* to talk to him, I can't reach him. I'd rather stay here than rattle around in my empty house if he's gone somewhere. I had to insist that

I start paying for my meals, however. I don't want to take advantage of the Howards' generosity."

"I know exactly what you mean," Mary said. "I wish I had a place to go so I wouldn't impose on them so much."

"You will soon," Claire said. "You are making progress."

Mary nodded but didn't look convinced. Instead, she picked up a puzzle piece and slid it into place.

It was later than their usual mealtime, and dusk was falling when Jane finally ushered them all into the dining room. The room was elegant, illuminated by candlelight, the table replete with linen and lace, mirrored tiles, flowers, crystal and lovely old china.

There was a breathless silence as the guests entered the glittering room.

"It's beautiful!" Stella finally exclaimed.

Louise, who was standing in the kitchen door with Jane and Alice, chuckled. "Jane's fixed something special for dinner. Alice got busy on the computer and made menus for you at each setting," Louise said.

"Take your places, please." Alice fluttered around the room. "Dinner is ready."

Patty sat down and picked up her personal menu.

Cold Cream of Cucumber Soup
Baby Greens with Cranberries
Dilled Salmon with Sour Cream Sauce
Wild and White Rice with Mushrooms
Brussels Sprouts with Pistachios
Chocolate Truffle & Toffee Cheesecake

"I've eaten in a lot of lovely places, but this is my favorite," Patty declared.

They'd all taken their places at the table, and Jane was about to serve the cold soup from a tureen on the sideboard when the doorbell rang.

"Who could that be?" Louise wondered out loud as she moved to get the door.

The others waited silently, and soon they could hear a male voice in the hall. The muted conversation went on for some moments. Then Louise reentered the room. She was followed by a tall, well-built man, handsome, with high cheekbones, a shock of thick brown hair and wide, hazel eyes.

"Claire, you have a visitor," Louise said.

Claire jumped to her feet. Pure delight lit her face. "Ben!" She ran to him, then threw herself into his arms. "What are you doing here?"

The man, eyeing the other women around the table, cleared his throat, obviously trying to decide if this was the time and place to say what he had to say.

He glanced again at Claire and made up his mind.

"I came to get you," the man said. "We need to talk."

"How did you find me?"

"I called the credit card company and found out where you'd been charging things. You purchased gas at the filling station in Acorn Hill so I drove over here to look for you. I saw your car parked here when I drove into town."

"You did all that to find me?"

"Of course I did. I love you, Claire." Ben's voice softened and he took her hands in his. "Please come home with me. I know I made you angry, but I'll make it up to you. I promise."

"There's nothing to make up for," she said, shaking her head. "I behaved like a spoiled child." She sighed. "Next year, if I want a birthday card, I'll write the date on your calendar in red letters."

Ben cleared his throat. "About that..."

Jane started to wonder if the rest of the group should leave the room, though everyone at the table was thoroughly enjoying the love story unfolding before their eyes.

"Yes?"

"I didn't forget your birthday, exactly. I remembered, but was off on the date. You have to come home. You're having a surprise party tomorrow night at our house."

"I am?"

"I invited people weeks ago," Ben said sheepishly. "I just planned the party for the wrong week."

A look of astonishment and then chagrin flickered on Claire's features. "You planned a party for me?"

"People are coming from all over. What would they have said if they'd arrived and you were nowhere to be found?" Ben put his finger into the tight ring of his shirt collar.

Claire turned to Louise. "It seems I'll be checking out tonight."

"I should say so!" Louise said delightedly.

After Claire ran upstairs to get her things, Ben apologized for interrupting the ladies' dinner.

Jane insisted that he sit down at Claire's place to wait for her.

Soon Claire returned with her suitcase. Her eyes shone. In one hand she carried the lap quilt she and Louise had been working on.

Claire stopped in front of Louise. "You have been so wonderful to me that I ..." she choked up.

Louise reached out and took the fabric from her hand. "Why don't you leave this with me. I'll put the binding on it and send it to you."

"You don't have to do that."

"I *want* to do it. We don't want you to forget your visit to Grace Chapel Inn and the new beginning that happened here, do we?"

"Oh, believe me, I'm never going to forget that." Impulsively she kissed Louise on the cheek.

"Jane, I guess you'll get your bed back tonight," Mary joked.

Ben got to his feet, and he and Claire began walking toward the door. Then he turned back. "By the way, ladies, we're having a big party at our house tomorrow night if any of you want to come."

The couple departed to gales of laughter.

"Louise, you're a marriage counselor," Alice said.

"Well, I'm not sure what just happened," Mary ventured, "but it was wonderful."

"Now can we eat?" Becky pleaded.

Jane went back to ladling the soup into bowls. "It's a good thing I'd planned a *cold* soup tonight."

The phone rang just as they were all finishing dinner. Louise went to answer it.

"Louise? It's Carlene Moss. I heard about your new guest." Carlene was the editor of the *Acorn Nutshell* and a dedicated journalist. "What a great story! Amnesia! I wanted to see if it would be okay for me to stop at the inn and interview her."

"Can you hold for a moment, Carlene?" Louise asked. "I'll speak to Mary." Louise laid the phone on the desk and hurried back to the dining room.

"Mary, may Carlene Moss, the editor of our local newspaper, take your picture for the next issue? She wants to do a story on you." She glanced at the clock. "I can put her off if you aren't up to it tonight."

"An article? I'd like that very much. I want my face out there where people can see it." Mary ran her fingers through her hair. "If she wants to do it tonight, I'd better find a comb first." She got up from the table and headed for the stairs.

Louise went back to the telephone. "It's fine with Mary for you to come now."

"Wonderful," Carlene said breathlessly. "I'll be there soon."

It wasn't even five minutes later when they heard Carlene's car tires crunching on the driveway outside. Jane was carrying the truffle cheesecake into the dining room with a flourish. Her friends always insisted that chocolate was a major food group, so she knew this particular recipe was going to be a hit. They heard Carlene's car door slam, and moments later she rang the bell. Alice got up to let her in. A heated debate over the merits of dark versus milk chocolate, and the value of store-bought pie crust, was raging when they returned.

After introducing her friends to Carlene, Jane explained the conversation she had interrupted. "We eat food, we cook food and we talk about food. Food has been at least sixty percent of the entertainment since my friends have been here."

"We will also take a reminder of Jane's food home with us," Becky said, patting her midsection. "And have to buy bigger clothing because of it."

"You look very businesslike," Louise said, taking in the camera bag and Carlene's ever-present notebook. Carlene's brown hair was pulled back into a short ponytail, and her reading glasses were perched on the top of her head. She was dressed in a khaki pants suit with a white shirt.

"I'm on my way home from Potterston. A young woman from there is part of a group traveling to Tanzania as part of a mission trip. I wanted to get a photo of the group getting on the bus to the airport."

"How wonderful," Louise said, ushering her toward an empty chair. "I enjoy hearing about young people making a difference in the world."

"She was quite excited, as was the rest of the group. The experience will be life-changing for them, I'm sure."

Carlene hiked her camera bag higher onto her shoulder. "And of course I heard about the amnesia story and knew I had to get that into the next issue."

"We're very eager to get Mary's story out," Alice said. "Maybe someone will come forward with information."

"It's a good idea. Many times eyewitnesses have no idea they've seen something out of the ordinary until they hear about an incident later." Carlene nodded approvingly.

At that moment, Mary walked down the stairs from the second floor. She was carrying Wendell, who was purring like a small motor. Mary settled Wendell on the floor. He made a figure eight through her legs before wandering off.

"This is Carlene Moss of the *Acorn Nutshell*," Louise said to Mary. "She's the one who has come to take a few pictures of you for the paper."

"That's wonderful. Maybe someone will recognize me." She turned to Carlene. "If you have any questions for me, I'd be happy to answer them."

Louise smiled. Asking Carlene if she had any questions was like asking Fred Humbert if he had any hardware. Newspaperwoman that she was, Carlene loved asking questions. "You can use the sunroom. The rest of us will be dallying over dessert for a while, no doubt. I'll bring you some while you visit."

○

Ethel arrived just in time to get the last piece of cheesecake.

"How is your project working out?" Jane inquired, referring to her budding friendship with LeAnn.

"Frankly, I think Florence is overdoing it a little, being neighborly, I mean. She's going to suffocate the poor woman with sisterly love. If I want to visit with her, I practically have to go to the post office and stand at the counter to do so."

"It sounds as though you and Florence are in competition for LeAnn's attention," Jane observed mildly. Ethel didn't seem to notice.

"The post office is an interesting place, however," Ethel continued. "I've caught up with people I haven't seen in months...like that poor Billings couple. *Tsk. Tsk. Tsk.* I really do love the people in this community and hate it when any of them are having troubles."

"I told Alice and Jane that I would talk to Mr. and Mrs. Billings the next time I saw them," Louise said. "Perhaps they'll confide in me. If so, I'd be happy to help them with their bookkeeping."

"You are such a dear person, Louise," Ethel said. "I only wish we could solve everyone's problems so easily."

Mary and Carlene came back into the dining room, interview finished. Carlene said her good-byes and left. Mary sat down wearily and motioned for them to continue their conversation.

"There are other troubles?" Jane asked, looking at Ethel questioningly.

Ethel nodded. "Like Jean Humbert not telling her mother she has a boyfriend in Australia."

"But Aunt Ethel, are you sure that's *true*?" Alice asked.

"Aunt Ethel, I know for a fact it *isn't* true," Louise said. "I was visiting with Vera and Jean today at the hardware store. Jean is working there this summer. Viola came in, and while we all were chatting she asked Jean if she had a boyfriend in Australia. Vera and Jean thought it was the funniest thing they'd ever heard. Apparently Jean has a steady boyfriend at college. Vera said she wouldn't be surprised if they considered marriage someday. Besides, Jean and Vera are very close. Jean would never keep something like that from her mother."

"No boyfriend in Australia? How can that be?" Ethel got an odd look on her face. "But my source is so dependable."

"It is lovely to hear of a mother and daughter that close," Mary said, unaware of Ethel's sudden turmoil or what the Howard sisters might be thinking of this new bit of information. "I wonder if *I* have children."

"You're sad because you don't even know if you are a mother, and ever since I arrived, I've been wondering why I had children in the first place. What an ungrateful person I am," Becky said.

Mary looked bewildered.

"Perhaps I need to explain," Becky said, recognizing the confusion the statement had caused around the room. Her gaze fell on Stella and Patty. "We've been having trouble with Blaine. He recently dropped out of school, quit his job, lost his apartment and came home to live with us. He's been living in his old room in our basement ever since. He watches television all day and shows no inclination or ambition whatsoever to look for a job."

"That's not the Blaine we've always heard about," Patty said.

"He goes out at night after we've gone to bed and comes home in the wee hours of the morning. His father and I have talked until we're blue in the face, but it doesn't faze him. It's as if he doesn't even hear us."

Becky reached for a tissue in her pocket. "His father is furious. He says that we've raised a 'lazy, good-for-nothing.' You know how much I dislike conflict. I'd go to any lengths to avoid it but now I'm living with it every day." She dabbed at her eyes. "I've been miserable."

"Just because your adult son is making decisions you don't like doesn't mean you have to blame yourself for it," Stella said. "You've been a great mom, but you can't mother your children forever. They need to try their own wings."

"I'm not sure he has wings," Becky said miserably. "I thought I was such a good mother. I taught my children morals and values. They know Jesus. They went to church, to piano lessons, to soccer and volleyball. We scrimped and saved to put them through wonderful schools and now...I thought I knew my children, but apparently I was wrong. What's worse—and completely selfish—is that I think it's a reflection on my parenting."

"Has he seen a doctor or a counselor?" asked Alice. "It could be that he is depressed."

"What would he have to be depressed about?"

"It's not always as simple as that," Alice said quietly.

"My husband says—"

"What do you say, Becky?" Patty asked.

Becky looked around the room silently, watching the faces of her friends. Then she stood up. "If you'll excuse me, I want to call home," she said just audibly. "I let my ego stand in the way of helping my son. If my son is in trouble and not just lazy as my husband believes, then … well … I'm not sure quite what I'll do yet, but I'll think of something."

∽

"We're a messed-up bunch, aren't we?" Stella mused as she, Jane and Patty sat on the darkened front porch later that evening. A bull-frog chorus rumbled in the distance. "I had no idea this trip would have such an effect on all of us."

"What's happened for you, Stella?" Patty asked softly.

Stella poured herself more iced tea from a carafe on the table. "I've realized how much I've missed my old friends. The people I know in the art world are acquaintances, but most of them aren't true friends. Right now I'm fairly 'hot.' I can't tell who actually wants to be my friend and who just wants to say they hang out with Stella Leftner."

"That's sad," Patty said, shaking her head.

"My husband says that old friends are the best. Despite all the people he knows, who does Al go hiking and watch baseball with? The guys he knew in high school and two college roommates. They have stood the test of time and he trusts them."

Stella's gaze was steady as she studied her friends. "Like you all," Stella murmured. "I can trust you."

"I had no idea you cared so much," Patty said.

"I've always admired you, Patty. We had our differences, but you were my role model, whether you knew it or not. I've always been impulsive, hurrying to finish something so I could go on to something else. You, on the other hand, are meticulous. You taught me how to pace myself and really evaluate what I was doing, especially in my art. I've thanked you silently many times over the years for your example." Stella smiled. "Even if you seemed just too good to be true sometimes."

"But I was jealous of you," Patty said, her voice barely a whisper.

"I would have given my pinkie finger just to look like you back then. I even considered coloring my hair blonde." Stella touched her dark hair. "We always fell for the same men and I was sure I was going to lose every one of them to you."

"I thought it was the other way around!" Patty marveled. "You were tiny, thin and exotic. You reminded me of a hummingbird, touching down at every flower. I could never keep up with you. If I'd been a bird, I would have had to have been … an ostrich."

"It would have made things easier if we'd known all this back then, wouldn't it?" Stella concluded cheerfully. "We certainly wasted a lot of time and energy wishing to be something we're not," Stella put her slender hand over

Patty's. "I'm glad that I got to say these things to you. Now that we are older and wiser, we can finally put that undercurrent of competition between us to rest."

Before Patty or Jane could speak, Stella continued, "Speaking of maturing, I'd like to run something by you, ladies. I'm thinking of having a face-lift."

"You can't have one of those unless you actually have something to lift." Jane pointed out.

"My jawline is looking a little soft, don't you think?" Stella cranked her head to the right and to the left. "There are some significant crow's-feet here." She pointed to her eyes.

"You need new glasses, not a face-lift," Patty said.

"You wouldn't tell me a big fib just to make me feel better, would you?" Stella looked cheered.

"We've quit comparing ourselves to others," Patty said, "remember?"

Stella turned to Jane. "How about you?"

"Honestly? Real friend to real friend?"

"Of course."

"This reminds me of a verse in Samuel," Jane said. "'The Lord does not look at the things man looks at. Man looks at the outward appearance, but the Lord looks at the heart' (1 Samuel 16:7)." Jane put her hand over her heart. "It's in *here* that people need a lift and there is only one Physician competent to do that."

"A spirit lift, huh?" Stella smiled. "You always did know how to put things in perspective."

They sat in companionable silence, each buried in her own thoughts until Stella glanced at her watch. "Ugh. I have to call the gallery tonight. Someone has questions for me about a piece of my work. If you'll excuse me, I'll take care of that now."

When she was gone, Patty turned to Jane. "Stella is offering me the friendship that I've longed for with her," she said quietly. "What if my deception spoils it all?"

"You were young," Jane said. "You've already paid a high price for what you did. It's time to come clean, Patty. Tell Stella. You heard what she said about true friends. Trust her to be one of yours."

"I know, I know," Patty sighed. "But it's too late tonight. Now it will have to wait until morning."

Chapter Fourteen

*J*ane found Alice at the computer early on Friday morning and paused to peer over her sister's shoulder.

"I couldn't sleep, so I'm doing research on missing persons," Alice informed her. "I'm trying to find something that will tell me about people who have been reported missing in Pennsylvania in the past week. Then I plan to look at all the states that border us. Surely if Mary wandered off, someone has reported her missing by now."

"Don't you think the police have already done that kind of search?"

Alice sighed and her hands dropped limply into her lap. "I suppose so, but I feel like I need to do *something*."

"Thanks to you she has a roof over her head, food to eat and clothing to wear, and soon," Jane said with a smile, "her very own lap quilt. She's safe, and we're praying for her. Don't sell yourself short, Alice."

"A social worker from the hospital said that as long as Mary was with us, she felt Mary was in good hands. But…"

"I understand. I've been thinking about it too. We can't keep her forever. Nor would she want us to."

Jane looked at the site Alice had put on the screen. "Maybe there's another way."

"There hasn't been any news coverage yet. The *Acorn Nutshell* article will be out next week, but maybe we can get more newspapers interested in her story." Alice spoke with determination. "What we need is to draw attention to her situation."

"And how do you propose we go about that?"

At that moment Stella drifted into the room in work-out clothes. "Go about what?"

"Good morning. Where are you going so early?" Jane asked.

"Jogging. I talked Patty and Becky into going with me. That should be interesting since neither of them has run in years. Would you like to come?" Stella peered curiously over Alice's shoulder just as Jane had.

"No thanks. I have a few things to take care of." Jane often enjoyed jogging in the morning, but she had her hands full making breakfast for the large group today.

"What were you talking about when I came in? 'Go about' what?"

"Alice is on the Internet trying to find out about persons reported missing in the last few days. She thinks we should put more effort into finding out who Mary is."

"Media coverage," Stella said nonchalantly. "When I'm opening a new show or my husband has something big at his gallery, we always try to get an interview with someone—a feature article or a radio interview on a morning show, for example. It's amazing how many people tune in while they drink their coffee and read the paper. Al does a casual tracking of where people have heard about the gallery events, and a number always say they heard it on the radio."

Alice nodded sagely. "Exactly. No one can come forward and identify her if they don't even know what's happened."

"Acorn Hill isn't really media central of the universe. How does one go about attracting attention?" Jane asked.

"You've got to have a hook," Stella said confidently. "An angle."

"Isn't a woman who doesn't know who she is angle enough?" Alice asked.

"Perhaps we're thinking on too large a scale," Jane said. "We need to start smaller. I'm sure there are lots of people right here in Acorn Hill who haven't heard about Mary."

"That's true," Stella acquiesced. "And she was found not far from town. Maybe someone saw or heard something and he or she doesn't even realize it. I'll talk about this with Becky and Patty on our run. When we get back,

we'll do some brainstorming. See you in forty-five minutes." She headed for the front porch where her friends
were waiting.

Alice followed Jane into the kitchen where Jane put on
water for tea and brewed a pot of coffee.

"What could we do that would make a difference?"
Jane asked. "We need to do something to keep Mary's
hopes up."

Alice, meanwhile, stared at the kettle as if she were
willing it to boil. The moment it started whistling, she rose
and poured the water into the teapot.

"What *do* you think happened to her, Alice?"

Alice brought the teapot and cups to the table and sat
down. "I've thought about it a lot. The first thing we have
to account for is the way Mary was battered and bruised
when she was found."

"There aren't too many ways to explain that, are
there?"

"It would be easy if she'd been in a car accident. That
would explain everything. The problem is that there was no
car."

"And therefore, no accident."

"That's what makes it so suspicious. If it didn't happen
in an accident, she must have been responsible for her
condition ... or someone else caused it."

The sisters were quiet as they contemplated the possibilities. Finally Jane stood up and walked to the refrigerator. She took out eggs and milk, then began to mix together some waffle batter.

A short while later, there was a commotion in the front hall as Stella and the others returned.

"We're starving!" Patty called into the kitchen. "Stella worked us like a fiend."

"I've never been so exhausted." Becky came into the kitchen and draped herself over a chair. "I may need chocolate to revive me."

"Hah! They walked and complained the entire way," said Stella.

"Here, have some fruit." Jane pushed a serving dish heaped with fresh fruit toward Becky. Becky frowned.

"I'm working on waffles."

"That sounds more like it," Becky said, dimpling sweetly as she smiled at Jane. "They're at least as good for me as a run, don't you think? Replacing carbs and all that?"

"See my problem?" Stella continued. "They don't take me seriously. Becky looked around, commenting on the birds, flora and fauna and how she needed to get out and sketch. Patty kept saying she was out of breath. The only reason she was out of breath was because she was talking so much."

"The woman is a general," Patty insisted, "barking orders, yelling at us to keep up."

"Sounds like not much has changed in twenty-plus years," Jane said. She poured some batter on the sizzling waffle iron.

Soon everyone was seated around the kitchen table. Mary came down and offered to pour coffee.

"Delish!" Stella took a bite of waffle and closed her eyes. "This is my new favorite food."

"Apparently a little fresh air did you all good," Louise observed as she entered the room.

Jane turned to Stella. "Maybe you'd better not take them running again. It seems to perk up their appetites. I may not have enough food in the house to feed them."

"It's your own fault," Stella retorted cheerfully. "You are too fine a cook, that's all."

Mary took a seat at the table. "I was thinking about jogging. I should try it, I guess. My body will tell me if it is something I've done before or not."

"You should do that," Jane said. "If you like it, great. If not, that's okay too."

Alice cleared her throat. "We were discussing your situation this morning, Mary. We'd like to think of a way to let more people know about your plight. It occurred to us that someone right here in Acorn Hill might know something."

"The police have sent my photo to a number of places, but they've had no response. It's as if I didn't exist at all. How could it be that someone here would recognize me?"

"Someone may have noticed a strange car going through town or driving down the road where you were found. Who knows?"

Jane snapped her fingers. "I've got an idea. You've mentioned how grateful you are that Finn found you. Why don't we have a little garden party and invite Finn and Kieran? I know Kieran would appreciate it. I've heard around town that he's telling people how proud he is of his 'rescue' dog. We'll just let it be known that it is an open house to honor Finn and that we're hoping that someone might have seen something and will come forward. We'd be grateful for anyone who might be able to help in any way."

"Won't that be a lot of work?"

"Jane could prepare for it with one arm tied behind her back," Alice said confidently.

"We talked only a week or so ago about having something here just to show off the flowers. I think this is a wonderful idea. Two birds with one stone, so to speak," Louise said.

"We'll call it a reception for you and Finn," Jane said. "You can never tell who might have information he doesn't even know he—or she—has. And the media might see this as a good hook," she said, smiling at Stella. "Besides, it will be fun. You all can get a feel for the people of Acorn Hill."

"The weather is supposed to be perfect on Sunday," Alice said. "Can we be ready by then?"

"Certainly. We'll make cookies and have Clarissa bake a cake at the Good Apple. We can use flowers from the garden for the table."

"And I'll polish the silver tea service," Louise announced.

Alice bobbed her head. "We'll take the long tables we've been using for our sewing machines outside. I'll cover them with our lace cloths."

"Oh my," said a small voice. Mary's eyes were huge and she'd gone very pale. "All this for me?"

"Do you mind?" Alice asked. "We should have asked your permission before we pushed ahead and started making plans."

"Mind? When you want to do something so wonderful for me?" Mary gave them a warm, thankful smile. "Perhaps someone will know who I am. And if they don't, at least we've tried. Besides, Finn *is* the real hero in this story. People should hear what an animal like Finn is capable of doing."

"So we can go ahead?" Stella asked, obviously itching to get started.

"Only if you'll tell me what I can do to help," Mary said.

"We can help Jane bake cookies," Becky suggested.

"If I remember correctly you always ate more than you baked," Patty commented.

"Okay, we can help with the baking," Stella said, "But there must be more that we can do. How about weeding the flowerbeds?"

"I like that idea," Jane teased. "Becky, can I borrow your camera? We'll need to have proof that you three ever picked weeds."

"Not to worry, girls. Weeds don't dare grow in Jane's garden," Alice said.

"That's a relief," Patty said. "I don't like weeding."

"We forgot one big item," Jane said. "Before we go much further we'd better see if Finn and his master can come."

"May I call him?" Mary asked shyly. "I'd like to be the one to invite them."

"Why don't you take the phone into the library," Alice suggested. "It's too noisy here. We'll get busy as soon as he gives us an answer."

Just after Mary went off to the library, the front door opened and Sylvia called, "Anybody home?"

"In the kitchen," Jane answered her.

"What's going on in here?" Sylvia asked when she entered the kitchen. "It smells divine."

"Pecan waffles. Want one?

Sylvia went to the cupboard and got a plate. "Is there coffee?"

"I just finished brewing a new pot."

Again, Sylvia went to the cupboard for a mug and poured a cup of coffee for herself.

"Thanks for making yourself at home here," Jane said. "Some days I need as many hands as an octopus has tentacles to get things done."

"Treat friends like family and family like friends," Sylvia said.

"I'd like to add to that," Stella said. "At Grace Chapel Inn they just treat everyone like royalty."

"Trust me," Jane replied, "we wouldn't serve royalty in our kitchen."

"What are you doing here so early in the morning?" Louise asked Sylvia.

"I lay in bed last night thinking about the quilts. I decided, if you'd let me, that I'd machine-quilt the tops for you. Because they're lap-sized, it won't take me more than an hour or two."

Sylvia sat down. "Then you'll each have your own special memory of Grace Chapel Inn to take home with you."

"How nice of you," Jane said, pouring some batter onto the hot waffle iron for a fresh waffle.

"Mine's a prayer quilt," Becky murmured. "As I sewed, I prayed for Blaine and the wisdom to know how to help him."

The room grew quiet as they considered her statement.

"I tried to call Blaine last night. He didn't pick up the phone, but I knew he was there. He's always home. Maybe he looked at caller ID, saw it was me and decided he didn't want to talk."

"He wouldn't do that to you." Patty hesitated. "Would he?"

"Frankly? I don't know what he'd do anymore. He's put a wall around himself. Nothing gets in and nothing gets out. I was tempted to give him a piece of my mind when the answering machine came on, but I decided against it. Instead, I told him that whatever else happened, I will always love him. He's my son no matter what he does with his life." Becky gave a small, humorless laugh.

"I'm sure what he needs most is unqualified acceptance," Stella said. "It's what we've all longed for at one time or another."

"I've been so upset with him that I've neglected to tell him how much I love him. I've never recognized until now how much of myself I've tied up in my children,"

Becky admitted. "Somehow I've got to learn to let go."
Everyone was suddenly silent as Patty gave Becky a warm
hug.

Jane saw that emotions were near the surface and
deliberately changed the subject. She put a stack of cook-
books on the table. "Here is some reading material, ladies.
There are decisions to be made. What kinds of sweets shall
we serve at our party?"

Louise quickly explained to Sylvia about the party, and
everyone started talking at once and moved closer to the
table. Jane then added to the stack one of the files that held
her tried-and-true cookie and candy recipes. "You might
also want to look in here. And let's think of a gift to present to Kieran as a small token of appreciation."

Chapter Fifteen

Viola Reed was behind the counter when Jane entered Nine Lives Bookstore. She'd left her friends in charge of picking out some recipes for the party, and she and Sylvia had walked to town, laden with lap quilts. Jane dropped off Sylvia at her store, then continued on to the bookstore to look for a gift for Kieran.

"Hello, stranger, I haven't seen you for a few days." Viola's face lit up at the sight of Jane.

"Hi, Viola. My college roommates are here for a reunion, so we've been busy at the inn. You may actually have heard of one of them." Jane mentioned Becky's name, and Viola's eyes grew wide.

"The illustrator?" Viola brought her hand to her throat and reflexively rearranged the rainbow colored scarf tied artfully at her neck. "I have some of the books she's illustrated here in the store. They're very popular." She walked to the children's section and pulled a couple of Becky's books from the shelf. "You don't think she would…"

"Stop by and autograph them for you?"

"Yes." Viola clasped her hands together.

"I'll ask her. I'm sure she will if she has time. Or you can bring them to her. We've got a lot on our plates these days. That's why I came to talk to you." Jane gave Viola the CliffsNotes version of what they were planning.

"... and I wondered if you could recommend a book that Kieran Morgan might enjoy. My friends and I thought that a book would be an appropriate gift. Nothing elaborate, just something to present to him as a token of appreciation."

"He comes in here every once in a while and looks at books on Ireland. I have a lovely picture book of the countryside. I also have CDs of Irish music." Viola looked a little embarrassed. "I like that kind of music. It makes me want to kick up my heels."

Jane tried to picture the thickset woman doing a sprightly jig, but couldn't quite imagine it.

"If you are free on Sunday afternoon, we'd love to have you join us," Jane said as Viola gift wrapped the book.

"Why, I'd be delighted to come."

"The party will be from two until five. Drop in any-time. Please let your customers know about it. We're counting on word of mouth." She started toward the door.

"I'll be happy to pass on the invitation. *Er*, Jane, before you go…" Viola hesitated. "Your Aunt Ethel was in here this morning saying the most peculiar things."

Jane turned back to Viola. "What kinds of things?"

"That she was afraid that Clarissa Cottrell might retire and move away from Acorn Hill. And something about an old couple who are in financial trouble. I didn't quite catch who they were. Surely *I* would have heard if any of that were true. I'm in the store every day and people, well, talk. But if there's anything we can do to help that poor couple, we should. Could you find out from your aunt who they are so we can see what kind of help they need?"

Jane had a suspicion she knew where Ethel's information came from. "I'll talk to her about it," Jane said, then smiled at Viola and walked out the door. Book tucked under her arm, Jane walked slowly back towards Sylvia's Buttons, her mind in a whirl. She should head to the inn, but she needed Sylvia's advice.

"While you ladies are looking at recipes, I think I'll go on an errand of my own," Louise announced soon after Jane and Sylvia had left. "On the way home I'll stop at the store for some eggs and butter. I imagine we'll be needing more."

She took a jar of homemade preserves from the cupboard and went upstairs for her purse. Louise had decided that now was as good a time as any to check on Nanette and Oscar Billings.

The elderly couple lived on the other side of Acorn Hill, but Louise decided to walk. She needed time to formulate what she might say to let this couple know that if they needed help in straightening out their financial affairs, she was available. She had to do it in such a way that would not insult them or have them think she was prying.

Lord, I pray for wisdom, tact and compassion. And for Your words on my lips.

Nanette and Oscar lived in a small green bungalow on a narrow lot in an older part of Acorn Hill. Louise remembered visiting the home with her father when she was a youngster. The Billingses must have been newlyweds at the time.

She lifted a hand to knock on the front door, but it opened before she could lower her knuckles. Oscar peered out at her like a friendly mole, blinking against the bright sun.

"Miss Louise, is that you?"

He'd always called the Howard sisters Miss Louise, Miss Alice and Miss Jane, a courtly gesture shown to three little girls.

"Hello, Oscar. I've been thinking of you lately and decided to pay you and Nanette a visit. I brought you a jar of Jane's preserves."

"Anything Miss Jane makes has to be delicious." He stepped aside. "Come in, come in. Nanette and I were in the kitchen, reading the papers."

The house's interior was just as she had remembered it—full of built-in, walnut bookshelves in the living room. In the dining room there was a floor-to-ceiling china cabinet filled with antique dishes. Most were flow blue—white dishes with blue designs that seemed to bleed into the pieces themselves and created a blurred effect. The china dated back to the late 1800s and, if Nanette ever wanted to sell it, the set would bring quite a price.

"Well look who's here!" A wavery voice greeted Louise. "How lovely of you to stop by."

Louise put the preserves on the table and gave the old woman a hug. "How are you? It's been far too long since I've seen you and Oscar."

Nanette tapped her hearing aid. "Can't hear very well at church anymore. These things aren't worth the plastic they're made from. Instead, we watch a TV preacher every Sunday morning and turn up the volume full blast. It's not as good as the real thing, of course, but God's with us too, just like you folks at church."

"I'm sure He is." Louise felt warmth spreading through her. She'd nearly forgotten how dear and sweet these people were.

"Can I get you something? Tea, coffee…?"

"No. I'm fine."

"Some fruit then? Will you eat a pear or a nectarine? We'll never finish them all before they go bad."

Louise looked to where Nanette was pointing. A large basket of fresh fruit sat on the counter.

"My daughter must think we don't eat our fruits and vegetables," Nanette cackled. "She sends us stuff like that all the time. Please, will you eat something?"

Louise agreed to a pear and watched as Nanette washed it, put it on a plate along with a small knife and brought it to her. The elderly woman had a spring in her step and a lightness to her carriage that belied her true age. And she didn't look the least bit worried about anything. Had Aunt Ethel been imagining things?

"I was just thinking about your father and mother the other day," Oscar said as he joined them. "What a fine couple they were."

The three of them spent the next few minutes reminiscing. Then Louise told them about the garden party on Sunday and invited them to come.

"It would be lovely to be at a party there again," Nanette said wistfully. "Your mother was such a fine cook and she loved to entertain."

"We'll be there with bells on," Oscar said jovially.

"No bells, dear," Nanette rejoined. "They are havoc for my hearing aids."

Louise was silently praying for guidance and for the right words to bring up the true reason for her visit when Nanette reached for a small photo album that was lying on the counter.

"You'll have to see photos of my grandchildren and great-grandchildren. We've got quite a family. They're such a blessing to us—and so much help."

"'Help'?" Louise echoed.

"We haven't had to worry about things for years. My grandsons come and paint the house. My daughter hires someone to do our windows. My son-in-law, an accountant, even does our taxes for us. We're retired in style, I'd say." Nanette sat back with a smile on her face."

"An accountant?" Louise stammered. "He does your taxes?"

"Has for years. He was an investment counselor for a while too. Thanks to him, we haven't had to worry about getting along financially in our golden years. Bless his heart."

If Oscar and Nanette have significant investments and an accountant in the family, it's not likely that they would have tax problems, Louise thought. *How had Aunt Ethel come to that conclusion?*

"He's recently been hired as a taxpayer advocate for the IRS," Oscar said. "And he's been sending us information from his office ever since. I've begun to wonder what the people at the post office must think with this blizzard of mail from the IRS coming our way."

"Now dear, he's being good to us, you know that. The least we can do is bring it home and look at it before we throw it away." Nanette turned to Louise. "Could you eat an orange, dear? Or a kiwi?"

Sylvia was in the back room using her long-arm quilting machine when Jane arrived at the store. Sylvia looked up and smiled as Jane walked in.

"I'm almost done with your friends' lap quilts. All they will have left is to sew the bindings. These quick little quilts have turned out rather well, I think."

Sylvia clipped a few threads and pulled Stella's three-by-three creation off the long arm and held it up. The rich colors made for a striking quilt, and Sylvia ran her fingers over the fabric fondly. "What do you think?"

"Fabulous. You're a genius. That's why I came to talk to you. You have to help me figure out what to do." Jane told Sylvia of her conversation with Viola and her suspicions that Ethel might be behind some of the other rumors currently going around town.

Sylvia ran her fingers through her hair. "'A little knowledge is a dangerous thing.' Ethel is probably gathering snippets of information and running with them. The rumors could be hurtful to the people involved."

"Do you think I should say something to her?" Jane asked.

Sylvia shrugged. "That's up to you. It might mean a lot to the individuals affected."

Jane sighed. "I think I'll stop by the carriage house and try to ask some tactful questions." They chatted for a few more minutes. Then Jane headed toward Ethel's house.

On her way, she met Rev. Thompson.

"Hello, Jane." He greeted her with a warm smile. "I haven't seen you out and about the past couple days."

"I'm having a minireunion at the inn for some college friends. We've been too busy talking to go out much."

As they chatted, an idea flashed into her mind. "Would you be willing to make a brief announcement for me at church on Sunday?" She told him about the garden party, Mary and Finn.

"I certainly will. Even if it's not strictly church-related, it is an act of kindness. We should all be supporting Mary in any way we can. How many people are you expecting?"

"I don't know. It doesn't matter, really, since we're having it outside and the time is flexible. All I have to make sure of is that we have enough tea, cold drinks and sweets."

"I know what kind of baker you are. The idea of the food alone may bring more people than you've bargained for."

Jane laughed.

"I'll spread the word, Jane. Today I'm doing church visits out near Fairy Pond. If anyone saw something, it would likely be someone who lives out there."

After she left the pastor, Jane kept on toward the carriage house. A lump formed in her stomach as she neared. How does one go about suggesting to one's beloved aunt that she is manufacturing and spreading rumors?

Of course, Ethel would never spread something she didn't think was true, but that didn't change the situation.

Jane knocked on the door and heard her aunt call "Come in."

Florence was with Ethel. Jane's heart sank. This would not be a good time to converse with her aunt. "You look busy."

Ethel gestured at a pile of flannel and some scissors on the table. "We're making items for layettes at church. A mother somewhere in the world will have some new things for her new baby. It's very exciting, don't you think?" Ethel said.

"Aunt Ethel, have you been bored lately?" Jane inquired impulsively, not quite sure where she was going with her question.

Her aunt tittered nervously. "Now why would you ask that?"

"Just curious, that's all. You've been spending a lot of time with LeAnn from the post office."

"A nice girl," Florence chimed in. "Much more relaxed than our other postmistress."

"What do you mean?"

"She is so much more open than Alma. LeAnn *says* things."

"Out of the ordinary things." Ethel jumped into the conversation. "Like who gets letters from interesting places."

"And she doesn't act so self-important either. You know how Alma is, laying all the letters face down on the counter, guarding the mail like someone might want to peek at it."

"She didn't happen to mention that someone in town was getting letters from the IRS, did she?" Jane tried to act nonchalant.

"She hasn't said that outright," Florence said, "but I saw … well, never mind. It just goes to show that we don't know our neighbors as well as we think we do."

"It certainly does," Jane said wearily. How could she ask her next question delicately? "Might it be best to make sure your information is correct before spreading it around town?"

"Oh, but I saw this with my own eyes," Florence said, nodding.

"Surely you have important tasks at the inn, dear," Ethel said. "Is there anything I can do to help?"

Jane sighed and decided she might as well ask her aunt and Florence to do what they were best at. She explained about the garden party. "You could let people know about the party and that we're hoping someone will step forward with information about the time Mary was found."

"We'll get right on it." Ethel turned back to her project, and Jane knew she had been dismissed.

Jane stood outside on her aunt's porch for a moment and sent up a quick prayer. *Lord, they mean so well. May there be a lesson for us in all of this.*

Jane headed back to the inn feeling particularly frustrated and yet sympathetic toward the two women. They definitely needed a new hobby.

Chapter Sixteen

*H*ow does this look?" Becky held up the sign she was making. Flowers erupted out of every corner, and a big red dog was sniffing at the posies in the lower right hand corner. The words on the poster read

Garden Party at Grace Chapel Inn

Sunday, 2-5 PM

Come meet Mary and Finn

"Very nice. It's not often that the bulletin board in the grocery store holds a piece of original art." Jane measured ingredients into a bowl for a batch of lemon bars.

"Okay. Then I'll make more signs like this one."

"You don't have to work that hard," Jane said. "I'm sure that Mayor Tynan's secretary Bella would color photocopy that one for us."

Becky winced. "I don't think so. I'll keep drawing while the rest of you bake."

"Don't you think we have enough, Jane? I've never seen so many cookies and bars in my life." Stella stood back to look at the tower of filled plastic containers and the trays covered with sugar cookies, ginger snaps and tiny squares of something made with coconut, chocolate and caramels.

"What doesn't get eaten will go into the freezer. I like to keep things on hand for guests. I often put a plate of cookies and a carafe of coffee on the sideboard in the dining room in the afternoon. It's a little extra welcoming touch."

"So we're doing slave labor for you, in other words." Patty put a dab of pink frosting on a small white cookie.

"Something like that."

"Does anyone recall the time we helped Becky bake for that guy she felt sorry for?"

"That was before I met my husband," Becky said primly. "Ancient history. I was a mere slip of a child back then."

"You weren't very mature, we'll give you that."

Becky glared at Stella which, of course, didn't stop Stella.

"Could I help it that he fell madly, head over heels in love with me? It was *cookies*, not gold I gave him."

"He didn't leave you alone after that until—"

"Never mind." Becky put her finger to her lips. "No one is interested in hearing this again—"

"Oh, come on. For old times' sake," Jane said.

Becky groaned while Stella told the story to Alice and Louise.

"She wanted him to stop following her around. One day Becky looked out the window of the front door and saw him walking down the sidewalk. She didn't have time to hide, and he would have seen her if she'd run to the back of the house."

Becky blushed the red of the geraniums in her artwork. "The only thing I could think of—I dropped to the floor in front of the door and lay there. I knew he couldn't see me so I thought that if I just lay still, he'd give up and go away."

"But he didn't go away," Patty picked up the story. "He kept knocking and knocking and when he didn't get an answer, he tried to open the front door so he could call inside."

"And there was Becky, lying on the floor, hiding out," Stella said.

"He never followed me again," Becky said with a sigh. "Of course he never spoke to me again either. I can't believe the things we did when we were young."

"We all did them, Beck," Stella said casually. "At least we outgrew our childishness. Not everyone does."

Patty drew a sharp breath but said nothing.

"You're shaking like a leaf," Alice observed. She and Mary were in the waiting room of the doctor's office in Potterston on Friday afternoon, looking forward to getting the doctor's take on Mary's improvement.

"I'm so nervous. I don't know if it's a good thing that I'm having faint recollections, or if that will be all I ever get. I need to know how to live if I never get my memory back." Mary gripped Alice's hands in her own.

"Let's not move to the worst case scenario quite yet," Alice said calmly.

"You may go in now," the receptionist announced to Mary.

Mary clutched Alice's hand. "Come with me?"

Instead of being shown into an exam room, they were invited into a private office. Dr. Broadmoor stood up, shook hands with them and gestured for them to sit down.

"You look much better," he said, examining the fading bruises on Mary's arms. He asked her some questions and made a few notes in a file. "Traumatic amnesia is usually transient," he said, "but the length of its duration often depends on the degree of the injury one sustains. You obviously had head trauma, but you've recovered well from your physical injuries."

Mary nodded. "Thanks to the Howard sisters."

Dr. Broadmoor smiled. "I understand how they could be good medicine." He shifted in his chair. "I've talked to a number of other doctors, experts about amnesia. What they all advise, at least for the time being, is that we be patient."

"There's that word again," Mary muttered.

"What, if anything, have you recalled since I saw you last?"

Mary told him about the things that had resonated within her.

"But I can't bring the memories fully to the surface."

"Still, it's progress. Things may come back gradually or pop into your head all at once. For now, our hospital social worker has told me that she has some good news. She's found several housing options for you. There are apartments in Potterston that ..."

Mary looked at Alice with panic in her blue eyes. "I know I can't stay at the inn forever, but perhaps there is a room somewhere in Acorn Hill?" she asked pleadingly. "I don't need much. Just a bed and ..."

"The housing facilities are maintained by the state and very low cost. Considering your ... financial situation, the social worker feels it might be best if ..."

"I'm sure we can find a temporary situation that Mary finds tolerable," Alice said quickly. "Grace Chapel has offered funds from their outreach program to help Mary."

"Are you sure? The facilities are carefully maintained."

Alice saw that Mary's eyes were wide with fear. "We'd like her to stay with us."

The doctor nodded. "That's your decision."

"In the meantime, what can I *do*?"

The doctor smiled. "Have patience."

"And pray," Alice added softly.

Chapter Seventeen

"My husband must be the dearest man on the planet," Stella announced to no one in particular as they all sat in the kitchen, watching Jane make their evening meal. Louise and Alice were bustling around the room helping to get the meal set up, and the aroma of fresh baked goods hung deliciously in the air.

"I just called to tell him what was happening, and do you know what he said to me? He said 'Sweet-ums, you just stay as long as you want. It sounds like a wonderful cause, and the gallery is practically running itself.' His secretary is dealing with my mail. All I have to do when I get home is go back to my studio and start painting again."

"'Sweet-ums,'" Becky echoed. "He calls you 'Sweet-ums'?"

"You didn't hear a word I said, did you?" Stella wagged a finger at Becky.

"Of course I did," said Becky, grinning broadly. "Al sounds awesome. But 'Sweet-ums'? Now really…"

Stella picked a carrot off a plate of crudités on the counter and waved it like a conductor with a baton. "What does your husband call you?"

Becky flushed. "That's not the point."

"It most certainly is."

"Yeah, Becky, what *does* he call you?" Patty leaned on the counter, her chin in her hands.

"It's none of your business," Becky said primly. "Stella *offered* to tell us what Al calls her."

"Let's have it," Stella said cheerfully. "Or we'll get the drawings out of your room and hold your frogs hostage."

Becky's eyes grew big. "It's Cuddles, if you must know. And leave my frogs alone."

"'Cuddles' and 'Sweet-ums'! I think I'm going to be sick," Patty groaned. "It's so sugary I feel cavities forming in my mouth as we speak."

"You three aren't helping," Jane said. "And quit eating the dinner before it gets to the table. Why don't you go into the living room and sit down and relax? We've all had a big day baking."

Jane shooed them out of the kitchen to carry on their silliness where they weren't underfoot, and the sisters worked in contented silence until a rap on the back door startled them.

Lloyd Tynan, mayor of Acorn Hill and Ethel's special friend, pushed open the door.

"Lloyd, come in." Jane gestured him inside. "We're just getting dinner ready. Would you like to join us?"

"Thanks, but I can't stay," he said quickly. He nodded at the others. "Alice, Louise, good to see you. Mind if I sit down?"

Then, without waiting for an answer, he took a chair at the table.

Alice and Louise exchanged a surprised look. Lloyd seemed upset.

"I've come to ask you ladies some questions. I may need help." He drew a deep breath as if to calm his nervousness. "I'll cut right to the chase. Have you seen a change in Ethel lately?"

"She and Florence are making every effort to be neighborly to the new postmistress," Louise said.

"And they are outdoing each other in the good deeds department," Alice added.

"They were both working on layettes to give away when I stopped in to see her," Jane said.

Lloyd's brow furrowed.

"There are worse things than an abundance of good deeds," Louise pointed out.

"Ethel enjoys LeAnn. She says she has interesting opinions on things." He scowled a little. "But she stops at my office with more speculation and gossip than ever before. Frankly, she seems anxious and upset."

"About what?"

"Mr. and Mrs. Billings, for example. She's sure that they've fallen behind on their taxes or some such nonsense. She told me that she knows that the IRS is hounding them. When I asked her how she had gotten that idea, she clammed up. You know Ethel. She can clam up pretty tight when she wants to."

The sisters nodded.

"Between this one-upmanship with Florence and her concern over people around town, she's just not been my Ethel lately."

"Perhaps I'll go to see her tonight," Louise suggested.

"Good luck." Jane smiled. "I tried to hint that they stop spreading rumors, and the two of them laughed and went right on with their business."

"I shall have to be more direct," Louise said calmly. "In fact, I'll do it right now." She stood.

"You'll miss dinner if you leave now," Jane said, glancing at the kitchen timer.

"I'll be back as quickly as I can, and I'll make do with leftovers if I must," Louise said gently.

Lloyd's face relaxed. "That sounds like a fine idea to me. Thank you, ladies. You've put my mind at ease."

Louise followed him out the door and walked across the lawn to her aunt's home. She knocked on the door and waited, unlike her aunt who always simply opened the door of Grace Chapel Inn and walked inside.

It took Ethel some moments to come to the door.

She'd been lying down. Her hair was mussed, and she was wearing her slippers instead of her shoes.

"If you are resting, I can come back later."

"No, dear, come in. I got up so early this morning that I felt a little tired. But right now, I'd enjoy your company." Ethel beckoned her inside.

As they had done so many times before, Ethel and Louise went directly toward the kitchen. Ethel filled the kettle and put it on the stove to heat, took out her tea things and filled a plate with Girl Scout cookies.

"You have Girl Scout cookies?" Louise sounded a little envious. Other than Jane's cooking, Girl Scout cookies were her only vice in the diet department. She would have dinner soon, but a few cookies couldn't hurt.

"I buy several boxes when I can get them. At my age, I've decided that once in a while it's acceptable not to have fresh baked goods in the house."

"That's fine at any age," Louise said. "If we didn't have Jane at the inn, Alice and I would eat very differently."

"She turned out well, didn't she?" Ethel said of Jane. "Sometimes I ached for that girl, not having a mother to raise her, but we must have done something right."

Ethel, Alice and Louise had all cared for Jane when she was a child. It was a wonder, Louise thought, that Jane had actually stayed sane with all of them bossing her around.

"Such a cute little thing, she was," Ethel reminisced fondly. "Always off making something—a wreath of fallen leaves, a twig house or an elaborate drawing in colored chalk on someone's sidewalk. I believe the entire town of Acorn Hill watched out for her."

Louise cleared her throat. "That's why I've stopped by. I'm watching out for you."

"Whatever do you mean, dear? I don't need watching. Lloyd makes sure that things are going well for me. He's always fixing a leaky faucet or moving my lawn sprinklers, you know that."

It was true, but that wasn't exactly what Louise had meant.

"You haven't been at the inn much lately."

"You're full to overflowing over there. You don't need me underfoot too."

"But you have been busy, haven't you?" Louise suggested. "We still haven't gotten to know your new friend from the post office. You've been keeping her to yourself."

"Florence and I have kept her busy," Ethel admitted. "Florence finds her fascinating. She's much more . . . open . . . about her job than Alma Streeter ever was."

Louise stayed silent, waiting for Ethel to continue.

"I guess I have been a little distracted lately," Ethel admitted.

"Well, I want to catch you up on a few things. As you know, the rumor about Jean Humbert's going to Australia is false," Louise said. "And I wanted to warn you against mentioning Wilhelm Wood's trip to South America to anyone. Wilhelm's mother would be very upset if she heard that from someone other than Wilhelm, and he hasn't told her yet. She worries about him when he travels. It would be a shame if she worked herself into a dither over it."

Ethel looked concerned.

"You know, some of the news going around town could be hurtful if it got back to the people concerned. For example, the Billingses are doing just fine financially, thanks to their son-in-law who is an accountant with the IRS. They'd be very distressed if they learned that people thought they were in trouble with the government."

Ethel looked down at her lap and nodded.

Louise made a few attempts at small talk, but they were greeted with monosyllabic responses, and their conversation soon ground to a halt. Finally, Louise gave her aunt a kiss. "Take care, Aunt Ethel. Displaying fruits of the Spirit doesn't mean you have to provide for the entire world, you know."

Ethel smiled weakly.

Chapter Eighteen

The house had quieted down for the evening, and Louise slipped out to the front porch to enjoy the cool night air. The moon was out, and she could hear night creatures in the bushes orchestrating a sweet song. It was in moments like this that she couldn't imagine living anywhere except Acorn Hill.

A rustling off to the right captured her attention. The sound of shrubs being brushed aside and soft footsteps made Louise sit upright. Who was coming across the yard this late at night?

Louise's question was answered when Ethel's face, pale in the moonlight, appeared. She mounted the porch steps. Ethel was dressed for bed. She wore fluffy slippers and a robe that was pulled shut at the neck and belted tightly at the waist.

Louise lifted a hand in greeting but didn't speak. Being the oldest of the sisters, she and her aunt had always had a particularly close relationship. Her heart softened as she watched her aunt shuffle up the steps and across the porch until she came to a rocking chair. She sat down heavily.

"Lovely evening," Ethel said finally.

"Indeed it is."

"Moon's out."

"So beautiful," Louise agreed.

They sat side by side in silence until Ethel began to rock.

Louise sensed that it was important that she not say anything yet. She began to rock as well. Eventually their swaying aligned itself. Back. Forth. Back. Forth. Louise wondered what her aunt had come to say, but was willing to give her the time she needed to get it out.

Back. Forth. Back. Forth.

Finally Ethel spoke. "Psalm thirty-four, verses twelve through fourteen."

Louise searched her memory for the verse. She'd learned a good many of them over the years. "Whoever of you loves life and desires to see many good days, keep your tongue from evil and your lips from speaking lies. Turn from evil and do good; seek peace and pursue it."

Although her senses perked up, Louise willed herself to remain relaxed.

Eventually Ethel's rocking slowed and she stood up. Without speaking she shuffled toward her niece and laid a kiss on the top of her head.

"Good night, dear."

"Good night, Aunt Ethel. Sleep well."

"I will." She disappeared down the steps, across the lawn and back to her own home.

She had just heard an apology of sorts, Louise knew, and she was sure that it had been difficult for her aunt to offer it. She smiled to herself. She had not directly told Ethel what harm her misguided gossip was doing, and Ethel had only indirectly confessed her wrongdoing. But it was as clear as if it had been written on a blackboard. Louise knew that now the odd bits of gossip would stop, and she would be very surprised if speculation reared its ugly head again for some time.

Lord, thank You for the sweetest, most endearing, most irritating aunt in the universe. We love her so much, and she loves us. Thank You for allowing us to have her in our lives. And Lord, will You please make sure she checks her facts before she starts telling stories in the future? Amen.

Then Louise rose and went to bed.

Chapter Nineteen

My head is swimming," Jane announced to no one in particular. The three sisters were gathered on the front porch on Saturday morning. Stella and Patty had walked to town. Becky was upstairs calling home. Mary, exhausted from all the attention she'd received from townspeople, was sleeping.

"I'm wracking my brain to think of anything we've missed."

"We're keeping this simple, remember?" Alice said. "We've contacted the Potterston papers. We've baked a ridiculous amount of food. If we've forgotten something, we'll just make do. Besides, we've got Mary and Finn, and they're the most important part."

"You are right, of course. I suppose the only thing left to decide is who will present Kieran with his gift and explain Mary's situation. I won't be able to do it because I'll be busy with the food, going back and forth between the garden and the kitchen."

"And Alice and I will be pouring tea and serving the cold drinks," Louise pointed out.

"Then we really do need someone who can fill in the gaps and keep things moving," Jane said.

"Maybe Carlene could do it," Louise suggested. "She's talked extensively with Mary and understands the situation fully."

"But she'll be taking pictures," Jane reminded her.

"There's Fred Humbert, I suppose, but Vera told me that he'd be coming to the party late," Louise said.

"How about Wilhelm Wood? He's charming and well-spoken," Alice suggested.

"That's a great idea. I'll take a walk and ask him right now."

On the way out of the house Jane paused to look over the yard. It was as pretty as she'd ever seen it. God's gift of nature was so miraculous that she felt a tightening in her chest every time she considered it. Many times she paused to look at a new bloom on a hibiscus plant or watch a hummingbird dip deep into a flower for nectar and marvel at the intricacy of every living thing. Each plant and creature was designed to perfection for the job it was meant to do.

She picked up her step. This party would be fun. Friends, neighbors, flowers and tea. There wasn't anything much better than that.

Time for Tea was open, and Wilhelm was behind the counter sorting his mail.

"Good, you're here."

"Where else would I be?" He chuckled "I can't wait for your party. I'm looking forward to examining the butterfly garden you started. I might do one for my mother."

"She'd love it. I'd never realized just how many plants there are that butterflies enjoy. We've seen so many in our yard since I put in that garden."

He picked up a stool on his side of the counter and carried it to the other so that Jane could sit down. "Rest a little."

"I'm not even tired. This get-together has been fairly simple. My friends have been awesome. We're still baking, of course, but that's pure enjoyment for me. I love the excuse to do it. Between them and my sisters, it's been easy to pull this together."

"Everyone loves a mystery or a good pet story," Wilhelm observed. "This has both. How can anyone resist?"

"I hope that's true for you as well," Jane ventured.

Wilhelm cocked one eyebrow in her direction. "What does that mean?"

"Louise, Alice and I will be busy keeping things running on Sunday. At three o'clock we plan to ask Kieran to tell us how Finn behaved when he found Mary. Then Mary will say a few words. She's eager for people to know how it feels to wake up not knowing who you are or anything about your surroundings. We want people in the community to recall whether or not they saw anything that night that could help the police determine what happened. If we can jog just one memory, it would be wonderful."

"Sounds like you've planned it perfectly."

"The one thing I don't have is someone to introduce Finn, Kieran and Mary."

"You will be doing that, won't you?" Wilhelm pushed a stack of letters to the side and put his hands, palms down, on the counter.

"I could, but my sisters and I will be busy with hostess duties. Would *you* do it for us? I can't think of anyone better. You are charming, eloquent, articulate—"

Wilhelm burst out laughing and held up his hands as if to stop Jane's onslaught of compliments. "Enough! You had me convinced at 'charming.'"

He paused a moment in thought. "Should I tell a joke or two?" he asked, "if I promise not to tell any old, tired ones?"

"Whatever you think is appropriate," Jane said. "Thanks, Wilhelm, this will free us up to give a great party."

She stood up to leave when he cleared his throat.

"I had an odd visit today."

"Oh?"

"Your Aunt Ethel stopped by this morning. We had a lovely but confusing conversation."

"What do you mean?" Jane asked cautiously.

"She appeared rather distraught. She told me she hadn't slept much last night, and that she knew she'd feel better once she'd talked to me."

"What did she say?"

"Frankly, I'm not quite sure." Wilhelm looked puzzled. "She carried on about misunderstandings and jumping to conclusions. She chattered about how very fond she was of my mother and that she'd never do anything to hurt her. She kept asking me if Mother was feeling okay. The next thing I knew she was vowing up and down that she would never, ever, make assumptions about anything ever again. She was quite distressed but eventually ran out of steam and just stood here looking up at me like a whipped puppy."

Poor Aunt Ethel!

"Then what?"

"I had no idea what she was talking about. I think she was apologizing for believing the rumor about my traveling to South America. Fortunately Mother never heard it through the grapevine, so I was able to break the news to her myself. No harm was done. After I told Ethel that, she seemed to relax. Next thing I knew, she was backing out of the door, smiling and waving." Wilhelm shook his head. "Odd. Your aunt is a sweet little thing. I've always liked her."

Thank You, God, for keeping an eye on Aunt Ethel and protecting her from herself.

On the way back to the inn, Jane was stopped by Nia Komonos, Acorn Hill's librarian. "Our library has been busy, thanks to you."

"What did I do?"

Nia laughed. "You've made everyone in town interested in dog stories, for one thing. And in books on amnesia. Everybody I've talked to is going to the party. Thanks to you, more than twenty books have been borrowed from the library."

"I guess that means that we can expect at least twenty people at the party. We'll find Mary's family yet."

Nia's dark eyes clouded. "How that poor woman must be suffering."

Mary felt safe at the inn with Alice and the rest, Jane knew, and the poor woman tried to put up a good front. But if she were forced to go out on her own right now . . . Jane hated to think of it. Mary was still so vulnerable.

As Jane continued down the street, Patsy Ley called out to her, "See you tomorrow."

Jane waved and smiled. Then she saw Lloyd Tynan coming toward her. Jane knew a meeting with him would likely turn into a lengthy conversation. Hoping to avoid that, she slipped into Craig Tracy's flower shop. It was cool and quiet inside. Jane drew a deep breath and walked toward the counter.

"How do you like it?" Craig was arranging a colorful bouquet with roses, tulips, lilies and other flowers.

"It's marvelous. Is the lucky recipient anyone I know?"

"A couple in Potterston have a wedding anniversary today. Their daughter ordered this to surprise them."

"How thoughtful."

"Yes . . ." Craig kept working on the bouquet, but continued to chat.

"By the way, I met Jean Humbert in the Coffee Shop this morning and she told me a quirky story. She said your aunt stopped by the house and kept apologizing for this rumor going around about Jean having a boyfriend in Australia. Jean told her that she and her mother had had a good laugh over it. Jean's had a pen pal in Sydney since she was in sixth grade."

"Oh my." Jane's heart went out to her aunt, running around town, apologizing for something that even the people who were involved in didn't quite understand. *Not that I understand it all myself*, Jane thought.

"May I make a corsage for Mary to wear on Sunday?" Craig asked as he put the finishing touches on the anniversary bouquet. "Something to lift her spirits?"

"She'd love that, Craig. That's very thoughtful of you."

"Good. It will be my gift to her," Craig said. "I want her to know that I'm cheering for her. It must be very difficult to be in her position."

"Everyone has been very kind. I'm hoping that someone at the party saw something—anything—to help her learn her identity."

"People have certainly been discussing the situation."

"Gossiping, you mean?" Jane sighed.

"The joys of living in a small town. Really, people are curious just because they care."

Becky was coming down the stairs as Jane entered. Her face was flushed.

Becky flung her arms around Jane and gave her a boa constrictor squeeze.

"Whoa," Jane tried to wriggle out of her friend's embrace. "I'm having a little trouble breathing."

Becky reluctantly let go but took Jane's hand, led her into the sunroom, and gestured for her to sit.

"I just got off the phone with my publisher. Not only do they love the frog sketches I faxed to them, but they are willing to consider a children's book based on my paintings of Fairy Pond."

"Fabulous!"

"And I want you to promise you'll provide all the information I'll need once I start the book."

"Me?"

"Who knows Fairy Pond better than you? Louise said you know every species of every creature that lives there." Becky leaned forward intently. "Would you consider it? It would help me so much. This is my chance to both write and illustrate a book."

"I'm happy to try, Becky," Jane said. "As long as you aren't disappointed if I'm not as informed about Fairy Pond as you seem to think I am. Trust me, I'm no expert."

"But you love it and spend a lot of time there."

"Of course."

"Then start thinking positively, Jane. I know you'll be able to help me. No negativity is allowed."

Jane laughed. "You came to this reunion with some negativity of your own. Did something happen to change that?"

Becky sat back in her chair. "Several things, actually."

"Do you care to share them?"

"I came here so stirred up about Blaine that I could barely stand it. Should I kick my own son out of my house? How could I discover what's troubling him? What was I to do? I kept rolling it over and over in my mind, never finding an answer. That was the problem. I've been trying to find my answer by relying on myself."

Jane tipped her head to one side and studied her friend.

"When I got here, I saw that you and your sisters put your trust in God every day. It's part of your way of living. He's not a God just for emergencies. You include him in all your decisions. It made me realize that I'd been praying on an as-needed basis, that I really hadn't entrusted Blaine to Him. I paid lip service to God but did I really trust Him to work this out? No."

Becky paused, but Jane sat quietly waiting for her to continue.

"...so I decided to try it your way. At bedtime I've been reading Scripture—Psalms and Proverbs mostly—and praying. It is clear to me now that God is the only One to get through to Blaine, and He doesn't need my help to do it."

Becky flushed. "So I decided to turn it over. I prayed, 'God, Blaine's Yours anyway, so I'll get out of the way and let *You* take care of him.'"

Jane leaned forward. "And what happened?"

"I really did turn over my son, Jane. I know that I'll do whatever I'm led to do for him, but I'm not going to obsess over it anymore. I have heavenly help in my corner now."

Jane reached out to take her friend's hand. Sunlight spilled across their clasped fingers.

"I called my husband and we talked rationally about Blaine. I told him what had changed in me. He promised he'd pray for Blaine."

"Amazing. When God is involved, remarkable things happen." No matter how many times Jane had experienced God's hand in her life, she was always filled with wonder.

"That's not the half of it. Blaine called me on my cell phone about forty-five minutes ago."

"*He* called *you?*"

"He told me that last night he'd had an overwhelming urge to talk to me. He wasn't sure why, but it was so strong that he finally decided he'd just dial my number."

"What did he say?"

"That he loved me." Becky's expression grew solemn.

"You don't look all that happy about it."

"My expectations were so high for my children." She looked pensively at a blue jay on the window ledge outside the sunporch. "Too high, apparently."

She was silent for a long while before she spoke again. "Blaine admitted that he froze when he tried to decide what to do with his life. He didn't want to disappoint us, so he kept going to school. It cost more and more money and he felt that he'd reached a place where it was too late to turn around and go back."

"What does that mean?"

"He went to school because he thought it was what I wanted, Jane. He wasn't doing it for himself, but for *me*." Becky's lips trembled. "Blaine has always loved animals and the outdoors. He said he always thought that the best job in the world must be to work on a ranch in the Southwest. He said he'd like to learn to train horses."

"Now, that is a switch."

"He's shut down because he can no longer follow a path I set for him, one he didn't lay out for himself."

"He's an adult. You didn't exactly force him to go to school."

"No, but can you imagine what I might have said if he'd announced he was dropping out of college to go to New Mexico and learn to rope and ride?"

"What would you have said?"

"I would have cried and stormed around the house and told him he was throwing his life away."

"And then?"

"Eventually I suppose I would have gotten used to the idea, realized that Blaine knew his own heart and encouraged him to go." Becky gave a teary smile. "And I probably would have decided that I should do some paintings in that part of the world, do a children's book in the Southwest, be wildly successful, buy my own ranch . . ."

Jane held up her hand as she laughed. "You don't have to wind it out quite that far. But you would have accepted his decision and let him go?"

"Of course."

"Then Blaine got it wrong too. He decided what *you'd* think. Didn't he? He chose the path he thought you'd like without regard to his own wishes."

"I meddled too much in his life. He was always a child who wanted to please me. If I hadn't been so controlling, none of this would have happened."

"He loved you enough to want to honor your wishes. That's admirable, Becky. It's your communication that fell apart. You made very big assumptions about each other."

"We did, didn't we? We're going to talk when I get home. There's so much to sort out. I told Blaine that if he needed to pursue his dream, that he should do so. The school won't go anywhere. He can always come back to it. He needs to know more about himself to make that decision."

Becky smiled tremulously. "Do you know what he said to me, Jane? He said, 'Mom, we should have had this conversation a long time ago.'"

"Sometimes God waits until we clear a path through our attempts to solve things. When we finally turn things over to Him, He can do the healing and blessing that He's been waiting for and wanting to do all along."

"And when I finally asked Him to help Blaine—and me—He was there, ready, willing and waiting," Becky marveled. "You know, Jane, if I travel for the rest of my life, no trip will ever stack up to this weekend."

Chapter Twenty

Mary knocked timidly on the partially open door to Jane's room. "Is this a good time?"

Jane waved her in. "It's always a good time for you. Go to my closet and pick out whatever you want to wear. If you can't find something here, Alice offered her closet too."

"I've never known such generosity..." Mary paused and smiled. "I don't think."

"Has anything else come back?"

"Things are beginning to seem...familiar. I hear songs that I recognize from somewhere in the past. It feels as though my memory—my personality—is hovering just below the surface, waiting to emerge."

"Then it will. We will just have to be patient."

"I'm just about out of patience," Mary said. "And there's not a thing I can do about it."

"Perhaps if you can manage to relax and enjoy the day, something will come to you unexpectedly."

"I guess it's worth a try."

Jane opened her closet door. It was, as Alice had said, as if a rainbow had exploded inside.

"How will I ever choose?" Mary gasped. She touched the soft fabric of a black silk dress, then reached for the next garment, a long flowing skirt.

"Choose what?" Stella and Patty had come upstairs to chat with Jane. Stella wandered into the room blowing little puffs of air on her fingernails to help them dry.

"What she'll wear to the garden party tomorrow."

"Does this mean we're going to have a fashion show?" Patty asked.

"Sure. Get Becky. We might as well do this by committee."

When her four fashion judges were seated, Mary went into the bathroom, slipped on a pale blue dress, came out and turned gracefully for the others.

"Pretty but not bright enough," Stella said nodding. "You'll be competing with a lot of flowers, you know. We want you to show up in the crowd."

"I don't think I'm a very showy person," Mary said shyly. "At least I don't *feel* showy."

"Let's see another one," Patty ordered, getting into the spirit of things.

Mary disappeared and came out in a little black dress.

Becky whistled.

"You look fabulous in that but it's too dark," Stella pronounced. "Let's see another."

"I think we need chocolate to make this decision," Patty announced. "Something to fortify us." She walked out of the room, and they could hear her footsteps descending the stairs. By the time Mary changed and came out again, Patty had returned with a plate of Jane's homemade truffles in her hand.

The party mood escalated from there. When Mary appeared in a colorful tie-dyed skirt and a military looking jacket with epaulets, they were all laughing.

"I'd better step in, or we're never going to find an outfit," Jane announced. "I may have just the thing." Instead of going into the closet, she knelt on the floor and pulled a dress box from beneath her bed.

Jane put the box on the bed and removed the lid. A cloud of tissue paper billowed up. She reached in and lifted out a sapphire blue sheath with Asian styling. She held it up and let the smooth silk fall to its full length, then held it up to Mary. The color brought out her eyes. "This is one of my favorite dresses," Jane said, smiling. "I wore it to a number of gallery openings, and it never failed to get a compliment."

"I couldn't borrow this. It's too beautiful!" Mary reached out and touched the smooth silk.

"That's why you *should* borrow it."

Mary looked longingly at the dress.

"You can't say no," Jane instructed. She turned to the fashion gang lounging on her bed. "Ladies?"

"It's you, Mary."

Mary looked hesitantly at Jane who nodded.

A puzzled expression flitted across Mary's features. "I think I just remembered something."

She suddenly had four rapt listeners.

"It's this color . . . I had a dress this color once, I'm sure I did." She closed her eyes. "I was small, I think. It feels like I was small but . . ." Her eyes flew open. "I lost it again."

"It's a good sign, Mary," Becky assured her. "It means the memories are coming back."

"A smile lit Mary's face. She looked at Jane. "I would be honored to wear this dress. Thank you."

"We're going to do an intervention," Becky announced as Patty and Jane sat in the sunroom playing a game of checkers.

"Let me guess," Patty sighed. "What's Stella doing now?"

"Another facial. Or a scrub. Or some sort of exfoliation. The woman spends more time on her skin than I do on my career."

Becky leaned over Patty's shoulder and made a move with one of Patty's checkers. "Have you noticed? She never comes out of her room unless her makeup is done and her hair is perfect."

"Are you talking about me?"

They all turned to look at Stella as she walked into the room looking as if she'd stepped from the pages of *Vogue*.

Becky blushed, but Stella smiled and joined them in the room.

"You don't understand," she said, taking a seat on a wicker chair. "You can all do your business in private. Becky, you have a home studio. Patty, people expect you to be in working clothes when you are at their homes. Jane, people would think it odd if you wore high heels every day. It's not that way with me. My studio is upstairs above our gallery."

She looked straight at Patty. "That's what I envied most about you, Patty, all of you really. None of you ever worried about how you looked."

"Yes, we did," Patty said, touching her hair unconsciously. "You just worried more."

"You did seem to spend a lot of time in front of the mirror," Becky said quietly.

"My mother always said that we are judged on first impressions." Stella sighed. "The underlying message was that if I wanted to be liked, I'd better look good."

Jane reached out and touched Stella's arm.

"My father ran a tight ship at our house," Stella said quickly. "When he came home from work he wanted the house tidy, dinner on the stove and my mother wearing a dress and earrings."

Stella looked down at the floor. "Dad had very fixed ideas about how things should be. Women should be thin and beautiful. Children should be seen and not heard. And any daughter of his had better represent him properly. Any time that I stumbled or made a bad decision, Dad took it personally."

"We never knew," Becky murmured.

"I never liked him very much back then. I *loved* him, but I didn't like him. I didn't agree with his strict rules. He had rules about everything—how I dressed, how I wore my hair, even my friends." She looked down at her hands. "He was very judgmental, but he was also my *father*."

Stella remained silent for a long moment. "I know we're supposed to honor our parents, but it's not always easy. Frankly, I looked forward to leaving home and going to school. I longed to be free."

"I'm so sorry, Stella," Patty breathed.

"But you're still listening to your father's voice in your head," Jane said.

Stella turned toward her.

"You're still living by his rules, aren't you?" Jane looked into Stella's eyes, and Stella quickly looked away. "You think there's a certain way you have to look, to act, to be," Jane said. "You're trying to make someone happy who isn't here any longer."

"I don't think...maybe...but..." Stella looked truly puzzled. "Am I?"

"What does your husband say when he sees you in the morning?" Patty asked.

"Al says I'm beautiful. He thinks I'm perfect the way I am."

Jane laughed. "So let me get this straight. You are trying to live up to an image that you've had in your head since you were young. You feel you'll never be good enough, yet you live with an *art connoisseur* who sees beautiful things and people every day and who says you're perfect." She smiled at Stella.

"Why don't you listen to *him* for a change?" Becky asked.

"Your husband sounds like a smart man to me," Patty said.

Stella appeared genuinely bemused, as if what she'd always believed to be reality was really smoke and mirrors.

"How did your parents feel about growing old?" Becky asked curiously.

"*Hmm?*" Stella said vaguely. "They hated it. Especially my mother. She knew how much Daddy cared about how she looked. It's odd, though. After he passed away, she started wearing blue jeans and funky shirts and threw out all her high heels. Once I caught her emptying her bathroom cabinet of makeup. She said she'd decided to go natural."

"How did she look?"

"She looked her age. She didn't try to hide her crow's-feet. She was really...beautiful. Graceful. Happy." Stella looked at the faces of her friends. "I guess Daddy's stern ways affected her too."

"I think that makes sense," Jane said quietly.

"Now she lives on the beach and walks in the surf every day. She's active in community functions. And she refuses to dress up for anything except church on Sunday."

They were all so silent that they could hear a clock ticking somewhere in the house and a woodpecker hammering on a tree outside.

"We loved him, you know. In so many ways he was a wonderful father and husband. He was generous, hard-working, reliable. I always felt safe with him. I knew that he would never let anything happen to me. He taught me to ride a bike and to change a tire. If I had run into trouble at school, he would have driven across the country to help me out." She looked out the window.

Suddenly Stella stood up. "I've got to think. I'm so confused...." Before anyone could stop her, she walked out of the room.

Patty, Becky and Jane stared at one another. Finally Patty spoke. "Boy, have I had things wrong about Stella."

Wendell, who had been sleeping soundly on a pillow on the floor, woke up, yawned so deeply everyone could see right down his pink throat and leapt into Patty's lap.

"Hey, big guy," Patty murmured as she scratched behind his ear. Wendell meowed once, turned around twice on Patty's lap and lay down.

"Looks like you have a new friend," Becky commented as the cat promptly closed his eyes and went back to sleep.

"Good," Patty brushed her hand slowly across Wendell's soft fur. "I need every one I can get."

Chapter Twenty-One

*E*arly on Sunday morning Jane stretched in the sunbeam that played across her bed. Wendell, who had sneaked into her room when she'd retired the previous night, was also stretching lazily at the end of her bed. He extended himself to his full length and even spread his toes as he roused himself from a good night's sleep.

"Ah, kitty," Jane murmured as she reached to scratch his exposed belly. "If only we could all be as relaxed and content as you." He rumbled a purr in reply.

Today was the garden party. Jane pushed her fingers through her hair and placed her bare feet on the floor. There was a gentle tapping on the door. Alice walked in and handed a cup of coffee to Jane.

"What time is it?"

"Early. I couldn't rest any longer. I believe I was counting lemon bars in my sleep."

"It's not that big a party," Jane said. She picked up a robe from behind the door, put it on and then sat down on the bed to enjoy the coffee. "But it's so important to Mary. Perhaps we've raised her hopes too much that someone will come forward with a clue to what happened to her."

Alice frowned. "Mary has so much hope that someone will have seen something."

"We've done all we can." Jane sipped the steaming coffee. A smile pulled at the corners of her lips. "At least we're not worried about having a good crowd. You know how people are here. They love a party."

"And goodies," Alice reminded her. "Maybe that's why I couldn't quit counting those lemon bars. I hope there are enough."

"We have plenty." Jane put down her cup and reached for the hairbrush on her bedside stand. "I think it will be fun, don't you? Patty, Becky and Stella are looking forward to it. They are eager to meet more of the locals. In their minds, Acorn Hill is a picture-perfect town." She stroked the brush through her hair. "That notion isn't far off, actually. We do live in a lovely spot."

"It's been quite a week, hasn't it?" Alice asked. "It seems impossible that we've accomplished all we have—quilting, baking, visits to Fairy Pond, caring for Mary. You have some amazing friends, Jane. I feel like I know you better, having heard their stories about you. I hope they will come back again."

"I hope so too. It's been a wonderful time for me. And for the others too, I hope." Jane gave a wide yawn and another catlike stretch that would have made Wendell proud. "I suppose I'd better get moving. I want to walk through the gardens to make sure no weeds raised their unwelcome little heads overnight."

"By the way, Pastor Ley and Patsy offered to come early and do what they could. I gave him the assignment of making sure cars didn't park every which way. We don't need a traffic jam."

"Good idea."

"Pastor Ley said he'd direct some of the people to park in the church parking lot."

"Perfect. This is working out rather well, isn't it? We may have to make it an annual tea party."

Another knock on the door announced Louise's arrival at the early morning get-together. She, too, was carrying a cup of coffee for Jane.

"My my, how do I rate?" Jane accepted the second cup, since she'd almost finished the first.

"You've been so dear and generous about Mary that it seems only appropriate that you deserve a little pampering yourself. That's why I took it upon myself to find some music for our tea party."

"I never even thought of that. I suppose if we were to have a real garden party we'd need some strings or a harp."

"Fortunately we can do something much simpler than that. I found some wonderful harp music on CDs. We can set a CD player beneath the serving table where it is hidden by a tablecloth. It will provide a little atmosphere."

"That sounds lovely, Louise. By the way, I talked to Craig Tracy for a moment yesterday," Alice added. "He is bringing Mary's corsage this afternoon after he delivers flowers to the hospital in Potterston."

"Maybe I don't have to get out of bed after all," Jane said. "Sounds like you've taken care of everything." Jane stared pensively out the window at the morning sky. "When things unfold so easily I can sense God's presence, can't you?"

After breakfast, Jane found Patty on the front porch holding a mug of coffee and staring off at some distant point. She leaned against the porch rail to study her friend.

Patty finally noticed Jane watching her. "How long have you been there?" Patty's hair was soft and golden in the sunlight, framing her face like a flaxen cloud.

"Just a few moments. You were certainly lost in thought."

"I've been lost there a lot this week."

"Still thinking about Stella?"

"I feel like such a fool. What I assumed was cockiness and overconfidence in her was insecurity. Because of my jealousy I ruined a relationship between her and someone she loved."

"When are you going to talk to her?"

"I don't know." She sighed. "It's been so busy that none of us have had a moment alone. I've waited this long. I can certainly wait until later. I want this afternoon to be perfect for Mary."

They both turned when they heard Sylvia Songer coming up the steps. She wore white linen slacks and a coral silk shirt.

"Hi, there. I just met Viola. She said that the Coffee Shop was buzzing with excitement yesterday. Everyone was trying to think of something they may have seen on the day of the accident. I think your problem might be too many sightings, not too few." She laughed. "I hope people don't begin to imagine they saw something."

Sylvia peered into Patty's nearly empty cup. "Is there more where that came from?"

Jane disappeared into the house and returned with a mug, a carafe of coffee and a plate of powdered doughnuts.

"Oh, this hits the spot," Sylvia said as she nibbled daintily on a doughnut. "I ran into Wilhelm Wood on his way to his store."

"At this hour? On a Sunday?"

"He said he needed to gather a few notes for this afternoon. I think he's pleased to help out." Sylvia took a sip of coffee. "I do hope we'll find out something about Mary. I know it's going to be a lovely party anyway, but if no one comes forward it will be disappointing."

"As Alice said this morning," Jane said softly, "the situation is in God's hands. We'll have to trust Him."

Ethel came out of her house with a watering can to water the moss roses encircling her mailbox. She looked surprised to see the gathering on the inn's front porch.

Jane waved her over. "What are you wearing to the party, Aunt Ethel?"

"I don't know yet, dear. I'm thinking of my yellow dress. Lloyd likes it." Ethel blushed like a schoolgirl. "Is Mary up?" Ethel asked. "I have something I want to give her today. I crocheted a bookmark for her with a little white cross. I purchased a Bible for her and made the bookmark to put in it."

"How nice of you, Auntie."

"Not so much nice as necessary, really. We need to care for those less fortunate than ourselves. Don't you agree? Sometimes I care a little too much," she said cryptically, "but my intentions are always good."

With that, she moved off again, faster this time, and disappeared into her house.

"What was that about?" Sylvia asked. "The part about her intentions being good?"

"You never quite know with Aunt Ethel, do you?" Jane answered. "Shall we go inside and see if the others are planning to go to church?"

After church and a light lunch, the women of Grace Chapel Inn fluttered about, getting ready for the party.

"How do you like this?" Stella came out of her bedroom after lunch and pirouetted in the hallway. She was wearing a hot pink dress and brightly colored jewelry. "Is it festive enough?"

"You look like a party all by yourself," Jane said.

"My husband likes me in pink." Stella studied herself in a hall mirror. "I look okay, don't I?"

"More than okay."

Stella followed Jane up to her bedroom. "After our conversation yesterday, I feel like a load has been lifted from my shoulders."

"I hope that you never forget you are beautiful, inside and out."

Stella turned to Jane with a look of deep gratitude. Jane smiled, then held up two dresses.

"Which should I wear, the navy or the orange?"

"Orange. You always did like bright colors. Be yourself." With that, Stella flitted out of the room and downstairs to check on Becky.

Grace Chapel Inn became part dressing room and part fashion show as everyone prepared for the party. Louise put on a full beige linen skirt, a dressy pale blue silk blouse and her signature pearls. Alice changed clothes three times before settling on a white piqué skirt and a peach blouse.

Mary was the only one who didn't take part in the chatter in the halls or gather with the rest of them in the living room. She stayed in her room with the door closed.

Sylvia, who had promised to come early and help set the tables, arrived a little after one o'clock.

"Don't you ladies look wonderful?" Sylvia said. "Like a bouquet of brightly colored flowers." She looked around. "Where is Mary?"

A noise on the staircase got their attention, and they all turned in that direction.

Mary stood shyly at the center of the staircase, her hand on the railing. Jane's bright blue dress skimmed her slender figure perfectly. Her hair, which she'd worn pulled back most of the time she'd been at Grace Chapel Inn, was down, softly framing her face.

Becky gasped, Patty clapped and Stella pronounced her "fabulous." Alice hurried to the stairs and took her hand. "You're beautiful, Mary."

"I feel like a little girl playing dress up." She drew a shaky breath. "I hope this works."

"Don't worry if our little party doesn't turn up something. Let's hope that the piece in the *Acorn Nutshell* or one of the larger papers will turn up some leads. Word will spread," Jane said.

"Today is as much about wanting you to know we're with you as it is about anything else. You do understand that, don't you?" Alice said quietly.

"I'm sorry." Mary smiled wanly. "Sometimes, when I think about it too much, I feel paralyzed with fear. Right now I should be telling you how grateful I am for all you've done, but there aren't words enough to express my thanks."

Alice leaned close to Mary. "Our reward will come when we find your family."

Chapter Twenty-Two

I'll start the music," Louise announced and bent to flip the switch on the CD player beneath the serving table. The sound of a harp floated into the yard.

Alice gave the flowers a last look, and Jane began to brew pots of tea and turned on the coffee urn. Wendell posed in the window, unmoving and so regal that he cut an impressive figure.

"How does it look?" Jane asked when the beverages were ready and she had returned to the yard. She was glad she'd done a lot of fertilizing earlier in the season, because now the flowers were thick and vibrant.

"It's lovely," Louise said.

Stella came out of the inn followed by Becky and Patty. Shortly afterward, Sylvia Songer rounded the side of the house and joined them in the center of the yard.

"I saw Lloyd knocking on your aunt's door," Sylvia said. "And there are several people walking down the street toward the inn. They kept looking at their watches to check the time. I suppose they don't want to be early but refuse to be a minute late either."

"Surely Acorn Hill knows the concept of an 'open house.'" Stella's brow creased. "Everyone doesn't have to come at the start and stay until the bitter end."

"I wouldn't count on that," Jane said with a laugh.

Sylvia peeked beneath a thin white dishtowel spread across a basket to see what goody was beneath. "*Mmm.* Pecan tassies." She put the towel back in place. "Florence was parading down the street with her husband and the postmistress LeAnn in tow."

"Where's Mary? She should be down here to meet the guests." Alice bustled off to round up their guest of honor.

"Where are Finn and Kieran? I'd hoped they'd come early so we could visit before everyone else arrived." Jane glanced toward the street.

Patty had gone to the front of the house to see who was coming down the sidewalk. She returned to answer Jane. "They just pulled up. You'll never believe how cute they both are. Did you realize that Finn's fur and Kieran's red hair are just about the same color? They both look as though they've been showered, shampooed and conditioned within an inch of their lives."

Finn and Kieran did look wonderful when they appeared in the garden. Kieran wore a bright green shirt and Finn had a matching scarf around his neck. The big dog had a happy expression as his tongue lolled out one side of his mouth.

Wilhelm Wood caught Jane by the sleeve and gave a little tug.

Jane turned. "Oh good, you're here. And don't you look handsome?"

"Will I do?" Wilhelm was dressed in a pair of navy trousers and a shirt so white Jane thought she might need her sunglasses to look at him.

"Perfect. I'm so glad you agreed to help us out. My sisters and I will be kept busy with the food and drink. Oh look, Kieran and Finn are already socializing."

Kieran looked proud enough to burst his buttons as an audience gathered around him while he retold the story of trying to call Finn home and of the dog refusing to budge from his spot near Mary.

"I don't know how long it might have been before anyone found her if it weren't for my dog," Kieran said. "I always knew he was a smart dog but I had no idea . . ."

Jane and Wilhelm smiled at each other. Things were off to a rip-roaring start.

"There's nothing for you to do until we start our little program," Jane began, "so just mingle and enjoy yourselves." She glanced at the table and her eyes widened. "The plates are already emptying. I'd better get busy."

A sudden hush fell over the gathering group. Jane looked up to see what had happened, and saw that Alice was ushering Mary over to where Finn stood with his owner. Finn held his head and ears high, taking it all in. When Finn saw Mary, he broke away from Kieran and headed directly for her. They met in the middle of the yard and to everyone's delight, Mary embraced the big dog. Finn responded by licking Mary's cheeks.

A few people clapped, and there was a ripple of laughter.

Rev. Thompson tapped a spoon on the side of a pitcher of iced tea. "If we can all bow our heads for a moment, I think this is an excellent time for a prayer.

"Dear Father in heaven, thank You for the bright sunshine, glorious flowers and sweet fellowship today offers. We ask that someone, somehow, will help Mary discover her identity—if not today, in Your own perfect timing. Bless the people of Acorn Hill, our families and precious friends. Amen."

"Amen," echoed those standing about.

The afternoon sun warmed the yard as people drifted around and enjoyed the refreshments while chatting happily with their neighbors.

Clarissa Cottrell was there, keeping an eye on her cake, cutting additional slices when needed. Vera and Jean Humbert talked animatedly with Craig Tracy, and Pastor Ley and his wife Patsy moved easily through the gathering. Mary was chatting with a reporter from Potterston, who was scribbling frantically in a notebook.

LeAnn had managed to free herself from Florence's orbit to stroll through the yard with Hope Collins.

"This is a wonderful idea, Jane," Hope said, moving toward her. She gestured in the direction of the new postmistress. "You know LeAnn, don't you?"

"Yes, we've met in the post office. How are you enjoying Acorn Hill?"

"It's a pleasant little town." She smiled, her brown eyes crinkling up at the corners. "Friendly." She pronounced. "Extremely friendly."

She glanced over at Florence, who was carrying a plate on which was a healthy selection of dessert bars and cookies. Her husband Ronald, his balding head shining in the sun, trailed a few steps behind her. They drifted across the yard to find chairs in the shade.

Jane looked at Florence and back to LeAnn. "Florence and my Aunt Ethel are a little overenthusiastic, but they mean well."

"Your aunt is a sweetie," LeAnn said. "I guess I'm just not really used to small-town life yet."

Jane tipped her head to indicate she was listening.

"I had no idea that people were so interested in one another."

"What do you mean?"

Hope chuckled. "LeAnn's not used to the gossip in a small town. She's not accustomed to everyone knowing one another and actually being interested in what's going on," she said, taking a bite of her lemon bar.

"Fortunately I've learned my lesson," LeAnn said and made a zipping motion across her lips as she glanced in Florence's direction. "If you know what I mean. And Alma will be back in a few weeks, so I guess it's just as well.

Before Jane could respond, Finn discovered Wendell sitting in the window and began to bark, causing a commotion. Jane started for the house to fix the situation, but was waylaid again.

"What a wonderful party you've organized," Florence said, appearing out of nowhere. "I see you were talking to LeAnn."

Jane nodded.

"When LeAnn came to Acorn Hill she was very lonely, you know." Florence frowned. "A little *too* lonely, perhaps."

"What do you mean?"

Florence glanced around and then leaned forward so only Jane could hear. "She was so desperate to meet people and make friends that I think she *talked* a little too much. She said things. Not much, mind you, but enough to get you thinking. She hinted, for example, at who was getting interesting mail from faraway places and if a lot of unusual mail was going to one address, little things like that." Florence looked disapproving. "She shouldn't do that. It's how rumors can get started, you know."

Florence looked as innocent as a newborn babe. "People in this town are trusting. When someone tells us something, we think it's the truth, not speculation or half-baked supposition."

Jane bit her tongue. She was not about to point out to Florence that she and Aunt Ethel had been just as eager to receive and dispense information as LeAnn had been to give it.

"Anyway, it looks like LeAnn has found a friend closer to her own age," Florence said, nodding toward LeAnn and Hope chatting by the tea table. "I think we did a good job of being neighborly, don't you?" With that, Florence dismissed the gossip fiasco. She waved at her husband, who was still seated in the shade. "Come on, Ronald. Don't dally. I need more tea."

Jane shook her head and started for the house again, but Louise came up behind her. "Look who stopped by," Louise said.

Jane turned to see their former houseguest Claire and her husband Ben standing nearby. Claire looked relaxed and happy.

Jane went up to Claire. "I'm so glad to see you here."

"We were driving through town, saw a sign at the gas station and had to stop. We couldn't miss it, not after knowing Mary personally," she said, taking her husband's hand. "I still can't believe that I was actually at your place when Mary came. Has anyone had a clue to her identity yet?"

"Not yet, but we have hope." Jane smiled at the young couple.

"I thanked Louise for all that you sisters did for me— and for Ben," Claire said to Jane. "I behaved horribly, but he forgave me." She turned shining eyes on him. "That's what really told me how much he loves me."

Ben gave a lopsided grin. "I think we've both come a long way toward growing up."

Jane left the couple smiling at each other, and then slowly made her way to the other side of the yard. Mary was standing there with Finn. She and the dog looked as if they'd been best friends forever. Finn looked up at her with liquid brown eyes, and she smiled down at him and gently stroked the top of his head.

Wilhelm stood beside them, glancing at his wristwatch. "It's three, Jane. Do you want me to start?" He ran his finger beneath the collar of his shirt.

"Nervous?"

"Not really." He smiled. "These people are family to me, to all of us. Just a twinge of stage fright to keep me sharp."

"Excuse me, excuse me please!" he spoke loudly into the crowd. Gradually conversation quieted, and soon he had everyone's attention.

"Our hostesses have asked me to say a few words. As you know, Mary was discovered about a week ago not far from Fairy Pond. Her memory has not yet returned, and Louise, Alice and Jane have invited you today to share in the hospitality of the inn, and to ask that if you—or anyone you know—saw anything, *anything* that might be even remotely connected with Mary's situation, that you come forward. You might have seen an unfamiliar car, a stranger, someone parked by the side of a road . . ."

Jane looked across the yard as she listened. The guests were paying close attention to Wilhelm. Lloyd and Ethel were leaning forward and listening with such intensity that they looked like they were walking into a strong wind. Carlene Moss was taking notes for her article and Pastor Ley had his eyes closed—praying, no doubt.

Jane's heart swelled with affection for these wonderful people who cared so much for a complete stranger.

By the time she returned her attention to Wilhelm, Mary had joined him. She had Finn's leash in her right hand and Kieran's hand in her left. When she spoke, her voice was soft but clear.

"This is the most wonderful opportunity for me to say thank-you to my rescuers," she began. "You all know my story by now, but perhaps you don't know that I was unconscious when I was found. I don't know how long I might have lain there or what might have happened to me had not Finn and Kieran come along. I believe I owe a huge debt of gratitude to Finn for finding me and sensing that I was in trouble, and to Kieran for respecting and paying attention to his dog's instincts. They are both heroes in my book."

Clapping erupted as well as a few cheers and whistles.

Kieran blushed the color of his hair.

Mary held out the gift that Jane had purchased. "This is a token of appreciation to you, Kieran. My gratitude is heartfelt." She turned to glance at Alice. "And we have something for Finn too."

At Mary's signal, Alice pulled a net bag of doggie accoutrements—bones, dried pigs' ears, toys, a box of flavored treats and even a plaid hat with holes where Finn's ears would go—from behind the tea table.

Finn's tail began to wag as Alice opened the bag and tossed him a rawhide bone. Completely, blissfully unaware of the attention focused on him, Finn lay down in the grass and began to chew.

"The Howard sisters are my other heroes. They took me in and generously shared their home without any expectation of compensation." Mary smiled ruefully. "Unfortunately I don't have a dime to my name... and I don't, for that matter, have a name... but I give them my eternal gratitude for the love they've shown me."

The guests again began to applaud.

Then Wilhelm stepped forward to wrap up the formal part of the party. "Be sure to greet Mary, Kieran and Finn, folks, and if you can think of anything that might help us, we'd all be so grateful."

Jane was about to return to her hostess duties when Aunt Ethel suddenly appeared beside her.

"Hello dear, what a lovely party." Her hair shone brightly in the sun.

"Are you and Lloyd having fun?"

"Oh my, yes. He's so proud of the people of Acorn Hill and how they've supported Mary."

Ethel put her hand on Jane's arm. "I just wanted to tell you, well, you know...it was all a misunderstanding, of course. It was unfortunate but we...wanted to make friends, you know...it seemed right at the time. I'm glad you said something...I just wanted you to know." Then Ethel brightened. "Did you know that Florence and I are going to be knitting baby afghans for the church? It's our new project." She smiled. "Oh, Lloyd is waving at me." She gave him a quick wave, then turned back to Jane. "I have to go. It was nice talking to you, dear." Ethel moved off, leaving Jane to ponder the mysterious conversation. Jane's heart filled with affection. Her dear, sweet, funny aunt. Life in Acorn Hill would be boring without her.

The sun hung low in the sky when the last stragglers finally left the party. Stella, Becky, Patty and the Howard sisters set to work quickly, and soon the lawn and kitchen were back in order.

"Let's sit down and enjoy the garden before we put away these last chairs," Jane said, looking around. "I think we deserve a few minutes with our feet up."

The fragrance of the flowers, the scent of freshly cut grass, and birdsong surrounded them.

"Did anyone come forward with new information about Mary?" Becky asked quietly.

"No." Mary shook her head. "Not yet."

Louise's eyes flew open, and she looked at Mary's crest-fallen face. "They still could, you know. Someone will tell someone about the party who will tell someone else, who will . . ."

"It was a wonderful party," Mary said with feeling. "You have all tried so hard to help me."

She squared her thin shoulders. "But I do think it's time I faced the fact that I might not recall or find out who I am for a long time. I guess I have to get on with my life."

"What will you do?" Patty asked.

"I've been thinking about it," Mary said. "I'll need to find a place to live, and I'd like to stay in Acorn Hill." People have been kind to me here. If I can find a job, and then a place to live, at least I will have friends." She looked shyly at Alice, Louise and Jane. "Like you."

"I think that's a splendid idea," Louise said. "Don't you agree, Jane?"

"Absolutely. But I wouldn't give up hope that your memory will come back. With time . . ."

"I know, but until then, I want to be in Acorn Hill." She put the tips of her fingers together and rested them beneath her chin. "I think I landed here for a reason. Even in my darkest moments, God has had His hand on me." Tears came to her eyes. "But that doesn't mean I'll quit praying for my family to come and get me—if I have one."

"Maybe we should go inside," Jane suggested as the light began to fade. "I've got a casserole to put in the oven. We all need something to counteract the truckload of sweets we've consumed today."

"Great idea," Becky said, and stood up. "I'm on a sugar high. I don't even remember how many brownies I ate. I was cutting them in the kitchen and the row was always crooked so I'd have to straighten it. You wouldn't want crooked brownies, would you?"

"I felt the same way about the lemon bars," Patty admitted. "I had so many that my teeth started to squeak."

"Teeth can't squeak."

"Yup, they can. Mine did."

One by one they meandered into the house.

"I'll set the dining room table," Alice volunteered. "The rest of you can go upstairs and get into something more comfortable."

"I wish we didn't have to leave tomorrow," Stella said. "This has been one of the most wonderful vacations of my life—wonderful friends, a beautiful location, fine dining, mystery and intrigue..."

"And don't forget the quilts," Becky said.

"...and creativity and learning."

"It has been nice, but I'm almost looking forward to going back home," Becky said wistfully. "In fact, I think I'll give Blaine a call before dinner. I want to see how he's doing." She glanced at Jane. "No meddling, I promise."

Before any of them could climb the stairs to the second floor, however, the doorbell rang. Two uniformed policemen stood on the porch.

"What is it?" Jane asked when she saw their somber faces. "Has something happened?"

Chapter Twenty-Three

We're looking for the woman with amnesia." The officers stepped through the door that Jane held open for them.

"That's me," Mary said nervously.

"Officer Briggs, Ma'am. And this is Officer Perry. We're with the Potterston police. We've discovered something relevant to your case." The policeman reached into his pocket and pulled out a driver's license and handed it to Mary. "Does this look familiar to you?"

Mary stared at the small rectangle. "The picture looks like me. It says this is someone named Lorna Carver..." She drew a sharp breath. "Is that me? Where did you get this?"

"We think we've figured out something. Is there somewhere we can speak in private?"

Mary looked around at the faces of the women she'd come to care about. "These women deserve to hear what happened too," Mary said quickly. The officers nodded.

"You'd better come in and we'll all sit down," Louise suggested. She led them into the living room. Everyone sat, creating a strange, anxious tableau as they waited for the officers to continue.

"An accident report came in late this afternoon," the shorter, huskier officer named Briggs said. "Someone reported a car on its side at the bottom of a ravine about five miles north of Acorn Hill."

"When we got to the site, we saw that it was not a recent accident," said the taller, fairer officer. "The car had been in the ravine quite a few days. It's a heavily wooded area, and the vehicle landed in a location that isn't easily seen from the road. If it hadn't been for the hiker who ran across it, it might not have been discovered for many weeks."

"Is that my car?" Mary whispered.

Officer Briggs nodded and continued. "We believe that after the accident you walked to the point where you collapsed. You must have gone nearly four miles from where the vehicle went into the gully. We aren't sure how long you were by the side of the road, but it's fortunate that the dog and his owner came along."

Mary stared at the driver's license in her hands. "So this is who I am?"

"We believe so." The policeman cleared his throat. "We did find some other items in the car. A suitcase, maps and a journal. From what we can gather, you were on a trip to Florida."

Mary continued to stare at the driver's license, tears in her eyes.

"We contacted the people at the address on your driver's license. They had assumed that you were traveling at first. Then when you didn't show up, they reported you missing. That was three days after you left home."

Mary looked up and clasped her hands to her ribcage. "Oh my." Then she took a deep, steeling breath. "It's what I've wanted. Why do I suddenly feel so afraid?" Mary—*Lorna*—sounded as if she was having trouble getting out the words.

"It's quite natural to be afraid of the unknown," Jane said gently.

"Now what?" Mary asked.

Officer Briggs continued his story. "It seems you hadn't been on the road long. Your home is only about eighty miles west of here. Your family started out as soon as we contacted them. They're waiting outside."

The silence in the room was absolute. Finally Alice broke it by saying, "What are we waiting for? Let's bring them inside." Then, realizing that this was Lorna's decision, she turned to her and added, "If you're ready, that is."

"I don't know when I'll be more ready," Lorna said uncertainly.

The two officers rose and went to the door.

"...or more scared."

Officer Briggs returned to the house, leading a man and a woman and two teenage boys. The tall gentleman was in his early fifties. There were furrows in his brow, but his eyes shone with kindness. The woman, Jane realized, looked a good deal like Lorna. So did the two jeans-and-T-shirt clad boys, who were obviously twins.

"Lorna!" The man took a step forward and then stopped himself. "They said I shouldn't go too fast. I don't want to frighten you, but we've been so worried."

"This is Jerry Carver, Ma'am, your husband." The police officer looked ill at ease. Obviously it wasn't often that he had to introduce a wife to her husband.

"Husband?" Lorna stared at Jerry. "But..." She looked down at her bare left hand.

"You'd lost a lot of weight recently," Jerry said softly, holding out a gold ring. "It was too loose. You were going to have it resized."

Lorna took the ring from his outstretched hand and examined it. She smiled at him weakly. She closed her hand around it and waited.

"And I'm your sister Mazie," the woman stepped closer. "And these are your boys, Kent and William."

Lorna stared at the youngsters, gangly teens shuffling from side to side, obviously wondering what to do with their hands—and their emotions. A smile brightened her features. "I have sons?"

"We don't want to rush you." Mazie looked to the officer for direction, then back to her sister. "This must be terrible for you. We love you, Lorna, and we're so sorry this happened to you. Just tell us what you want us to do."

The boys squirmed under their mother's intense examination until one of them exclaimed. "Quit staring, Ma! You're making me nervous."

Everyone burst out laughing, breaking the tension in the room.

"French Fry," Lorna blurted unexpectedly.

Jane and the others exchanged concerned glances, but Lorna's family didn't look surprised.

"French Fry and Big Mac!" she said delightedly.

The boys grinned from ear to ear.

"Frenchy and Mac!"

"What does it mean?" Alice asked gently.

"I don't recall my sons yet, but I remember our cats!" She was half laughing, half crying. "It will come back,"

Lorna said, now assuring her family. "Frenchy and Mac are Siamese kittens. If I know that, the rest is bound to follow." She moved forward and held out her hands to her husband and sons. "Now that I've found you, I can wait patiently for the rest."

Jane smiled and backed out of the room, gesturing for the others to follow so that Lorna could have time with her family.

Chapter Twenty-Four

*I*t was after ten when Lorna's family left the inn, assuring her that they would be back in the morning.

"Are you certain you don't want to go along?" Alice inquired. "They seemed very eager to have you go with them."

"Even though I *know* they are my family, I don't remember them," Lorna sighed. "I've got to ease into it." She looked around. "Right now *this* is the only home I remember. Thank you, Alice, for offering to drive me to Potterston in the morning. It will be good for my family to meet with the doctor. It will help them understand what's happened to me."

"How about you, Lorna? Are you okay?" asked Alice. "Really okay, I mean. A lot has happened for you today."

"I'm fine. Much better than I was before I knew that I had a family." She hesitated briefly. "They seem nice, don't they?"

"They're wonderful. It's obvious how much they love you and how frightened they were while you were missing."

"I don't understand why they didn't report you missing immediately," Becky said.

"Apparently I'd been on my way to visit my sister in Florida." Lorna shrugged. "I was planning to take my time driving. My husband…" she smiled a little at the word on her lips, "was out of town on business, and the boys were staying with friends. Jerry had been leaving messages on my cell phone, but no one was at home to check in with me, and Mazie didn't expect me right away. Each thought the other was in touch with me. I guess I just fell through the cracks for a few days." She shuddered. "I really fell through them, didn't I?"

They all smiled.

"Once my husband and the boys returned home and realized none of them had heard from me, they called my sister. She hadn't heard from me either. By that time, I was already here at the inn. They realized I was missing and panicked."

"Are you going to put on your wedding ring?" Louise asked quietly.

Lorna pulled it out of her pocket, where it had been since her husband gave it to her. "It doesn't fit." She slid it on her finger to demonstrate. "Apparently one of the reasons I was so excited to see my sister was to show her how much weight I'd lost."

"At least now we know how you got all the scratches and scrapes," Alice said. "You'd been making your way through trees and brush trying to get out of that ravine."

"If I'd been on the road, I might have been seen earlier, the police said, but because I followed the bottom of the gully, no one noticed until I made it to the road where Finn found me."

"You have no idea how worried we were that you'd been dropped off there on purpose and..." Jane's voice trailed off.

"I couldn't think of a reason that anyone would leave me there unless they wanted to get rid of me." Lorna shook off the thought. "But everything has turned out all right." She smiled. "I don't really remember my husband, but I already *like* him. My family will be here for me while my memory returns."

"You're on your way. Remember French Fry and Big Mac."

Her gaze traveled over the women and rested for long moments on each of the sisters. "God bless you people. You did a wonderful thing for me." Lorna put a hand to her lips. Too choked up to speak, she turned and went upstairs.

"I'm so exhausted that I'm not even taking off my makeup before I go to bed." Stella drooped dramatically against the banister.

"What about your pores? Aren't you afraid of having them plug up overnight?" Becky teased.

"Tonight I'm going to live dangerously."

"What a risk taker," Becky muttered, "living on the edge."

"What a weekend," Stella sighed. "I can't imagine that anything more exciting than this could happen."

Monday morning Jane had coffee brewing by five. After mixing a batch of scones to bake and putting out jars of orange marmalade and raspberry preserves, she glanced at the clock. It was early, and she'd given everyone strict instructions not to set their alarms, so she didn't expect to see anyone downstairs before nine. She knew her sisters were sleeping soundly because she'd checked on them before she'd come downstairs.

That was why Jane was surprised to see Stella tiptoeing into the kitchen carrying her running shoes.

"You're up early."

"I'm wired from last night. I thought a nice long run might burn off some of my excess energy. Want to come?" Stella sat down on a stool and slipped on her shoes.

"Are you kidding? I'm not going to do anything more strenuous today than walk upstairs to take a nap." Jane pushed a cup of fresh coffee in Stella's direction.

"It's been an amazing week, hasn't it?" Stella savored the aroma of the brew before taking a sip.

"Remarkable."

"It's changed things for me, you know. Until this weekend I had no idea how completely I was still listening to my father's voice in my head. He was a good man, Jane. Misguided, yes, but I believe he tried his best."

"You forgive him?"

"I'm starting to wish I'd done that much earlier in my life." Stella rolled her eyes. "It would have made things a lot simpler."

She clapped the palms of her hands against her thighs. "I'd better get going, or I'll convince myself not to do it. I'll be back in half an hour or so."

"Have fun," Jane said to Stella's receding back.

Jane poured herself another cup of coffee and broke open a cranberry muffin left over from the day before. She'd eat again when the others awoke, but she expected that to be a couple of hours later.

She watched the birds flock around the feeders as she waited for the oven timer to ring. Then she took the scones out and laid them on the counter. She was surprised to hear more footsteps on the stairs. This time Patty entered the kitchen. Her blonde hair was uncombed, and she still wore her pajamas. There were dark rings beneath her eyes. She looked worn out.

"Did you sleep?"

"If I did, I can't recall it. I tossed and turned like a fish on the bank."

"Too much excitement?" Jane handed her a scone and a cup of coffee.

"Last night was wonderful. All the turmoil was in my head after I went to bed."

"Stella?"

"I have to tell her, Jane. Time's running out. We're leaving this afternoon." Patty groaned. "I have to get it out, but I'm dreading it so much."

"She's out for a run. Why don't you catch her when she comes in? That way the two of you can talk in private."

"I want you to be with us."

"Wouldn't it be better to do this without me?"

"She won't strangle me if you're watching."

Jane chuckled. "So I'm supposed to protect you? Frankly, I don't think you're in much danger, my dear."

"I'd still feel better if you were with us."

"If you insist. But I think you should do it alone."

"Do what alone?" Stella asked from the doorway. She was panting and there was perspiration on her forehead.

"You weren't gone long," Jane said.

"I didn't go very far," Stella said sheepishly. "I've really let myself slip this week. I felt like I was running through mud. Do you have any more coffee?"

"Gallons." Jane filled a cup.

"Now what is it Jane wants you to do alone?" Stella said to Patty as she joined them at the table. She reached for a scone, broke it open and spread it with butter. When she looked up her eyes were sparkling. "Real butter. No more margarine for me. I'm going to live a little."

"I have something to tell you," Patty began, "and Jane knows what it is. I asked her to stay with us because...you might want to scream at me, and I know that we all behave better when we're around Jane."

Jane rolled her eyes. When had she become the man-ners police?

"I can't think of a thing that would make me want to do that," Stella said frankly. "This week has made me realize that I love you guys more than ever."

"Maybe you'll want to take that back when I'm done," Patty warned.

Stella stared at her, comprehending the gravity of Patty's mood. "What is it?"

"Remember when you were going with Barry when we were in college?"

"Yes." Now Stella looked really confused.

"You loved him, didn't you?"

"Well, yes, but what does that have..."

"You might have married him if the two of you hadn't had that terrible fight, right?"

"We'd talked about it," Stella admitted. "Of course, we were awfully young."

"Have you kept track of Barry over the years?"

Stella smiled. "Actually I have. It took a long time, but we were finally able to talk again. He's done quite well for himself. He owns a manufacturing business. They make gadgets for airplane engines, I think. He's a pilot himself. He owns a of couple airplanes. He's still good-looking too, better, actually, than he was when we were in school."

Patty groaned. "It's worse than I thought then."

"What on earth are you talking about?" Stella nibbled on her scone.

"Barry is handsome, successful . . ."

". . . charming, debonair, and the father of five children. Can you imagine? Five!"

"I was hoping you'd say he was chubby, bald and delivered newspapers for a living."

"You have got to tell me what this is about," Stella ordered. "You're upset, and I have no clue why."

"Remember the day you and Barry broke up?"

Stella rolled her eyes. "How could I forget? I haven't been in a bigger argument before or since. He was furious with me and I with him."

"Over the lost necklace?"

"I didn't lose it," Stella said firmly. "Something happened to it, but it wasn't my fault. Of course Barry didn't believe that. He acted like I'd tossed it in the trash."

A flicker of sadness passed over Stella's features. "Frankly, that's why I reconnected with him. I needed him to know that wherever that piece of jewelry went, it wasn't my fault."

"It *wasn't* your fault," Patty echoed.

"I know but..." Stella looked at her oddly. "Why are we having this conversation?"

Patty dipped into the pocket of her pajamas and pulled out the necklace. She laid it on the counter between them. "It was *my* fault, Stella. I'm the reason you and Barry broke up."

"Don't be ridiculous. And where on earth did you find that necklace?"

"I've had it all along—since we were in school."

Stella registered this information in slow motion. "If that's the case, why didn't you give it to me back then? You could have saved me a million tears."

Patty drooped like a thirsty flower. "I didn't give it back because I was the one who took it."

"Took it? You mean you...intentionally...why?"

"Because I was so jealous of you and Barry. I thought I loved him, but he never even looked at me. He only had eyes for you. Stella, I'm ashamed to admit this, but I was so jealous of you back then that I could *taste* it. I took it because I knew that it would cause trouble between you and Barry. But when it caused you to break up, well, I knew I'd gone too far, but it was too late to admit what I'd done."

Stella looked at Patty as if she were speaking a foreign language.

"You had it all: looks, brains, personality and Barry. I wanted to hurt you."

Tears streamed down Patty's cheeks. "I am so sorry for what I did. I was all wrong about you. You were hiding so much pain, and all I saw was your shell, not your heart. And now you'll never speak to me again, and this friendship we've renewed is ruined."

The situation was so uncomfortable that Jane wanted to turn away from Patty's pain, but instead, she put a hand on her friend's shoulder.

"Who says it's ruined?" Stella asked.

Patty's head snapped up. "What?"

"Who says it's ruined?"

"How can you even look at me after what I did to you?"

"What, exactly, do you think you did to me?" Stella was remarkably calm.

"I ruined your life, that's what. If I'd stayed out of it, you and Barry would probably have married. You'd be the one with five children and a huge house and . . ."

"Five children? I don't think so. And a huge house? Patty, have you ever seen my home? Al and I are going to sell it because it's too large for us. Stuff doesn't matter to me. Love is what matters."

"And I messed it up for you because I was eaten up by jealousy."

"Patty!" Stella said firmly, "look at me!"

Patty lifted her head.

"You have been blaming yourself all these years for ruining my life? Patty, you probably did me the biggest favor in the world."

Patty narrowed her eyes. "I don't understand."

"If I'd married Barry, I never would have found and married Al." Stella leaned forward. "All that business with Barry is history, water under the bridge. Sure, I was devastated for a while, but not nearly long enough."

Now both Patty and Jane looked at Stella questioningly.

"If I'd been as deeply in love with Barry as I thought I was, I wouldn't have been dating someone else within six weeks. My wounds would have taken considerably longer to heal, don't you think?"

"But I meddled in your life."

"Yes, you did, but without that meddling, I may never have met Al. He's been my anchor throughout my career. Barry didn't care about my work. He always joked that he didn't understand it. Do you think I would have been happy married to a man who didn't respect my art? Al, on the other hand, admires me both professionally and personally. He's crazy about me, Patty, and I feel the same way about him. Barry wasn't the one for me. I would have discovered it sooner or later. I understand that now. You just made me figure it out sooner. If he broke up over something as absurd as my losing a necklace and refused to believe me when I said I hadn't misplaced it, why would I want him?"

"You aren't furious with me?"

"Oh, I'm disappointed, I guess." Stella put her hands on her hips. "It's not what you expect to hear from one of your closest friends. But it's the past, Patty." Her expression softened, "Besides, I can see that you've suffered enough. There's nothing I could do or say that's worse than what you've done to yourself. I see the pain in your eyes. I wouldn't have punished you for all these years."

Patty stared at Stella, slack-jawed. Then she tipped her head back and groaned. "You aren't going to yell at me? Tell me you'll never speak to me again?"

"I always knew it was you who was keeping the four of us from getting together," Stella said. "I never knew why, because you'd see Becky and Jane separately but…"

"I didn't want to see you because it brought up all the remorse I felt."

"Frankly, I'm glad to know why it happened, Patty. I never understood."

"You never said anything."

Stella gave a wry laugh. "Remember me? The girl who wanted to be perfect? I always thought you didn't want to see me because of something I did. Patty, I'm actually happy to know what happened. I thought I was to blame."

Patty looked at Jane, who was quietly slicing fruit into a bowl. "You've got something tumbling around in your head right now, don't you?"

"Funny, isn't it, how the Bible speaks to everything, to every situation?" Jane said mildly.

"Let's hear it," Patty sighed.

"Proverbs 10:9: 'The man of integrity walks securely, but he who takes crooked paths will be found out.'"

Patty looked from Jane to Stella and back again. "If it weren't for me, we could have had weeks like this every year. I'm so sorry."

"Then we'll have to start making up for it," Jane said. She put her hand on Patty's arm. "That means *you* plan our next reunion."

"When's the next one?" Becky shuffled into the kitchen in her slippers and pajamas. "Tell me right away so I get it on the calendar. Let's make it at a time I'm not under deadline. . . ." She paused, seeing the streaks of tears on Patty's face. "What's going on here?"

"It's a long story," Jane said, shaking her head. "But a good one."

Chapter Twenty-Five

*L*ouise, Alice and Lorna found the others already at the dining room table when they came down for breakfast. They were looking at old photos Jane had dug out of a trunk.

"I suppose it's time to start bringing the suitcases down so we can load the van," Stella said with a sigh.

"I don't want to leave," Becky said glumly. "This has been too perfect." Then she brightened. "But Jane and I will get together soon. She's going to help me with a book I'm writing on Fairy Pond."

"Can we join you?" Stella asked. "You'll be much more creative with us around."

Lorna watched them without speaking.

"What's going on in your head, my dear?" Alice asked. "You're thinking so hard I can practically hear you."

Lorna put her arm around Alice's shoulder. "I was wondering about the people I call my friends. Could they possibly be as wonderful as all of you?"

"I don't see why not. Like attracts like, you know," Alice said.

"I'm still frightened," Lorna admitted. "I'm glad I now have an identity, but my life ... I just don't know."

"From now on you'll have us too," Alice reminded her. "Perhaps you and your husband or sister can come back for a visit."

"I'd like that." Lorna's chin quivered.

Before she could say more, someone knocked at the front door.

Alice went to open it and was met with a gigantic bouquet of flowers that nearly filled the doorway. Craig Tracy's face peered through the greenery.

"Delivery for 'The Women of Grace Chapel Inn.'"

"For us. Why?"

"I guess you'll have to read the card to find out." Craig came through the open door, marched into the dining room and set the floral arrangement in the middle of the table.

Louise plucked a small, white envelope out of the mass of blooms, opened it and read aloud the enclosed card.

> *To the caring women who kept our*
> *Wife, mother and sister safe.*
> *We will always be grateful.*
>
> > *Lorna's Family*

Lorna looked as delighted as if she'd been the one to receive the flowers. Her face glowed as she announced, "They *are* as nice as I'd hoped they'd be. How thoughtful."

"And grateful," Alice added.

"Generous too," Jane commented, eyeing the size of the bouquet.

"Looks like you have a winner of a family," Stella commented. "And we know that they're fortunate to have you."

Lorna burst into happy tears, and, as if on cue, every one of the women began to dab at her own eyes. Craig carefully backed out of the dining room and onto the porch, then closed the door quietly behind him.

That evening, the three Howard sisters sat once again on their wide front porch and watched the daylight fade.

"It's going to be very quiet around here without all our guests," Louise said.

"I already miss them," Alice added. "It's a good thing we have reservations for next weekend."

"How do you feel, Jane? It's been an especially challenging week for you."

Jane looked out across the lawn and toward the little town they all loved. "I feel grateful. I wondered if I'd feel restless or dissatisfied when I saw my old friends and heard about what they were doing. Instead I feel peace. This *is* where I'm supposed to be, and it's where I'm happiest."

"It's where we all belong," Louise said with confidence. "It's where God has planted us."

Alice nodded emphatically. "All we have to do here is grow."

"Amen," her sisters said in unison. "Amen."

About the Author

*J*udy Baer is the author of more than seventy books for adults and teens. She has won the Romance Writers of America Bronze Medallion and has twice been a RITA finalist. She lives in Elk River, Minnesota, with her husband.